Praise for
THE LOST FLEET: DAUNTLESS

"A solid, thoughtful, and exciting novel loaded with edge-of-your-seat combat."
—Elizabeth Moon, Nebula Award–winning
author of *Marque and Reprisal*

"Jack Campbell's dazzling new series is military science fiction at its best. Not only does he tell a yarn of great adventure and action, but he also develops the characters with satisfying depth. I thoroughly enjoyed this rip-roaring read, and I can hardly wait for the next book."
—Catherine Asaro, Nebula Award–winning
author of *Alpha*

"Black Jack Geary is very real, very human, and so compelling he'll leave you wanting more. Jack Campbell knows fleet actions, and it shows."
—David Sherman, author, with Dan Cragg,
of the Starfist series

D0011556

THE LOST FLEET
DAUNTLESS

JACK CAMPBELL

ACE BOOKS, NEW YORK

THE BERKLEY PUBLISHING GROUP
Published by the Penguin Group
Penguin Group (USA) Inc.
375 Hudson Street, New York, New York 10014, USA

Penguin Group (Canada), 90 Eglinton Avenue East, Suite 700, Toronto, Ontario M4P 2Y3, Canada
(a division of Pearson Penguin Canada Inc.)
Penguin Books Ltd., 80 Strand, London WC2R 0RL, England
Penguin Group Ireland, 25 St. Stephen's Green, Dublin 2, Ireland (a division of Penguin Books Ltd.)
Penguin Group (Australia), 250 Camberwell Road, Camberwell, Victoria 3124, Australia
(a division of Pearson Australia Group Pty. Ltd.)
Penguin Books India Pvt. Ltd., 11 Community Centre, Panchsheel Park, New Delhi—110 017, India
Penguin Group (NZ), Cnr. Airborne and Rosedale Roads, Albany, Auckland 1310, New Zealand
(a division of Pearson New Zealand Ltd.)
Penguin Books (South Africa) (Pty.) Ltd., 24 Sturdee Avenue, Rosebank, Johannesburg 2196, South Africa

Penguin Books Ltd., Registered Offices: 80 Strand, London WC2R 0RL, England

THE LOST FLEET: DAUNTLESS

An Ace Book / published by arrangement with the author

PRINTING HISTORY
Ace mass-market edition / July 2006

Copyright © 2006 by John G. Hemry writing as Jack Campbell.
Cover art by Pat Turner.
Cover design by Annette Fiore.
Interior text design by Kristin del Rosario.

ISBN: 0-441-01418-6

ACE
Ace Books are published by The Berkley Publishing Group,
a division of Penguin Group (USA) Inc.,
375 Hudson Street, New York, New York 10014.
ACE and the "A" design are trademarks belonging to Penguin Group (USA) Inc.

PRINTED IN THE UNITED STATES OF AMERICA

10   9   8   7   6   5

To Christine and Larry Maguire.
Good people and good friends who've made our lives
richer by their being here.

For S., as always.

ACKNOWLEDGMENTS

I'm indebted to my editor, Anne Sowards, for her valuable support and editing, and to my agent, Joshua Blimes, for his inspired suggestions and assistance. Thanks also to Catherine Asaro, J. G. (Huck) Huckenpöhler, Simcha Kuritzky, Michael LaViolette, Aly Parsons, Bud Sparhawk, and Constance A. Warner, for their suggestions, comments, and recommendations.

ONE

THE cold air blowing in through the vents still carried a faint tang of overheated metal and burned equipment. Faint echoes of a blast reached into his stateroom as the ship shuddered. Voices outside the hatch were raised in fright and feet rushed past. But he didn't move, knowing that if the enemy had resumed the attack there'd be alarms sounding and many more than just one blow struck to the ship. And, attack or not, he had no assignment to run to, no job to fulfill.

He sat in the small stateroom he'd been given, arms crossed and hands tucked in to try to drive away an inner cold that never seemed to leave him. He could hear the sounds of the ship and her crew, and as long as the hatch remained closed he could try to pretend the ship was a ship he knew and the crew were people he'd served with. But those ships and those people were gone, as by all rights he should be as well.

He shifted position slightly, clenching his hands tighter against the cold that welled up from within, as one knee brushed against the rough edge of the small desk this stateroom boasted. He stared at that edge, trying to grasp what it meant. The future was supposed to be smooth. Smooth and clean and bright. It wasn't supposed to be rougher and more worn than the past. Everybody knew that. But then, wars weren't supposed to be apparently endless, going on and on and draining the smoothness and brightness from a future that could now only afford efficiency.

"Captain Geary, your presence is requested at the shuttle dock."

The announcement took a moment to penetrate. Why did they want him? But an order was an order, and if he lost the structure of discipline now he might find he had nothing left at all. He exhaled heavily, then stood, his legs stiff from inner and outer cold. He braced himself before opening the hatch, not wanting to face the people outside, but finally yanked it open and began walking.

The passages of the Alliance battle cruiser *Dauntless* were crowded with enlisted personnel and a leavening of other officers. They made way for him as he walked, creating a narrow path that seemed to magically open and close just before and behind him as he plodded steadily toward the shuttle area. He kept his eyes unfocused, looking straight ahead and not seeing their faces. He knew what would be reflected on those faces. He'd seen the hope and awe, neither understanding nor desiring it. Now he knew that awe would be joined by anguish and despair, and he wanted to see those faces even less than before. As if he'd let them down, when he'd never promised them anything or claimed to be anything more than he really was.

The crowd suddenly jammed solid before him, and he had to halt. A junior officer looked back and saw him. "Captain Geary!" she exclaimed, her face lighting with irrational hope. The junior officer had dirty hydraulic fluid smeared across one side of her face and a light cast on one arm to cover an injury from the recent battle. Her uniform showed scorch marks on the side of the injured arm.

Geary knew he should say something to the officer, but

he couldn't find any words. "Shuttle dock," Geary finally stated.

"You can't get there through here, Captain," the lieutenant offered eagerly, fatigue falling away from her and oblivious to the lack of reaction from Geary. Her sudden enthusiasm made her seem impossibly young and somehow made Geary feel even older. "It's sealed off while they repair battle damage. You felt that last shock, didn't you? We had to jettison some fuel cells before they blew. But we'll be ready again soon. We're not beaten yet. Are we? We can't be."

"I need to get to the shuttle dock," Geary repeated slowly.

The lieutenant blinked. "Shuttle dock. Go down two decks and forward from there. That should be clear. It's good to see you, sir." Her voice broke on the last sentence.

It's good to see me? Geary thought. A momentary heat of anger warred against the ice inside him. *Why?* But he just nodded and replied without inflection. "Thank you."

Down the ladders two decks and forward again, Geary moved alone through the crowd that still parted and closed as he walked. Despite his attempts to avoid seeing, he caught glimpses of faces now, faces with the same anguish and lit with the same insane optimism when they caught sight of Geary.

Admiral Bloch waited at the entry to the shuttle dock, along with his chief of staff and a small crowd of other officers. Bloch motioned to Geary and drew him aside to speak privately. Unlike the others, Bloch seemed less despairing than stunned by the recent battle, as if he still weren't quite able to grasp what had happened. "The Syndic leaders have agreed to negotiations. They insist that I and every other flag rank officer participate in person. We're in no position to refuse their demand." The Admiral's voice sounded dull, very different from the booming enthusiasm Geary had grown used to hearing. His eyes were dull, too. "That leaves you the most senior officer in our absence, Captain."

Geary frowned. He hadn't really considered that before now. His seniority dated from the day he'd been promoted to Captain. That had been a very long time ago. And with that seniority would come responsibilities. "I can't—"

"Yes." Admiral Bloch drew a deep breath. "Please. Captain. The fleet needs you."

"Sir, with all due respect—"

"Captain Geary, I wouldn't blame you for wondering if you'd have been better off if we hadn't found you. I thought, a lot of people thought, it was a harbinger of good luck. 'Black Jack' Geary, back from the dead to accompany the Alliance fleet to its greatest victory." Bloch closed his eyes for a moment. "Now I need to leave the fleet in the hands of someone I can trust."

Geary grimaced, wanting to yell at Bloch, tell the admiral that the man he wanted to leave in charge of the fleet wasn't the man actually standing here, that such a person had never existed. But Bloch's eyes weren't simply dull, Geary now saw. They were dead. He finally just nodded slowly. "Aye, aye, sir."

"We're trapped. This fleet is the Alliance's last hope. You understand of course. If something happens . . . do your best. Promise me."

Geary fought down another impulse to shout out his objections. But breaking the ice inside him would be too hard, and a stubborn sense of duty insisted he couldn't refuse Admiral Bloch's request. "I will."

"*Dauntless* . . . listen, Captain." Bloch leaned close, speaking even more softly. "*Dauntless* has the key onboard. Do you understand? Ask Captain Desjani. She knows and can explain. This ship *must* get home. Somehow. The hypernet key must get back to the Alliance. If we can do that, there'll still be a chance, and the ships and the people we've lost won't have been in vain. Promise me, Captain Geary."

Geary stared, not understanding, shocked even through his numbed senses by the pleading in the admiral's voice. But it wasn't like Geary would be in charge forever. Bloch would negotiate with the Syndics, then return and be back in command. Geary would never have to learn any details about some "key" on the *Dauntless* that somehow related to a method of traveling between the stars that was much more rapid than even the system-jump faster-than-light transportation method used in Geary's time. "Yes, sir."

"Good. Thank you. Thank you, Captain. I knew if there was one person I could count on, it'd be you." If Geary's reaction to the admiral's statement showed on his face, Bloch gave no sign. "I'll do my best, but, if worse comes to worst . . ." Bloch stood silent for a moment. "Somehow, if you can, save what's left of the fleet." He raised his voice as he led Geary back to the others. "Captain Geary is in command of the fleet in my absence."

Everyone turned to stare at Geary. Surprise, elation on the faces of the younger officers, skepticism showing on some of the older officers as they all murmured acknowledgment of the admiral's order.

Geary brought his hand up in the formal salute he'd always known but hadn't seen among this fleet. He didn't know when saluting had ceased to be a normal military courtesy in the Alliance fleet, but he was damned if he'd just wave good-bye to a superior officer. Bloch gave a rusty half-salute in reply, then turned and passed quickly through the entry area toward the waiting shuttle, followed by a couple of the older officers.

Geary watched the shuttle depart, unmoving, wondering what he should feel. Command of an entire fleet. Or what was left of it, anyway. The pinnacle of a Navy officer's career. His command was just for a little while, of course. No matter how bad things were, they didn't really want him in command. Admiral Bloch was just making a small gesture toward the legendary Captain "Black Jack" Geary, granting a symbolic honor before the Admiral got back with whatever agreement he'd managed to arrange. The negotiations might take a while, but Geary had once known and dealt with representatives of the Syndicate Worlds, and while he'd never liked the Syndics, he was certain they'd cut a deal now rather than face the losses the trapped Alliance fleet would otherwise inflict as it died.

He became aware that the remaining officers were watching him, expectation now warring with their other expressions. Geary turned to face the group and nodded. "Dismissed." They all turned to go, except for two who paused to awkwardly salute in acknowledgment of the order. Geary returned the salutes, wondering why and at what point such things had gone out of style.

Then he stood, watching them leave, uncertain what to do next. Where did the acting fleet commander belong? On the bridge of the *Dauntless*, perhaps. With everyone watching him and nothing really to do. *What possible difference does it make where I go now? I can give orders from my stateroom if I need to, but I won't need to, and what would I do if I could? Everything I knew, everyone I knew, is gone. I'm so very tired. I spent almost a century in survival hibernation, sleeping away the lives of my friends, and I'm still tired. To hell with it.*

He returned to his stateroom, sat down at the rough-edged desk and tried to look at and think of nothing again. But he couldn't, because he did after all have a job to do now. After several minutes, the long habits of duty nagged him into motion. Geary squinted at the communications panel set next to the desk, making sure he'd push the right buttons. "Bridge, this is Captain Geary. Acting fleet commander. Please notify me when the shuttles from the fleet reach the Syndic flagship."

"Aye, aye, sir." The enlisted sailor visible on the screen nodded rapidly, his eyes filled with awe at seeing Geary. "Estimated time of arrival is fifteen minutes from now."

"Thank you." Geary hastily shut off the screen, unnerved by the hero worship on the man's face. He tried to settle back into his numbness, but duty dug its heels into Geary's shoulder and kept poking at him. Rather than keep fighting it, he reached for other controls. The flagship's combat system balked at first from letting him see the latest fleet status data, but somewhere it picked up the information that Geary was now acting commander and grudgingly provided the necessary access. Geary read down the list of ships slowly and methodically, feeling pain beginning to finally gnaw against the deadness inside of him. So many ships lost. So many of the remainder damaged. Small wonder Admiral Bloch had gone to seek terms from the Syndics.

"Captain Geary. Our shuttles have reached the Syndic flagship."

"Thank you." Geary didn't want to think about Admiral Bloch being herded through the enemy ship to beg and bluff for whatever concessions he could squeeze out of the victorious enemy. Geary had never cared for the way the Syndics treated their own people, let alone how they handled others. But they could be reasoned with.

"C-captain Geary. Th-this is the communications watch."

Geary looked toward the screen. The officer there seemed rattled beyond what Geary had seen elsewhere. Far more rattled. "What is it?"

"A . . . a message . . . from the Syndic flagship. Captain. Th-they sent it to all our ships."

"Show me." The image of the officer dissolved. Geary saw Admiral Bloch and the other senior Alliance officers, standing next to a bulkhead on what must be the Syndic flagship. The view pulled back, showing the location to be a shuttle dock, and revealing a Syndic official with the impeccably tailored uniform, brilliant rank insignia and instantly recognizable arrogance of a Chief Executive Officer facing the camera.

"Alliance Fleet, your Admiral came to us to 'negotiate' for terms of surrender." The CEO made a gesture.

Geary felt his mouth go dry as a group of Syndic special troops stepped forward, one per Alliance officer, and fired point-blank into Admiral Bloch and the others. Bloch and some of the others tried to remain at attention but crumpled as blood stained their uniforms. Within moments, every senior Alliance officer lay unmoving and unquestionably dead.

The Syndic CEO waved negligently toward the bodies. "There is nothing to 'negotiate' with your former leaders. Anyone else who tries to 'negotiate' will suffer the same fate as these fools. Those Alliance ships and officers who surrender unconditionally will receive reasonable terms. We have no quarrel with those who were forced to fight us by misguided leaders such as these." Even through his shock, Geary wondered if the Syndic CEO knew how insincere that statement sounded. "But those who attempt to 'negotiate' will die, though perhaps not as quickly as your Admiral."

"You have one hour to surrender your ships. After that, we will move in and crush any resistance."

Geary stared at the screen after it blanked and the face of the communications officer returned, gazing back at Geary with despair. Geary had known the Syndics to be ruthless, but he'd never known them to commit this kind of atrocity. Like other things Geary had encountered, it seemed the Syndics had changed over the long course of this war, and not for the better.

It took a long moment for it to sink in that his command of the fleet was no longer a temporary thing. A fleet decimated in battle and trapped, facing overwhelmingly superior numbers. With one hour's grace. And here was this communications officer, and uncounted others like him, hoping and praying that Geary could somehow do something.

Geary took a deep breath, knowing the emptiness he had felt since his rescue was helping to keep his face composed. "Get me Captain . . ." What was the name Admiral Bloch had mentioned? "Desjani. Captain Desjani. Now."

"Yes, sir! She's on the bridge, sir."

On the bridge. Geary belatedly recalled that Desjani was *Dauntless*'s commanding officer. Had he met her? He couldn't remember.

Within moments, Captain Desjani's face was displayed

on the screen. Middle-aged perhaps, her face worn with the strain of time, experience, and the recent disastrous battle, so that Geary couldn't even have guessed at how she'd look in a time and place of peace and calm. "I was told you wanted to speak with me."

"Captain, are you aware of the recent Syndic message?"

She swallowed before answering. "Yes. It was sent to all ships, so every commanding officer saw it."

"Do you know why the Syndics killed Admiral Bloch?"

Desjani's mouth twisted in a snarl. "Because they're soulless scum."

Geary felt a twinge of anger. "That's not a reason, Captain."

She stared at him for a moment. "They decapitated our leadership, Captain Geary. A Syndic fleet would be crippled if left leaderless, and they're assuming we'll work the same way. They want to dishearten us by showing a massacre, and by openly killing all of our leaders they're trying to make sure we won't be able to organize any more resistance."

He stared back, unable to form words at first. "Captain Desjani, this fleet is not leaderless."

Desjani's expression shifted and her eyes widened. "*You're* in command?"

"That's what Admiral Bloch said. I thought you'd have been aware of it."

"I was informed, but . . . I was uncertain how you'd respond, Captain Geary. But you *will* exercise command? Praise the living stars. I need to inform the other ships. I was monitoring their discussion about what we should do when I was notified to call you."

Geary forgot whatever he'd intended saying next as the possible implications of Desjani's statement sunk in. "Discussing? What are the other ships' captains discussing?"

"What to do, sir. They're discussing and debating what to do following the death of Admiral Bloch and all of the other flag rank officers."

"They're *what*?" Inside Geary, ice cracked. "Weren't

they also informed I'd been placed in command of the fleet by Admiral Bloch?"

"Yes . . . sir."

"Haven't any of them contacted the flagship for instructions?"

Desjani's face, recently radiant with hope, now picked up another emotion, the wariness of an experienced officer when his or her boss showed signs of cycling off of the nearest bulkhead. "Uh . . . no, sir. There've been no communications addressed to the flagship."

"They're *debating* what to do and they haven't even contacted the flagship?" Geary couldn't quite grasp the idea. Letting the custom of saluting fall by the wayside was one thing, but individual ship captains ignoring the presence of higher authority? What had happened to the Alliance fleet he'd known? Captain Desjani was eyeing him, waiting for the explosion she seemed certain was coming. Instead, he spoke with forced calm as the right words came from somewhere inside him, spooling out like an ancient recording brought to life. "Captain. Please contact the commanding officers of every ship. Inform them that the fleet commander requires their presence at a conference onboard the flagship."

"We have less than a hour left before the Syndic deadline, Captain Geary."

"I'm aware of that, Captain Desjani." *And I'm increasingly aware that I need to show these people I'm in command before this fleet falls apart, and I need to learn something about them before I seriously misjudge anything critical. I know too damn little about everything.* "Admiral Bloch showed me his conference room. He said he could gather his captains for a virtual meeting there."

"Yes, sir. The necessary data net is still functioning within the fleet."

"Good. I want them ready at that conference in ten minutes, and to acknowledge that order individually within five minutes, and if any one of them tries to beg off, tell them attendance is mandatory."

"Yes, sir."

He remembered with a start of guilt that he'd been ordering around the captain of a ship on her own vessel without any special courtesy. He'd hated that kind of thing, once, when it'd been done to him. He needed to remember that now. "Thank you, Captain. Please meet me outside the flag conference room in . . . eight minutes."

If his memory served, the conference room lay about five minutes' walk from his stateroom. Geary took advantage of the three minutes that left him to call up the fleet disposition again, staring intently at the way the ships of the Alliance fleet were formed up and mentally tallying their degrees of damage. What had once been a dutiful intellectual exercise had become something he must grasp as well as he could within three minutes. He noticed something missing from the display, something he knew ought to be there and added it in, then he stared at the display a little longer, trying to understand why it didn't make sense to him.

Once again through the passageways of the *Dauntless*, once again the faces of the crew harkening to him. Geary remembered his promise to Admiral Bloch and tried to look like he knew what he was doing. He'd been a junior officer once, so he'd learned that trick long ago. He wasn't sure what else he might've learned that could really help now.

An Alliance Marine stood at rigid attention outside of the flag conference room and saluted as Geary approached. The gesture startled him for a moment, until he realized that if anyone would retain old traditions it would be the Marines.

Captain Desjani stepped forward. "Captain Geary, all ships' commanding officers are present."

He looked toward the conference room, seeming to be empty from this angle and outside of the viewing area. "All of them."

"Yes, sir. Most of them seemed very happy to receive your order, sir," Desjani added in a rush.

"Happy." Of course they'd been happy. They hadn't known what to do. But now they had him to turn to. Desjani, too, who seemed to have shed at least a decade of age since Geary had told her he'd exercise command. *Waiting for the hero to save the day*, Geary thought bitterly. *But that's unfair. After what they've been through* . . . He thought about how he felt, the emptiness inside, and wondered what emptiness these others might be feeling with their own universe suddenly changed beyond expectation. He gave the *Dauntless*'s Captain a searching look, trying to see beneath the weariness she projected. "What shape are they in?"

She frowned as if uncertain of the question. "They've given us the latest status reports on damage to their ships, sir. You can access them—"

"I already have. I don't mean their ships. You talked to them. I assume you know them. What shape are *they* in?"

Captain Desjani hesitated. "They've all seen the message from the Syndics, sir."

"You already told me that. Now tell me your honest opinion of those ship commanders. Have they been beaten?"

"We're not beaten, sir!" But the words seem to falter at the end, and Desjani's eyes shifted toward the deck for a moment. "They're . . . tired, sir. We all are. We thought this strike at the Syndic home system would finally tip the balance, finally bring about an end to the war. We've been fighting a very long time, sir. And we've gone from that hope to . . . to . . ."

"This." Geary didn't want to hear the plan described again. Admiral Bloch had explained it a score of times when talking to Geary. A bold blow, made possible by something called the hypernet, which hadn't existed in Geary's time, and by a Syndic traitor. An alleged Syndic traitor, anyway. "Am I right in assuming the ships we're confronting represent the bulk of the Syndic fleet?"

"Yes, sir. Damn near the entire Syndic fleet." Desjani's

voice wavered, and she visibly fought for control. "Waiting for us. Our leading elements didn't stand a chance."

"The main body fought its way clear."

"Yes. But at considerable cost. Black—Excuse me. We can't hope to defeat the Syndic forces out there with what we've got left."

Geary frowned, only half-noticing the way Desjani had abruptly changed what she was saying. More important, at the moment, was what she'd actually said. No hope. According to the ancient legend of Pandora's box, hope was supposed to be the one gift the box had contained amidst its ills. Something to keep people going when nothing else was left. But if these people had truly lost hope . . . Then he looked squarely at Captain Desjani and saw again what he didn't want to see. Hope did still exist there, in eyes focused on him.

"Sir." The *Dauntless*'s Captain spoke in an oddly stilted manner. "By your leave, sir. We need you, sir. They, we all, need something to believe in. Someone who can get us out of this."

"I'm not a legend, Captain, or whatever you think I am." There. He'd finally said it. "I'm a man. I can't work miracles."

"You're 'Black Jack' Geary, sir! You fought one of the first battles of this war, against overwhelming odds."

"And I *lost*, Captain."

"No, sir!" Geary frowned again, startled by Desjani's vehemence. "You held off the attack, you ensured every ship in that convoy got away! And then you still held the enemy, letting the other escorts escape. Held the Syndics off until you ordered your crew to save themselves while you remained behind and fought the enemy until your ship's destruction. I learned that story in school, sir, just like every child in the Alliance!"

Geary stared at her. *It wasn't like that, Captain*, he wanted to say out loud. *I fought because I had to. Because that was what I'd taken an oath to do. Then we stayed because my ship'd been too badly damaged to run. I told the* crew to evacuate, yes, but that was my duty, too, not hero-ism. Someone had to provide covering fire a little longer so the escape pods could get away, and that was my job.

I didn't want to die. When my ship's last combat system was knocked out, I set the power core on self-destruct and tried to get away using a remaining survival pod. A dam-aged pod that was further damaged when my ship blew up. No working beacon. Just another piece of junk in a system filled with junk from the battle. No one found me. Not until almost a hundred years later, when your mighty fleet came sneaking through that backwater system and stumbled across me.

To finally wake me up and tell me the Alliance has turned me into something I didn't recognize. Promoted in the wake of my supposed death during my "last stand" to the rank of Captain in the fleet and legendary hero of the Alliance. I think I can be a Captain. How can anyone liv-ing be a legendary hero?

But Geary said nothing, because looking at Desjani he knew she wouldn't believe it, and because he now knew that if she did believe, he'd be killing her last hope. I prom-ised the Admiral I'd save this fleet if I could. I don't see how I can do that. But maybe this heroic idol they believe in has a chance of somehow doing it. "That was a long time ago, Captain," he finally replied softly. "But I'll do my best." And pray it may be enough. "Now, before this meeting, what's this 'key' business about?"

Desjani looked carefully up and down the passageway before answering, and then spoke so quietly Geary could barely hear her. "The Syndic hypernet key is onboard the Dauntless."

"What the hell does that mean?"

She looked startled. "I'm sorry. I forgot you didn't have hypernet."

"All I know about it is that this hypernet provides much faster interstellar travel than the system jump drives do."

"Much faster. Yes, sir. The exact advantage over system jumps varies based on some science I frankly don't understand, but it's usually by a factor between ten times and one hundred times as fast."

"Damn."

Captain Desjani nodded, looking around quickly to once again ensure no one could hear them. "Unlike the system jumps, which use the gravity wells from stars, a hypernet has to be created, and when a hypernet is set up, the entire net is aligned to what's usually called a frequency, though it's actually something more complicated than that. Each gate is assigned a sort of subfrequency. To use a particular hypernet, you need what's called a key. It allows you enter that net and select the gate you want."

Geary nodded, trying to absorb the implications. "So having a key to the Syndic hypernet let's us use it. Where'd *Dauntless* get a Syndic key?"

"We got it from the traitor." Her face twisted. "The double traitor. It made our strike at the Syndic home system possible."

"I see. They gave you the means to get here and then waited for you." *Guessing you'd never be able to resist such an opportunity.*

Desjani grimaced. "Yes, sir."

"Then the Syndics know we have this key. Why's the fact it's on *Dauntless* so important?"

"Because they know we *had* it, but they don't know what ship it was on. They don't know if it's been destroyed already. They don't know if one of the surviving ships still has it. If they knew it was on *Dauntless* . . ."

"They'd immediately throw everything they had at her to make sure the key was destroyed."

"Yes, sir."

"They can't just change the, uh, frequency of their hypernet?"

Desjani shook her head. "That's impossible, Captain Geary. Once the net is constructed, its fundamental characteristics can't be changed."

Geary thought for a moment, all too aware of how much he had to learn but also knowing that he had to get into the conference room quickly to meet with the gathering ship captains. "How big is this key?"

"Too big for someone to carry, if that's what you mean. It's large and heavy."

"Can we duplicate it? Make copies and give some to other ships?"

"No. Copying a hypernet key is beyond the capabilities of any ship in the fleet. Back home, in Alliance space, there are worlds with that capability."

He thought for another moment, thought about what that key would mean to the Alliance if it could be returned home. One more responsibility for the great hero to shoulder. "Let's go meet the ship commanders." People who looked like him but apparently didn't quite think like him. How long would it take him to figure out the differences forged by a hundred years, a hundred years spent at war? He'd have to listen carefully to everything they said . . . "Wait. One more thing. A few moments ago, when you said we didn't have any chance of defeating the Syndic fleet here, you started to say something else. What?"

Desjani looked uncomfortable, her eyes shifting to look past Geary. "I . . . I started to say that Black Jack himself couldn't defeat this Syndic fleet. Sir."

Black Jack himself couldn't do it. The expression had the ring of something used all the time. For a moment, Geary couldn't figure out how to respond to that. Then a twinge of self-mockery came to his rescue. "Well, Captain Desjani, we'd better hope you're wrong about that, hadn't we?"

She stared at him, then unexpectedly grinned. "Yes."

Geary went inside. Desjani followed him into the room, then when he paused, she indicated one seat not far from the door. The conference room wasn't all that large in reality. Geary had seen it with the conferencing systems off, just a moderately sized room with a moderately sized table to accommodate those who might actually sit in here. But with the systems on, as Geary came to his designated seat at the table, he saw it stretching out with scores of seats, each seat occupied by the commanding officer of a fleet ship. Geary couldn't help staring a little at them, amazed at how each officer looked exactly like he or she was sitting here instead of on their own ships. As his eyes focused on each, their image came close, as if they were now sitting nearby, and a small tag popped up with their name and ship clearly identified. In the center of the table, easy to see from every seat, a large projection showed the disposition of the Alliance Fleet and of the Syndics. Virtual image technology had clearly improved during his long sleep.

I guess it's a lot easier to hold meetings now. Geary took a moment to wonder if that was a good thing, or if that was one of the things which had sapped the spirit from the fleet. He stood at his seat, wondering if anyone should or would call everyone else to attention, but when that didn't happen, he sat stiffly.

No one spoke. With the exception of Captain Desjani, who'd taken a real seat just to his left, every other officer was looking at him. Geary looked back at them, one by one, letting his gaze linger on each briefly before moving on. Some gazed back with carefully blank expressions, hiding their thoughts. A number of others held challenges in their eyes, plainly not receptive to Geary's authority. But the majority stared at him with the desperation of the dying, praying for deliverance. To varying degrees, all of them seemed weary and worried.

Geary took a deep breath, deciding to deliberately avoid the informality he'd seen among this fleet in favor of the formal speech and actions he'd always known. "For those of you who haven't met me, I am Captain John Geary. When Admiral Bloch left the *Dauntless*, he placed me in command of the fleet. I intend to carry out that responsibility to the best of my ability." He wondered what his voice sounded like to them, what the words meant to them.

A woman who must be approaching retirement age gave Geary an acidic look. "Did Admiral Bloch provide any reason for that action?"

Geary frowned at her, feeling a slow glow of heat forming inside and welcoming the relief from the coldness he'd felt since being rescued. "I'm personally not accustomed to asking my superiors to provide me with reasons to justify their decisions." A ripple ran through the ranks of the ship captains, but what it meant he couldn't tell. "Admiral Bloch did, however, inform me that I was the senior officer in rank and length of service remaining with this fleet."

The woman's eyebrows shot upward. "Length of service? Are you serious?"

"Are you suggesting we compare dates of rank, Captain . . ." he looked at the identifying tag floating near her, "Captain Faresa?"

"That would be meaningless, as you are aware."

"No, I am *not* aware." Geary let the growing heat enter his voice. "If this fleet begins picking and choosing which rank and seniority factors matter, it will dissolve into chaos, and *you will all die.*"

A moment of silence followed before another officer broke in. Captain Numos of the *Orion*, Geary saw. "Are you suggesting you can somehow offer us salvation? There are only two options available to us as a fleet, Captain. We die fighting, or submit to, at best, living slavery and slower death."

Geary found himself smiling wearily. "I can die fighting. I imagine it's easier the second time around."

Captain Duellos, of the *Courageous*, laughed. "Very good, Captain Geary! If that's our fate—"

Numos interrupted again. "There's another option. If we break up, every ship for itself, some of us may win through to the hypernet gate—"

"Break up?" another captain demanded. "You mean every ship for itself?"

"Yes! The slower and more heavily damaged ships are doomed anyway. There's no sense—"

"My ship took damage because it absorbed enemy fire that would've been aimed at yours otherwise! And now you want to leave us to Syndic labor camps?"

"If there's no alternative—"

"Quiet." It wasn't until everyone stared at him that Geary realized he'd spoken. From their expressions, he wondered what his voice had sounded like this time. "This fleet will not abandon any ships."

Numos spoke again and Geary could see some of the other officers nodding in agreement with his words. "That's not a reasoned judgment because you're not qualified to command this fleet. You know that. Your knowledge of weapons and tactics is hopelessly outdated. You lack understanding of the current situation, here and at home. You—"

Something inside Geary flared to full life in a blast of heat. "Captain Numos, I am not here to debate command issues with you or any other officer of this fleet."

"You're not qualified to command! You don't know—"

"I *know* I'm in command by virtue of seniority and the last order of Admiral Bloch, and that if I require information to support *my* command, then my *subordinates* will provide that information."

"I'm not—"

"And if you or any other ship commander feel themselves to be incapable of supporting me properly or following orders, I *will* relieve them of command and replace them with officers I can depend upon. And, I might add, officers that other ships can depend upon to support *them*." Numos's face flushed. "Do *you* feel incapable of supporting me properly, Captain Numos?"

Numos swallowed, then spoke with stubborn insistence but without the confidence he'd shown earlier. "Captain Geary, your seniority is a fluke, as you yourself know. Your date of rank is almost a century old because your promotion to Captain was granted *posthumously*. No one knew you were still alive. A century in survival hibernation does not impart any experience." Some of the other captains made small motions of agreement, apparently emboldening Numos again. "We must choose a commanding officer based on their ability to deal with the current situation, and that requires current knowledge."

Geary stared back at Numos so coldly that he leaned back as if being threatened. "In the Alliance Fleet I know, no one 'chose' their commanders. I have no intention of allowing you or anyone else to interfere with my command authority."

A stout man down at one end of the table cleared his throat. "Captain Geary is senior. He's in command. End of discussion."

Geary nodded toward him, fixing the name and face in memory. Captain Tulev of the *Leviathan*. Someone Geary could count on.

Then a woman in the uniform of the Alliance Marines spoke. Colonel Carabali, who must've inherited her command when the Marine general accompanying the fleet died along with the other flag officers. "We're sworn to obey our commanders and defend the Alliance. The Marines understand that Captain Geary is our commander under Alliance Fleet Regulations."

Another ship's Captain spoke up, her voice ragged. "Dammit, if he can't get us out of this, who can?"

All eyes focused on Geary again as the woman openly voiced what so many of them had been thinking. He wanted to avoid those faces, but he had to meet their hope and skepticism dead on. Geary couldn't hide anymore. "I'm going to try."

TWO

SILENCE hung in the room for a moment, then Captain Faresa spoke again, her voice and expression still harsh. "How, Captain? What magic will you use? We have less than an hour remaining before the Syndic deadline expires."

Geary gave her an equally harsh look, but he could gaze down the ranks of ship commanders and see that his command authority hung on a knife-edge. For the first time, he noticed how young many of them were. Younger than the ship captains he'd known a century ago and clearly less hardened or experienced than those captains. Too many of them were watching and waiting, ready to jump in any direction. And if they started jumping, the entire fleet might fall apart and leave the Syndics with easy pickings. "Then we'd better use that time thinking instead of hurling barbs at each other, shouldn't we?" He pointed at the center of the table, where the display portrayed the ships of the Alliance fleet. The most heavily damaged ships had formed into a rough sphere. Between them and the looming wall of the Syndic fleet, a rectangular wall of Alliance ships spread out, bent into a crescent facing the enemy. It looked impressive, until you totaled up the ships involved and realized the waiting Syndic sledgehammer would shatter the Alliance crescent as if it were made of glass.

Captain Duellos pointed as well. "Unfortunately, this display is accurate, and neither the realities of war nor the laws of physics have changed since your last battle, Captain Geary. We're here, the Syndics are here only two and a half light-minutes away from our leading elements, and the hypernet gate is"—his hand swung around to an area on the other side of the enemy fleet—"here, thirty light-minutes from us, on the wrong side of the enemy."

"If we could have a few more hours to repair our damaged ships," someone suggested.

"A few more hours or a few more days wouldn't help," another shot back. "The Syndics are repairing their damage, too. And they can count on reinforcements and resupply coming through that gate behind them!"

Duellos nodded to Geary. "I agree. Time is not on our side, even if the Syndic deadline is not enforced."

Geary nodded back, his eyes once again tracking along the officers ranked around the table. "We can't hold off an attack. Nor can we attack them and have any expectation of survival."

Numos spoke again, his face red. "Individual ships might be able to—"

"To what, Captain? Get to that . . . gate? Then what?" Geary heard a collective intake of breath. "This fleet has a Syndic hypernet key. I know that. But I assume the ships using it must go through together." A murmur of agreement came. "I repeat, an-every-ship-for-itself plan will not be followed by this fleet, and any commanding officer who tries it will be court-martialed by me if I can catch them, or killed by the Syndics when they reach that gate *alone* and can't get through it." Silence.

Geary sat back and rubbed his chin. "That's what we can't do. But it's not every option. Perhaps one of you can explain this to me." He hesitated over the display controls, finally finding the right ones. "Here." Geary pointed to a spot slightly behind and off to the side from the Alliance forces. "Twenty light-minutes away from the Alliance ships nearest to it. Why isn't this guarded?"

Everyone frowned and craned to look. Finally, Captain Faresa gave Geary one of her looks, one that seemed capable of eating away metal. "Because it's meaningless."

"Meaningless." Geary let the word hang for a moment, wondering as he did so if he could figure out a legitimate way to avoid having to see Faresa's face again. "That's the system jump point." Shrugs met his statement. "Dammit, why can't we use that to get out of this?"

Duellos spoke slowly. "Captain Geary, there's likely only one or two stars within jump range of that point."

"There's only one," Geary stated flatly. It hadn't been hard to look up that piece of information. "Corvus."

"Then you see the problem, sir. The system jump method is too limited in range. The Corvus System is itself only a few light years away, and still deeply buried within Syndic territory."

"I know that. But from Corvus we could jump to any of"—he checked his figures—"three other systems." Geary could see the other officers exchanging looks, but no one spoke. "From one of those systems we could jump to others."

Captain Faresa shook her head. "You aren't seriously suggesting getting back to Alliance space by using system jump drives, are you?"

"Why not? It's still faster-than-light."

"Not nearly faster-than-light enough! Do you have any idea how deep in Syndic space we are?"

Geary openly glared at her. "Since the shape of the galaxy hasn't altered appreciably since my last command, yes, I do know how deep we are in Syndic space. So we've got a long haul out of here. It's a chance. Do you prefer dying here?"

"Better that than commit slow suicide! We don't have the supplies to sustain that kind of journey. It would take many months. Perhaps years, depending on the route. But that's irrelevant, because the Syndic fleet will simply get there ahead of us and destroy us as we arrive!"

Geary was trying to tamp down his anger enough to formulate an answer, when Captain Desjani began speaking as if to herself. "Corvus System isn't on the Syndic hypernet. The Syndic fleet couldn't beat us there." Desjani looked around. "They'd have to follow us through the same system jump point. That'd take time."

Captain Duellos nodded eagerly. "Yes! We'd have a free window to transit Corvus to our next jump point. Not a long one, but time enough. Then the Syndics would have to guess what our next destination would be."

"We don't have the supplies!" Faresa insisted. Duellos glared at her in a way that made it clear there was no love lost between them. "Who even knows what's at Corvus?"

"It can't be that important," someone suggested. "Not if the system isn't on the Syndic hypernet."

"We don't know what's there!"

"Captain Faresa." She turned to glare at Geary as he gestured to the representation of the Syndic fleet. "We know what's here, don't we? Can anything in Corvus be worse? We'll face better odds no matter what, and we'll have the transit time in jump space to repair internal damage to the ships."

Heads nodded and smiles started to appear. "But, supplies . . ." Faresa tried to insist.

"I assume there's something at Corvus." Geary craned his head to look at the data. "This says there was a Syndic self-defense base. Do those still stock supplies that Syndic ships passing through could draw on?"

"They used to . . ."

"They'll have something. And there's an inhabited planet in that system. There'll be some off-planet facilities, in-system traffic. Stuff we can get parts and food and other essentials off of." Geary studied the display, lost for the moment in calculation and momentarily unaware of the other officers. "It'd be a snatch-and-grab through Corvus.

The Syndics will be coming out of that jump point behind us as fast as they can, so it'll be a race to get our slower and more heavily damaged ships through the system before we can be caught." He looked around, seeing uncertainty on many faces. "We can do this."

Captain Tulev spoke again. "Captain Geary, I must warn that getting to the jump point here will not be easy."

"It's not guarded."

"No. But the Syndic fleet is close, and they have some very fast ships. They can leave their slower ships behind to catch up. We can't."

Geary nodded. "Very true. Ladies and gentlemen, I will stall the Syndics as long as I can. But as soon as we start moving—"

"Captain." A short woman, her eyes intense, leaned forward. "We could maneuver the fleet, look like we're reorganizing to meet an attack, and get those damaged and slow ships closer to the jump point under cover of those movements."

Geary smiled. Commander Cresida of the *Furious*. He'd have to remember her, too. "Do you have some ideas?"

"Yes. I do."

"Let me see them as soon as you can work them out."

"It'll be a pleasure, Captain Geary." Cresida leaned back again, her scornful gaze directed toward the area where Numos and Faresa were sitting.

Geary looked at everyone again. *Still shaky. But I'm giving them something to do. Something that might work, even if seems such a long shot they wouldn't even consider it without me pushing them. Face it, Geary, without you they wouldn't have even thought of it because they were all fixated on that hypernet gate, doing the enemy's job for them by closing out their own options.* "Then let's get going." Instead of responding directly, the other captains all exchanged surprised looks. "What's wrong? Somebody tell me."

Captain Desjani spoke with visible reluctance. "It's customary for proposed courses of actions to be finalized, then debated by the senior officers and ship commanders, with a vote afterward to affirm support."

"A *vote*?" He stared at her, then around the table. No wonder Admiral Bloch had sometimes struck him as a politician running for office. "When the hell did this 'custom' begin?"

Desjani grimaced. "I'm not personally familiar—"

"Well, I don't have time for a history lesson right now. And we don't have time to debate what to do. I may not know what everything is like now, but one thing I do know is that waiting, paralyzed, for a snake to strike is the worst possible course of action. Indecision kills ships and fleets. We have to act and act decisively in the time we have. I will not conduct any votes while I am in command. I am open to suggestions and proposals. I *want* input from you. But I am in command. That's what you want, isn't it? You want Black Jack Geary to lead you out of this mess, don't you? Well, then, by the living stars I *will* lead you, but I will do so in the best way I know how!"

He subsided, watching them, wondering if he'd pushed too far. A long moment passed. Then Commander Cresida leaned forward again. "I've got orders to follow. Orders from the fleet commander. I don't have time for nonsense when there's work to do on the *Furious*. Captain Geary?"

Geary gave her a grin. "By all means, Commander."

Cresida vanished from her place at the table as she broke the connection. Then, as if her words and action had been a domino falling, all of the other officers hastily rose and bid farewells. Geary got the sense that, ironically, many of them saw further debate as a harder option than following Geary at this point.

Geary watched them vanish with an odd sense of longing. There ought to be handshakes and conversation as they all filed through the hatch, a few moments of personal interaction forced upon everyone by the need to move a lot of people in a big room through one small doorway. But not here, and not now. The figures of his subordinates simply popped out of existence, and the apparent great size of the room and its massive conference table dwindled as its virtual occupants vanished, until within moments it was an unremarkable compartment dominated by an unremarkable conference table.

However, aside from the real presence of Captain Desjani still standing nearby, two small clusters of officers remained. Geary frowned at them, noticing for the first time that their uniforms differed in small ways from that of the Alliance fleet. He concentrated on their identification. One set of officers belonged to the Rift Federation, while the other slightly larger group were part of the Callas Republic. He remembered both associations of planets. Neither the Rift Federation nor the Republic had contained many inhabited worlds in his time, and both had been neutral. Events had clearly drawn them into the war on the side of the Alliance, though. Geary nodded toward them, wondering just how much authority he could wield over these allies. "Yes?"

The Rift Federation officers looked toward the Republic officers, who made way for a woman in a civilian suit. Geary fought back a frown as he saw her. *I didn't say no one but ship commanders could attend, did I? I don't think so. Who is this?* The identification tag next to her image read "C-P Rione." *What does that mean?*

The woman eyed Geary, her face impassive. "Are you aware that under the terms of our agreement, our ships may be withdrawn from Alliance control if competent authority should determine they are not being employed in the best interests of our home worlds?"

"No. I didn't know that. I assume you're the 'competent authority' in question?"

"Yes." She inclined her head very slightly toward Geary. "I am Co-President Victoria Rione of the Callas Republic."

Geary glanced at Captain Desjani, who shrugged apologetically, then back at Victoria Rione. "I'm honored to meet you, ma'am. But there's a great deal to do—"

She held up one hand, palm out. "Please, Captain Geary. I must insist upon a private conference with you."

"I'm sure there'll be plenty of time—"

"*Before* I commit our ships to your command." She looked toward the Rift Federation officers. "The ships of the Rift Navy have agreed to follow my recommendations on the matter."

Well, damn. Another glance at Desjani earned a shake of her head. He'd have to go through with this. "Where . . . ?"

Desjani stepped away. "Here, Captain Geary. I'll leave the room, and a virtual privacy shield will drop around you and the co-president. When you've finished the private conference, say 'end private conference end' and you'll both be able to interact with the other officers again if you want to." She hastened out the hatch as if happy to be able to avoid this engagement at least.

Geary watched her go, composing his face as carefully as he could. Wishing he could return to the numbed state he'd endured since being awakened, he turned to face the politician, whose cold stare apparently hadn't left Geary at any point. "What is it you want to talk about?"

"Trust." Her voice wasn't a single degree warmer than her expression. "Specifically, why I should entrust the surviving ships of the Republic to your command."

Geary looked down, rubbing his forehead, then back at her. "I could point out that the only alternative is to entrust their fate to the Syndics, and we've recently seen how the Syndics do business."

"They might deal differently with us, Captain."

Then go get your precious rear end shot off by the Syndic special forces and see if I care! But he knew he'd need every ship he could, and part of him hated to think of leaving anyone behind, willingly or not. "I don't think that'd be a good idea."

"If so, *explain why*, Captain Geary."

He took a deep breath and matched her glare. "Because the Syndics massacred Admiral Bloch and everyone with him when they tried to negotiate with all the ships we've got left backing them up. You'll be negotiating with a fraction of that amount of backing. Do you think the Syndics will deal better within someone in a much weaker position?"

"I see." She looked away at last and began pacing back and forth down one side of the room. "You don't think the combined ships of the Republic and the Federation will impress the Syndics."

"I don't think the combined ships of the Republic, the Federation, *and* the Alliance have a snowball's chance in hell of surviving against an all-out attack by the forces the Syndics have arrayed out there. We could hurt them, maybe badly, but not survive. And unless the Syndics have completely changed since I knew them last, they never deal fairly. The stronger party imposes whatever terms it thinks it can enforce."

Rione stopped pacing, looking down at the deck, then back at him. "That's right. You've thought this out from more than a purely combat viewpoint."

Geary reached for the nearest seat and slumped into it. He hadn't exerted himself this much, physically or emotionally, since his rescue, and the fleet physicians had clucked anxiously over him on just those counts after he'd been thawed out. No telling what results such a long hibernation might have on Geary's physiology, they'd warned. *I guess I get to field-test the question.* "Yes, Madam Co-President. I did try to think it out."

"Don't patronize me. These ships are the life of my Republic. If they're destroyed—"

"I want to get every ship that I can home."

"Really? Instead of regrouping and trying to stage a brilliant counterattack resulting in a glorious victory? Isn't that what you really want, Captain Geary?"

Geary just looked at her, not bothering to hide his weariness. "You seem to think you know me."

"I do know you, Captain Geary. I've heard all about you. You're a Hero. I don't like Heroes, Captain. Heroes lead armies and fleets to their deaths."

Geary sat back, rubbing his eyes now. "*I'm* supposed to be dead," he reminded her.

"Which makes you all the more a case in point." Rione took two steps toward the situation display still visible on the conference table and pointed to it. "Do you know why Admiral Bloch took this chance, why he gambled so much of the Alliance's power on this operation?"

"He told me it looked like a way to finally force an end to the war."

"Oh, yes." Rione nodded, her eyes still on the display. "A daring and bold blow. An operation worthy of Black Jack Geary himself," she added softly. "That's a quote, Captain."

Geary stiffened. "He never said anything like that to me."

"Of course not. But he said it to others. And invoking the spirit of the great Black Jack Geary helped win approval for this attack. Which as you see, has gone so well."

"Don't blame me for this! I'm going to get what's left of this fleet out of it if I can, but I didn't put it here to begin with!"

She paused, as if listening intently to Geary. "Why did you assume command?"

"Why?" He waved one hand toward the hatch. "Because Admiral Bloch asked me to. Ordered me to! And then . . . they . . ." He glowered at the deck, unwilling to look at her. "I didn't have any choice."

"You fought to assert your authority. I saw that, Captain Geary."

"I *had* to. Without someone taking command, someone with a legitimate right to command, this fleet would've fallen apart and been destroyed in detail by the Syndics. You must've seen that, too."

She bent down, and her eyes sought his. "Can I trust Black Jack Geary? That's who you are."

"I'm an officer of the Alliance. And . . . I have a job to do. If I can." He tried to bite off the last three words and failed, not wanting to show any weakness of spirit, not sure how that might harm the fleet's already slim chances. "That's all I am."

"All? Not the hero of legend?" She came closer, peering at him. "Who are you, then?"

"I thought you said you already knew that."

"I know Black Jack Geary, and I fear that the great Black Jack Geary will try to do something heroic that will seal the fate of this fleet and perhaps that of the Alliance and of my own people as well. Are you Black Jack Geary?"

He laughed, unable to control it. "Nobody could be him."

She spent a long moment watching him, then turned and walked a few steps away again. "Where's the hypernet key?"

"What?"

She spun, eyes flashing. "The Syndic hypernet key. I know there's one still in the fleet. If it had been destroyed, you'd have told everyone that to ensure they followed your plan. It still exists. Where is it?"

"I'm sorry, but—"

"*Does* it still exist?"

He met her eyes, trying to decide what to do, what to say, and hating the idea of lying. "Yes."

"Where?"

"I'd prefer not to say."

"Suppose I said I'd agree to place my ships and those of the Federation under your command if you told me?"

He managed a crooked half-smile. "I'd still prefer not to say, but for the sake of those ships, I'd tell you."

"You'd agree to that? You know the importance of that information?"

"Yes. And yes, I'd agree to tell you, if that's what it took to get those ships out of here with the rest of the fleet."

Co-President Rione's eyes narrowed. "I could then trade that information to the Syndics in exchange for safe passage."

That hadn't occurred to him. He glared at her. "Why the hell are you telling me that?"

"To let you know that misplaced trust can be deadly. But you were willing to grant trust to me. I'll be blunt, Captain Geary, I'm agreeing to this only because I don't see any other choice. The ships of the Republic will remain in this fleet, and I'm certain the Rift Federation ships will follow my recommendation to do so as well. But I reserve the right to remove those ships from your command whenever I see fit."

He shrugged. "It doesn't look like I've got any other choice, either, do I?"

Rione actually smiled. "No, you don't."

"Thank you." Geary paused, then stood carefully, one hand supporting himself on the chair. "There's something I'd like from you." The co-president frowned. "I need a politician. Someone who can make an argument last as long as possible. Someone good with saying lots of words that don't mean what they sound like, and avoiding commitments."

"Why, thank you, Captain Geary." Apparently Co-President Rione did have a sense of humor buried somewhere inside her.

"Don't mention it." He waved at the display, where the wall of Syndic ships loomed over the Alliance fleet. "The Syndic deadline isn't more than half an hour away, now. We're going to need every minute we can get to repair damage and reposition our fleet in readiness to bolt for that jump point. Can you speak to the Syndics, string them along and try to keep them from moving in as long as possible?"

"You mean on behalf of the Republic and the Rift, or of the entire fleet?"

"Whatever works. Whatever will keep them talking. Just buy us some time, Madam Co-President. As much as you possibly can."

She nodded. "That's a reasonable request, Captain

Geary. I will open the talks with the Syndics as soon as I board my shuttle."

He stared at her. "Shuttle? You're not going to—"

"The Syndic flagship? No, Captain Geary. I'm coming here. To the *Dauntless*. I want to keep a personal eye on you. And on a certain very important piece of equipment. Oh, yes. You told me nothing. But I believe I can best safeguard the interests of my people by being on your ship."

Geary took a deep breath, then nodded. "I'll notify Captain Desjani you're coming."

"Thank you, Captain Geary." Another smile, as challenging as her eyes. "Now I shall attempt to frighten the Syndics into giving us all more time." With that, her image vanished.

Geary sat for a moment looking at the spot that Rione had seemed to occupy. *Maybe she* can *frighten the Syndics into holding off a little while longer. She sure scares me.*

CAPTAIN Desjani took the news of Co-President Rione's imminent arrival as if it were just one more malign event in a day filled with them. "At least we've still got those ships with us."

"Yes." Geary looked around. "Captain Desjani, where's Admiral Bloch's staff?"

"His staff?"

"Yes. All the officers assigned to him as fleet commander. Where are they? I'd think they'd have sought me out."

Desjani looked briefly puzzled, then her expression cleared. "Oh, I understand. You're thinking of the old days. I'm sorry," she added hastily in apparent response to the reaction she saw on Geary's face, "but much has changed. We've been short of experienced officers for a long time. The staffs you knew have been cannibalized so those officers would be free to be assigned to ships."

Geary shook his head. "Losses have been that bad?"

"Bad?" Desjani hesitated. "We've lost many ships over

the course of the war. The Syndics have lost more," she added hastily.

"I was wondering why many of the ship commanders seemed so young."

"There's . . . not always the luxury of allowing officers a long career before they're needed to command ships."

"I understand," Geary stated, even though he didn't really understand at all. All these young commanding officers, all these new ships . . . he felt the ice inside him again for a moment as he realized all of the ships whose data he'd examined were new or nearly new. Geary had assumed that was because older ships had been left behind since they were less capable. Now he wondered just how many older ships there were, just what the typical lifespan of the officers, sailors, and ships of the Alliance had dwindled to under the pressure of this war.

Captain Desjani was still explaining, as if she felt the need to personally justify the situation. "Losses haven't always been bad. But sometimes we lose a lot. A century of war drains a lot of ships and sailors from a fleet." She looked both angry and weary. "A lot of them. Admiral Bloch did have two senior aides assigned. You may not have seen them board the shuttle with him to go to the Syndic flagship, along with Admiral Bloch's chief of staff."

"No. *But then I wasn't aware of much of anything at that point.*

"They're all dead now, of course. There's some junior officers who were seconded to the staff, but they're all ship's company. They've got primary jobs on the *Dauntless.*"

"I assume they're needed there right now."

"Yes, although one of them's dead and another's too badly injured to leave sick bay. I would like to continue using the other two in their primary duties—"

Geary held up one hand to forestall further words. "By all means. I'll see them when conditions permit. Can you tell me how Admiral Bloch ran a fleet with such a small staff?"

Desjani made a face. "By only doing what needed to be done and leaving the rest to his ship commanders, I suppose. And the support systems available to you are very effective." She checked the time and looked alarmed. "Captain Geary, with your permission, I really must get back to the bridge."

"Permission granted." Desjani was hastening away even as Geary's arm quivered in anticipation of returning a farewell salute that never came. *Am I going to have to get used to that, or am I going to have to change the way they do things?* He looked over at the Marine, still standing at attention outside the entry to the conference room a short distance away. "Thank you." The Marine obliged with a rigidly proper salute, which Geary returned.

He started to head after Desjani, knowing he should be on the bridge as well, but felt his legs suddenly wavering as if their strength had fled again. Geary put out a hand, leaning on the bulkhead, and when certain of his balance, began walking slowly toward his stateroom.

He dropped gratefully into the chair, breathing heavily. *I can't afford this now. There's too much to do.* He dug inside a drawer, coming up with a med-pack containing the fleet physicians' best estimate of what he'd need to keep going. *They told me this stuff won't interfere with my thinking. What if it does? But if I don't take it I won't be able to do my job anyway.*

I need to stop getting into situations where all my options are potentially bad.

He slapped the med-pack against his arm, feeling the slight tingle that meant it was doing its work. It'd take a few moments to feel the effect, so he called up the support systems that Desjani had mentioned.

As soon as he did so, he saw a message from Commander Cresida of the *Furious*. It contained the plan she'd promised to reposition the fleet ships in preparation for fleeing to the jump point. Geary studied it as carefully as he could, feeling the pressure of time weighing on him. Less than half an hour, perhaps, before the Syndics moved;

less than that if they'd lied about how long they'd give the Alliance ship commanders to make up their minds. Once all the Alliance ships were in position, or once the Syndics started moving if that happened first, the plan called for the code name Overture to signal the fleet's withdrawal toward the jump point.

He felt a surge of frustration as he scanned ship names, wishing he knew more about how they'd move and how they'd fight. *Numos was right that my knowledge is outdated, but my ancestors know I'm still a better commander than he'll ever be.* And as he'd told Numos, right now acting instead of waiting was paramount. Muttering a quick prayer, he marked the plan approved and tagged it to be transmitted to the fleet.

He started to stand up, felt a quiver of unsteadiness still there, and sat again, forcing himself to wait a few more minutes. Turning back to the fleet statistics, Geary began scanning through them, trying to absorb as much knowledge of the ships as he could. As he'd suspected, they were all new or nearly so. If the average age of those ships meant what he thought it did, losses must have been, must still be, staggering.

The loss of a ship didn't necessarily mean the loss of the entire crew of course, but you'd still lose a lot of people.

Geary stared at the rough edge on his desk, finally realizing what it told him. Ships being churned out as fast as they could be built to replace losses in battles. Officers and sailors being rushed through training to crew those ships, then promoted quickly to replace those also lost in combat. And as those inexperienced crews in hastily constructed ships were hurled into battle, they kept taking heavy losses, dying too fast to learn. How long had the fleet been caught in that death spiral? *No wonder they forgot to salute. No wonder they've forgotten how a fleet should be commanded. They're all amateurs. Amateurs with the lives of their shipmates and the fate of the Alliance in their hands. Am I the only trained professional left in this entire fleet?*

What happened to all the ships and people I knew? Did they all die in battle while I slept?

Not wanting to think about that, Geary tried to concentrate on the data before him again, scrolling it quickly so he'd have to pay close attention. He frowned, suddenly half-aware of something he'd just skimmed over, and looked back again carefully. There it was. Alliance battle cruiser *Repulse*, commanding officer Commander Michael J. Geary. *Michael Geary was my brother's name. But he has to be long dead, and he never entered the fleet that I know of. Not before I went to sleep for a century, anyway.*

Do I have time to follow up on this? But we're going into battle, and if something happens I might never know. Geary hesitated, then punched in the code to speak to the commanding officer of the *Repulse*. It took a few moments, then an unnervingly almost-familiar face appeared. "Yes, sir?"

Neither the tone nor the expression of the *Repulse*'s commander seemed welcoming, but Geary couldn't stop from asking, not after seeing that face. "Pardon me, Commander Geary, but I'd like to know if we're related."

The other's face stayed hard and unyielding. "Yes."

"How? Are you—"

"My grandfather was your brother."

The ice threatened to take him again. His brother. A few years younger than him once upon a time. Geary was looking at a face reflecting the inheritance his brother had passed on to a grandchild, and suddenly the loss of his own time felt unbearable, and not just because the *Repulse*'s commander looked to be quite a few years older than Geary's own apparent age. His grandnephew had beaten the odds by surviving this long, but that didn't seem to have brought him any joy. "What . . ." Geary looked away and took a deep, shuddering breath. "I'm sorry. I don't know anything about you and . . . and . . . my brother. What happened to him?"

"He lived and he died," Geary's grandnephew stated flatly.

Something about the hostility brought Geary's temper out. "I know that. He was my brother, you cold bastard."

"Do you need anything else, sir?"

Geary glared at the man, seeing the signs of age there along with lines imparted by strong emotions. His grandnephew was certainly a couple of decades older than Geary, and those years hadn't been kind to him. "Yes. There is something else. What the hell did I ever do to you?"

The other man actually smiled, though the expression held no humor. "You? Nothing. Not to me, or to my father, or to my grandfather. Grandfather used to say he'd have traded the honors for having you back, but then he lived in the glow of Black Jack Geary, Hero of the Alliance, not in the shadow of that Hero."

Geary heard every capital letter as the commander of the *Repulse* pronounced the words, and he let his anger show. "That's not me."

"No. You were human. I figured that out. But to the rest of the Alliance, you weren't human. You were the perfect hero, the shining example to the youth of the Alliance." Commander Michael Geary hunched closer to his screen. "Every day of my life has been measured against the standard of Black Jack Geary. Do you have any idea what that's been like?"

He could guess, having seen the emotions that had greeted him on so many faces. "Why the hell did you join the Navy?"

"Because I had to! Just like my father. We were Gearys. That's all there was to it."

Geary squeezed his eyes shut and pressed his hands against his head. *I've only lived with this image of myself for a few weeks. To live a lifetime in its shadow . . .* "I'm very sorry."

"*You* didn't do it," his grandnephew repeated.

"Then why do you so obviously hate me?"

"It's hard to break the habits of a lifetime."

I want to hear about my brother, and what happened to

*his children, and whatever you could tell me about my
other friends and relatives, but I can't do that with someone who's hated me all his life and isn't the least bit reti-
cent about showing me that hate.* "Damn you."

"You already did."

Geary reached to break the connection, then fixed his
grandnephew with an icy glare. "Do you feel capable of
following my orders to the best of your ability?"

"Oh, yes. I can do that."

"If I see you balking or in any way hazarding other
ships by your actions, I'll relieve you of your command in
a heartbeat. Do you understand? I don't care if you hate
me." Which was a lie, and he was sure the other man knew
it was a lie, but it had to be said. "But I will not tolerate any
actions that will imperil the ships and sailors of this fleet."

The other Geary quirked a half-smile. "I assure you I
will carry out my duties as if Black Jack Geary himself
were my commander."

Captain Geary stared again. "Tell me that's not a common phrase."

"It's a common phrase."

"I don't know whether to curse you again or shoot myself."

The smile grew. "You hate it, too, don't you?"

"Of course I do."

"Then perhaps, for Grandfather's sake, I can wish you
well. It's hard, and even harder seeing you younger than
me, but you'll have to live with Black Jack Geary now,
too."

"You're expecting me to fail, aren't you?"

"Fail is a relative term. I've had to deal with pretty high
standards in my life. You're going to have to deal with
much higher ones."

Geary nodded, as much to himself as in answer to his
old and bitter grandnephew. "And you'll be there to watch
me fail to live up to the standards of a demigod. Fair
enough. I've got a job to do. So do you."

"Yes, sir. Permission to get back to my work? *Repulse* was severely damaged in the battle, as I'm sure you know."

No, I hadn't been sure of that. Too much to learn too fast. "Very well, Commander." Geary broke the connection, then sat gazing at the blank screen for a long moment before trying to stand again. His left leg trembled a bit, so Geary balled his hand into a fist and punched his thigh hard enough to possibly raise a bruise. Then he headed for the bridge of the *Dauntless*, grateful for even the minor distraction caused by the lingering pain in his leg.

The sailors who'd crowded the passageways of the *Dauntless* in the immediate aftermath of battle were partly gone now, most having reached the places they needed to be and devoted themselves to what needed to be done. The remainder made way for Geary, but something had changed in the way they regarded him. He could see their faces carrying not just the unwelcome awe and hope, but also growing confidence. Confidence in him or because of him, it didn't matter which. He had to be their commander now, though, so he met those faces and tried to reflect the confidence back at them.

The semicircular bridge wasn't a very large compartment, either, but then large compartments made no sense in spacecraft, especially warships. The captain's seat, which normally dominated the space, had been moved to one side and another seat with a fleet commander's flag embossed upon its back had been fastened to the deck beside the captain's. Captain Desjani sat strapped into her seat, gazing intently at the virtual display screens floating before her, occasionally directing a command or question to one of the officers and enlisted occupying various watch-stations filling the half-arc of the compartment in front of her. Geary took a moment to absorb the scene, finding a welcome measure of comfort in watching the familiar rituals of ship command.

Then a watch-stander noticed him and gestured to Captain Desjani, who turned far enough to see Geary and offered a brief nod in greeting before she went back to monitoring repairs and preparations for further combat. Geary walked to the admiral's seat a bit stiffly, pausing to run the fingers of one hand over the embossed flag for a moment. Somehow, it seemed to him, actually sitting in that seat would mark an irreversible step. At that point, he'd be actively commanding a fleet. It was a very bad time to recall that his previous largest command had been of a three-ship escort force.

Geary sat down and looked around, trying to accustom himself to this new role. "Captain Desjani, is Co-President Rione aboard yet?"

Desjani gave him a quick, carefully neutral look as she replied. "So I've been informed. Her shuttle docked several minutes ago."

Geary checked the time. "She must've bought us some time. The Syndic deadline expired over ten minutes ago."

"Perhaps she did." Desjani leaned closer and lowered her voice. "How much does Rione know? About *Dauntless*?"

Geary tried not to flinch. "Too much."

"Admiral Bloch may well've told her, you know."

He hadn't thought of that, but it seemed reasonable that Rione could have made the same demands on Bloch that she did on Geary, and already knew where the key had been located. *So why ask me? Maybe to find out how honest I'd be with her. I guess I managed a passing grade.* "At least she didn't come to join us on the bridge."

"I'm sure she's still talking," Desjani deadpanned.

Geary found himself grinning briefly despite everything, then sobered as he called up his displays. A situation display appeared, floating at his eye level, the Syndic ships holding steady in their formation, while speed and direction vectors showed a good portion of the Alliance ships shifting in various directions, the slower ships tending toward the jump point and others moving on different vectors to conceal the fleet's intentions. *So many ships in this fleet. If I try to focus too much on one area, I'll lose the big picture.* He moved his gaze toward the enemy formation and felt his guts tighten. *And so many Syndic ships. What if they're faster, or we're slower, or somebody just does the wrong thing?*

What if I'm that somebody?

He studied the controls, then tried to pull up data on the Alliance ships. Instead, personnel files for every officer in the fleet appeared. Muttering angrily, Geary tried another command. This time he got a readout of statistics for each class of ships. Not exactly what he'd wanted, but still useful. Now, if he only had a few more minutes to learn more about these ships, how they differed from those he'd known. He gestured to Captain Desjani. "I'm looking at specs for the ships, and I recognize most of the weapons."

She gave a quick command to one of her subordinates, then nodded to Geary. "Yes. The basic weapon concepts haven't changed in most cases, even though the weapon capabilities have become a lot better. We still use hell-lances as the primary weapon, but their charged particle 'spears' are faster, longer-ranged, carry more energy, and the launchers can recharge much quicker than in your last ship."

"And you're still using grapeshot."

"Of course. It's a simple and deadly weapon. The rail-guns can impart higher velocities to the rounds than in your day, and targeting system improvements let us use grapeshot at slightly greater ranges, but it's still a fairly close-in weapon because once the patterns disperse too widely, the odds of overwhelming or significantly weakening enemy defenses are too small."

"What's a specter?"

"Basically a meaner version of the missiles you were used to."

"Wraiths, you mean?"

"Yes. Specters are autonomous missiles like the old wraiths, but they're more maneuverable, carry multiple warheads to give them a better chance of punching through shields and into an enemy's hull, and have better survival chances against enemy active defenses." She gestured outward. "Defenses have improved, too. Shields are stronger, rebuild and adjust coverage faster, and the ships' physical hulls have some better survival characteristics."

There hadn't been a radical change in weaponry, then. The ships still used missiles at longer ranges, augmented by hell-lances and grapeshot when they got close enough. Heavier weapons but deployed against stronger defenses. "What's this—"

"Captain?" Both Geary and Desjani jerked their heads around to look at the sailor who'd spoken, Geary taking a moment to realize the call hadn't been directed at him. The sailor in turn seemed uncertain who to report to. "The Syndic fleet is broadcasting a demand for individual ships to announce their surrender immediately."

Geary fought down an urge to grimace, all too aware everyone was looking at him for his reaction. Rione's efforts to stall had obviously hit their limit. He wondered whether simply remaining silent would cause the Syndics to waste time repeating their demands. "Captain Desjani, I'd appreciate your estimate of what will happen if we don't respond."

She hesitated, then spoke in a rush. "I can't be sure what the Syndics will do, but if we don't reply, there's a chance some of our ships may respond on their own. And if some begin surrendering—"

"Damn." As much as he hated to admit it, Geary knew from what he'd seen in the conference room that she was right. He couldn't stay silent and risk that outcome. "I want to talk to the Syndic commander."

"Private channel, sir?"

"No. I want everyone to see and hear us."

"We'll send a hail to the Syndic flagship. It's a few light-minutes away." Desjani pointed toward the communications watch, conveying her order with the motion. That sailor nodded and began working his controls. Several minutes passed, then the sailor gestured forward. Geary followed the gesture with his eyes and saw a new display spring to life. Centered in it was the familiar image of the

Syndic CEO who'd announced the murder of Admiral
Bloch and his fellow Alliance senior officers. *"Dauntless?"* the CEO asked. "You were Bloch's flagship, were
you not? Are you capable of surrendering the fleet en
masse, then?"

Geary straightened, trying to keep his temper down, but
not bothering to hide his own feelings. "You're not talking
to the captain of the *Dauntless*. You're talking to the fleet
commander."

The Syndic flagship was slightly behind the lead elements of the enemy fleet, placing it close to three light-
minutes away from *Dauntless*. Geary kept his answer as
short as he dared, then waited for his reply to reach the
other ship, knowing the built-in time lag would automatically help buy more time for his fleet.

Three minutes from *Dauntless* to the enemy flagship,
then three minutes back. At about six minutes after Geary's
reply, he finally saw the Syndic CEO's eyes shift in annoyance. "I don't care what you style yourself. I've been
very generous out of humanitarian concern for the well-
being of fellow humans, but your time is up. Broadcast
surrender, drop your shields, and deactivate all offensive
and defensive weapon systems immediately or you will be
destroyed."

Geary shook his head for emphasis. "No."

Six minutes later, he saw the Syndic fleet CEO frown in
response to the brief reply. "Very well. *Dauntless* will be
destroyed. Now if you don't mind, I'm sure other ships
will be trying to surrender."

"The ships of this fleet are under my command, not
yours, and they will fight under my command," Geary
stated, trying to put all the ice that had once filled him into
his tone. He knew his reply would be heard by his own
ships far quicker than it would be received by the much
farther-away enemy flagship, and would hopefully forestall any individual Alliance commanders still tempted to
trust their fate to surrender. "The Alliance fleet is not
beaten and will not surrender." He hoped the words con-

veyed a confidence he didn't really feel. But as long as he seemed confident on the outside, his own ships and the Syndics wouldn't know what was going on inside Geary.

The long-distance conversation had been continuing for almost twenty minutes when Geary saw the Syndic CEO looking off to the side, apparently checking one of his own displays. "It seems I'll have to have my intelligence staff reeducated. I find no match for you in my database of Alliance officers."

"You're not looking in the right place," Geary advised, letting a small humorless smile show. "Try looking under deceased officers. As far back as your files go."

Another six minutes. "You're dead, then?" The CEO shook his head. "A stupid ploy and waste of time. You're not listed. A search through the entire database, including every Alliance officer known to have served in this war doesn't produce any matches at—" The Syndic CEO stopped speaking, his eyes still locked on whatever his display was showing.

Geary smiled again, this time baring his teeth. "I assume you found me. About a century ago."

By the time Syndic CEO's latest reply came in, his face had reddened with anger. "A simple, foolish trick. If you think I'd be stupid enough to believe that, you are sadly mistaken. You're simply stalling for time. I will not tolerate further delays."

"I don't care what you believe." Geary let the next words come out slowly, all too aware that the rest of his own fleet was listening in on this conversation. "I am Captain John Geary. I am now in command of the Alliance fleet. You're dealing with me now. These are my ships. Back off."

The CEO was glowering when his latest message arrived. "Even if you were that person, there's nothing you can do. You're outnumbered, outgunned, and cut off. You have no options but surrender! I repeat, I will tolerate no more delays. My patience is at an end."

Geary tried his best to look unimpressed. "I beat the

Syndics once, and I can beat them again." He knew what he had to say. He was still speaking as much to his own ships as to the Syndic CEO. Maybe he'd give the Syndic pause, and hopefully he'd give his fleet some more confidence. Geary actually found himself enjoying this a little. Being Black Jack Geary to Alliance sailors had been a constant trial, but using his legend to rattle the Syndics was actually a bit of fun. "There's always something a good commander can do. I repeat, this fleet isn't beaten. If you're foolish enough to try attacking, you'll find we're ready to kick you halfway to the next star system." He knew that wasn't true, but halfhearted bluffs weren't going to gain him anything at this point.

Another six minutes. The Syndic CEO eyed Geary, wariness apparent now even though the CEO was still trying to project arrogant assurance. "That's nonsense, as you're well aware. Your situation is hopeless. Unless you surrender now, you will die. This conversation is at an end. I expect your next response to contain your surrender."

Geary ignored the latest ultimatum. "Sorry to disappoint you. The Syndic fleet thought it'd already killed me once. What makes you think you'll have more luck this time? You, on the other hand, haven't died even once yet. And after watching what you did to Admiral Bloch, I'd be more than happy to send you to your ancestors."

The Syndic CEO had been keeping his expression carefully controlled, but Geary thought he could read uncertainty there. Which was very good if true. Rattling an enemy commander's confidence could go a long way to ensuring their defeat.

On the other hand, Captain Desjani and the other *Dauntless* crew members who Geary could see seemed to be torn between happiness at Geary's taunting of the Syndic commander and concern that the taunting would provoke an immediate Syndic attack.

Geary waited, watching out of the corner of his eye as the ships of the Alliance fleet continued slowly repositioning. How much longer would he be able to stall before all of his ships would be ready to bolt for the jump point?

"I have neither time nor patience to deal with a fool," the Syndic CEO finally spat out six more minutes later, then broke the connection.

Geary sighed and relaxed his stiff posture. "Captain Desjani, how much longer until all of our ships are in position?"

She checked her own displays. "Your, um, negotiations with the Syndic commander bought us about a half hour, but I estimate another half hour is still needed, sir. *Titan* is lagging, though. She took a lot of damage," Desjani added quickly.

"Yeah." Geary checked *Titan*'s status. Perhaps he should order the crew to evacuate . . . No. *Titan* was an auxiliary, a mobile fleet-repair-and-rebuild ship. Essentially a small shipyard accompanying the fleet to repair damage too serious for ships to fix on their own, and to manufacture replacement items from raw materials. There'd been two *Titan* class ships with the fleet, Geary saw. The other had been blown to fragments during the recent battle. There were other repair-and-rebuild ships still surviving, but none of them had *Titan*'s range of capabilities. *I need* Titan *if I'm going to get this fleet home. But she was slow to start with, and now she's got battle damage to her engines slowing her more. All I can do is pray I rattled that Syndic goon enough to keep his fleet passive for another half hour.*

As far as Geary could tell, the Syndic fleet hadn't yet moved, maintaining the same position relative to the Alliance fleet. As a result of the redeployment, Geary's own ships had shifted out of their crescent into a rough oval, which on the displays looked like a shield protecting the most heavily damaged and slowest Alliance ships that had fallen back in a hopefully inconspicuous way toward the jump point. Geary watched the symbols representing his ships crawling across space, praying for a little more time.

"We're picking up movement by the Syndic ships. Blue shift."

That meant the Syndics had increased their speed toward the Alliance fleet. Geary cursed under his breath and stared at the display showing the enemy forces. The Syndic fleet hadn't changed formation at all, maintaining that wall of firepower, but as he watched, *Dauntless*'s long-range optical sensors tagged ship after ship with movement vectors indicating they were accelerating toward the Alliance fleet. Like every other ship commander Geary had ever known, he wished for a magic detection system that could've provided information at faster-than-light speed. But like communications, sensors in normal space were still limited to light-speed. *Which means they started moving less than three minutes ago, so they've already got the jump on us.* "They're holding formation. The slowest ships are setting the pace."

Desjani nodded, her face tense. "That must mean they don't suspect your plan."

My plan. Yeah. I hope it works. "How do I call the fleet?" he asked Desjani.

She tapped some buttons. "You're on."

Geary took a deep breath. "All ships, this is the fleet commander, Captain John Geary. Execute Overture immediately upon receipt. I say again, execute Overture immediately upon receipt." There wasn't time for a neatly executed maneuver, coordinated in advance so that every ship would have time to receive the signal before the fleet moved in unison. But the fleet wasn't dispersed too widely. Every ship should receive the message within a minute and begin moving as soon as they heard the order.

On his display, ships flared with green dots as they acknowledged the order, the wave of green spreading out from *Dauntless*'s position on all sides as ships received the order and replied. In the same way, beginning with the ships closest to *Dauntless*, the Alliance fleet raggedly surged into motion toward the jump point. *Dauntless*'s own engines kicked in, steering the flagship toward the center of the force. Geary watched his ships accelerating, seeing some of the faster ships falling in around the slower ones to act as escorts, eyeing the Syndic advance for the first signs they'd realized what he was doing, that the Alliance fleet wasn't simply falling back in a bid to delay an inevitable battle within this system but was planning to jump out of immediate danger.

"*Titan*'s still lagging."

Geary nodded in response to Desjani's words, feeling a tightness in his guts as he watched the big, slow ship's movement. "I wish she could've gotten closer to the jump point."

"Given the amount of damage she's sustained, *Titan* got as close as she could in the time available and given the plan's constraints."

Geary gritted his teeth, though not in anger at Desjani. She was doing exactly what she should do—tell him the truth as she saw it. But he'd approved the plan. He'd seen *Titan* in it, in the short time he had to look at that plan, and hadn't known the huge repair ship would be a concern. Hadn't known that she'd move so slow. It wasn't like they'd had a lot of time to move her or that they could be too obvious about it, but he'd approved the plan, they hadn't been able to stall the Syndics long enough, and now *Titan* was in real trouble.

Because now he could see signs that the enemy was reacting, finally realizing that the Alliance fleet was fleeing toward the jump point. The time-late images of the wall of Syndic warships showed it stretching out of shape toward them as the faster ships began to pull away from their slower counterparts. *Three minutes for them to see what we were doing, some time more for them to figure out what it meant, and then three more minutes for us to see them act on that information. They'll be closing on us now, and the information will get more and more timely, but that's not a good thing since it means the enemy will be getting closer to being able to engage our rearmost ships.* He couldn't call it a rear guard, because the ships farthest back were there from necessity, not design.

Geary found himself wishing for hidden squadrons of ships, waiting to leap out from some impossible concealment to lop the head off of the Syndic formation. But he had no such squadrons, no such means of hiding them, and any ship he sent to hit those exposed ships at the head of the Syndic advance would be unable to retreat to safety before the Syndic main body closed in.

Geary kept watching the ships and their movement vectors slide across the display and didn't need to calculate the result. His own experience with understanding relative motion provided the answer as the minutes crawled by. "The Syndic interceptors are coming on too fast. *Titan* won't make the jump point before some of them get within engagement range of her."

Desjani nodded. "Concur."

"Can *Titan*'s escorts stop them?"

She pondered the question for a moment, then shook her head. "Not just with their stern weaponry. They'd have to turn."

"And then they'd be doomed." *I might have to do that. Might have to order that. I don't want to lose those ships, those crews, but if it's them or* Titan, *and* Titan*'s necessary for everyone else to get home* . . .

Another nod from Captain Desjani. "We can abandon *Titan*. Try to pick up some of her crew."

"We need that ship."

Desjani hesitated, then she nodded a third time. "Yes."

"Then we can't abandon her." Desjani gave him a worried look. *Trying to figure out how the legendary Black Jack Geary can get out of this mess? If you do figure out how, let me know. How to buy time for* Titan? Geary scowled at the displays, trying to find some way to change the physics and coming up with only one answer no matter how he tried.

Trade at least a ship for a ship. Either a squadron of lighter ships, or some ship powerful enough to single-handedly stave off the onrushing Syndic lead elements but less "important" than *Titan*. *I can't use* Dauntless. *Wouldn't it be a relief if I did? Another last stand, and this time end it all for sure. No more burden of command, no more legions of desperate people looking to me as their only hope. No more fate of the Alliance, perhaps, hanging on my head, and no more hearing about Black Jack Geary, the Hero of the Alliance. But I can't. The key's onboard. I made a promise. Even if I hadn't, I can't abandon my duty to all of these people. But then which ship do I choose instead? Who do I send to their deaths?* His eyes searched among the ships, trying to make a choice he hated.

And then he saw something else. "What's *Repulse* doing? She's falling back."

Desjani gestured to her crew, then waited for a reply. "I'm informed *Repulse* has notified the fleet that she'll be maneuvering independently."

"What? Get me their commanding officer." *Repulse* was still only thirty light-seconds away, so it took only a minute for *Dauntless* to send its request and *Repulse* to reply. The newly familiar face of *Repulse*'s commanding officer appeared before Geary. "What are you doing?" Geary demanded without preamble. "You're going to be overtaken by Syndic ships soon unless you get your speed back up. Return to your place in formation."

A minute later, instead of answering directly, Commander Michael Geary just grinned triumphantly. "You screwed up, Great-Uncle Black Jack. You know that, don't you? *Titan*'s in trouble. Cresida's not a bad officer, but she's not as experienced as she'd like to think. And she can be a hothead, jumping without thinking first. You should've checked her plan better. It takes a lot of time sailing around *Titan* to realize what a slow tub she is under the best of conditions. That means there's only one option if *Titan*'s going to saved."

Geary tried to use his fingertips to push back a growing pain in his temples. "I understand *Titan*'s in trouble. I know we need to do something. But there's different ways of executing that option."

Another minute, while the Syndic pursuers grew closer. Geary watched them, impressed despite himself by the acceleration of which these modern warships were capable.

Repulse's commander officer shook his head. "All of the options come down to the same thing. And you know it. Well, I'm going to do you a big favor, Great-Uncle Black Jack. I'm going to save you the trouble of choosing who dies. *Repulse* is close to the line between the closest Syndic ships and *Titan*. My ship's well positioned for this action, and she's got the necessary firepower. She's also got damaged main drives that I've been pushing too hard and are threatening to fail, so she may not be able to keep up with the fleet regardless. Feel better?"

Geary felt the coldness inside again, but he could only find one word in answer. "No."

The *Repulse*'s commander's grin stretched wider at Geary's response, becoming a bit grotesque. "Because of your mistake, I'll finally get to live up to the legacy of Black Jack Geary! My ship holding off the entire Syndic fleet! My ancestors, *our* ancestors, will be proud. How long do you think my ship'll survive, Great-Uncle Black Jack?"

Geary barely kept from snarling in frustration. A ship would die because of him. At least one, because if *Repulse* didn't hold the enemy off long enough, then *Titan* still wouldn't make it to the jump point in time unless Geary sent more ships back to screen her. And this man he wanted to embrace as a link to his dead brother couldn't let go of his anger even now. "Hold them off as long as you can. They'll try to slip some ships past you."

A minute later, Michael Geary shook his head again. "They won't make it. I'll have clean shots at their flanks when they try." The grin finally wavered and went away. "This isn't easy, is it? I understand a bit now. I truly didn't want this. You do what you have to do, though, and it's up to your ancestors how it all turns out. You just have to . . .

the Syndics will capture any of my crew who get off before *Repulse* dies. I know you can't wait around to pick them up now. Promise me that some day you'll try to get them out of the Syndic labor camps. Don't forget them."

Another promise, another demand on him, from someone who knew damned well that he wasn't a demigod but still needed to believe in him. "I swear to you I won't forget them, and I'll do everything I can to someday get them home."

"I'll remember that! And our ancestors heard you as well!" Michael Geary laughed sharply, his gaze shifting rapidly as he looked off-screen at his own ship's bridge. "It's going to get very hot any moment now. I need to go. Get the fleet out of here, damn you." He hesitated. "I've got a sister. She's on the *Dreadnought*, back in Alliance space. Tell her I didn't hate you anymore." The connection broke leaving Geary staring at the ghost memory of his grandnephew's face.

He became aware that Captain Desjani was looking at him, wondering what his private conservation with the *Repulse* had involved. Geary spoke to her, trying to keep his voice flat and controlled. "*Repulse* is going to attempt to hold off the Syndic ships long enough for *Titan* to get to the jump point."

Desjani hesitated, her eyes widening. "Sir, you should know, the commanding officer of *Repulse* is—"

"I know who he is." Geary guessed his voice sounded rough, harsh, and had no idea how that would seem to the bridge crew of the *Dauntless*, and he didn't really care at the moment.

Desjani stared at him for several seconds, then looked away.

Every minute after that seemed impossibly long, Geary watching *Titan*'s achingly slow progress and the vectors of the Syndic warships piling on speed as they closed the distance. The fastest Syndic ships had pushed their velocity up past .1 light and were still accelerating. "Isn't there any way to make *Titan* go faster?" he finally snapped.

The others on the bridge exchanged glances, but no one answered. Despite his earlier determination to keep an eye on the big picture, Geary focused on the *Repulse*, knowing that what happened around her would determine the fate of other ships. The rest of the Alliance fleet was accelerating toward the jump point, limiting its speed to keep from leaving slower ships behind, but drawing steadily away from *Repulse*. The damaged battle cruiser had ceased accelerating, coasting along behind the rest of the fleet as if her propulsion systems were totally blown. She was almost forty-five light-seconds away from *Dauntless* now, and losing ground by the moment. Geary did a quick estimate in his head, figuring that by the time the Syndic pursuers reached *Repulse*, the badly damaged ship would be over a light-minute behind the rest of the fleet.

The wall once formed by the Syndic fleet had stretched into a sort of ragged cone, with the bulk of the Syndic ships back in the base, while the fastest ships had charged forward as quickly as they individually could, their tracks converging on an intercept with *Titan*. Geary saw the great opportunity the extended Syndic formation offered for a vicious counterblow, just the sort of opportunity a mythic commander like Black Jack Geary would surely take. *But I know what would happen to my fleet after I blew away those leading Syndic ships and the rest of the Syndic fleet caught up to us, and I'm not the Black Jack Geary these people think I am.*

Like members of a grand ballet corps sweeping together for a finale, the Syndic ships gracefully arced down toward *Titan* and the lone Alliance warship, *Repulse*, barring their path. Three Syndic Hunter-Killer ships that must have strained their drives to the utmost were in the lead as they tried to race past *Repulse* at better than .1 light speed, aiming directly for *Titan* and her escorts. Geary watched the battle on the display floating before him, knowing the events he was watching had already played out a minute earlier, seeing the shape of the *Repulse* slowly turning to face the pursuers. Too slowly. Her damaged main drives had apparently lost much of their maneuvering and acceleration capability, leaving *Repulse* unable to move with any speed.

According to Repulse*'s last update, her propulsion system wasn't that badly damaged. Why is she wallowing like that?* Then Geary noticed the Syndic HuKs not altering course to further avoid *Repulse* and realized what his grandnephew was doing. *He's pretending to be in worse shape than he is. It's his only ace, and he's playing it very well. If only I'd had some time to get to know that man.*

Repulse, swinging slowly and majestically up and around, barely managed to bring her main weapons to bear and fired her kinetic grapeshot, patterns of large metal ball bearings aimed to intercept the path of the oncoming HuKs. At the speed the HuKs were moving, relativistic effects would mean they'd have a distorted image of the outside universe, which together with the time-late lags caused by the distances involved meant the Syndic ships would lose vital time in seeing and responding to any threats.

Whether because they had too little warning time to react or simply chose to ignore the barrage, the HuKs swept directly into the grapeshot kill patterns, their leading shields sparkling with impacts as they absorbed the barrage. The Syndic warships surged onward, still fixated on the *Titan*. "No hits," Geary commented tonelessly.

Captain Desjani shook her head. "There wasn't much chance of one, but all those head-on strikes against the HuK shields by the kinetic rounds must've depleted the shields a great deal. The relative speed of the impacts was huge. They'll have to shift a lot of power from the sides and rear to try to rebuild their front shields."

"I see." And now he did. Or rather, he was seeing what had happened over a minute ago. The HuKs sprinting past *Repulse* obviously weren't worried about taking any more shots from the Alliance ship. But before the projected paths of the Syndic ships began to pass *Repulse*'s position, the battle cruiser had rolled with sudden speed and agility, changing aspect to bring her main batteries to bear on points the HuKs would pass through. The Syndics probably didn't see the maneuver in time to react, maintaining their courses and allowing *Repulse* to target the spots they'd occupy as the enemy tried to race past.

A barrage of hell-lances erupted from the Alliance ship, racing outward to reach a point in space just as one of the Syndic warships passed through the same spot. The charged particle spears slashed into the HuK, then as *Repulse* kept rolling to bring her weapons to bear on another intercept point, another barrage fired and slammed into a second HuK. At fairly close range, the bolts of energy tore through the weakened side shields and the thin underlying armor, then ripped apart the guts of the Syndic ships.

Still moving at better than .1 light, the wrecks of the two HuKs raced onward, no longer accelerating, no longer living warships, no longer threats to *Titan* or any other Alliance ship.

But Geary's eyes were locked on the third HuK, as *Repulse* brought her bow up and around in a wrenching maneuver to face it. He felt a familiar tension inside as if the display were showing events in real time, rather than revealing the light of actions already over a minute old now. The display showed what looked like a massive glowing ball leaping from the *Repulse* on a course that carried it straight into the HuK's path. The ball seemed to hesitate a moment as it flared against the HuK's shields, then it plowed through the weakened barrier and into the ship. Where the ball hit, the HuK simply vanished, a third of the ship gone in an instant, and the remaining pieces tumbling away as they were wracked by secondary explosions.

"What the hell was that?" Geary whispered.

Captain Desjani bared her teeth. "A null-field. It does exactly what the name says, temporarily nullifying the strong force that holds atoms together."

"You're joking."

"No." She pointed at the remains of the HuK. "Inside the null-field, atomic bonds fail. Matter simply falls apart."

Geary stared at her, then at the display. Matter. Matter making up a ship, and matter making up its crew. Falling apart and gone. Not just dead, but vanished into nothing. "Does every ship have one of those null-fields?"

"No. Just the capital ships, and not all of them." Desjani's fierce grin faded. "They're fairly new, short range, and they take a long time to recharge. I know why he fired it when he did. It was the only way to stop that HuK. But he may not get off another shot from it, and I doubt any Syndic capital ships will let him get close enough to nail them."

"Can a shield stop those things?"

"A powerful enough one, yes." She looked frustrated now. "Null-fields can't be charged if you're too deep in a significant gravity well, and the charge can only be held for a very brief time before you have to fire. As a result we haven't been able to employ them against Syndic planetary targets, yet."

"Planetary targets? You mean planets, don't you?"

Frustration shifted to annoyance before Desjani cleared her expression. "Of course."

Of course. Hitting an inhabited planet with something which would make pieces of it fall apart into component particles was just a matter of "of course." *What's happened to these people? How can they talk regretfully about not being able to destroy worlds that way?*

His attention was jerked back to *Repulse*. Another brace of HuKs had tried to get past her, but the Alliance ship pivoted again, with an agility at odds with her tonnage, so most of her hell-lance batteries could bear on the path of one of the HuKs. Running head-on into that concentrated barrage, the HuK's forward shields flared and failed, letting the hell-lances ravage the length of the ship and turn it into high-velocity junk.

Captain Desjani pointed, drawing Geary's attention to the fact that *Repulse* was volleying specter missiles as fast as the ship's launchers could pump them out. The remaining HuK took out the leading specters with its defenses,

but then the torpedoes began getting through, hitting the
shields and then punching holes through the ship. Within
moments, that ship, too, was out of the fight.

"That was most of her remaining specters, Captain
Geary," Desjani advised. "*Repulse*'s captain is using
everything he's got to stop the leading Syndic ships."

Geary nodded slowly, trying not to reveal his emotions.
*He's leaving precious little for dealing with the following
Syndic ships. But, then, that won't matter, will it? Not in the
big scheme of things, where getting* Titan *out of here intact
is critically important. Damn the big scheme of things and
damn the Syndics.*

He studied the movement vectors, getting the feel of
them with those first five HuKs gone, and could see the answer. "He might've done it."

"But not yet," Desjani advised.

The next wave of HuKs met another barrage of
grapeshot and hell-lances. Here and there, a specter crept
through the confusion to hammer Syndic shields, but four
of the five HuKs made it past. Three had been slowed appreciably, though, losing velocity to the impacts of the
grapeshot and acceleration capability to damage. The
fourth had clearly expended a lot of weaponry just getting
safely past *Repulse*.

"He's done it," Desjani stated, her voice rising with elation. "I recommend that you tell the *Titan*'s escorts to hit
that leading HuK with a half-dozen specters fired out of
their stern launchers. The HuK won't be able to survive
that after everything it tossed out to get past *Repulse*, not
unless it deviates from its course, and if it does that, it
won't be able to get to *Titan* before *Titan* jumps."

"Very well. Order them to do that, if you please." He
didn't listen as Desjani passed on the order, watching instead as more HuKs, this time with light cruisers in support, came up on *Repulse* and lashed the Alliance ship with
fire as they dashed past. Even though the Syndic ships
were moving too fast to have undistorted views of the outside universe, *Repulse* had taken more damage and was too

badly hurt to maneuver quickly enough to avoid shots aimed at her estimated position. *Repulse* got off another shot from its null-field, but the light cruiser it'd been aimed at danced aside, taking only a glancing blow to its shields.

The battle was now seventy light-seconds away from *Dauntless*. The displays could only tell Geary what had been happening one minute and ten seconds ago, but Geary still knew exactly what it was like on the *Repulse* at this moment. He'd been in the same situation, though facing better odds. The expendable weaponry, the grapeshot and the specters, would be used up. The ship's shields would be flaring almost constantly on all sides, as incoming fire drained and shredded the outer defensive layers. Then would come the occasional impact of hits on the hull as the shields suffered spot failures, like random blows from the hammer of a blind giant, before the shields failed completely. The hell-lance batteries would keep firing, falling silent individually or in clusters as they or their power supplies were shattered. And, coming faster and faster, balls of metal and spears of superheated gases would race through the hull from side to side and end to end, smashing anything and anyone in their paths.

"*Repulse* is launching survival pods."

It was getting hard to tell exactly what was happening. The battle had thrown out so much junk that some of it was obscuring the view of the action. But *Dauntless*'s systems could still spot the beacons as survival pods were ejected from the *Repulse*. *Dauntless*'s systems automatically calculated intercept options to the survival pods, telling Geary what he'd need to do to try to pick up survivors from *Repulse*. He stared at the courses, seeing how they crossed through the thick of the oncoming Syndic fleet, knowing he couldn't help the sailors in those pods now. They'd be picked up by the Syndics once the main battle was over, doomed to life in the Syndic labor camps. *But I won't forget my promise to you, Michael Geary. If it's humanly possible, I'll get them out of there someday.*

Syndic ships were passing *Repulse* almost continuously now, none of them stopping to engage, but simply firing as they passed and letting their numbers overwhelm the lone Alliance ship. Heavy cruisers began sweeping by, adding their weight to the weapons pounding *Repulse*.

"As of seventy-five light-seconds ago, *Repulse* was no longer firing. All weapons appear to be disabled or destroyed."

Geary simply nodded, not trusting himself to speak. The survival pods were still coming out occasionally, but too few of them.

"We've received a core-destruct initiation signal from *Repulse*."

"How long until the core blows?" Geary didn't recognize the voice at first, then realized it was his own.

"Uncertain. The same for the intensity of the overload. We don't know how much damage the core has already taken."

"Understood." *Repulse* might already be gone, the light from the event not yet having reached *Dauntless*. He'd know for certain soon. Geary pulled his attention away from the battle for a moment, seeing the ships of the Alliance fleet plunging into the special area of the gravity well around this star where conditions were right to enable the transition into the jump space where other stars were only weeks or months of travel away. "Commander Cresida's plan said ships today can make jumps at up to point one light speed."

"That's correct," Desjani advised. "The jump drive systems reached that capability before the hypernet stopped further research and development."

"Good," Geary commented tonelessly. "None of our ships will have to slow down to make the jump."

Titan was almost there, the movement vectors of the leading Syndic ships closing frantically. The closest Syndic HuK, the one that had barely made it past *Repulse*, shattered into huge fragments as specters from *Titan*'s escort slammed into it. Other Syndic ships were vainly

reaching toward the big Alliance ship and just falling short
of intercepts in time to stop her and her escorts as they vanished into jump. More of the leading Syndic ships, all light
units, started coming apart as those heavy Alliance ships
that hadn't yet jumped threw barrages at them. The surviving Syndic HuKs braked and frantically changed vectors,
trying to cripple some other Alliance ship before it could
jump, without getting annihilated themselves.

Geary looked back, and *Repulse* was gone. A spreading
zone of wreckage and gases in the midst of the oncoming
Syndic fleet marked the site of her death. *May the living
stars guide you, and our ancestors welcome you, Michael
Geary. Farewell until we meet again in that place.* "All remaining ships. Jump as soon as possible. I say again. Jump
as soon as possible. Now, now, now."

THREE

JUMP space hadn't changed in the slightest. Geary knew he shouldn't have expected it to have changed (what was a human standard century to the life of the universe?), but he'd been haunted by the thought that the new hypernet systems would somehow be visible threading through the emptiness. Instead, jump space presented only the same vista of an endless drab black that always seemed just on the verge of turning into darkest gray. Splayed across that vastness were rare splashes of light, following no understood pattern and representing something that remained unknown even now.

"The sailors say the lights are the homes of our ancestors."

Geary looked toward Captain Desjani. "They said that in my time as well." He didn't feel like talking but felt he should. She'd taken the time to come see him, in this large stateroom that'd once belonged to Admiral Bloch and was now his home. Geary didn't add that since being rescued he couldn't look at the gray infinity of jump space without having his bones start to ache as if the cold they'd experienced in hibernation would never leave them.

Desjani stared at the display for a moment before speaking. "Some of the sailors are saying you've been there. In the lights. That you were waiting there until now, when the Alliance needed you."

He started laughing, unable to resist even though he could hear the strain showing through the sound. "I think if I'd had any choice in the matter, I wouldn't have come back now."

"Well, they're not saying it was a time you chose. They're saying you were needed."

"I see." Geary stopped laughing and gazed at her. "What do you think?"

"The truth?"

"That's all I ever want from you."

Desjani smiled. "Fair enough. I think that *if* our ancestors were to intervene directly in events, and *if* they had chosen to bring you to this fleet when they did, then it was a very good thing."

"Captain, in case it hasn't become clear to you yet, I'm not that Black Jack Geary you heard about in school."

"No," she agreed. "You're better than that."

"What?"

"I'm serious." Captain Desjani leaned forward, gesturing with one hand for emphasis. "A legendary hero can inspire, but they're not much help when it comes to concrete actions. I'm not sure the Black Jack Geary I always heard about would've led this fleet out of the Syndic home system. You did."

"Because you all think I *am* Black Jack Geary!"

"But you are that man! If you weren't, then any of us who'd survived would currently be on our way to Syndic labor camps. You know that's true. If you hadn't been there, the fleet would've been destroyed."

Geary made a face. "You're assuming no one else would've risen to the occasion. You, or Captain Duellos, for example."

"Captains Faresa and Numos are both senior to me in length of service, and to Captain Duellos as well. They wouldn't have followed us. Maybe a few of us would've thought to try fleeing through the jump point, but not enough to have a chance of surviving the long trip home. No, the fleet would've fallen apart and died ship by ship." Desjani grimaced, then smiled again. "You prevented that."

Geary shrugged, avoiding directly responding to what she'd said. "You told me you had something for me?"

"Yes. You've received a message from Commander Cresida on the *Furious*."

He gave her a confused look. "Transmitted just before we jumped?"

"No. A means to transmit messages in jump space was developed quite a while ago. We can't run high-rate data streams, but we can send simple messages."

"Oh." He pondered "quite a while ago" for just a moment before recalling what had prompted the question. "What does Commander Cresida want?" Desjani passed Geary a notepad. He looked down at it, reading the short message. "She's offering her resignation?"

Desjani shook her head as Geary looked at her. "I didn't read the message, Captain Geary. It was 'personal for' you."

"Oh." *I've got to stop saying that.* "Well, she is. She's offering to resign because of *Repulse*." Saying the name made the very recent memory hit him like a blow in the gut.

"But you ordered—"

"The Captain of the *Repulse* volunteered," Geary stated, his voice sounding bleak even to him. "No. Because the plan she developed required the sacrifice of another ship to ensure *Titan* made the jump." Geary slumped, staring at the notepad and wondering if he needed another boost of meds or if he was just reacting to the stress of thinking about what had gone wrong and what that had cost. *She tried. When just about everyone else was sitting around planning their funerals, Cresida offered to work that plan. Michael Geary liked her, I think. And I approved that plan. Me.* "I don't think there was any other way to get *Titan* out of there. Not with what she had to work with." Desjani watched him, saying nothing. "Can I write my response on here?"

"Yes," she replied. "The shorter the better, of course."

Geary took the stylus and wrote. *To Commander Cresida, ASN* Furious. *Request denied. You retain my full confidence. Respectfully, John Geary, Captain, ASN.*

He handed it back to Desjani, who looked a question at him. Geary indicated she should read. She did so, nodded, then smiled slightly. "Just what I'd have expected of you, sir."

Geary watched her, feeling an emptiness inside. *Everything I do, they interpret as being what they'd expect of Black Jack Geary. Or someone even better than the legendary Black Jack Geary! Ancestors help us all. Why can't they just know me, as I really am?*

But, then, how much do I know them?

He took another look at Captain Desjani, trying to see her as if for the first time. "What's your first name, anyway?"

She smiled briefly. "Tanya."

"I don't think I've known anyone named Tanya before."

"The name became fairly popular at one time. You know how that goes. There's a lot of women in my generation named Tanya."

"Yeah. Names do come and go, don't they? Where're you from?"

"Kosatka."

"Really? I've been to Kosatka."

Desjani looked disbelieving. "In-system or landfall?"

"Landfall." The memories tumbled out and left a pleasant glow in their wake. "I was just a junior officer, then. My ship got sent to Kosatka as part of an official Alliance representation for a royal wedding. Some really big deal. The whole planet went sort of manic over it, and they fell over themselves being nice to us. I've never gotten so many free drinks and meals." Geary smiled at her, then saw the lack of recognition on her face. "I guess it didn't make history."

"Uh, no. I suppose not." Desjani smiled politely. "Kosatka doesn't pay nearly as much attention to the royal family as it used to."

Geary nodded, trying to keep his own smile in place. "Yesterday's unforgettable pomp and circumstance got forgotten pretty quickly, I guess."

"But, still, I'm not sure anyone remembers you were on Kosatka. That's something special. Did you like it?"

His smile turned genuine again. "Yeah. I don't remember any spectacular scenery or anything like that, but it seemed like a real welcoming, comfortable place. Some of the crew talked about going back there to live once they'd retired." He forced a laugh. "I bet it's changed, though."

"Not that much. I haven't been home in a long time, but that's how I remember it."

"Sure you do. It's home." They sat silent for a moment, then Geary exhaled heavily. "So, how is home?"

"Sir?"

"Home. The Alliance. What's it like?"

"It's . . . still the Alliance." She shook her head, looking older and more tired than just a moment ago. "It's been a very long war. So much has to go into the military, to build new ships, new defenses, new ground forces. And so many of the young have to go into those same things. All of our worlds have such wealth when combined, but it's being worn away."

Geary frowned down at his hands, not wanting to see her face just then. "Tell me the truth. Are the Syndics winning?"

"No!" The answer came so quickly that Geary thought it must reflect some sort of faith rather than professional analysis. "But neither are we," Desjani conceded. "It's too hard. The distances involved, the ability of each side to recover from losses and field new forces, the balance in weaponry." Desjani sighed. "It's been a stalemate for a long time."

Stalemate. It made sense, for exactly the reasons Desjani gave. Both the Alliance and the Syndicate Worlds were too big to be defeated in less than centuries of war. "Why the hell did the Syndicate Worlds start an unwinnable war anyway?"

Desjani shrugged. "You know what they're like. A corporate state run by dictators who call themselves servants of the people they enslave. The free worlds of the Alliance were a constant threat to the dictators of the Syndicate Worlds, living examples that representative government and civil liberties could coexist with greater security and prosperity than the Syndics could ever dream of. That's why the Rift Federation and the Callas Republic ended up joining with the Alliance in the war. If the Syndics succeeded in crushing the Alliance, they'd go after any remaining free worlds next."

Geary nodded. "The Syndic leadership was always worried about revolt by some of its worlds. That's why they attacked us when they did? Because turning the Alliance from an attractive alternative to a wartime threat was the only way to keep control of their own populace?"

This time Desjani frowned slightly, then shrugged again. "I suppose, sir. To be honest, the war started a very long time ago. I never really studied the exact circumstances. All that matters to me, and to everyone else in the Alliance today of course, is that the Syndics launched an unprovoked attack on us. Or rather, on our ancestors. We can't allow them to benefit from that."

"Have they?" Geary asked.

"Not that I know of," Desjani replied with a fierce grin. Then her smile faded. "Nor have we, needless to say."

"Nobody's benefiting, and no one can win. Why not end the thing, then? Negotiate."

Her head whipped up, and she stared at him. "We can't!"

"But if neither the Alliance nor the Syndics can win—"

"We couldn't trust them! They won't honor any agreement. *You* know that. The attack you held off so long ago

was a surprise blow, an unprovoked stab in the back! No."
She shook her head, with anger this time. "Negotiations
are impossible with creatures like the Syndicate Worlds.
They need to be crushed so that their evil won't spread further, won't result in the murder of more innocents. No matter what it costs."

He looked away again, thinking about what a century of
warfare can do not just to economies but also to minds. *I
guess Desjani's right that the exact reasons the Syndics attacked a century ago aren't that important anymore. But
I'll have to try to remember to look it up sometime, try to
find out what exact reasons caused this war instead of just
laying it at the feet of the immoral nature of the Syndic
leaders. Not that the Syndics haven't already shown themselves to be capable of horrible acts. Admiral Bloch could
certainly testify to the futility of negotiations with them.
But if neither side can win and neither side will negotiate,
that dooms everyone, good or bad, to endless war.* Geary
glanced back at Desjani and saw she was watching him
now with calm certainty. *Certain I'll agree with her, because aren't I the legendary Black Jack Geary?*

As if reading his mind, Captain Desjani nodded at that
moment. "You see how important it is that we get home.
The strike at the Syndic home system might've been the
means for us to finally tip the balance. It failed, but if we
can get the Syndic hypernet key home and get it dupli-
cated, the Syndics will face an impossible situation.
They'll have to either take down their own hypernet or
know we can use it against them at any time and any place
on the net."

Geary nodded back. "And if they took down their hypernet, the Alliance could shift forces so much faster than
the Syndics that we'd be able to concentrate forces again
and again, crushing the Syndics piecemeal while they
scramble to try to catch us. It'd be a huge advantage on
those grounds alone. I can only imagine the economic advantage the Alliance would gain. Why'd they risk giving
us one of their keys?"

Desjani made a face. "From their perspective, the plan probably looked foolproof. Dangle the bait of the Syndic home system, offer us a key there through a supposed traitor, and then trap us so far from home we couldn't possibly escape." She grinned. "But they didn't know we'd have *you*."

Oh, for the living stars' sake. But as long as she brought it up . . . "How'd you find me? After all that time? Why didn't someone find me earlier?" The questions had occurred to him before, of course, but he'd never pursued the answers, not wanting to delve into the events that had separated him from his own time and left him here among these familiar strangers.

Desjani tapped on the small table between them, bringing up a display of star systems. "Did you know you could do this? Your last battle— Excuse me, what we thought was your last battle, took place here." She pointed to an unremarkable star. "Grendel."

Geary nodded and swung his own finger along a line of stars. "It was part of a standard transit route. That's why my convoy was heading through the area."

"Yes. But it was also close to Syndic space, which is why the convoy had a routine escort. Right?" Geary nodded as Desjani's hand waved to indicate the stars beyond. "They could jump straight into Grendel's system. Which they did when they attacked you." She sat silent for a moment. "Afterward, well, my understanding is the system was swept, but there were Syndic forces jumping in and out constantly, hoping to catch more shipping. Everything had to be done under combat conditions, the accumulated battles left more and more wreckage and flotsam drifting through the system, and eventually Grendel was effectively abandoned except for some automated early-warning systems to let us know if the Syndics were coming through. It just made more sense to jump safely through Beowulf, Caderock, and Rescat than run the gauntlet through Grendel." Another shrug. "And once the hypernet was set up, nobody even needed to do that."

Geary gazed at the display, cold seeming to seep in through the walls around him as he thought of the decades his survival pod had spent tumbling through space in a system empty of everything except the wreckage of war. "But you went through there."

"Yes. We needed to jump into a Syndic system where one of their hypernet gates existed, and Grendel offered a perfect jumping off point. Isolated, quiet, empty." She swung one finger slowly through the representation of the lonely star. "Our sensors are better, more sensitive, than they used to be. They picked up the power being used in your survival pod and the tiny amount of heat that it was generating. It might've been power leakage from a Syndic spy drone, so we investigated." Desjani pursed her lips. "The fleet physicians estimated you had only a few more years of survival time left, at best, before power in the pod was exhausted."

The cold bored into him, threatening to freeze his breath in his throat. "I hadn't heard that."

"They're not supposed to keep anyone alive that long, you know. The only reason it kept going all that time is because you were the only one aboard. If there'd been even just two survivors drawing down power to sustain hibernation . . ."

"Lucky me."

Desjani had her eyes locked on him again. "Many believe it wasn't a matter of luck, Captain Geary. An awful lot of things had to work out just right for you to end up alive on this warship just when the Alliance needed you. Just when *we* needed you."

Great. More proof to the believers that I've been sent by the living stars to . . . do what? Are they "only" expecting me to somehow lead this fleet to safety, or is that just the start of their dreams?

How do I tell them otherwise? And what happens when they learn I'm just a very fallible man upon whom fate played a lot of nasty tricks?

Geary realized she was watching him with concern. "What? Is something wrong?"

"No! It's just . . . you were silent a long time, not looking at anything. I did get a bit worried."

The last batch of meds must've started wearing off, or recent events had just overwhelmed even what the meds could do. "I guess I need to rest some."

"There's no reason not to now. It's three weeks transit time to Corvus in jump space. Plenty of time to recover." Desjani looked briefly guilty. "The fleet physicians want to see you again as soon as possible. I'm supposed to tell you that."

I bet they do. Am I better off avoiding them or seeking them out? "Thanks. And thanks for everything else, Tanya. I'm glad I'm on *Dauntless*."

It was amazing how a smile could transform Captain Desjani's face. "As am I, Captain Geary."

He sat for a few minutes after she'd left, unable to work up the mental or physical energy to do anything else. Three weeks to Corvus. Not so long, but an eternity of time for a fleet of ships whose futures had once seemed confined to the space of an hour.

The bedding had been changed at some point, saving Geary the dilemma of either asking for help getting new bedding or sleeping in Admiral Bloch's sheets. He slept for a long time, his sleep restless with vivid dreams that he couldn't recall at all during brief periods of waking.

Eventually he got up, unable to sleep through the muffled sounds of the working-day life of the *Dauntless* that came to him even inside the well-insulated stateroom. Grateful to find himself feeling stronger, he rummaged in compartments, trying to ignore anything that looked like a personal possession of the late Admiral Bloch, and found some unopened ration bars that, for all he could tell, were as chronologically as old as he was.

It wasn't like he felt like enjoying food, though, so the ration bars sufficed for a small breakfast.

Now what? Now he had the luxury of time. The Alliance fleet would be in jump space for weeks. He could actually find out a little bit more about what had happened since he'd entered that survival pod and started his long sleep. From what he'd heard and seen already, much of recent history wouldn't make pleasant reading, but he had to know it if he wanted to understand these strangers he'd been thrust into commanding.

As it turned out, the modern version of the *Sailor's Manual* contained what appeared to be a decent condensed history of events since his "last stand."

Geary skipped hastily over the account of what had once been his final battle. He'd never been comfortable hearing even routine praise for himself, so the idea of reading a worshipful account of his actions made him feel almost ill. Especially when even levelheaded and experienced officers like Captain Desjani seemed to think he'd been sent back by the living stars to somehow save the Alliance.

But as he started to read past the story of "Black Jack Geary's Last Stand" he stopped to stare at the date. Almost one hundred years ago. *To me, it all happened less than two weeks past. I remember it so clearly. I remember that battle and those people in my crew and getting into that survival pod with my ship being ripped apart around me and Death riding on my shoulder. It was only two weeks ago. To me.*

They're all dead. The ones who died on my ship and the ones who got away safe. All the same now. And even the children of those who survived are dead, too. All that's left is me.

He put his head down and couldn't think of anything but grief for a long time.

EVENTUALLY, Geary made it through the history, finding it to be a relentlessly positive account of battles lost and won, making even what sounded to Geary like defeats seem like they'd somehow been part of a master plan. But that was an official history for you. What Captain Desjani had told him, of a stalemate lasting for decade after decade, was obvious when he read between the lines. As the history drew close to the present day, it seemed to become almost shrill in its patriotic exhortations, a sure sign to Geary's way of thinking that morale was perceived as shaky.

The *Sailor's Manual* had always been intended to teach the basics, so its contents couldn't confirm Geary's belief that the officers and sailors of the Alliance fleet were, on average, young and minimally trained. But as fleet commander he could access any personnel files he wanted, and those he checked at random all told the same story. Most of the personnel in the fleet had painfully little experience. A few had survived through luck or innate skill long enough to really know what they were doing, but they were a small minority. Each of the great victories celebrated in the history Geary had read had obviously taken a serious toll. Even though the official history didn't admit to any defeats, Geary figured those had cost plenty as well.

He wondered how officers like Captains Numos and Faresa had stayed alive while so many others had died. Granted he'd only seen them briefly, but he hadn't gained the impression that either of them were especially skilled. He suspected they were like some officers he'd once known, the ones who somehow managed to always let someone else take the risks, who worked hard at maintaining their image while avoiding actions that might hazard them or their image. But he had no proof of that, so for the time being at least all he could do was watch Numos and Faresa in the hope of either confirming or refuting his suspicions.

Having stalled as long as he could, Geary steeled himself and called up the record of Commander Michael Geary. As he'd guessed, and as had been apparent from the way he'd fought his ship, his grandnephew had been one of the experienced and skilled survivors. Not because he'd held back in action, either. Michael Geary had indeed spent a lifetime trying to live up to the heroic standards of

Black Jack Geary. He'd finally achieved that goal by dying in battle.

A lot of amateurs and a few survivors. No, they were all survivors, of a war that'd kept going for a long, long time, with occasional cease-fires that had apparently only been agreed to so that both sides could rearm after particularly heavy losses.

I need to talk to these people. Geary stared at the door to his stateroom, grateful for the protection it offered but also knowing he couldn't keep hiding here. *I have to get to know them, see how well they can still hold up under pressure. Based on the people I've met so far, they'll keep trying for a while because of their irrational faith in me, but what happens after I've made enough mistakes, after I've made it clear that I'm not the mythical Black Jack Geary but really just Commander John Geary, promoted to Captain after his "death" and not sure what the hell to do or how to get them home safe? What then?*

The only way to learn the answer to that question was to get out past that stateroom door.

For the next several days, Geary devoted perhaps half his time to studying and the other half to walking through the *Dauntless*. He'd set an informal goal of trying to walk to every compartment in the ship, if for no other reason than he knew letting the crew see him would be important for their morale. He also desperately wanted them to see him as human, before he proved his fallibility again, but he wasn't sure he was making much progress on that account.

On one such walk, he stopped by the compartment containing *Dauntless*'s null-field projector. The null-field's crew stood around, smiling, as Geary stared at the massive, squat device. Something about the size and shape of the weapon made him think of a mythical giant troll, resting on its haunches as it waited patiently for a victim to come close enough. Geary did his best to hide his misgivings and smiled back at the crew. "The weapon's ready to employ?"

"Yes, sir!" The crew chief, who looked so young Geary wondered if he'd been shaving for very long, laid a possessive hand on the monster. "It's in perfect condition. We run checks every day, just like the manuals say, and if anything looks even a little off, we make sure it's fixed."

Another of the null-field's crew spoke up, her proud tone matching that of the crew chief. "We'll be ready, Captain. Any Syndic warship that gets within range is gonna get fogged real good."

It took Geary a moment to realize that "fogged" must refer to what would be left after a null-field shot reduced anything, and anyone, within its target area into subatomic particles. Somehow, he nodded and smiled in response to the boast. Gunners loved their guns. They always had and probably always would. That's why they were gunners. And his ancestors knew the fleet needed good gunners. "The next time we get up close with the Syndics, we'll see if we can give you that shot." The crew grinned and pumped their fists into the air. *I don't have the heart to tell them that* Dauntless *can't be risked if I can help it. But there's all too great a chance we might end up getting close to Syndic warships whether I like it or not before this is all over.*

The hell-lance battery crews weren't quite as enthusiastic, but then unlike the null-fields, their personal toys weren't brand-new weapons that they'd gotten to be the first to play with. Geary easily recognized the hell-lance projectors, even though these bulked three times the size of the ones he'd known.

A veteran Chief Petty Officer at a hell-lance battery patted one of the weapons. "I bet you wish you'd had one of these girls along on your last battle, eh, Captain?"

Geary managed that polite smile again. "It would've come in very handy."

"Not that you needed one, sir," the chief added hastily. "That battle of yours . . . everyone knows about it. This stuff today is great, but they don't make ships or sailors like that anymore."

Geary knew the truth of the statement, but he knew another truth as well. He looked at the dull surface of the hell-lance for a moment, then shook his head. "You're wrong, Chief." Then he cocked one eyebrow at the others present. "One of the advantages of being fleet commander is that I get to tell a chief he's wrong." They all laughed, then stopped when Geary spoke again, his voice measured. "They still make great ships and great sailors. You all saw *Repulse*." His voice caught on the last word, but that was okay because he saw the sailors' reactions and knew they understood and felt the same way. "We'll get the damage to our ships repaired, we'll restock our expendable weapons, and the next time we meet the Syndic fleet, we'll make them pay a hundred times over for *Repulse*."

They cheered. He felt like a fraud, mouthing words he didn't really believe. But they had to believe in themselves, and mistaken or not, they believed in him.

As he turned to go, the chief yelled over the cheers. "We'll make you proud you commanded us, Black Jack!"

Ancestors help me. But Geary turned and spoke as the crowd fell silent to listen. "I'm already proud to command you."

And they cheered again, but that was okay, because what he'd said this time was completely true.

He had to be escorted by Captain Desjani when he went to see the hypernet key in its secured area. About half as large as a cargo container, the device took up most of the space in the compartment where it rested. Geary walked around the outside, seeing the power cables snaking into it and the control lines weaving in and out. He looked at it for a long time, wondering at how something so ordinary in appearance could be so important.

"CAPTAIN Geary." The only good thing about Co-President Victoria Rione's expression was that it was marginally less cold than her tone of voice.

"Madam Co-President." Geary stepped back to allow her into his stateroom. He'd been trying to wean himself off the meds and hadn't taken any today, which had left him feeling even worse than usual and in no mood for a visitor. But given her authority over some of the ships in the fleet, he couldn't send Rione away. "To what do I owe the honor of this visit?"

Apparently, he didn't quite manage to keep the irony out of his voice, because Rione's expression dropped a few more degrees toward absolute zero. But she walked into the stateroom, waited while Geary closed the door, then eyed him silently.

If she's trying to unnerve me, she's doing a good job. Geary tried not to let Rione anger him, since he had a feeling that Rione used such emotions to trick her opponents into saying and doing things they'd probably regret. "Would you like to sit down?"

"No." She turned and walked the three steps that took her to the far bulkhead, apparently absorbed in studying the picture there. It was a legacy of Admiral Bloch, of course, a stunning starscape that was just the sort of thing you'd expect to find in a naval officer's stateroom. Rione spent perhaps a minute looking at the picture, then turned toward Geary again. "Do you like starscapes, Captain Geary?"

Small talk. He hadn't expected that, and it made him warier than ever. "Not particularly."

"You can change it. You can put any picture from the ship's graphic library on here."

"I know." He refused to add that he hadn't been able to bring himself to wipe out the picture because it represented a legacy of Admiral Bloch's former presence here.

Rione eyed him for several seconds longer before speaking again. "What are your intentions, Captain Geary?"

My intentions are purely honorable, ma'am. The incongruous thought arose totally unbidden, causing Geary to pretend to cough so he wouldn't laugh instead. "Excuse me. Madam Co-President, as we discussed earlier, I intend to try to get this fleet back to Alliance space."

"Don't evade the question, Captain. We're en route to

the Corvus System. I want to know what you intend doing next."

If I knew for sure, I'd tell you. But perhaps Rione's visit wasn't such a bad thing after all. She was apparently one of the few people on this ship who didn't worship the space he sailed through, she'd already made it clear she wouldn't hesitate to express her opinions, and as far as he could tell from their earlier conversation she had a good head on her shoulders. Granted, she also didn't try to hide her dislike of him, but unlike the hostility he'd seen from people like Captains Numos and Faresa, at least the Republic co-president's disdain seemed tempered by some degree of common sense. "I'd like to discuss that with you."

"Really?" Rione's skepticism was clear from both her tone and her expression.

"Yes. Though I ask that our discussions remain confidential. I hope you understand."

"Of course."

Geary took one step to the table and painstakingly worked the still unfamiliar controls to call up its display. Stars glowed in the air above the table's surface, then winked out. Cursing under his breath, Geary tried again, and this time the display remained steady. "We're got some options."

"Options."

"Yes." *If she can talk in one-word sentences, so can I.* Geary carefully manipulated the controls, and the stars were replaced with a miniature picture of how the Alliance fleet would currently appear to a godlike observer. "We're likely to have a head start through Corvus before any Syndics come through the jump exit behind us. A few hours, at least."

Rione frowned and came to stand near him, one arm almost touching his, but apparently as unreactive to his personal presence as if he were another wall. "The Syndic fleet was in very close pursuit when we entered jump.

Surely they'll still be right behind us when we enter the Corvus System."

"I don't think so." Geary pointed toward the display. "We'll be disposed like this when we leave jump. It's a decent formation. More important, we've got plenty of heavy firepower toward the rear of the formation."

"Heavier than the Syndics?"

Sarcasm definitely didn't become Co-President Rione, Geary decided. "Locally, yes. When we entered jump, the Syndics were focused on trying to stop or slow some of our big units long enough for their big ships to catch up and destroy them. But the situation will be different on the other side of the jump if the Syndics come through right behind us. They're all strung out. Their light stuff would run head-on into our main strength. We could send our own slow units on ahead while our best ships stayed at the jump exit and trashed the light Syndic ships as they came through." He paused, then shook his head. "No, they won't have followed us through immediately. They'll have to take time to reform their forces. They can't make a jump in that wall formation of theirs because it's spread so wide the outer portions wouldn't be within the jump point. They'll call back the HuKs and other light units, get the heavies rearranged, and then . . ."

She raised one eyebrow. "Then?"

"That's a big question." Geary looked at her, trying to figure out if he could trust Rione or her judgments. *Trust them or not, she may think of something I haven't.* "I'd like your thoughts on something."

Rione gave him a guarded look, her skepticism still obvious. "My thoughts."

"Yes. On what we do next."

"Then before you say anything else, let me say this. Don't misjudge your strength, Captain Geary."

He frowned, feeling the weakness in his body, resenting that weakness and Rione's apparent allusion to it. "What exactly does that mean? I'm physically capable of—"

"No. Not your personal strength. The strength of this

fleet." Rione waved one hand dismissively toward the depiction of the Alliance fleet. "Those give you a surface picture. They don't tell you what's inside."

"Are you saying I can't trust my information?"

"The information on the fleet is accurate as far as it goes." She gestured again in apparent frustration. "I don't know the right word to describe the problem. This fleet is like a piece of metal that seems very strong. But when struck, it breaks fairly easily. Do you understand?"

He did. "Brittle. You're saying the fleet's brittle. Strong-looking but too easily shattered by a blow. Is that right?"

Rione appeared surprised. "That's exactly what I meant."

"But not physical weakness. Not flaws in ship construction or weaponry."

"I begin to feel certain you know that is not what I'm referring to."

And I begin to feel certain there's more to you than meets the eye, Co-President Rione. "I appreciate your assessment."

"You don't seem to be startled by it. Frankly, I thought you'd react angrily."

Geary gave her an obviously false smile. "I like surprising people." *Which is one reason why I won't tell you that I've no intention of letting this fleet stay brittle if I can help it. Metal can be reforged, tempered. So can this fleet. I hope. Though whether I or anybody else could succeed in doing that under these conditions is another question.* "I've been trying to get to know—" He almost said "these people" before checking himself. "This fleet. They're good, but as I was told some time back"—a little more than a week ago—"they're tired."

"This isn't the type of tiredness that can be cured by a good night's sleep, Captain Geary."

"I know that, Madam Co-President."

"If you commit these ships to a major battle, even under the conditions you describe, they may fail you."

Geary looked down and bit his lip. *That's exactly what I'm afraid of, but I don't know what she might repeat to others.* "I don't intend seeking a major fleet engagement at this time."

"That is *not* a reassuring statement. It is critically important to the Alliance, as well as to the Callas Republic and the Rift Federation, that these ships return to Alliance space!"

"I know that, Madam Co-President."

"We must avoid losing more ships."

Geary glowered at her. "Madam Co-President, contrary to whatever you appear to believe, I am not in the habit of spending ships and the lives of sailors as if they were loose change rattling around in my pocket." Her eyes narrowed, but Rione stayed silent for the moment. "I don't intend to seek out a fleet engagement. I have no idea whether or not the Syndics will be able to force such an action. But I will do all I can to maximize the odds in our favor, no matter what."

Rione stayed silent a little longer before answering. "That's hardly a promise, Captain Geary."

"I don't make promises I can't keep. I can't control what the Syndics do, and I can't be certain what kind of situations we'll face. Surely you understand military realities enough to know that sometimes units must be risked?"

"Units like *Repulse*?"

Geary glared at her. "Yes," he rasped.

Instead of speaking again, Rione just seemed to study Geary for several seconds. "Very well, Captain Geary. I must add that in the case of the *Repulse,* I have been remiss." She inclined her head slightly toward him. "May I offer my personal condolences on your family's loss, as well as my official condolences, and thanks for your family's sacrifice, on behalf of the Callas Republic."

He looked down at the deck, composing himself, then nodded back. "Thank you, Madam Co-President. I didn't know you were aware I was related to the commander of the *Repulse*." He knew his voice sounded rough and knew he couldn't do anything about it.

"Yes. I should've expressed my sympathies much earlier, and beg your forgiveness."

"That's all right." He straightened himself and took a deep breath. "There've been many, many sacrifices." Rione still didn't look friendly, but she seemed perhaps a few degrees warmer. The last thing he wanted to do now, though, was talk about the dead, so he changed the subject without worrying about being obvious. "As I said earlier, I'd appreciate your assessment on something." Looking away from her, Geary concentrated on the controls for the table and once again called up a display of stars. "We're jumping in here, inside Corvus System. We'll swing through, picking up whatever supplies we can grab in the time available."

He indicated the jump exit, then swung his finger to point out another area. "This is the jump point out of Corvus. We've got three possible destinations." He highlighted a star. "Yuon's one of them, and it's pretty near along a straight shot back to Alliance space." Another star. "Voss, which goes a bit back the other way, deeper into Syndic territory." And the third. "Kaliban. Which just sort of carries us along inside Syndic space, but sets us up to potentially jump to four other stars." He paused. "Suppose you were the Syndic commanders, Co-President Rione. Where would you expect us to go?"

She didn't hesitate. "Yuon."

"Because?"

"We're running, Captain Geary. The fleet is running for its life. And Yuon offers the fastest route home. Not fast, by any means, compared to hypernet. But significantly faster than the alternatives."

He looked down at the display, rubbing his jaw. "Doesn't that make it too obvious a choice? Too obvious a place for the Syndic fleet to jump into and wait for us?"

"I repeat, our fleet fled the Syndic home system. We're in hostile territory. Running is the only reasonable option."

"Alright, I agree we need to run. We also need to avoid getting caught, which means we need to steer clear of an obvious route."

"In theory, yes. But we're constrained by the realities of our condition. The Syndics will know you want to go to Yuon, Captain Geary."

Geary gave her a twisted smile. "But I *don't* want to go to Yuon, Madam Co-President."

She stiffened, and Geary could swear he saw ice forming inside her eyes. "Voss! You're planning on jumping back toward the Syndic home system, then jumping in again, hoping the defenses will be surprised and the fleet off chasing us—"

Geary held up both hands, palms out. "No."

"No?" Rione took a step to the side, as if circling him warily, and watched his face.

"No. In a perfect world, maybe." *In a perfect world, we wouldn't be fighting a war that's a century old.* "But I can read those damage reports on our ships, and I can total up the weapons we've expended and the state of our supplies. Just as well as I can guess at the current ability of this fleet to handle another major battle." Geary shook his head. "It'd be an insane risk."

"I agree." Rione said that cautiously, as if still waiting for Geary to spring a trap.

"But the Syndics will have to defend against that chance, won't they? That means putting a blocking force in Voss and keeping some reinforcements for their home system close at hand. Just in case I'm insane," he added dryly. "That'll deplete the forces they have to chase us."

"So you *are* going to Yuon?"

"No. I want to go to Kaliban."

"Kaliban?" Rione's eyes shifted rapidly from Geary to the star display. "What does Kaliban grant us?"

"Time and the greatest degree of relative safety." He raised another palm, forestalling more objections. "I know time is our enemy, too. But it gives the fleet more time to recover. Our auxiliaries are building more expendable

weaponry now, grapeshot and specters, and we'll pick up
materials to build more while we're in Corvus, I hope.
We'll get more damage fixed. Yes, once we reach Kaliban,
we'll need to jog toward home. And we'll be in desperate
need of resupply, so we have to find enough of what we
need there. But we'll have a couple of good star options for
our next jump, one okay option, and one risky option.
That'll leave the Syndics with four places to guard even if
they've been able to localize our fleet by then."

Rione looked thoughtful as she nodded. "And what of
this degree of relative safety?"

Geary indicated the stars again. "We've been beat up,
and the Syndics have us badly outnumbered. But the Syndic fleet doesn't have an infinite number of ships. The
more they divide what they've got to try to catch us, the
better the odds we'll face if they do catch us. Here," he
pointed to Yuon. "They need to put enough ships there to
at least hurt us a lot more if we go through that system. But
they also need to put ships into Voss to protect against that
possibility. And they've got to keep the pressure on us,
which means a strong force pursuing us through Corvus."

"I see. That leaves little for Kaliban. If you're right. But
how sure can you be that the Syndics will disregard the
chance you'll go to Kaliban?"

"I don't think they'll disregard it," Geary corrected. "I
think they'll consider it by far the least likely objective for
us, and they'll regard it as much less critical a matter than
if we went to Yuon or Voss. Going to either of those stars
would create an immediate problem for the Syndics. If we
go to Kaliban, we're still a problem, but one they'll think
leaves them time to deal with us." He stared down at the
representation of Kaliban. *I just wish I knew what the Syndics had at Kaliban. The little intelligence we have is more
than a half-century old. Hell, I wish I knew what they had
at Corvus.*

"Why are you explaining this to me?"

He glanced at her. "As I said, I want your opinion."

"You sound like you've already made up your mind."

He tried not to sound irritated. "No. I'm trying to formulate a plan, and I'm thinking through options. You have a different way of looking at things, so I value your impressions."

For a moment, Geary could swear Rione looked slightly amused. "Then I tell you that I'd go through Yuon."

"I see—"

"I'm not finished. *I'd* go through Yuon. But what you've said is true, and I myself warned you that we must avoid a major battle. I now believe as you do that Kaliban will be the best option."

Geary gave her a wry smile. "Then may I assume the ships of the Republic and the Rift will follow my orders and go to Kaliban?"

"Yes, Captain Geary." Her expression shifted. "Getting the rest of the Alliance fleet to go there will be your task alone, I'm afraid."

She thinks that'll be a problem. I hadn't thought that far. The fleet's ship commanders followed me out of the Syndic home system. But they were facing imminent death, and even then some of them wanted to debate things.

And they're all tired and want to get home.

Rione was once more apparently studying the starscape. "I regret to say I know little of your personal life, Captain Geary. Did you leave anyone behind?"

He pondered the question. "It depends how you mean that. My father and mother were still alive. My brother was married. He didn't have any kids, yet, though." Funny how he could say that and somehow emotionally divorce it from the image of the older man who'd been his brother's grandson, and who'd died on the *Repulse*.

"No life partner?"

"No." He realized she was looking at him and wondered how a one-word answer could reveal so much to her. "Nothing that worked out."

"A blessing, perhaps?"

"In light of what happened to me, yeah." Geary shook

his head. "I always thought they'd have finally figured out how to extend the lifespan by now."

"Alas, no." Rione was, to all appearances, studying the starscape again as she spoke. "You know what's happened every time they've tried. Nature will let us keep humans healthy and strong nearly up to the end, but come the end still does, even though scientists have taken the human body apart down to the quantum level and rebuilt it in an effort to change that."

Geary, feeling tired again, sat down and leaned back, closing his eyes for a moment. "It's enough to give someone religion."

"It's certainly enough to make someone think about it." She glanced at Geary. "Is there an ancestral home?"

"Not unless they've built one since the last time I was back."

"Where will you go when we return to Alliance space?"

"I don't know." He stared at nothing, his mind wandering. "There's somebody I need to look up on the *Dreadnought*, wherever that ship is."

Rione didn't mask her surprise. "You know someone on a ship back in Alliance space?"

"Not really. I have a message for her, though, that somebody asked me to deliver." Geary brooded on that for a moment while Rione waited, then shrugged. "After that, maybe I'll go to Kosatka."

"Kosatka?"

"It was a nice place, once. I hear it's still nice."

"Kosatka," Rione repeated. "I do not think your fate lies on Kosatka, Captain Geary."

"Do you foretell the future as well as read minds?"

"All I read are people, Captain." Co-President Rione walked back to the hatch, pausing in the entrance. "Thank you for your time, and for your confidences."

"You're welcome." He half-rose as she left, then sat back down heavily, weary once again and wondering why his stomach felt so tight.

"KALIBAN?" Captain Desjani stared at Geary. "But the way home lies through Yuon."

"Captain, the Syndics know you're thinking that. They'll be there."

"But not in enough strength—"

"How can you know that?" Geary realized he was snapping at Desjani and reigned in his temper. "You told me yourself. The Syndic ships in their home system could hypernet to, uh, Zaqi and then jump to Yuon in a little less time than it'd take us to get to Corvus, transit that system, and jump to Yuon. They could have their entire damned fleet there, except for the ships pursuing us, which would come out of the jump exit and hit us from the rear."

"But Yuon . . ." Desjani's voice trailed off.

Geary saw the desperate weariness in her and felt a stab of shame at his own anger. "I'm sorry, Tanya. I know how much you want to get home. I want to get us there, too."

"The Alliance needs this fleet, Captain Geary. And it needs *Dauntless* and what *Dauntless* carries. The sooner the better."

"The Syndics'll be waiting for us at Yuon, Tanya. If we go that way, we *won't* get home."

She finally nodded. "They understand us too well, don't they?" When Geary didn't answer immediately, Desjani continued. "The Syndics knew we'd jump at the bait they offered, the chance to hit their home system, and now they'll know we'll head straight home through Yuon."

"I'm afraid so."

"But you see clearer than that. You know we must take a longer route."

Geary suppressed a groan of exasperation. *Maybe I just don't have the same emotional need to get home as badly as you other people do!* "I'm going to notify all ships of our planned destination before we leave jump—"

"Captain!"

"What?"

Captain Desjani adopted a formal posture. "Sir, you

must inform the ships' commanding officers of this decision in person."

He tried to dampen an immediate flare of annoyance. "I've been told that if we transmit it in jump there's zero chance of the Syndics ever intercepting the message. And in any case I'm not going to put it to a vote."

"I'm not saying you should put it to a vote, Captain, but you need to tell them yourself." She must've read his feelings on his face. "I know this isn't how you did things in the old days, but it's how we're used to doing things now." Another pause. "Sir, you must lead personally! You can't do that by sending a brief text message."

The last thing he wanted to do was face that crowd of officers again, knowing that some believed in him with all the fervor of Captain Desjani and some thought him a living fossil who needed to be cast aside. "Tanya, we're probably going to be awfully busy every second this fleet is in the Corvus System. Even if the Syndics don't send ships jumping into the system right on our tails, they'll still be coming at some point. We don't know what kind of defenses the Syndics have in Corvus. We'll need to decide what facilities to ransack, overcome, or overawe any resistance . . ." Desjani just looked back at him stubbornly. *Face it. My gut tells me Desjani is right. I had to convince her in person about Yuon. If she's refusing to be convinced now, it's because her professional judgment says I need to talk those other ship commanders into going to Kaliban.*

Nice to know Desjani won't cave when she thinks I'm wrong even if she does believe I'm the ancestors' gift to this fleet.

Geary nodded, not bothering to hide his reluctance from her. "Okay, Tanya. You win. As soon as we're certain no immediate Syndic pursuit is coming out of the jump point on our tails, I'll call a conference and tell everyone in person that we're going to Kaliban and not Yuon." She didn't answer. "Okay. I'll also tell them *why* we're going to Kaliban and not Yuon."

"Thank you, Captain. I hope you understand—"

"I do. And I thank you for making clear your recommendation."

"Whatever waits for us at Corvus can't be too dangerous, Captain Geary. They won't even know the outcome of the battle in the Syndic home system."

"Yeah." *Maybe we'll be able to use that somehow.* "But Corvus is so close to the Syndic home world it might be a tough nut."

Desjani made a dismissive gesture. "It's not on the Syndic hypernet."

Geary thought about the way she'd said that. "That obviously means more than I realize. Explain it to me, please."

She looked surprised, then nodded. "I just assumed you knew, but how could you? The hypernet lets someone go very quickly from wherever they are to wherever they want to be. They don't have to go through other places to get there."

"Oh." *Damn. I said it again.* "With the system jump drives you have to jump through systems within range to eventually reach where you're headed."

"Yes." Desjani nodded again. "Many, many systems only mattered because people had to go through them to get to somewhere else. They didn't have any special resources or other significance. Once a hypernet is up, all that passing-through traffic vanishes."

Geary thought about that. "I can't imagine that benefited the bypassed systems."

"No. The only reason someone will go to them now is if they have personal reasons or because the system has something special. But if the system does have something special, it'll be on the hypernet."

He had a vision of many broken branches withering away even as the main tree flourished. "What's happened to them?"

She shrugged. "Some have put their resources into trying to get hypernet gates, but few have succeeded. Some have tried to make themselves special in some way so others would lobby for a gate for them. Again, few have managed that. Most were never that wealthy to begin with and have been slowly declining as trade bypasses them and they lose touch with technological and cultural developments being shared through the hypernet. The best and brightest people from such systems always seek to emigrate to hypernet-linked systems as well, of course."

"I see." *A bit like me. Isolated and increasingly outdated. Bypassed by the hypernet and by history. I wonder how some of these Syndic systems will react when I bring the Alliance fleet through? At least they'll be part of history again.*

We'll exit jump at Corvus in another week and find out just how that system has fared since being bypassed by the Syndic hypernet. I'd better work on my speech to the ship commanders, and keep praying that the Syndic plan wasn't devious enough to include setting a trap inside Corvus for any Alliance ships that managed to jump out of their home system.

FOUR

THE star known to humanity as Corvus glowed like a tiny, bright coin against the star-dappled black of normal space as the Alliance fleet leaped out of jump. Geary, trying hard not to show how tense he was, looked down toward his armchair controls and saw his hand gripping the chair so tightly his fingers were white. He took a deep breath and stared at the display, willing it to produce the information he needed.

"No mines," Captain Desjani reported.

Geary just nodded. If there had been a minefield laid at the jump point exit they'd have already found it the hard way. But he'd felt safe in gambling that there wouldn't be mines here. Even when system jump drives had been the only way to get from star to star, there hadn't been many jump points guarded by minefields because they were as much a hazard to friendly shipping jumping back into normal space as they were to enemies. Deep inside Syndic territory, or Alliance territory for that matter, resources never would've been wasted on deploying and maintaining minefields.

Which was the only nice thing Geary could think of about being trapped so deep inside Syndic territory.

"No nearby shipping detected on initial scans," a watch-stander reported.

Geary nodded again. The report didn't mean much. They'd exited the jump point about a billion kilometers from Corvus, but Geary had long ago stopped thinking in terms of kilometers when it came to space navigation. Instead, he paid attention to the light-distance readout that reported they were eight and a half light-hours from the star. If the very old records they were relying on had been accurate, the main inhabited world orbiting Corvus was about 1.2 light-hours from its star. That meant whatever the fleet's sensors were now seeing and analyzing around that world was a picture well over seven hours old.

Aside from that single habitable world, Corvus boasted only three other satellites worthy of the name planet. One was a battered rock in a slightly eccentric orbit less than a light hour from the star, another a gas giant about six light-hours out, and farthest out a frozen snowball of a world, the orbit of which had it not much more than a half light-hour away from the jump point. Which meant that frozen world was also about a half light-hour away from the Alliance fleet.

"Captain Desjani." She turned to look at him. "It used to be routine for the Syndics to maintain defensive bases near jump points. The same sort of thing we did. I understand the Syndics have kept a lot of those bases active."

Desjani scowled. "We always assume the old bases remain active. If a hypernet gate is built, that gets new defenses. But for stars without hypernet, Alliance policy has been that if defensive bases are to be kept in-system, then it's not worth the cost of moving them. The Syndics seem to have followed the same policy."

"That makes sense. Why waste money? The question is whether they'll have bothered with maintaining a base this far inside their territory." Geary rubbed his forehead, watching the display where a slowly expanding sphere around the fleet's ships marked the area where something like a real-time picture could be established. The sphere still looked ridiculously small against the size of the star system they were invading. Fortunately, it would soon cover the orbit of the frozen world. "That means if they still have a base here, it'll be there," he added out loud.

Captain Desjani nodded. "We'll know soon. Initial optical and full spectrum scans show installations with heat signatures, so something's still active there, but we need more data. There's definitely not a major naval force nearby, though. We'd be seeing some signs of that by now even if the information was time-late."

Thank the ancestors for not-so-small blessings, Geary thought irreverently. In fact, space traffic in the system seemed light. Geary, unconsciously anticipating the sort of system jump traffic he'd been used to, instead saw no interstellar shipping passing through en route to the various jump locations. What in-system traffic had been spotted, running between the inhabited planet and what must be various off-planet mining and manufacturing sites, was confined to the plane of the system and clustered among the inner planets. *Where the hell is everybody?* Geary couldn't help wondering, even though he knew that thanks to the hypernet "everybody" didn't have to go through Corvus or systems like it anymore.

Geary tapped a communications circuit, having painstakingly learned how to use his controls during the jump to Corvus. "This is Captain Geary for Captain Duellos and Captain Tulev. You are to take the Second and Fourth Battle Cruiser Squadrons and assume positions covering the jump exit. If any Syndic forces come through there in immediate pursuit, they must be destroyed before they can get past you."

Geary could almost hear the anticipation of one-sided slaughter in Duellos' and Tulev's voices as they rogered up for the order. On his scan, Geary watched the heavy combatants of the two squadrons swinging around and moving back toward the jump point. The battle cruisers were able to accelerate quickly for their size but were comparatively lightly defended since their acceleration had been purchased by adding more propulsion power at the expense of defensive-screen capability. He'd have to hold them there long enough to nail any Syndics coming through on the heels of the Alliance fleet, but not leave them isolated as the rest of the fleet moved away. Just a simple matter of timing, with seven big warships and the lives of their crews riding on Geary's ability to get it right.

Mines. How could I have forgotten that until now? I don't care how much Syndic shipping gets disrupted. "Captain Duellos. Have your ships lay a minefield around the jump exit, slaved to the local star so it maintains position."

Duellos acknowledged the newest order, sounding definitely gleeful this time. The Alliance fleet had taken some heavy loses in the Syndic home system from mines laid as part of the ambush, so Geary didn't begrudge any desire by Alliance sailors for retaliation on that count.

Another tap on a circuit to communicate with the entire fleet. "All units, with the exception of the Second and Fourth Battle Cruiser Squadrons, are to assume standard fleet-attack formation Alpha Six immediately upon receipt of this message." The units of the fleet, jumbled by the battle in the Syndic home system and the pell-mell retreat through the jump point, hadn't been able to reform while in jump space and now needed to resume the semblance of an orderly formation again. Geary watched on his display as the ships and squadrons slowly acknowledged an order that took a few light-minutes to reach the farthest ships, trying not to shake his head at how scattered the fleet was.

"The fleet is still proceeding in-system at point one light speed," Desjani reminded him. "It's going to take some of those ships quite a while to reach their assigned positions."

"Yeah." Geary studied the display, still essentially empty of real-time threat information. "If we slow the fleet, individual ships will have an easier time taking station. But I don't want to risk slowing the fleet until we've learned more about whatever Syndic force we're hopefully surprising here."

"Holding back never won a battle," Desjani stated approvingly, in the manner of someone quoting a lesson.

Geary was still mentally shaking his head at Desjani's statement when a chime sounded to call attention to the display. He watched as the time-late data from the inhabited world scrolled by. Analysis of imagery and things like chemical by-products in the atmosphere indicated the world was still running an industrialized economy, but with signs of inactive facilities and apparently not as heavily populated as expected given the length of time humans had been settled there. That matched what he'd heard about those systems that had been bypassed by the hypernet system slowly dying on the vine. A score of objects orbited the world, seven tagged as cold and probably mothballed and two labeled as likely military installations. No military shipping was visible in the more than eight-hour-old picture.

"The installation on the fourth world is active and assessed military," the reconnaissance watch reported. "Two minor combatants are active near the base as of forty-one minutes time-late."

Geary jerked his head around and stared at the system display of the frozen planet. They still didn't have anything like a real-time picture of the area near the Syndic base, but as of forty minutes ago there'd been two Syndic ships there. *We arrived in system less than ten minutes ago, so they won't see us for another half hour. By then, we'll be a lot closer to them.* "Is the identification of those Syndic ships accurate? We're sure that's what they are?"

Desjani frowned, probably taking the questioning of her ship's displayed information personally. "The IDs on the ships near the base? Yes, Captain Geary. Type and Class ID is certain. Model is tentative."

"I'll be damned." Desjani gave Geary a wondering

look, so he pointed at the display. "We called those things nickel corvettes in my time."

"Nickel?"

"Yeah. Like the coins. They're useful, but they don't last long if you need to use them. Those ships were half-obsolescent when I . . ." Geary let his words trail off, not sure how to refer to his apparent death in battle a century ago. "When I was last in combat," he finally stated.

Desjani snorted in amazement. "I've never seen that class of ships before. I suppose those corvettes must've been left here because it was easier to leave them in the hands of the local Corvus authorities than it would've been to dispose of them."

"Probably." For a moment, Geary imagined himself at that Syndic base or on those ships as the Alliance fleet came pouring out of the jump point. If the age of those Syndic ships was any indication, this system didn't even really qualify as a backwater in the war. Decades, at least, since Corvus had been involved in the Alliance–Syndicate Worlds war, aside from sending in taxes and doubtless occasional shipments of draft-age young adults. For a few more minutes or a few more hours, depending on where in the system they were, they'd still think they were a backwater. Then they'd finally begin to see the Alliance fleet arriving, ship after ship becoming visible as the light from their arrival finally reached the various Syndic watchers. And they wouldn't believe it for a few minutes, would they? Wouldn't believe that here was the war arriving, in sudden and overwhelming force.

The fleet communications circuit came to life. "Captain Geary, this is Commander Zeas on the *Truculent*. We're within weapons range of an active radar emitter focused on the jump point."

"This is Geary. Take it out." He glanced at Desjani. "I know that's just a navigational aid, but it's probably sending contact reports to that base."

"I concur," she agreed. "Though the reports will be

going at light speed, so they won't get there before visual sightings of us can take place from the base."

"Every couple of minutes helps. Is the base itself sending out any active sensor emissions?" Geary checked the display even as he asked, knowing the answer should be there somewhere.

"No, sir." Desjani indicated the proper data fields. "Did you expect that?"

"No." Geary almost bridled at the question, then found a moment's amusement in it. "Even in my primitive time it was obvious that radar would take twice as long to spot something as a visual sensor would, since the radar pulse has to go and return while the light from the object only has to travel that distance once." The difference in time was insignificant on a planet's surface, but when the size of a battlefield was measured in light-hours it mattered a lot.

Desjani gulped visibly. "I didn't mean any disrespect—"

"I know that. I also know I'm out of date in a lot of ways, so I'd rather you keep on assuming I don't know something. We're safer that way, and frankly, Captain, I trust you with knowledge of my fallibility."

"Yes, sir." Desjani grinned. "You already know the trust that I and my crew have in *you*."

This time, Geary tried not to wince. Trying to change the topic, he nodded toward the display. "I wish this wouldn't take so long. Too bad we can't do faster-than-light microjumps inside star systems."

"Yes. The waiting has always been the hardest part for me," Desjani confessed. "We can see the enemy, we know where they are, but it'll still be almost four and a half hours before we get close enough to that base on the fourth world to turn it into craters."

A new voice answered her. "You could go faster." Both Desjani and Geary turned to see that Co-President Rione had come onto the bridge of the *Dauntless*. Rione looked directly at Geary. "Couldn't you?"

Geary shrugged, trying to ignore the disdainful expression he could see out of the corner of his eye on Desjani's face. "We could. I don't want to."

"Why not?" Rione came forward and sat in an unoccupied seat designated for observers, strapping herself in with carefully precise movements.

"Because among other things, the ships of this fleet are already averaging point one light speed. We're in normal space and subject to the rules there. That means the faster we go, the worse we'll run into relativistic effects." Rione eyed him, plainly awaiting elaboration and leaving Geary wondering yet again how much she really knew and how much she was testing him. "To put it in the simplest possible terms, our perspective of everything outside of this ship gets increasingly distorted the faster we go. At point one light, we can still figure out what we're looking at with some accuracy. As we get closer to the speed of light, it gets harder to tell where everything really is. I'm having enough trouble now figuring out where the enemy is located and where their ships are going. The last thing I need is to have to wonder where my own ships are, too."

Rione waved at the display. "I understood these presented images that compensated for relativistic effects when necessary."

Captain Desjani, her ship's honor apparently at stake once more, answered. "Madam Co-President, the systems can fairly accurately compensate for relativistic effects on this ship because they know what this ship is doing. For any other ship, the systems can only estimate from what it can observe. We'd get a time-late and distorted picture of the other ship, and the resulting corrections vary in accuracy. The image we get could differ significantly from where the other ship is actually located and from what its actual course and speed vectors are at any moment."

Any further questions from Rione were forestalled by the communications watch. "Captain Desjani, we've received a challenge from Syndic defense forces in-system."

Desjani looked at Geary, of course. He frowned at the display and the time. "That was quick. Correct me if I'm wrong, but that base on the fourth planet must only now be picking up visual on the first fleet ship coming out of the jump point."

"Agreed." Desjani swept her gaze across the bridge. "That signal must've come from a Syndic source about fifteen light-minutes out from the jump point. Find it," she ordered her watch-standers.

It only took a few moments, thanks to the fact that the fleet was spread out so much. Using the bearings from which the Syndic signal had been received by different, widely separated ships, the source was easily localized. Full-spectrum sensors focused on the spot, finally picking out a small object. "It's tiny," the communications watch reported. "That's no ship. Not a crewed object, either. Assess the source of the signal to be an automated traffic management assistant."

"Why didn't we spot it before now?" Desjani demanded.

"It seems to have been out here a long time, ma'am. Very heavily pitted. Preliminary sweeps assessed it as most likely an ancient piece of debris drifting through the system."

Geary, pondering how that description also matched the last century of his own existence, rubbed his chin as he studied the display. The closest ship to the object, the cruiser *Ardent,* was less than a light-minute away. *That thing won't be equipped with weaponry, but it might have stuff that'll help the Syndic base track us, and it could have a self-destruct capability that could damage any ship that wanders too close. Better safe than sorry.* "*Ardent*, this is Captain Geary on the *Dauntless.* Get rid of that thing."

Then he had to wait almost two minutes for a response. "*Ardent*, aye. It's gone." Geary watched his display, knowing that it would be several minutes at best before he'd see the indications that *Ardent* had blown away the satellite.

"Should we answer the signal, Captain Desjani?" the communications watch persisted.

She looked to Geary again. "It must've sent a report to the base."

"Yeah. That report will arrive a little after they get visuals on us, I guess." Geary thought the problem through, aware that he was setting in motion events and decisions that would play out for the next several hours. He tried not to think about how many lives in Corvus System and the fleet rested on what he decided now.

"Captain Desjani," Geary stated carefully, thinking again of the shocked defenders of Corvus System. "Please inform the Syndic authorities that we are here to accept their surrender. Broadcast that through the entire system."

She gave him a puzzled and disappointed look. "So far, everything indicates there's very little in the way of defenses here, and what they have is hopelessly outdated. Defeating them won't be hard at all."

"No. But we'll get a lot more supplies and usable parts off of them if they surrender quietly than if we have to smash them into submission. We may even convince them to pony up more if they think it'll keep us from wrecking everything in this system."

"Isn't it better to ensure that their capability to resist is eliminated?"

"No." Geary shook his head firmly. "Losing the Syndic assets in this system would mean nothing to the Syndicate Worlds, but every ship damaged and weapon expended here means something to the Alliance. We're better off winning without a fight. If we broadcast a surrender demand now, it'll arrive everywhere in the system about a half hour after our presence has been detected. They'll have had time to realize how much force we have relative to them, time to get really scared, and that's when our demand will arrive."

Desjani still looked disappointed but held back whatever else she'd intended arguing. A few minutes later, *Dauntless* broadcast the message as the Alliance fleet continued falling toward the inner system at a tenth of the speed of light.

Geary watched his display, willing time and distance to pass more quickly. The Syndic base should've spotted the Alliance fleet by now, but even if the nickel corvettes got moving immediately, the *Dauntless* wouldn't see that movement for another ten minutes. He concentrated on his own ships, trying to sort out the tangle of movement vectors so he could figure out how well they were doing at getting into formation. Judging from how hard it was to read their movements, his ships weren't doing all that well. Granted, the fleet's speed made repositioning more difficult, but still the individual ships seemed to be doing a poor job of straightening themselves out.

"The Syndic commander has responded to our demand that they surrender," Captain Desjani grumbled.

"Okay." Geary checked the time, confirming that the response to his surrender demand must've been sent very quickly. He took a moment to pick the right control, then found himself gazing at the image of an elderly man in an obsessively neat but worn Syndic Executive Class Officer uniform.

The Syndic Executive visibly gulped, but he shook his head and tried to look resolute. "This is to acknowledge receipt of your transmission. Your request must be denied. I am not permitted to surrender any forces or installations within this system. Transmission end."

Oh, for . . . Geary let out an exasperated breath. "Our request must be denied? Is he kidding? It sounds like he thinks we asked permission to hold a dance."

"In a few more hours we'll bring his headquarters down around his head," Desjani replied cheerfully.

"Maybe. Until then, there's no reason I can't keep trying to get the idiot to see reason." Geary almost smiled at Desjani's expression. "Don't worry. I won't beg."

"I didn't—"

"Don't worry about it. Let me send this transmission personally." Geary paused to order his thoughts, then pressed the right command sequence. "This is the Alliance fleet, Captain John Geary commanding, entering Corvus

System. We're here to accept your surrender," Geary announced, not missing the irony of his demand after the Syndic CEO had used pretty much the same words to him a few weeks ago. "As you can tell from our arrival vectors, we've come from the Syndicate Worlds home system. Our work there is done for now." Geary tried to put the right amount of victorious arrogance into that misleading statement. If the Syndic commander thought it meant the Alliance had trashed the Syndic home system, it might help overawe him. "We expect all Syndicate Worlds military forces and any local forces to lay down their arms, deactivate defensive systems, and cease any form of resistance. It should be obvious to you that we have more than enough firepower to enforce our demand, and that any resistance on your part would be meaningless. Failure on your part to surrender quickly guarantees the futile deaths of your defenders and serious damage to installations within this system. I expect your next message to be an agreement to surrender."

He leaned back, looked toward Desjani, and shrugged. "If that doesn't get through to him . . ."

"A hell-lance will," Desjani finished.

"Yeah. If it comes to that." Geary frowned at the display. "Still no movement by the corvettes as of ten minutes ago. Interesting. They're just maintaining the same positions in orbit relative to the Syndic base."

"Perhaps they're planning to use them as part of the perimeter defense of the base."

"That'd be awfully dumb, tying down ships into static defensive positions, even if we didn't outnumber them so hugely." He studied the picture. "I think there's another reason, but—"

"Syndic cruiser detected orbiting the fourth planet!" the recon watch announced.

"Just one?" Geary watched the report scroll in. He didn't recognize the class of the light cruiser, but the system declared it to be an obsolete design. "Are these specs right?"

A dozen people on the bridge hurriedly checked. Desjani answered for them all. "Yes, sir."

"Wow. Look at the propulsion system on that thing! Why'd they stick so much propulsion capability on a light cruiser?"

Desjani frowned, studying the data. "We don't know. The design hasn't been encountered and is known only through intelligence sources. Apparently, only a few of those were built, and if they saw battle, the records didn't get back to us."

Geary nodded absently, thinking that the only reason the records wouldn't have gotten back was if the Alliance force involved had been cut to ribbons. The light cruiser wasn't heavily armed, though. It just had that honking big propulsion system. *Hopefully I won't have to worry what the idea was behind that. If the Syndic commander surrenders, I can ask someone. Otherwise, that cruiser will be a lot of junk floating in close formation after we blow a million holes in it.* "The cruiser and the corvettes are still hanging around the planet. That's a hopeful sign."

"It'll make them easier targets, anyway."

Another hour had almost gone by when the Syndic commander's response was received. "I am in receipt of your last communication," the executive in the worn uniform stated precisely. "Standing Syndicate Fleet Fighting Instructions, Article Seven prohibits surrender. Article Nine requires all military installations to be defended in the most vigorous possible manner. Article Twelve states there are no situational exceptions to Articles Seven and Nine. Therefore I must again deny your request."

Geary stared at the image for a long moment. "How can he be that stupid?"

Co-President Rione answered. "He's a bureaucrat, Captain Geary. Look at him. Listen to him. He lives to enforce rules regardless of whether or not those rules make sense." From her tone, Rione had met more than her share of such people already.

Geary almost laughed at the absurdity of it. *A bureau-*

crat. *Some guy who's probably spent his entire career making sure every letter of instruction laid down decades ago and light-years away are followed down to the last subclause. The sort who thinks following every petty rule matters more than anything else. Who else would end up in command of a system where the war was never supposed to come? Who else would want to hold that command for year after empty year?*

Then the reality of what the bureaucrat's petrified insistence on following Syndic Fleet Fighting Instructions, Articles Seven, Nine, and Twelve would cause came back to Geary. He'd have to kill enough of the people serving under this bean counter to force a surrender. *Damn him.*

Geary punched his communication controls viciously. "To the Syndicate Commander in Corvus System. Surrender is your only option. If you force us to destroy your defenses, I assure you that I will make every effort to ensure that you personally share the fate of your front-line personnel." He broke the connection, then turned to Captain Desjani. "Have your communications people try to ram some messages directly through to the corvettes and the cruiser telling them we'll accept their surrender." Desjani let disapproval show for a moment, but she nodded and gave the orders. *Give it a rest, Tanya Desjani. There's no glory in smashing people facing impossible odds.*

Still three hours until the fleet got close enough to the base to engage its defenses. Desjani's eyes strayed to the section of the display showing the battle cruisers gathered around the jump point, and it wasn't hard for Geary to read her thoughts. Duellos's and Tulev's ships would get to draw blood, but *Dauntless* would apparently have to be content with accepting the surrender of a few outdated ships. Desjani wasn't happy about that.

The ships of the Alliance fleet fell deeper into the Corvus System, while the individual ships crawled with widely varying speed and precision to the positions they were supposed to occupy relative to the flagship, the time-late images of the Syndic corvettes dithered around near their base, the Syndic light cruiser apparently continued to orbit the fourth world, and Geary watched it all with growing irritation. He started out trying to note every Alliance ship that was laggard about moving into the new formation, but it wasn't too long before he'd had to switch to spotting those ships that were assuming their positions with relative speed. There were simply too many laggards to keep individual track of, and distressingly few good performers.

The leading units of the Alliance fleet were supposed to be assuming a formation resembling a huge rectangle, with the flat face toward the enemy. The main body was supposed to be in another even-larger rectangle behind that, then the support ships and their escorts were supposed to be arrayed in a cube farther back yet. Two smaller cubes off to either side were to hold screening forces ready to screen against actions by enemy forces in those areas.

Instead, the intertangled swarm of Alliance ships looked to Geary for all the world like a single distorted wedge, with the fat end toward the enemy.

An alert pulsed, and symbols sprang to life on the display. Geary held his breath as *Dauntless* picked up Syndic ships exiting the jump point. Modern ones, moving fast. Geary felt adrenaline surge even though he knew he was watching events that had taken place ten minutes ago. And whatever defense his battle cruisers had carried out had also played out ten minutes ago.

Geary barely had time to register the presence of a squadron of Syndic Hunter-Killers formed up around a single heavy cruiser before he watched short-range concentrated fire from Duellos' and Tulev's battle cruisers ripping the HuKs to shreds. Moments later, the Alliance attacks swamped the cruiser's defenses and riddled it before it could get off more than a few shots that were absorbed harmlessly by the battle cruisers' screens. On the heels of the visual sighting of the battle, reports from the battle cruisers began arriving, confirming what Geary had already seen.

Geary waited, but nothing else came through after the reports of the first ships. They'd been an expendable force, sent through on the off-chance that the Alliance fleet had continued fleeing in panic and hadn't tried to defend the jump exit.

Expendable. Geary had always thought that was an ugly word and an uglier concept. Apparently, the Syndics didn't share that feeling.

Around him, cheers had erupted on the bridge of the *Dauntless* as they watched the small Syndic force get slaughtered. The sound wore at Geary's nerves, leaving him looking for something to vent his anger on. He tapped the fleet communications circuit again. "All units not yet in standard attack formation Alpha Six are to expedite their movement."

Desjani gave Geary a surprised glance, but quickly hid her reaction. Not that the *Dauntless*'s captain had to worry. As flagship, the unit every other ship had to take position relative to, the *Dauntless* was defined as being in position the moment the order was issued. "Do you think that's their entire fast-pursuit force?" she asked so quickly that Geary suspected she was just trying to change the subject.

How the hell would I know? Geary wanted to snap back. Instead, he thought about the question for a moment. "I think so. If they were sending through more, why leave an appreciable gap between their arrival times?" He paused. "That wasn't a big force, though. They should've been able to get it through the jump point right on our heels."

"They were just over an hour behind us." Desjani appeared to be thinking, then nodded. "They hesitated, then sent through a small force just in case it might find us unprepared."

Hesitated. Yes. Geary nodded back. "They sent something so they could tell their superiors they'd maintained a hot pursuit. Enough to make it look serious, but nothing big enough that they'd mind losing it." And too bad for the sailors on the ships their bosses didn't mind losing.

"Yes. Human life means nothing to them." Captain Desjani looked straight into Geary's eyes, her voice flat.

"Point taken." *I'll have to remember not to misjudge Captain Desjani. She has what she believes are good reasons for everything she does.* Geary bit his lip as he studied his display. If that was the entire Syndic fast-pursuit force, he could order the battle cruisers to rejoin the rest of the fleet. But the Syndics could've deliberately paused between waves to mislead defenders into thinking they wouldn't be sending in anything else for a while. But those battle cruisers were already ten light-minutes away from the rest of the fleet. Ten minutes away for receiving messages. Ten minutes away from Geary even knowing if those ships were in trouble. At least an hour away from being able to help them. And they were getting farther away every moment. "Captain Duellos, Captain Tulev, this is Captain Geary. Well done. Please rejoin the fleet as expeditiously as possible. Have your ships assume assigned positions within standard fleet attack formation Alpha Six."

Ten minutes for Duellos and Tulev to get the message. Then they'd have to get their ships up to speed and start a long stern chase to catch up with the fleet. It'd be quite a few hours before they were in formation.

But at that, it seemed those battle cruisers would be in formation before anyone else achieved that goal. Instead of resolving into the ordered rectangles, the Alliance fleet seemed to be rushing to further fatten the end of the rough wedge facing the Syndic base.

What the hell is going on? Geary pulled back the display, trying to see if he was missing some large picture inside the more detailed view. No. It still didn't make sense. Only the slower units like *Titan* seemed to be in their assigned positions. And crippled *Titan* didn't have any choice in the matter, slowly crawling across the system in the wake of the faster warships

It only gradually dawned on him that *Titan* was distressingly unaccompanied. "Where're the ships that are supposed to be acting as close escort on *Titan*?" He expanded his look at the situation again. "*All* the support craft accompanying the fleet are missing their escorts. Where the hell are the escorts for the auxiliaries?" No one on the *Dauntless*'s bridge answered.

He'd avoided verbally blasting most of the other ships in the fleet again for being slow to get into formation, not wanting to give in to what he suspected was bad temper as opposed to professional judgment. But falling back into formation should've been a relatively quick and easy maneuver for the assigned escorts. If they'd actually been headed for their positions, they must have been in them by now. This was simply too careless— Careless? Or something else? Geary took another look at the way the ships in his fleet were strung out, then pulled the view back to get the two Syndic corvettes into the focus.

It took him entirely too long to figure out what was going on, but he finally did. "Ancestors save us all!"

Desjani stared at him, clearly wondering if the vague outburst this time referred to her own ship. "Captain Geary?"

Geary just concentrated on his display, trying to get control of his anger and voice before speaking. Finally, he pointed at the movements of the Alliance ships. "Those . . . fools . . . aren't getting into formation because they're all trying to get in on the kill when we make contact with those corvettes." Now that he'd realized what was happening, it seemed obvious, the way almost the entire Alliance formation had bent and stretched toward the place where the fleet would intercept the Syndic corvettes. Most of Geary's fleet had abandoned or ignored their assigned positions, and their assigned duties in the larger scheme of things, just so they could possibly get a lick in when the corvettes were annihilated by a ridiculously overwhelming force.

Desjani looked as if she were hesitant to speak, then finally began talking. "Aggressiveness is the primary—"

"Aggressiveness! That's what you call this?"

" 'Close with the enemy,' " Desjani stated in a way that again sounded like a quote to Geary. Then she confirmed it. "That was one of the final orders given at Grendel." Desjani watched him, knowing he'd make the connection.

And Geary remembered, trying once again not to let his emotions show. Because, after all, those events during a battle a century before in the Grendel Star System hadn't been much more than a month ago for him. His ship had lost communications with the other units in the convoy as they battled the Syndics. But before the loss in communications, one of the last orders he'd given his own ship, which would've been heard over the command net, had been "close with the enemy." "You're not seriously telling me that . . . that . . ."

She nodded, radiating pride now. Pride in herself, in the fleet, and in Geary. "That's our primary rule of engagement in the Alliance fleet. Be aggressive. Never hesitate, never delay. Close with enemy, just as Black Jack Geary ordered long ago," Desjani declared, her face glowing.

Geary wanted to grab her and shake her. *You idiot! All of you idiots! That's not a one-size-fits-all solution to every tactical situation! It's not even smart a lot of the time!* "By every ancestor of every sailor in this fleet, Captain Desjani, discipline matters as much as aggressiveness! A few frigates can take down those corvettes. I was going to send a single squadron of them to do it."

"They know they're fighting under the eyes of Black Jack Geary, sir! They want to show you how good they are!"

"They're not! They're acting like an untrained mob! They're ignoring my orders!" Geary bit back whatever he might've said next. Desjani and the other members of the *Dauntless*'s crew were staring at him as if he'd just slapped Desjani. "Look, aggressiveness is all well and good in its place, but if it's not matched to intelligent tactics and co-ordinated, disciplined actions, it's a recipe for disaster."

Desjani's pride had shaded into stubbornness. "It's

served us well, sir. The Alliance fleet is proud of its fighting spirit."

Instead of shooting back another harsh reply, Geary
took a deep breath. *Yeah, it's "served you well."* No wonder the fleet had lost so many ships. No wonder the fleet
had snatched eagerly at the bait the Syndics dangled and
ended up on the verge of destruction. And they were doing
these things out of a totally warped view of Geary's own
philosophy. *I don't even know whether or not to feel guilty.
Is it my fault if the example of Black Jack Geary they're
blindly following isn't actually true and never was?*

*It's going to take time to change this. I can't just tell
them they're wrong. If they accept that, it'll crush their
spirit. If they don't accept it, they won't change, and my
own authority will be even shakier than now.*

He nodded with deliberate care to Desjani. "Fighting
spirit is immensely important, Captain. From what I have
seen, the Alliance fleet is right to be proud of its spirit."
She grinned with apparent relief at Geary's words. Glancing around, Geary saw similar expressions on the faces of
the rest of the bridge crew. "But we do need to apply that
spirit properly, to make sure we do"—*What's the right
phrase?*—"maximum damage to the enemy. It's like aiming a weapon to make sure it hits the target dead on."
Geary indicated his display. "Right now, this fleet isn't as
well aimed as it could be." *And aren't I the master of un-
derstatement.* "We'll work on that."

But even as Geary spoke the last sentence, he saw that
the leading ships in the Alliance fleet were accelerating
past .1 light speed, abandoning all pretense of maintaining
any sort of formation as they raced each other to reach and
help destroy the two Syndic corvettes. Amazingly, the now
five-minute-old images from around the Syndic base
showed that the corvettes still hadn't tried to run, but were
maintaining a blocking position not far from the Syndic
base. Geary was still trying to decide if they were brave or
foolish or simply paralyzed with fright when the reason finally became apparent—a courier ship sighted launching

from the base and accelerating away. The Syndics were trying to get a report off through one of the jump points around Corvus. *I wonder what Syndicate Fleet Fight Instruction article mandates sending a report?* Geary wondered bitterly. *That idiot in charge of them wouldn't do it if it wasn't spelled out as a requirement.*

The forward elements of the Alliance fleet were still accelerating, past the speed where they could effectively target the enemy ships. *That's it. It's past time I tried to regain control of this goat rope.* Geary mashed the communications control with his thumb. "This is Captain Geary. All units of the Alliance fleet are ordered to return to their places in formation. All units are to reduce speed as necessary to ensure they are not exceeding .1 light." He hated giving that order going into a battle, where individual ship commanders should've had the flexibility to alter speed as they fought, but Geary couldn't see how else he could slow down all the ships crowding to reach the Syndic corvettes.

Geary bit back another curse. The displayed positions of many of his own ships were increasingly uncertain, and it would take several minutes for the farthest out to receive his last order. "Ships of the Third Frigate Squadron are ordered to engage the Syndic corvettes. Any unit in a position to intercept the Syndic courier vessel is ordered to make every effort to stop it."

He paused, waiting to see what would happen, knowing there was nothing else he could do at the moment. It'd be a few minutes before he knew whether anyone was listening to him this time.

At least he could tell the battle cruisers were on their way back. They wouldn't catch up with the trailing elements of the fleet for three hours, but at least they were doing what they were told.

Within the next fifteen minutes, it became apparent that a little more than half of the Alliance ships charging toward the Syndic corvettes had somewhat sheepishly begun following Geary's last order. Unfortunately, as some of the ships slowed and others kept accelerating, any semblance

of order within the Alliance fleet vanished. The leading
edge of the wedge had become a twisted blob in which
many of Geary's own ship positions were far from certain.

The display picture of the outer fringes of the Alliance
fleet flickered in an almost strobelike way as the time-late
images updated and jerked from point to point. It looked
like close to a score of Alliance ships had come around and
were trying to accelerate toward an intercept with the Syndic courier vessel. *Orion*, far out of range of any possible
intercept, for some unfathomable reason had pumped out
several specters aimed at the courier, even though the distance and relative speeds were too great to expect any
chance of a hit.

And the Syndic light cruiser's position had jumped
wildly as *Dauntless* finally saw it accelerating toward the
Alliance fleet. *What's he doing? He's in no position to help
screen that courier.* The blob that made up the Alliance
fleet had now stretched out in three directions, one thin
arm reaching "up" and to the side toward the courier's
path, another larger mass of ships still heading for the Syndic corvettes and their base, which were now less than an
hour away from contact, and a spreading cloud of ships at
the back where Alliance units were finally dropping back
toward their assigned positions. The Syndic light cruiser,
having come around the fourth planet, seemed to be accelerating under the force of its huge propulsion system as if
aiming to skim along the bottom of the Alliance blob.

Geary stared at the display, trying to understand what
the light cruiser was up to. Estimated speed and directional
vectors for the Syndic warship kept jumping around as it
exceeded .1 light and kept accelerating. It was also apparently altering its course slightly again and again, so that as
Alliance ships picked up time-late observations distorted
by relativistic effects, the "compensated" position of the
cruiser also jerked from spot to spot and its projected
course swung wildly through space. Only two things
seemed certain. The cruiser was still accelerating and it
was still heading toward the Alliance fleet.

Why? If he's just running away, why run away through the Alliance fleet? But how is he planning to engage us? As close as he is and going that fast, he'll shoot past our ships with no better idea of where they are than they can tell where he is. Even with his propulsion system, by the time he'd be able to slow down to fighting speed he'd be—.

"Damn!" Geary didn't even notice the reaction on the bridge of the *Dauntless* to his explosive curse. *I should've seen it. I should've figured this out a long time ago. A ship built with that much propulsion capability must be intended for a special kind of attack.* He gestured at the general area of his display where the representation of the Syndic cruiser was flickering from point to point. "He's headed for *Titan.* "

"What?" Captain Desjani followed Geary's movement with an expression of shock. "How could it? He'd never be able to figure out exactly where *Titan* was at the speed he's going."

"It's what he's designed for, Captain Desjani! I should've known as soon as I saw it!" Geary jabbed his finger at the display again, drawing an arc through the front of the Alliance fleet and ending at *Titan.* "Major propulsion capability so he can accelerate quickly to speeds high enough that the relativistic effects make targeting him damn near impossible. Once he's dashed through defending units that can't target him worth a damn, he'll spin around and use that same propulsion power to brake hard enough that he can slow down to a speed that allows him to engage whatever soft targets the warships are protecting."

Desjani actually snarled as she studied the display. "Ancestors forgive me. He'll be at maximum velocity when he pierces through our lead units. We'll have very little chance of achieving hits on him unless we can fix his course exactly—"

"We can't! We can't exactly project his course because we don't know exactly where he is now!" Geary paused, then bared his teeth. "But we know exactly where he's going."

"*Titan?*" Desjani's hands played across her controls. A hugely elongated cone appeared, the broad end centered on where the ship systems estimated the Syndic cruiser was now. "Here. If that cruiser is headed for *Titan* and has to brake down to a velocity low enough to get high-probability targeting data on *Titan* as he passes within weapons range, he'll have to start braking about here, and that'll mean he'll intercept *Titan*'s course *here*." Her finger pointed at the place where the cone had shrunk down to a narrow needle.

Geary nodded, feeling a momentary surge of exultation. That was why the Syndics hadn't built more ships like that light cruiser. Once you figured out what their target was, escort ships behind the main body could intercept it short of the target. But Geary's elation quickly faded as he studied the area around the course Desjani had drawn in. *There's nothing in place to stop that cruiser.* Titan*'s escorts are still too far off from chasing after those worthless corvettes, the reserve squadrons are scattered all over the place, and* Titan*'s fallen even farther back because the fleet has been accelerating away from her.*

And the commander of that Syndic light cruiser had been smart enough to see what was going on and to see that *Titan* was the Achilles heel of the Alliance fleet. *Smarter than me*, Geary admitted. *That's a very good sailor out there. Too bad I have to do my best to kill him or her.*

The first thing to do was to make sure that the light cruiser had something else to worry about. "All ships in Cruiser Squadrons Eight and Eleven are to pursue the Syndic light cruiser." That was far more ships than should be needed, but Geary couldn't tell how many of the ships in those squadrons were actually close enough to the Syndic cruiser to worry it. None of them could possibly catch the cruiser before it reached *Titan*, but if Geary could slow it down, perhaps they could play a role. "All other ships engage the light cruiser if it comes within effective weapons range."

He took a moment to check on the corvettes. Their screening of the courier launch over, the Syndic corvettes had turned to run. Geary shook his head. *They're too slow, and they waited too long.* There were Alliance ships less than a half hour behind them, and the corvettes couldn't accelerate worth a damn. "Captain Desjani, please inform those two corvettes that if they do not surrender immediately, they will surely be destroyed."

"Yes, Captain Geary." Desjani kept her thoughts to herself this time.

Up and to the side, the Syndic courier ship had depended on speed and relativistic uncertainty to get past the onrushing Alliance ships, but an Alliance destroyer had taken advantage of the luck of its position relative to the courier and rolled in from below in a perfect intercept. Geary had only a moment to realize he hadn't offered the courier a chance to surrender before the destroyer opened fire, its hell-lances dancing along the path the courier was following. The courier ran into the barrage, which punched right through the thin defenses of the Syndic ship. The courier's engines blew, and the entire ship vanished as the explosion shattered it into small pieces. *Pity. Good intercept, though. Who was that destroyer? Rapier, one of the Sword Class ships. I'll need to remember her.*

"One of the corvettes has broadcast surrender," *Dauntless*'s communications watch announced, unable to keep a trace of dismay from her voice.

"Tell"—Geary checked the display hastily. —"*Audacious* to overtake and board the corvette and ensure it's stripped of anything we can use." He paused, thinking about how poorly orders had been followed so far, then hit his own controls. "All units in the Alliance fleet, this is Captain Geary. I have personally accepted surrender of the Syndic corvette PC-14558." Desjani stared at him, eyes wide. Geary avoided her gaze, looking stubbornly at his own display. He'd just told everyone that the surrendered corvette was effectively under his personal protection now. It was an extreme measure, but he had an ugly feeling that otherwise even a surrendered ship wouldn't be safe from attack by some of his overenthusiastic commanders.

He switched his gaze back to the battle cruisers far astern, wishing they could somehow teleport next to *Titan*, then searched for the Syndic cruiser.

And found it racing past the leading Alliance ships.

Geary watched with a sense of helplessness as the Alliance ships closest to the Syndic cruiser scrambled to intercept it, and saw all of them fail as the cruiser's velocity, now up past .2 light, so effectively confused Alliance targeting systems that they kept misjudging their predictions. A few specters came close, trying to follow right up the cruiser's path. But all of them were caught in a stern chase with low relative speed. They died in flares of light as they were taken out by the Syndic cruiser's defenses, which had only to fire backward, knowing any pursuer would be coming from directly astern.

Everyone was looking at him now. They weren't saying anything, but Geary knew what they were thinking. *What do we do, Black Jack? How do you get us out of this mess?* Because he knew they'd be certain he could. Idiots. If they kept getting into terrible tactical situations, how long would it be before Geary couldn't figure out any way out?

Damn and damn again. That Syndic commander spotted the weakest point in the fleet. If we lose Titan *our chances of getting home go way down. But he doesn't have to kill* Titan. *He just has to slow her down some more, leaving us to either wait around for the main Syndic fleet he no doubt guesses is coming after us, or abandon a ship this fleet needs.*

No, Titan's *just one of the weakest points in this fleet. The other weak point is the lack of discipline that led* Titan's *escorts to abandon their responsibilities. I can't do anything to lessen our need for* Titan, *but I can sure as hell try to fix the discipline in this fleet.*

If I get the chance.

Geary's eyes ranged across the display, ignoring the combat system's uncertain guesses at the Syndic cruiser's exact position and vector, letting his instincts judge the chances of any Alliance warships getting to the Syndic cruiser before it could reach *Titan*. He barely registered the rapid death under an avalanche of Alliance hell-lance fire of the second Syndic corvette, the one that had tried to flee rather than surrender, as Geary realized there was in fact one ship still far enough back to interpose herself in time.

Dauntless.

That cruiser could be on a suicide run. Dauntless should be able to take it easily in terms of firepower, but if it decides to ram Dauntless or run in close and self-destruct, I could lose this ship. Even if the cruiser doesn't want to ram anybody, his ability to see what's ahead of him in time to do anything about it is severely compromised by his speed. Just trying for an intercept could cause a collision bad enough to annihilate both ships.

I promised Admiral Bloch I'd get this fleet home with the hypernet key. I can't risk Dauntless.

But if I don't risk Dauntless, I may well lose Titan.

But Bloch and Desjani both said the hypernet key on Dauntless is more important than anything else in this fleet.

He had a sudden memory of a very old myth, of a hero trying to make it home from a long war and losing his ships one by one, his followers one by one, until only he was left to come back. In the myth, that had been a triumph of sorts. And he had a vision of *Dauntless* limping back into Alliance space, alone, the wreckage of scores of other Alliance ships thrown to the wolves behind it, littering the path home.

And he knew that wouldn't be a triumph of any kind in his eyes.

Even if it would, it's too high a price.

And how long will these people follow me if I hang back and let them die?

Geary refocused on the people around him, watching

him, and realized only a couple of seconds had elapsed while he'd been debating within himself. "Captain Desjani, I want *Dauntless* to take out that Syndic cruiser before it gets within range of *Titan*."

Desjani grinned as the other sailors on the bridge uttered whoops of joy. "It'll be a pleasure."

"He's very fast, and he's good, Captain Desjani. Don't take any chances. We have to ensure a kill, and we're only going to get one shot at it."

"Yes, sir."

Dauntless jumped forward under Captain Desjani's commands, arcing over and down at her highest acceleration, Geary feeling a surge of excitement himself as the ship headed for her prey. He watched, not wanting to give orders over Desjani's head directly to her crew, but fearing Desjani would misjudge the Syndic cruiser's course. If they shot past the cruiser, the time required to turn and catch up would doom *Titan*.

Desjani was playing it smart, though. Geary watched the course she was pushing her ship down and realized Desjani was ignoring the combat system estimates. Instead, she was bringing *Dauntless* down to an intercept well ahead of the path the cruiser would have to follow to get within weapon's range of *Titan*. At the speed the Syndic cruiser was going, it probably wouldn't be able to see *Dauntless*'s maneuver until too late to react. *Unless that Syndic commander guesses* Dauntless *will move to an intercept. But what can they do? If they alter course they won't pass close enough to* Titan *to engage her. If they slow down to screw up the course projection, my other ships will be able to get close enough to throw enough junk at the general location of that cruiser that something will be bound to hit. And they can't speed up more because they wouldn't be able to brake down to engagement speed in time to shoot at* Titan *and have any reasonable chance of a hit.*

I hope.

Geary watched on his display as *Dauntless* curved

down toward a point where she'd cross the projected path of the Syndic cruiser and felt a strange pang of fellowship with whoever commanded the enemy ship. They obviously knew how to drive a ship and had a well-trained crew. How long had they been out here, exiled to Corvus System, waiting for the very unlikely chance that any Alliance force would ever arrive here? How easy it would've been to let things slide, to assume they'd never see combat, to let the ship and the crew deteriorate. But whoever they were, they hadn't let things slide, they'd kept their ship and crew in top shape, and the efforts had almost paid off. Might still pay off.

The Syndic cruiser's estimated position jerked again. "He's going to have to start braking soon," Desjani noted.

Geary nodded. "Do you think he's seen us yet?"

"Unlikely, sir. He's got old combat systems. They'll be severely stressed by all the ships out here and trying to compensate for relativistic distortion at the speed he's going. But even if he sees us, he won't get past us," Desjani promised in a soft voice.

"I know."

Desjani grinned fiercely at Geary's simple statement of confidence in her, but she kept her eyes on the combat display as she brought *Dauntless* down on the charging cruiser. Geary frowned. Dauntless had to be able to hit that enemy cruiser, but at the combined speeds of the *Dauntless* and the Syndic cruiser, they'd flash past each other in an instant without any chance for the targeting systems to engage. Had Desjani spotted that? Or was she so focused on reaching the enemy that she hadn't realized what would happen? Should he say anything to Desjani? Overrule her, perhaps, in front of her crew?

The paths of the two ships kept converging, the remaining distance to the Syndic cruiser scrolling down at a fantastic pace. Geary finally cleared his throat. "Captain—"

But Desjani held up one hand, palm out, her eyes still riveted on the combat display. "I have it, Captain Geary."

He wasn't nearly as certain as she was of that, but

Geary kept his silence. It was one of those moments he recognized, when you had to either have confidence in someone or else show everyone that you lacked confidence in that person. And Desjani had seemed very capable to him.

So Geary tried to look like he trusted her while inside he prayed to his ancestors that Desjani knew what she was doing.

"He should be braking now." Captain Desjani rapped out orders, pivoting *Dauntless* around so her main propulsion system faced forward. "All ahead full." *Dauntless* shuddered as her drives started braking her own velocity, the ship's structure groaning with stress, and Geary feeling the force pressing him hard into his seat. A high-pitched keening noise filled the air as *Dauntless*'s inertial dampers fought to keep the stresses on ship and crew within bearable limits.

Dauntless's projected course was altering quickly, bending down toward the path the Syndic cruiser had to be taking en route *Titan*.

Closer. Geary tried to swallow without showing it.

Desjani's eyes were fixed on the display. "He should be down below point-two light now if he's braking to engage *Titan*." The image of the Syndic cruiser, only light-seconds away now in the closest thing to real time that naval engagements often saw, seemed to be very close to the course Desjani had predicted. "Set grapeshot to fire in sequence as we cross the cruiser's estimated path," Desjani ordered. "Charge null-field and stand-by."

Dauntless, still braking hard, swept across the projected path of the Syndic cruiser at an angle, its grapeshot launchers hurling out their ball bearings down that path at millisecond intervals as each crossed it.

"Fire four specters, two to starboard and two to port." The missiles swept out, each braking itself farther as its onboard sensors sought out a good fix on the Syndic cruiser undistorted by relativistic effects, then accelerating again toward their target.

Desjani paused. "Fire null-field."

Geary watched on the display as the huge glowing ball that represented the null-field charge shot up and backward from *Dauntless*, toward the bottom of the Syndic cruiser's current course.

And suddenly the Syndic cruiser was there, the range scales scrolling downward incredibly fast as it swept forward, either still unaware of *Dauntless*'s actions or trusting in speed to get it past *Titan*'s last defender. Even though he should've been expecting it, knowing the cruiser had to be braking, Geary was still surprised when he realized he was looking at the stern of the cruiser as it used its massive propulsion system to slow its progress.

Lights sparkled as the Syndic cruiser ran tail-on into the barrage of grapeshot, each ball bearing impacting the cruiser's shields and vaporizing in a flash. The cumulative impacts slowed the cruiser as if it were plowing through a close-set succession of brick walls, even as they seriously weakened its rear-facing shields. Geary watched the display, his jaw tight, thinking about how that extra deceleration was probably overwhelming the ability of the cruiser's inertial dampers to compensate, and what effect that'd be having on her crew. But there were too many lives in the Alliance fleet riding on stopping the Syndic cruiser. *I can't let the fate of the cruiser's crew affect my decisions. And, damn, but that was a nicely done intercept.* "Very nice job, Captain Desjani."

Her face actually flushed with pleasure at the praise, but Desjani kept her voice dispassionate. "He's not dead yet."

A moment later the cruiser raced into contact with the null-field. Weakened by the successive impacts of the grapeshot volleys, the shields flared and failed as the weapon dug a swath along one side of the fast-moving ship like a knife slashing through butter. The Syndic light cruiser reeled from its course as the charge tore a trench through a long section of the hull and partway inside. Through the glow of the gas cloud, which had been solid parts of the cruiser moments before, Geary watched with a sort of sick fascination as the crippled Syndic warship shot past above the *Dauntless*. In that brief moment, Geary thought he could see secondary explosions and escaping atmosphere as compartments once safely inside the cruiser were now suddenly open to space.

He was wondering if the *Dauntless* would need to catch up to the Syndic cruiser in order to finish it off when the specters fired earlier came angling in from either side, their target now slowed appreciably. Somehow, a defensive system on the cruiser was still working and managed a lucky hit that made one specter flare and disappear. The specter's companion missile went into a series of evasive maneuvers, but even as it did so the two specters on the other side looped straight into the cruiser's beam.

Twin explosions blossomed two-thirds of the way down the cruiser's hull, and the ship broke apart. Moments later, the smaller aft portion erupted into a larger explosion as the power core blew it into nothingness.

The forward part of the cruiser, crippled and torn, spun off, then took another blow as the last remaining specter rammed into it and blew a huge chunk away.

Geary became aware that the bridge of the *Dauntless* was echoing with cheers. He took a deep breath, watching the remains of the Syndic cruiser tumble off into space, then tore his gaze away and saw Captain Desjani watching him, her mouth stretched in a broad, triumphant grin.

"Why aren't you cheering, Captain Geary?" she asked.

Geary closed his eyes. "I never feel like cheering when brave people die, Captain Desjani. Those Syndics had to be stopped, but they fought well."

She shrugged, still smiling. "They'd be cheering if the shoe was on the other foot."

"Maybe. But I don't model myself on the Syndics." He nodded toward his display, not looking at her. "You did an outstanding job on that intercept, Captain Desjani. There're no more Syndic combatants active. I'd like your recommendation on the possibility of getting boats over to the wreck."

"It'd be hard to intercept, and after what we did to it there's unlikely to be anything left salvaging."

"There might be survivors, Captain Desjani."

She remained silent for a moment. "I'll see what can be done."

He heard disagreement in her voice again but didn't really care.

FIVE

COLONEL Carabali's image saluted Geary. "My Marines are prepared to secure the Syndic base, Captain Geary."

Geary looked down at the frozen world, less than a light-minute away from *Dauntless* now. "Make sure your Marines know that we want as little broken as possible when that base is taken. After we've salvaged whatever we can use from the base, we'll destroy anything left with military potential, but I want to make sure we don't put holes through anything we're going to want for ourselves."

"They've been briefed to avoid collateral damage to the maximum extent possible, Captain Geary."

Geary started to ask if that meant they'd actually follow those orders scrupulously, then stopped himself. Unless things had changed a lot more than he could imagine, you just didn't ask whether or not Marines would follow orders. You assumed that they did, and that was all there was to it. "Very well. Get your landing parties on the way. *Arrogant*, *Exemplar*, and *Braveheart* have taken out the antispace defenses near the base and will maintain positions overhead in case you need their firepower."

"Thank you, Captain Geary. My Marines will have that base for you in short order. Intact," Colonel Carabali added with a brief twist of her lips that might've been a smile.

Geary leaned back, rubbing his forehead and wondering why things seemed to alternate between happening too slow and too fast with no real transition between the two states. He looked back at the display, where the ships of his fleet not involved in capturing the Syndic base had braked themselves down to .05 light. No longer facing any enemy combatants to lure them away, they were finally forming into a semblance of order. *Titan* and the other fleet auxiliaries had escorts again and were veering slightly above the rest of the fleet to take a direct path to the jump point they'd use to exit Corvus System several days from now.

He frowned as his eyes rested on the battle cruisers still hastening to rejoin the rest of the fleet. *How much time do I have in this system? How long would it have taken the Syndics to reorganize their fleet, to decide how much to send through the jump point after us, and to actually get into jump space? I've gone over this a thousand times, and it always comes down to just not having any way to know. But aside from those mines I had Duellos leave at the jump point, I don't dare leave anything else there on guard.*

Geary studied the remaining Syndic activity in Corvus System. He could tell where the light waves showing his fleet's arrival could be seen by watching a sphere expand at scale light speed across the depiction of the system. It was odd to think that the arrival of the fleet, and the hours-later destruction of the three Syndic ships, wouldn't even be known by the inhabited world for some time. War had come to Corvus, but most of the inhabitants of the system would remain blissfully unaware of that for a few hours yet.

He hadn't heard from the Syndic commander again. Either the man was pouring over the Syndic Fleet Fighting Instructions for what to do next, or he'd died in the preliminary bombardment of the base. Thinking of the lost crews on the two Syndic ships that had fought to the death to no purpose, Geary couldn't help hoping for the latter.

He fiddled with his controls, finally finding one that provided reports on the Syndic base nearby. Some of the images seemed to confirm that the base had indeed been maintaining stockpiles of supplies on hand for any passing ships that needed them. It'd been a safe assumption that the supplies would still be there even if the base had been abandoned, since shipping out the matériel would've cost more than they were worth, and keeping those supplies deep-frozen and unaffected by weather was rarely a problem on worlds that were usually far enough from their stars to lack meaningful atmosphere. *The stockpiles are supposed to be for Syndic warships, of course, but I've no intention of being picky at this point. I hope Syndic fleet food is better than what the Alliance serves, but I doubt it.*

Ancestors. I made a joke to myself. I wonder if I'm starting to really thaw out.

I wonder if I want to thaw out.

"Captain Geary." He glanced back and saw Co-President Rione still in her seat on the bridge, her face revealing no emotions. "Do you believe all Syndic resistance in the Corvus System has been eliminated?"

"No." Geary gestured at the display before his chair, wondering how much of it Rione could see. "As you've seen, our Marines are in the process of taking the military base on the fourth world. There's a couple of military bases around the second world, that's the inhabited one. They don't even know we're here yet."

"Will they be a threat to the fleet?"

"No. They're obsolete and designed to defend the planet, which we have no interest in messing with. I don't intend bothering with them if I can help it."

Captain Desjani gave Geary a surprised look. "We should eliminate all Syndic military capability in this system."

"Those fortresses aren't any threat to us and wouldn't be worth the Syndics moving anywhere else," Geary replied. "But I'd have to divert some ships to take them out, expend weapons in the process, and worry about damage to civilian targets on the planet from any pieces of the fortresses that enter atmosphere."

"I see." Desjani nodded. "There's no sense in using up our limited supply of weapons on them, and you don't want to split up the fleet."

"Right." Geary gave no sign he'd noticed Desjani didn't acknowledge the point about civilian casualties. Out of the corner of his eye, he saw Rione watching them both intently.

The Co-President gestured toward Geary's display. "You've recalled the forces guarding the jump point?"

"Yes. If anything comes through there now, it'll almost certainly be too powerful for my battle cruisers to handle, and I'm not prepared to sacrifice them or any other ships just to blunt the nose of a Syndic pursuit force."

Rione studied the display again. "You don't think they could retreat quickly enough to rejoin us?"

"No, Madam Co-President, I don't." Geary moved his finger across the display as he spoke. "You see, anything coming out of the jump point will probably be at pursuit speed. Say point one light, just like we were. While they were on guard, my battle cruisers were matching the movement of the jump point in the system, but that's a lot slower. The Syndics would have a big speed advantage, too big for my battle cruisers, or any ship in this fleet, to overcome before they got battered into wrecks."

Desjani had been following the conversation silently, but now looked toward Rione. "If we had some automated warships, we could expend some of those on the mission without the risk of losing personnel. But we have none of those."

Geary frowned, sensing from the expressions on Desjani's and Rione's faces that the statement had considerable history behind it. "Has that been proposed? Building fully automated warships?"

"It has been proposed," Rione responded dryly.

Captain Desjani's expression hardened. "In the opinion of many officers, we would gain great advantages in situations such as this if the construction of uncrewed ships controlled by artificial intelligences would be approved."

Rione met Desjani look for look. "Then I'm afraid those officers are doomed to disappointment. One of my final acts before departing Alliance space with this fleet was participating in an Alliance Assembly vote regarding such a program. It was overwhelmingly defeated. The civil leadership of the Alliance is not willing to entrust weapons and weapons employment decisions to artificial intelligences, especially when those AIs are to be given control of warships capable of inflicting great harm on inhabited worlds."

Desjani flushed. "If oversight AIs were also installed—"

"They'd be subject to the same potential failures, instabilities, and unpredictable behavioral development."

"Install an override!"

Rione shook her head implacably. "Any AI capable of controlling a warship would also be capable of learning how to bypass an override. And what if our enemies learned to access this override through experimentation or espionage? I've no wish to give them control of warships we've built. No, Captain, we don't believe we can trust AIs to operate independently. I assure you the Assembly is in no mood to bend on this point. Not now, and not at any point in the foreseeable future."

Desjani, glowering, made a barely respectful nod and turned back to her display.

"Anyway," Geary continued, pretending the argument hadn't happened, "now that we've taken out the Syndic naval forces in the system, I'm going to threaten the inhabited world into sending us some cargo ships full of stuff we need. Food, mostly. Maybe some power cells, if we can adapt some of the Syndic stuff to work with ours."

A officer with gray-streaked hair to Geary's right shook his head. "We can't, sir. They're deliberately designed to be noncompatible. Just like their weapons. But if we can get the right raw materials, *Titan* and *Jinn* can manufacture more weapons. *Titan* can also build more power cells, and so can *Witch*. "

"Thank you." Geary tried to look as appreciative as he actually felt for the quick and to-the-point briefing. "Can those ships tell me what they need?"

"We've got the information onboard *Dauntless*, sir. Assuming their last updates to us are accurate, of course."

"You're supply?"

The gray-haired man saluted awkwardly, as if the gesture were long unused. "Engineering, sir."

"I want you to make sure we know what the highest priorities are for each of those ships."

"Yes, sir!" the man beamed, apparently honored at being given a task by Geary.

Geary turned to Desjani. "At least that way I'll be sure to demand the right tribute from the Syndics in this system."

Co-President Rione stood up and took a couple of steps to lean near Geary and murmur just loud enough for Geary and Desjani to hear. "By so making your demands, Captain Geary, you'll also be telling the Syndics exactly what your greatest needs are."

Desjani made a face. Geary thought she looked unhappy, too, but had to admit Rione was right. "Any suggestions?" he murmured back.

"Yes. Include some misleading demands. The Syndics will not know which demands represent real needs for us and which are luxury items, for want of a better term."

"Good idea." Geary gave her a lopsided grin. "Would you by any chance also have any suggestions as to who should present our demands to the authorities here?"

"Are you drafting me, Captain Geary?"

"I wouldn't want to say that, Madam Co-President. But you do have the necessary skills, and it'd be nice if you agreed to volunteer before I gave you the job."

"I'll consider it." Rione nodded toward Geary's display

again. "I understand most of what's happening now, but
not that activity around the surrendered corvette."

"It's being stripped for any useful parts," Geary assured
her. He focused on the information himself, then frowned
and studied it closer. He gave Desjani a questioning
glance, but she indicated she didn't see anything odd,
which also bothered Geary. He reached for his communications controls. "*Audacious*, why are all the survival pods
from the Syndic corvette enroute to you?"

The other ship wasn't far away, so the reply came so
quickly that it almost seemed real time. "There are materials on the Syndic survival pods we can cannibalize, sir.
Emergency life support and emergency rations, mostly."

"Do you intend leaving the corvette intact?" Not that it
was all that much of a threat, but Geary hadn't intended
leaving any enemy warship in functional condition behind
them, regardless of whether or not its combat systems had
been trashed.

"No, sir." *Audacious* replied. "The corvette will be destroyed by triggering a power core overload after we've
finished stripping it."

Geary waited, but when *Audacious* said nothing more,
he tapped his communications key again. "*Audacious*, how
do you intend disposing of the corvette's crew?" He didn't
want to have to divert a ship to deliver prisoners to a
planet's surface or some other safe location.

"They're on the corvette, sir." The voice from *Audacious* sounded surprised at the question.

Once more, Geary waited a moment for *Audacious* to
finish replying to his question. He was moving to tap the
communications key again when he suddenly realized with
a growing sense of horror that the other ship *had* finished
answering him. *"How do you intend disposing of the
crew?" "They're on the corvette, sir."* The corvette that
was going to be destroyed by its own power core.

Geary looked down at his hand, the finger still poised
over the communications key, and saw that his lower arm
was trembling. He wondered how much of the rest of him

was reacting to the shock of what he'd realized. *They're going to simply blow up the prisoners with their own ship. Ancestors, what's become of my people?* He looked over at Captain Desjani, who was talking with one of the *Dauntless*'s watch-standers and seemed unconcerned about Geary's conversation with *Audacious*. Rione was apparently seated behind him once again, out of his sight.

Geary closed his eyes, trying to order his thoughts, then slowly opened them again and finally, moving his finger with great care, keyed communications. "*Audacious*, this is Captain Geary." *You're about to commit mass murder, you bastards.* "Return the survival pods to the Syndic corvette."

A few seconds passed. "Sir?" *Audacious* asked. "You want the survival pods destroyed, too? We could use some of their components."

Geary stared straight ahead and spoke with a flat voice. "What I want, *Audacious*, is for the crew of that corvette to be allowed to evacuate that ship in their survival pods prior to the destruction of the corvette so they can reach safety. Is that absolutely clear?"

A longer pause. "We're supposed to let them go?" The captain of the *Audacious* sounded incredulous.

Geary noticed Captain Desjani was staring at him now. Ignoring her, he spoke again, letting each word fall slowly and heavily like falling hammers. "That's correct. The Alliance fleet does not murder prisoners. The Alliance fleet does not violate the laws of war."

"But . . . but . . . we've—"

Captain Desjani was leaning toward him, whispering urgently. "The Syndics—"

Geary's control snapped. "I don't care what's been done before!" he roared at both the communications circuit and the bridge of the *Dauntless*. "I don't care what our enemies do! I will not allow any prisoners to be massacred by any ship under my command! I will not allow this fleet and the Alliance and the ancestors of all aboard these ships to be dishonored by war crimes committed under the all-seeing eyes of the living stars! We are sailors of the Alliance, and we *will* hold ourselves to the standards of honor our ancestors believed in! Are there any further questions?"

Silence reigned. Captain Desjani was staring at him, her face frozen, her eyes reflecting shock. Finally, *Audacious* replied, her Captain's voice hushed. "The survival pods are on their way back to the corvette, Captain Geary."

Geary struggled to control his voice. "Thank you."

"If you wish my resignation—"

"No." It had been several days since the last wave of weakness had hit him, but one seemed to have come on now, and Geary tried to fight it off without resorting to a med-patch. "I don't know everything that has led to this. I have every reason to believe you were carrying out your duties as you understood them. But I must emphasize that whatever violations of the laws of war that took place before this must stop. We are the Alliance. We have honor. If we hold to that, we will win. If we don't hold to it . . . we don't deserve to win."

"Yes, sir." It was hard to tell from the voice of the Captain of *Audacious* what he thought of what Geary had said, but at least he was doing what he was told.

Geary slumped in his chair, feeling as if in the last several minutes he'd aged the century he'd slept through. Captain Desjani was staring at the deck, her face troubled. *She's a good officer. Like the Captain of the* Audacious. *Just misguided. Somewhere along the line a lot of important things got set adrift.* "Captain Desjani—"

"Sir." Desjani swallowed and shook her head. "Forgive me for interrupting you, sir, but while you were speaking to *Audacious*, the Marines reported they have taken the Syndic base and are conducting mop-up operations."

"Thank you, Captain Desjani. I wanted to say—"

"Sir. The Marines have taken prisoners of most of the garrison of the base."

Geary nodded, trying to understand why Desjani kept interrupting him.

"The rest of the fleet heard what you told *Audacious*.

However, the Marines would not have been monitoring the communications circuit you used with *Audacious*."

Then he got it. Prisoners. Lots of them. And Captain Desjani, whether she agreed with Geary or not, was going to keep interrupting him until he realized what might well be going on at that base. "Get me Colonel Carabali."

"She's out of communications for some reason, sir, but we have an audio and video feed from the ground force command-and-control net."

"Give me a link to that!" His display blinked, and the three-dimensional projection of ships and the Corvus Star System was replaced by a panel made up of at least thirty individual pictures ranked side by side and in vertical columns. It took Geary a moment to realize he was looking at video depictions from what were probably each squad leader in the Marine assault force. He reached forward as if to touch one, and the image expanded, pushing the other images to the side. Geary touched another, and it and the first image adjusted so both were the same size, the other small images ranked around their borders ready for access. *Wow. That's a pretty neat toy. I wonder how many commanders have played with it while they lost track of the big picture?*

Geary scanned his eyes across the images, searching for signs of prisoners or any obvious indication that one of the images represented a link to the commander of the assault force. His eyes paused on one image, watching the metal of a corridor wall warp as something firing large solid slugs punched numerous holes in it. Symbols flowed across the image, he saw an arm gesturing within the view, then he could see Marines dashing forward, looking inhuman in their combat armor. Two fired some sort of barrage in the direction from which the shots that hit the wall had come, then a third leveled a large tube and fired it.

The view shook. Marines dashed forward, the image Geary was viewing jerking as the Marine broadcasting it ran with the others. Around the corner and down a long corridor with some sort of security station at the end.

Geary, expecting to see mass devastation from whatever weapon had been fired from the large tube, instead saw only bodies sprawled about in armor different from that of the Marines. *A concussion weapon? I guess the Marines used that because of their orders to limit collateral damage to the installation. That might mean those Syndic soldiers are still alive.*

The thought brought Geary's mind forcefully back to his current mission. He searched the images again, finally noticing one scanning across some sort of large room or hanger with a big crowd of people in it. He touched the image, and it grew. *That's it. Those are Syndics.* "Captain Desjani, how do I talk to someone using this?"

She indicated a communications symbol at the bottom of the image. "Just touch that."

"Have you reached Colonel Carabali yet?"

"No, sir."

Then I'll have to bypass her. Geary touched the symbol. "This is Captain Geary."

The image jerked once. "Yes, sir."

"Who's this?"

"Major Jalo, sir. Second-in-command for the landing force. Colonel Carabali ordered me to oversee mop-up operations to secure the main installation while she checked for any pockets of resistance in outlying areas."

"Are these all the Syndic prisoners?"

"Not yet, sir. The mop-up sweeps are bringing in some final holdouts."

"What . . ." *How do I ask this?* "What are Colonel Carabali's orders regarding the prisoners?"

"I haven't received orders on final disposition, sir. Standard procedure is to turn the prisoners over to the fleet."

That's interesting. Do the Marines know what happens to prisoners? Or do they pretend everything's okay to keep their consciences clear? Geary was about to ask another question when the view in his image jerked again. Everyone visible within the image swayed on their feet. "What was that?"

Major Jalo's voice came faster, hyped and ready for action. "Some sort of heavy explosion, sir. There's another," Jalo added unnecessarily as the image jerked again. "Somebody's hitting the area with heavy ordnance."

Heavy ordnance? The Marines have already taken the surface around the base, and the ships overhead have taken out the anti-space defenses. Ancestors. The ships overhead. "Captain Desjani! Are any of the ships positioned near the Syndic base firing?"

He watched the image from Major Jalo dance a few more times as Desjani answered. "*Arrogant* is firing upon an area near the base, Captain Geary. I don't know what the target is."

"Hold those prisoners until you get further orders from me," Geary barked at Major Jalo, then he leaned back and scowled at the array of images. "How do I get the fleet display back?"

Desjani reached over and tapped a control. There was the representation of Corvus System, with the ships of Geary's fleet spread all over the place. He fumbled at the communications key for a moment, fuming inwardly. "*Arrogant!* Identify the target you're firing upon!" Geary waited, his temper rising, as no reply came and *Arrogant* continued to pound the surface near the Syndic base. "*Arrogant*, this is Captain Geary. Cease fire. I say again. Cease fire."

The other ship was only a few light-seconds away, but a full minute passed with no response. Geary counted to five inwardly, thinking through his options. "Captain Desjani. *Exemplar* and *Braveheart*. Which has the best commander?"

She didn't hesitate. "*Exemplar*, sir. Commander Basir."

"Thank you." Geary tapped the communications key. "Commander Basir on *Exemplar*, do you copy?"

"Yes, sir," the reply came within less than a half minute.

"Can you identify the target being fired upon by *Arrogant*?"

A longer pause this time. "No, sir."

"Have you, *Braveheart*, or *Arrogant* received requests from the Marines to fire upon any targets on the surface?"

"No, sir. Not *Exemplar*, and I overheard no requests to *Braveheart* or *Arrogant* on the coordination net with the Marines."

I don't know what that idiot on Arrogant *is doing, but if that ship keeps throwing heavy weaponry at the surface, she's liable to hurt our own Marines, not to mention damaging supplies at the base. And now I know for certain that* Arrogant*'s not responding to any threat to her or the Marines.* "Thank you, *Exemplar*."

Geary glared around at the personnel on the bridge of the *Dauntless*. "Can I control *Arrogant*'s weapons? Do we have a way to remotely override local control?"

Everyone shook their heads, but only Captain Desjani spoke. "No, sir. As previously discussed," she added, somehow glowering toward Rione without actually looking that way, "it is believed that allowing ship systems to be controlled remotely opens up vulnerabilities that can be exploited by the enemy."

Rione's voice came. "Enemy intrusion into the remote command systems, avenues for delivering disabling viruses—"

"And a lot of other things that good emissions warfare can do even if it isn't supplemented by espionage. Thank you, I know. I spent a moment hoping someone'd found a way around all that during the last century." Geary bared his teeth as a thought came to him. "But I do have one thing on *Arrogant* that I can control."

Desjani raised one eyebrow in question.

"*Arrogant*'s got Marines on board, right?"

She nodded.

Geary tapped his communications control. "*Arrogant*, this is Captain Geary. You are endangering our personnel on the surface. You will cease fire immediately, or I will relieve your commanding officer of command and give direct orders to the Marine detachment aboard *Arrogant* to place that individual under arrest. I will not repeat my order again."

Even though he was royally ticked off at the moment, Geary couldn't help wondering how the fleet would take that kind of ultimatum. But Captain Desjani seemed grimly pleased. Apparently *Arrogant*'s commanding officer wasn't popular with her, at least.

"*Arrogant* has ceased fire," Desjani reported a few seconds later in a carefully bland voice.

"Good." *Shooting at shadows is one thing. When you're in combat, it's all too easy to think there's an enemy target where there's nothing. But that fool on* Arrogant *was too stubborn or dumb or both to realize the mistake or stop shooting when I ordered it. I need to get rid of* Arrogant's *commanding officer as soon as I can swing it.* Just one more thing to worry about.

"Sir?" Geary and Desjani both looked toward the watch-stander who'd spoken. "We have Colonel Carabali on the circuit again."

Carabali looked as furious as Geary had been moments before. "My apologies, Captain Geary. The unit I was with was forced to take shelter within a shielded bunker, so we were unable to communicate with anyone."

"Forced to take shelter? Is there still that much Syndic resistance around the base?"

"No, sir." Carabali seemed to be fighting to keep from snarling. "We did initially pursue some Syndic forces into the bunker. But as we were preparing to leave it, the area we were in started being bombarded by one of our own ships."

Arrogant. *Firing on a location occupied by our own people. That stupid sorry excuse for a ship commander.* "Did you lose anyone?"

"By the grace of our ancestors, no, sir."

"Good." *Although if you* had *lost someone I could've hanged that fool on* Arrogant. "Any idea what *Arrogant* was shooting at?"

"I was hoping you knew, Captain Geary," she said slowly.

Geary almost smiled at the carefully understated words, but he managed to keep his expression stern, knowing the Marine commander probably wasn't yet in the mood to see the dark humor of the situation. "No. My apologies for the time required to get *Arrogant* to cease fire. I will ensure steps are taken to make certain this sort of thing isn't repeated."

"Thank you, Captain Geary. Major Jalo tells me you were in communication with him regarding the prisoners."

"That's correct." Geary paused, wondering how to word his next statement. *Were you planning on murdering your prisoners, Colonel?* "I don't know what the standard procedure has been regarding prisoners."

Carabali's eyes narrowed. "Standard procedure has been that we turn them over to the fleet, sir." Everything in her tone and posture clearly communicated a further message to Geary. *I'm certain you know what the fleet does with them once they're out of our hands.*

The exchange brought Geary's temper rising again. *How dare she be holier than thou about this? It seems the Marines kept from being directly involved in killing prisoners by looking the other way. That's not exactly the most virtuous of actions. Though at least they kept their own hands clean. I have to give them credit for that much.* But all he said was, "That's changed. You will maintain responsibility for the prisoners and make arrangements to ensure the prisoners are confined in an area with adequate life support and the means to call for rescue once we depart."

Carabali's expression shifted. "I understood the base was to be totally destroyed, sir."

"Sufficient living space, food, water, and life support to keep the prisoners alive until rescued will be kept intact, along with one primary and one backup means of basic communications with the inhabited world in this system." It was so easy for Geary to reel off the requirements.

Everyone had known them once. Every officer had been required to know them. And to follow them. "The prisoners will be kept under guard and treated in accordance with the laws of war until we depart. Are there any questions?"

Carabali was watching Geary as if studying him. "I understand these orders are to me, personally? That they cannot be overridden by any other fleet officer without your concurrence?"

"Yes, Colonel. I have every confidence that you will faithfully execute the spirit as well as the letter of my orders."

"Thank you, Captain Geary. I understand and will obey." Carabali rendered a precise salute, then the image blanked out.

Geary leaned back, rubbing his eyes, then looked toward Desjani again. "Thank you, Captain Desjani."

"I just did my duty, sir." Desjani was looking away, refusing to meet Geary's eye.

Geary looked around the bridge, seeing the other officers and sailors also finding anything else to stare at rather than look him in the face. "Captain Desjani—"

"Standard procedure," she interrupted in a low voice.

Geary stopped and took a deep breath. "How long?"

"I don't know."

"Official?"

This time Desjani paused, then shook her head, still not looking his way. "Never official. Never in writing. Just understood."

So you all knew it wasn't right. Couldn't be right. Or you'd have written it down.

But as long as you didn't write it down, you could pretend it really was okay. Just unwritten.

Desjani spoke again, her voice thin. "We heard your reaction, Captain Geary. We saw your reaction. How could we have let this happen? We've dishonored our ancestors, haven't we? We've dishonored *you.*"

Even though Desjani was still avoiding his gaze, Geary found himself looking away from her. *They did. They've*

*done something horrible. They're good people, and
they've been doing something horrible. What do I do?*
"Captain Desjani . . . all of you . . . your past actions are
between you and your own ancestors. Ask them for forgiveness, not me. I wish . . . I wish to remind you all that
someday we will be judged for our actions. I will not judge
you. I don't have that right. But I'll not permit dishonor-
able actions by forces under my command. I'll not permit
some of the finest officers and enlisted personnel I've ever
met to sully their own service. And you *are* fine officers
who command fine sailors. Sailors in the Alliance fleet. All
of us are, together. There are things we don't do. From this
moment forth, let us all ensure our every action reflects
well on us and our ancestors. Let us live to the highest
standards, lest we win this war only to find ourselves staring in the mirror at the face of our late enemy."

A murmur of replies followed. Geary looked around
again, and this time everyone met his gaze. It was a start.

For the first time, he wondered if missing the last century had actually been a blessing of sorts.

THE conference room once more appeared to be occupied
by the apparently endless table with every commanding
officer in the fleet seated along it, even though Geary knew
only Captain Desjani was actually here in person with him.
Right now the images of the other ship commanders were
staring at him with expressions that ran the full gamut from
faithful to hostile, with plenty of surprise thrown in for
good measure. "Kaliban?" the harsh voice of Captain
Faresa demanded. She made a dismissive gesture toward
the navigational display of local stars that floated above
the table. "You actually want us to jump to Kaliban?"

Geary nodded, tamping down his temper. It had gotten
to the point where even thinking about Captain Faresa, or
Captain Numos for that matter, made him angry. He
couldn't afford that kind of distraction. Besides, it was unprofessional, and he couldn't demand professionalism

from others if he didn't try his best to practice it himself. "I explained my reasons."

Captain Numos shook his head in a way that somehow reminded Geary of the bureaucratic Syndic commander. "I cannot agree to such a rash and senseless course of action."

Captain Tulev broke in, frowning. "It seems to make a great deal of sense to me."

"That's hardly surprising," Numos stated in a disparaging tone.

Tulev flushed but continued to speak in an even voice. "Captain Geary has analyzed the likely enemy reactions to our current situation. I can't fault his reasoning. The Syndics are not fools. They'll have a major force waiting for us at Yuon."

"Then we'll deal with them."

"This fleet is still recovering from what happened in the Syndic home system! Our losses can't be replaced until we reach home. Surely, even you realize we can't risk getting caught by superior forces again."

"Timidity in the face of the enemy—" Numos began.

"We aren't in this situation because of timidity," Captain Desjani interrupted, ignoring the angry look Numos sent her way. "We're here because we were more concerned with acting aggressively than with thinking about what we were doing." She subsided while the other officers stared at her in either disbelief or incomprehension.

Captain Faresa made what was apparently her best attempt to speak in a condescending voice. "Are we to understand that the commanding officer of a ship in the Alliance fleet regards aggressiveness as a negative quality?"

Geary leaned forward. "No. You are to understand that aggressiveness without forethought is a negative quality. That's *my* opinion, Captain Faresa."

Faresa's eyes narrowed as she opened her mouth to speak, then froze in that position. Geary watched her, not letting his amusement show. *You were going to cite fleet traditions, weren't you, Faresa? Maybe even quote Black*

Jack Geary. But I'm the one person you can't use that against.

Farther down the table, a commander spoke, his words rushed. "It's common knowledge that prolonged survival sleep affects people." He paused as he became the center of attention, then spoke quickly again. "This isn't the officer whose example has inspired this fleet for a century. Not any more."

Everyone looked toward Geary, who realized that the commander had brought into the open something his enemies must have been whispering since he took command. To his own surprise, the charge didn't anger him. Perhaps because Geary disliked the heroic image of Black Jack Geary so much that he didn't mind having someone else disassociate him from that mythical construct. Geary could also tell from the expressions around the table that most of the officers present disapproved of what had been said. Many still clearly worshipped Black Jack. Others seemed unhappy with the unprofessionalism of the comments made by the commander. He hoped at least a few were actually trusting him because of his actions so far.

So instead of reacting with passion, Geary deliberately leaned back and looked directly at his opponent. A name tag immediately sprang into view, identifying the man and his ship. Commander Vebos of the *Arrogant.* Of course. "Commander Vebos. I don't claim to be more than human. I am, however, the officer who led this fleet out of the Syndic home system when it was threatened with imminent destruction. I know how to command a fleet. I know how to give orders. That's because I learned how to take orders, a necessary skill in any officer. Don't you agree, Commander?"

Vebos turned pale at the pointed reference to his actions in bombarding the Syndic base. But he bulled ahead anyway. "Other officers could've done better. Captain Numos. He'd have us halfway home by now!"

"He'd have us in Syndic work camps by now," Captain Duellos noted dryly. "Though he was willing enough to try to get away alone in *Orion* while the Syndics were busy finishing off our damaged ships."

It was Numos's turn to flush red with anger. "I will not—"

Geary slammed his hand onto the table, and silence fell. "I do not wish to have my officers publicly malign other officers," he stated.

Captain Duellos rose and inclined his head toward the place Numos occupied. "My apologies to Captain Geary and to Captain Numos."

Geary inclined his own head in return. "Thank you, Captain Duellos. It is critical that we remain focused. This fleet is transiting the Corvus System en route to the jump point that leads to Kaliban. We are currently in negotiations with the Syndic authorities on the second planet. They are being told to provide us with supplies and raw materials as we pass through the system, on pain of having the fleet inflict extensive damage to their world." Geary thought that of those present, only Captain Desjani would guess that Geary had no intention of actually bombarding an inhabited world simply to punish the people on it. "I am certain that the Syndics will be awaiting us with force at Yuon. I will take this fleet to Kaliban. And our ancestors willing, I will take this fleet home."

A number of commanders still looked unhappy or skeptical, but most of the officers made their at-least-grudging agreement clear. Geary looked along the ranks of ship commanders, trying to identify those who looked to be trouble, then stopped himself. *I won't turn into a Syndic CEO, playing political games and purging officers suspected of "disloyalty." But by the living stars, Commander Vebos won't still be commanding the* Arrogant *when we leave this system. That man isn't simply disloyal and insubordinate. He's stupid.*

The number of officers around the table dwindled rapidly as they broke the connections that had presented their images at the conference. Once again, the apparent size of the table, and the room itself, shrank along with the reduction in officers whose images had been present. Many of the officers paused, their images suddenly seeming to stand before Geary, and expressed brief words of support. Geary acknowledged them as gracefully as he could, trying to not grimace at how many of them looked at him with the worshipful eyes of those seeing Black Jack Geary in the flesh.

Captain Duellos was the last to leave, giving Geary a big grin. "Maybe you should've left Numos and *Orion* guarding the jump exit," Duellos suggested.

"Why would I have wanted to do that?" Geary asked.

"You could've left him there!"

Geary laughed despite himself. "His crew doesn't deserve that."

Duellos smiled again. "No. I expect they suffer enough as it is."

"Sorry I had to slap you down when you and Numos started to get personal," Geary said. "I trust you understand why I did that."

"I did, sir. Though I must confess I don't regret making the remark and reminding my fellow ship commanders of the course of action Numos tried to endorse back in the Syndic home system." Duellos paused. "I want you to know that you have my unconditional support."

"Thank you."

"Not Black Jack Geary. You."

Geary raised one eyebrow. "You've figured out I'm not that person?"

"I'm glad you're not," Duellos confessed. "The man always scared me."

"That makes two of us."

"Captain Desjani is a very good officer. You can trust her."

"I already know that." Geary made a face. "Speaking of trust, do you have any officers you'd recommend for command of *Arrogant*?"

"I can give you some names. A word of advice, Captain Geary?"

Geary nodded. "I never refuse to listen to advice from good officers."

Duellos made a small bow. "Thank you. Don't replace that idiot Vebos with an officer certain to be loyal to you. It will raise concerns of a loyalty purge."

Geary bit his lip, trying not to show his surprise that Duellos had echoed his own earlier thought. "Surely that hasn't actually happened in the Alliance fleet."

For the first time, Duellos looked grim. "Captain Geary, I know that you have already learned of some of the things that have happened in the Alliance fleet."

"Damn," Geary whispered, then shook his head. *Loyalty purges in the Alliance fleet. Unbelievable. When? Where? I don't really want to know.* "Thank you, Captain. I'll remember your advice. It's very good to have officers like you and Desjani whom I can trust implicitly."

"We can always trust in our ancestors as well," Duellos offered. "I do not regard myself as an overly religious man, nor have I subscribed to the belief that the dead Black Jack Geary would somehow return when he was most needed. But it is nonetheless heartening even to me that you came to us when you did."

Geary snorted. "I suppose I shouldn't complain about being found since I'd have been dead for real before much longer. But I'm not sure even my ancestors can help me much with this situation."

Duellos made a sweeping gesture and grinned. "Then perhaps mine can assist with avoiding the enemy fleet and looting bystanders. By dint of experience, that is. My ancestors include a few pirates."

"Do they? I guess there are some skeletons in everyone's family closet. A few of my ancestors were lawyers."

"Ah! My condolences."

"We've learned to live with it."

Duellos stepped back and saluted. "You reminded us all of how our actions have dishonored our ancestors, you know. But you did it as well as such a thing could be done. You spoke of 'us' and 'we,' placing yourself alongside us.

And placing us alongside you. There are many who will not forget that."

Geary returned the salute, thanking whichever ancestor had inspired him to use those words. *Because I sure didn't think that out beforehand.* "Thank you."

"It is only the truth, sir." Duellos lowered his hand, and his image vanished.

GEARY sat down heavily in his stateroom, staring glumly at the display he'd activated. It showed the situation in Corvus System, with a few ships from the Alliance fleet finishing up their work at the Syndic base on the frozen world while the rest of the fleet proceeded through the system in a halfway decent formation. *Fourteen hours since we entered this system. How much longer until serious Syndic pursuit shows up?*

I can't believe how tired I am. Do I dare sleep? Will the fleet fly apart again if I'm not watching it?

The hatch chime sounded. Geary heaved himself up into a more formal position. "Come in."

"Captain Geary." Co-President Rione spoke formally, her expression as controlled as usual. "May we speak?"

"Certainly."

Geary waved her to a seat, but instead Rione walked over to stare at the starscape that dominated one bulkhead. "First of all, Captain, I hope my interventions on the bridge did not adversely affect your work."

"Not at all. You had some good input. I appreciated the advice."

A momentary smile twisted Rione's lips, then vanished. "More so than Captain Desjani, I would assume."

"She's the Captain of *Dauntless*," Geary pointed out in a carefully neutral voice. "The bridge is her throne room, if you will. The place where her authority finds a center. Any ship Captain would be a little touchy about someone else appearing to exercise authority on the bridge."

Rione turned her head for a moment to give Geary a searching look. "Does she react this way to you, as well?"

"No. I understand the protocol, and I have an established role. I let her run her ship while I try to run the fleet. That sort of thing is well understood. But there's no real protocol for having a high-ranking civilian on the bridge. There's bound to be some friction. Captain Desjani's a good commanding officer, though. She'll get used to your appearances on the bridge, and she won't act improperly toward you."

"Thank you, Captain Geary." Rione inclined her head in a brief gesture. "I wish you to understand that for my part, I did not take amiss Captain Desjani's strong words regarding the issue of robotic warships. The argument is never-ending, and I truly appreciate the thoughts of those who actually fight, but I cannot imagine fully entrusting weapons to artificial intelligences."

"To be perfectly honest, I agree with you." Geary shrugged. "It's the same problem we had in my time. If an artificial intelligence isn't smart enough to employ a weapon all by itself, you can't trust it very much in battle. If the AI *is* smart enough to employ a weapon all by itself, you can't trust it at all."

Rione's lips made another very brief smile. "True. But it's time I addressed the issue that brought me here." Geary waited while Rione stared at the depiction of the stars. "I find it necessary to confess something to you, Captain Geary. You have shamed me."

"If this is about the prisoner thing—"

"It is. I suppose you're tired of hearing us express our feelings?"

"That's not how I meant it."

"No. I didn't think so." Co-President Rione seemed to be studying the starscape again. "Captain Geary, I'm not one of those who believes that the past was always a better place. That the old ways were necessarily better. But I have known for some time that the pressures of this war have warped those who fight it. How much so is easily overlooked. We have forgotten some very important things."

Geary frowned and pretended to be looking at his hands. "You've all been through a lot."

"That's an explanation, but it's not an excuse." Rione had bent her head again, her mouth a thin, hard line now. "It is all too easy to become like the enemy you hate, isn't it, Captain Geary?"

"That's why we have the laws of war. That's why we try to teach honor to those who have to fight."

"The laws of war mean nothing if those charged with following them do not believe in them. Honor can be twisted, turned upon itself, until it appears to justify the most evil actions. You know this, Captain Geary."

Geary nodded heavily. "I'm in no position to judge anyone, Madam Co-President. I had the luxury of avoiding the many years of war that led to this state of affairs."

"Luxury? You don't appear to have enjoyed the experience." Rione raised her head, but she still didn't look toward Geary. "In the last few hours, as time permitted, I've gone back through my classified archives, studying the true history of the war and trying to determine how we reached this state. I want you to know it wasn't the result of any deliberate process. I could see where the rules got bent here and there, always for what seemed good reasons. The next time they got bent some more."

"For the best of reasons," Geary stated without emotion.

"Yes. Step by step, over the course of time, we grew to accept things. We grew to believe that the deplorable actions of the Syndicate Worlds justified deplorable actions on our part. Even I accepted this as an unfortunate reality of the war." She finally looked at Geary with an expression he couldn't read. "And then you reminded us all of what our ancestors would think of those actions. Only you could do this, because no one else could speak so clearly from the past to us. You reminded us that this war began because we were different than the Syndicate Worlds. Because there were things the Syndicate Worlds would do that the Alliance would not."

Geary nodded again, uncomfortable under Rione's gaze. "I never believed that the Alliance somehow made a decision all at once to start violating the laws of war. I guessed it had been like you said. Starting down the slippery slope and ending up at the bottom without even realizing how you got there. All because of the old argument that we had to do some bad things to win because it was important to win."

"An old argument and a false one, isn't it?"

"I think so. If the Alliance starts modeling its actions on those of the Syndicate Worlds, I'm not sure what the point of winning would be."

"I heard you say that. I agree." Rione bowed her head toward him. "You reminded us of who we once were, Captain Geary. And you had the courage and fundamental decency to stand by the truly honorable things you believed in, even at the risk of alienating those in this fleet who believe in you and follow you."

Geary shook his head. "I'm not a courageous man, Madam Co-President. I just acted on instinct."

"Then I hope that you will continue to do so. When first we met, I told you that I had no use for heroes and expressed my concern that you would lead this fleet to ruin. I freely admit that thus far you have proven me wrong." Rione inclined her head again and left.

Geary rubbed his forehead, thinking over Rione's words. *She didn't exactly give me unconditional approval, did she? "Thus far" I haven't lived up to her worst expectations. But that's okay. She'll help keep me honest. I don't want to end up believing I deserve all those worshipful looks I keep getting from people in this fleet.*

He thought about going back to the bridge of the *Dauntless*, and then thought about having to face all the others there. *I think I've had enough drama for now.* He paged the bridge instead, telling them he'd be catching some sleep and making sure they'd wake him if anything important happened.

Seven hours later a buzzing sound jerked him awake. "Geary here." He tried to come fully awake, shocked at how long he'd slept and how tired he still felt. Obviously, he hadn't recovered as much from his long survival sleep as he'd been imagining.

"Captain Geary, this is the bridge. Sorry for waking you, sir. You asked to be notified—"

"Yeah, yeah. What is it?"

"We've sighted major elements of the Syndic fleet exiting the jump point. Captain Desjani assesses it to be the main pursuit force."

SIX

"**CAPTAIN** Desjani, I'm afraid I have to agree with your estimate." Geary totaled up the ships that had so far been seen exiting the jump point. A swarm of HuKs led the way, with multiple squadrons of heavy cruisers right behind. Since the Alliance fleet was looking straight back at the jump exit, the leading Syndic ships tended to obscure those behind them, but several squadrons of battle cruisers and battleships had been confirmed bringing up the rear. "There's a lot of junk blocking the view of the jump exit."

Desjani grinned. "You ordered mines placed at the exit, sir."

Oh, yeah. Geary took another look. "How many did we get?"

"They swept the mines with HuKs and light cruisers, sir. The hard way. We estimate they lost or suffered severe damage to about fifteen ships. The debris fields we can see correlate to the destruction of most of those."

Coming out of jump space and running right into a minefield. They probably never knew what hit them. "Do you think what we can see is everything?"

Desjani gave him a look that implied she thought Geary wanted more enemies to fight, then studied her display. "There could be a follow-on wave. But if this is it, we can take this force."

Geary noted that Desjani's voice seemed torn between excitement and worry at the prospect. All of her training called for charging into action, but the last time the Alliance fleet had faced a major Syndic force, it had gotten its butt kicked hard.

"We could," Geary stated with a confidence he didn't really feel. After watching his fleet make a mishmash of the engagement with minor Syndic forces, he wasn't looking forward to a much bigger battle anytime soon. But he knew he had to outwardly express confidence in the fleet. If word got around (and it surely would) that he'd even implied the fleet lacked the ability to win, it could cripple the fleet's chances before the next shot was even fired. "But we'd have to turn back to engage them. I don't see any reason to do that." He tried to make it sound like the pursuing Syndic forces weren't worth the trouble. "I hadn't planned on any more battles in this system."

Apparently, he succeeded to some extent. Desjani and the watch-standers on the *Dauntless*'s bridge all nodded knowingly.

Geary fiddled with his controls, trying to make the display calculate the chances of the Syndics catching up with the Alliance force. "Have I got this right?" he muttered to Desjani.

She looked over, then after a moment nodded again. "Yes. We're only about four light-hours from the jump exit now. Forty hours of transit time if we stay at .1 light speed, but even if we had to slow for some reason, we've got a very big lead. We'll be at the jump point to Kaliban well before they can catch up to us and delay us further." Desjani grinned. "Some of the fleet captains questioned why we didn't take more time to loot this system. This should answer them!"

Geary smiled briefly, unsettled both by Desjani's endorsement of what she clearly saw as Black Jack's once-again demonstrated infallibility and by the news that some of his captains had been grumbling about his decisions openly enough for someone as clearly loyal to him as Desjani to have heard. Then he finally noticed something else on his display. "What's this? Who're these guys?" Geary pointed at a group of ships coming up at an almost leisurely pace from the direction of the inhabited world. Even though the ships were moving slower than the Alliance fleet, they'd been coming from ahead and so were on course to intercept the Alliance force. "They're Syndic, but they're marked as nonthreatening?"

Desjani curved the edges of her lips in a very brief smile. "That represents the fruit of our Co-President's efforts at diplomacy. Twenty merchant ships, supposedly loaded with food and other materials we asked for."

"Twenty ships?" Geary couldn't help grinning. "That'll be a decent amount of supplies."

"Yes," Desjani agreed with visible reluctance at the idea of being in debt to Co-President Rione.

"How are we set up for the rendezvous?"

"They're merchants, so they can't accelerate worth a damn, but they've been told to use their propulsion systems without regard for economy, and they appear to be doing so. By the time we meet up with them, they should've been able to get up close to our speed. If we have to brake, it won't be by much." Desjani's finger raced across the display, pointing out details. "The merchants are headed to join up near the positions of our big auxiliaries. That'll minimize the time needed to transfer the supplies over." She paused. "We've confirmed their identity as merchant transports by visual and full-spectrum scans. No weapons are visible."

Geary nodded, feeling a surge of relief that everything had been handled well, even though he'd been dead to the world. "What about security?"

"I took the liberty of contacting Colonel Carabali. Detachments of Marines will take boarding shuttles to each of the merchants, conduct searches for hidden weapons, and maintain a watch on the crews."

"Very good. That's exactly what I'd have told the Colonel to do." Desjani beamed at the praise in a way that seemed incongruous in a woman her age. "Where's Co-President Rione now?"

"I believe she's resting." Desjani made "rest" sound like an unmilitary activity, apparently forgetting that Geary had just spent several hours doing the same. "She did record a report for you."

"Thanks." Geary pulled up the file.

On the recording, Rione looked weary. "Captain Geary. After substantial negotiations, hindered by our distance from the inhabited planet, I convinced the Syndicate Worlds authorities that we would be willing to forebear from annihilating them if they would provide suitable tribute. Captain Desjani's crew provided me with an estimated number of large cargo ships in this star system as well as how many had been seen in time-late images near the inhabited world. This information enabled me to insist on twenty such ships carrying supplies listed on both our real and false needs lists. The Syndicate Worlds authorities provided remote signing of an agreement not to attempt any action using the cargo ships against the Alliance fleet in exchange for our promise not to launch further attacks within the system before our departure. The text of that agreement is attached. Please do not hesitate to contact me if questions arise."

Geary read through the agreement, finding nothing that raised alarms in his mind. Rione seemed to have covered everything. *Then it's just a matter of trusting the Syndics at this point. And I'd be crazy to trust the Syndics. But what can they pull with Carabali's Marines breathing down their necks?*

He looked back at Captain Desjani. "Those merchant ships are a little farther from the jump exit than we are, but they must've seen the arrival of the pursuit force by now."

"But they're not altering course," Desjani agreed, answering Geary's unstated question. "Perhaps they're afraid we'll run them down if they try. They're close enough and cumbersome enough that by the time they managed to get turned and going away from us, we could have destroyers all over them. Or perhaps they're afraid that if they run, it'll provoke an attack on the inhabited planet."

"Good possibilities." Despite the appearance of the Syndic pursuit force, everything seemed well in hand. *Unfortunately, it's usually just when you think everything's under control that everything and its brother starts going to hell in a handbag. So what can go wrong?* Titan? *She looks like she's not in trouble for once.*

"Sir." Both Geary and Desjani turned at the operations watch-stander's hail. "*Titan* reports she has another primary propulsion unit back on line."

"Praise our ancestors." Geary had tensed in dread as *Titan*'s name came up on the heels of his worries. It had taken him a moment to realize it wasn't bad news after all. Now he checked the statistics for *Titan*, noting its best acceleration had improved significantly. *But she's still too damn slow. What idiot labeled those ships Fast Fleet Auxiliaries? The only thing fast about them is how quickly they can get into trouble.* "What are the chances *Titan* can strap on a few extra primary propulsion units at some point?"

The operations watch-stander looked startled, then glanced at the engineering watch-stander, who also looked surprised, then thoughtful. "It might be possible, sir." His face began to take on the glow of an engineer presented with a complex problem that he might have the means to solve.

Geary leaned back, taking in the entire situation slowly, trying to make sure he hadn't missed anything. But aside from the Alliance fleet itself, the Syndic pursuit force and the twenty merchants headed steadily for their rendezvous, nothing else seemed to be moving in Corvus Star System. All the other Syndic shipping had headed for the nearest place to dock and hope the Alliance fleet didn't send any ships that way. *Dauntless*'s combat systems were estimating that the Syndic pursuit force had pushed up to an average velocity of slightly more than 30,000 kilometers a second, but against the vast scale of space, that still left them crawling at not much more than a tenth of light speed. "They're not trying to catch us," Geary noted.

Desjani frowned, her eyes darting to the representation of the Syndic warships. "They're not?"

"No. Not if these readings are right. They're not accelerating anymore. Not that they could catch us before we reach the jump point even if they did push up to point two light. But they're not trying."

"They're . . . just chasing us?"

"Herding us," Gearing corrected. "They want us to keep going."

"To the jump point?"

"To Yuon. I'd stake my life on it." *Come to think of it, I am. Worse, I'm staking the lives of every man and woman on these Alliance ships on it. What if the Syndics have already guessed that I won't run straight for home? What if they know Kaliban is the best alternative?*

No. They can't risk this fleet getting safely through Yuon, so they'll be there in force. They don't have any choice.

But they still might've seeded Kaliban with enough mines to rip this fleet to shreds. Has there been enough time for that? Would the Syndics have that many mines close enough to Kaliban to get them there before we get there? Have they even considered the possibility that we'll go there?

There's no way to know. I can't afford to second-guess this. I can't afford to let the possibility of disaster keep me from making and acting on decisions, because no matter what I do there'll always be that possibility.

He took a long, deep breath, momentarily blocking out his surroundings. When Geary opened his eyes, he saw Desjani giving him an approving look.

"I don't know how you can be so relaxed at times like this," she confessed. "But I know it impresses my crew."

"It's, um, something I work at."

It gradually became obvious that nothing was going to happen for a while. Geary checked the timeline for the rendezvous with the Syndic merchants and saw that the Marine shuttles wouldn't launch for another two hours. Fighting off an irrational urge to keep watching everything for fear it might come unraveled without his personal attention, Geary stood up. "I'm going to get something to eat," he told Captain Desjani. She nodded. Geary noticed as he left that the watch-standers on the *Dauntless*'s bridge were all watching him admiringly. *Ancestors help me if I ever start to believe everything I do is as perfect as these people think. If I tripped and fell on my butt, they'd probably think it was Black Jack Geary's way of preparing for action, and they'd all start doing it.*

However, the interaction with the personnel on the bridge had reminded Geary of the importance of letting the crew see him. He'd been thinking longingly of holing up in his stateroom again and gnawing on a ration bar, safely hidden from the eyes of both those who worshipped the decks Black Jack Geary trod and those who thought John Geary was an ancient relic totally out of his depth. Instead, he walked to one of the mess areas, joined the line and got a meal, then sat down at a table with several sailors at it.

They watched him with wide eyes as he took a bite of something tasteless. "How are you folks doing?" Geary asked. Instead of answering, they all looked at each other. Geary glanced at the petty officer sitting next to him and asked the one question he could be sure would get a clear answer. "Where are you from?"

"Ko-Kosatka, sir."

The one thing you could always get sailors to talk about was home. "The same as Captain Desjani?"

"Yes, sir."

"I've been to Kosatka." The man's jaw actually dropped in amazement. "It was a while ago . . . of course. I liked it. What part of the planet are you from?"

The man started talking about his home. The others got

drawn in, as Geary learned another one of his tablemates was also from Kosatka. As in Geary's time, each ship seemed to draw much of its crew from one particular planet, with the rest of the sailors from places scattered across the Alliance. The others were from planets Geary had to confess he'd never visited, but just his expressions of interest kept the sailors happy.

Eventually, one of them asked the question Geary knew would come. "Sir, we're going to get home again, aren't we?"

Geary finished chewing a bite that had suddenly gone dry as well as tasteless. He took a drink, not willing to risk his voice cracking. "I intend bringing this fleet home."

Smiles broke out on all sides. Another sailor spoke quickly. "Any idea how long, sir? My family . . . well . . ."

"I understand. I don't know for certain how long it'll take. We're not going straight back." Smiles faded into stunned silence. "The Syndics would expect that, you see. They'd set another trap." Geary smiled in what he hoped was a confident way. "Instead, we're going to bedevil them every light-second of the way home, go places they don't expect, hit them by surprise." He'd been thinking how to phrase things right, how to make a desperate retreat sound like a victorious march. "We lost a lot of friends in the Syndic home system. We had to leave in a hurry, as you know. But we're not going to let that stand. We're going to jump around, hit the Syndics again and again, and we're going to make them pay. By the time we get home, the Syndics are going to wish they'd never messed with the Alliance."

There were smiles all around the mess area now. Geary stood up, praying to his ancestors to understand why he'd said something he knew misrepresented things, and kept his own smile in place as he left the compartment.

Apparently, his little speech spread through the ship faster than he could walk. Hardly surprising, since any one of the sailors within earshot could've recorded it with their personal comm units, and several undoubtedly had done

so. Geary found himself speeding up, trying to get to his
stateroom without looking like he was running, trying to
get away from all the sailors and officers who believed
he'd somehow be able to make true everything he'd said.

An hour later, he forced himself out of the sanctuary of
his stateroom and returned to the bridge. Desjani was still
there, studying something on her palm unit. The position
of the Syndic pursuit force relative to the Alliance fleet
hardly seemed to have altered, though if the Syndics had
done something different within less than four hours, the
light showing the images of that event wouldn't have
reached *Dauntless* yet. The Syndic merchant ships bringing the supplies the Alliance fleet had demanded were
much closer, though, their paths through space forming
wide arcs that were converging steadily on the course of
the Alliance ships.

The merchants had come from the inhabited world,
ahead of and beneath the Alliance fleet's track through
space, but because of the Alliance fleet's velocity, they had
been required to aim for a point even farther ahead in order
to achieve a rendezvous at matching speeds. During the
merchants' slow journey, the fleet had swung past the orbit
of the inhabited world, and now the merchants were coming up from only slightly below, still moving ahead but
slower than the fleet, so that their courses were curving
gradually up to meet the Alliance ships.

Captain Desjani shook her head over what she was
reading, made some notations, then turned to Geary. "Personnel issues," she confided to Geary. "I wish someone
would figure out how to keep crew members from forming
disruptive personal relationships."

"My first commanding officer wished the same thing,"
Geary responded dryly. "Not about me personally,
though."

Desjani looked shocked. "Of course not, sir."

Geary very briefly considered the idea of jumping
Tanya Desjani right there and then in order to convince her
that he was in fact human. It had, after all, been more than

a century since his last physical encounter with a woman and that was a long dry spell no matter how you counted it. The thought gave him enough perverse amusement to lift his mood a bit. "It could've been about me. There was this raven-haired lieutenant who I thought was hotter than a plasma field. Fortunately for good order and discipline, she thought I was a geeky young ensign without many redeeming qualities."

Desjani smiled politely, clearly not believing him. "Colonel Carabali asked that you contact her before the Marine shuttles launch. I was just about to have you paged."

"Glad to know my timing is good." Geary called up the Colonel, momentarily surprised to see that Carabali wasn't in combat gear herself. *But then she couldn't be. Her responsibility is to exercise overall command of the teams going to the ships. She can't go along with one of them.* "Yes, Colonel?"

"Captain Geary, I wished to know if you had any special instructions for my Marines before their shuttles depart."

"I don't believe so, Colonel. My experience is that Marines know their jobs better than I know their jobs. I assume there's no need to say I don't trust the Syndics."

Carabali grinned. "My people will be in full combat load-out. Even if those merchant ships are packed full of Syndic assault troops, my Marines will be able to fight their way out."

"If that happens, Colonel, I assure you that my warships will make certain none of those merchant ships survives. But hopefully it won't come to that. I'd like to have those supplies they're carrying."

"Understood, sir." Carabali glanced to the side. "Ten minutes to shuttle launches. I'll keep you informed of any developments."

"Thank you." Geary relaxed again, reassured by Carabali's cool competence. *It's damn good to have the Marines backing you up.* He scanned the fleet display, noting which warships were in the best positions to engage the Syndic merchants if necessary. *It looks like we're ready for anything.* The thought brought to mind his old executive officer, long dead now even though Geary's memories of him were only several weeks old. Geary had said the same thing to him once, only to have his XO look worried and comment that it made him wonder what they might've overlooked. *Well, Patros, you're safe with your ancestors now, and I'm* still *wondering what I might've overlooked.*

Geary spent the next few minutes trying to fight off the dark mood that remembering his old shipmate had thrown him into. Patros didn't belong here on the bridge of the *Dauntless,* but then neither did Geary. *Two ghosts. That's what Patros and I are. What the hell am I still doing here, alive and fighting a war that belongs to our descendants now?*

The Marine shuttles finally began launching on schedule, giving Geary something else to concentrate on, each shuttle being tracked as it arced toward the particular merchant ship that was its target. Geary felt himself tensing as the shuttles, small and swift next to the large, ungainly merchant ships, swooped down toward the merchants

It felt oddly like watching a volley of specters homing on their targets, until the shuttles turned and began braking instead of accelerating to impact, as missiles would have. Geary, sweating for news of the Marines, belatedly remembered the video panel available to him and punched controls until it popped up again. Twenty screens flashed into existence next to Geary's display, each showing the view from a Marine squad leader.

This time there wasn't anything else he should be watching, so Geary watched, fascinated, as the Marines entered the merchant ships, conducted searches and posted guards in important areas like engineering and the bridge. It all went smoothly, with no resistance from the Syndics, who acted stiff and formal but not openly hostile. Unlike the large crews of warships needed to handle the special requirements of combat and combat damage, the merchant

ships only had crews of about a dozen each, making it easy
for the Marines to keep an eye on them all.

Geary had seen the interiors of Syndic merchant ships
before, during the period before the war when his ship had
been ordered to conduct inspections of ships passing
through Alliance space. He recognized some of the features on the Syndic merchants here, causing him to wonder if the ships themselves were that old or if the design
features had been retained for so long. He guessed either
possibility could be true in a system bypassed by the hypernet.

One by one, the Marine squad leaders reported in, de-
claring the merchant ships to be to the best of their knowledge unarmed and proceeding peacefully to the rendezvous.
But Geary noticed that the Marines watching the Syndic
crews didn't relax, remaining on full combat footing. Once
again, he had a moment of empathy, wondering how it felt
to the merchant sailors to have the armored figures of
Marines looming nearby, alien visitors to the familiar compartments of their ships. *As long as they don't try anything,
they'll be safe. They should know that, after the way we
handled the prisoners at the base. That should keep anyone from doing anything foolish.*

The merchant ships crawled closer to the Alliance fleet,
Geary watching the streaming images of the Syndic merchant crews as seen by the Marines on one side, while on
the other his display showed the twenty Syndic merchant
ships proceeding at what felt like a leisurely pace toward
their rendezvous with the Alliance auxiliaries.

Nothing seemed to be wrong. Nothing at all. *What
could I be overlooking?* Geary searched his brain for anything, but he kept coming up empty. *Maybe for once we
did cover everything.*

"Captain Geary, this is Colonel Carabali."

A new window had appeared, showing Carabali's face.
She didn't look happy. "Sir, there's something about this I
don't like."

And maybe we didn't. Geary glanced toward Captain

Desjani and gestured for her attention. "The Colonel's unhappy about something."

Desjani frowned and keyed into the conversation.

"Go ahead, Colonel," Geary ordered.

Carabali pointed at something Geary couldn't see. "Are
you watching the video from the Syndic ships, sir?"

"Yes."

"Does anything seem odd about their crews to you, sir?
As a fleet officer, sir?"

Geary frowned, too, and studied the pictures more
closely. There was something odd about them, now that
Carabali had drawn his attention to it. "Are the senior merchant officers all supposed to be on their bridges?"

"Yes, sir, they are."

Desjani made a brief noise. "The Syndics seem to grow
their senior merchant officers very young, don't they?"

Carabali nodded. "Yes. Exactly. I assume the Syndics
called for volunteers to crew these ships, but as far as I can
tell from visual examination, there's not a man or woman
aboard those ships older than their twenties."

"Interesting batch of volunteers," Geary said slowly.
"Most of the merchant captains I knew wouldn't have left
their ships to someone else, even for a run like this."

"I've questioned my Marines. They indicate there was
a definite lack of familiarity with the ships by many of
these so-called crew members. They thought that was due
to volunteers being assigned to the ships from the pool of
available merchant sailors, but I'm not so sure that's the
reason."

Geary thought about that and didn't like it. Merchant
ships tended to have older officers, people who'd learned
their jobs and worked their way up through long years of
experience. It was a very different kind of professionalism
than the fleet officer kind, but strong enough in its own
way. He took another look at the alleged merchant crews.
"Young and physically fit, too, aren't they?"

"Look at their eyes, sir. Look at the way they carry
themselves," Carabali urged.

"Damn." Geary exchanged a glance with Desjani. "Those aren't merchant sailors. They look like soldiers."

"I'd stake my career on them being military," Carabali agreed. "And not just any military. They're trying to slouch around and act like civilians, but they don't really know how to relax like that anymore. They've been too highly trained. They look to me like the sort of people you find in shock troops."

"Shock troops." Geary inhaled slowly. "The sort of troops you send on desperate missions."

"Or one-way missions. Yes, sir."

Desjani looked ready to order mass murder, and for once Geary didn't blame her. "Alright, Colonel. What do you think they're planning? Some sort of attack?"

Carabali chewed her lower lip. "Not a conventional assault. They're too few, they're not in armor, and they can't have weapons easily accessible because we'd have found them. If there were sailors guarding them, they might still be able to overwhelm the guards, but not with my Marines on watch in full combat gear."

"That's what I'd think. Then what? We've confirmed there's no weapons on those merchant ships."

Desjani jerked as if struck by a thought, then leaned toward Geary and spoke in a low but urgent voice. "They have a weapon, sir. Their power cores."

Geary blinked, trying to digest the information and seeing Carabali pale slightly as she heard Desjani's statement. "Their power cores. Do you think they mean to overload their power cores when they get close to our ships?"

Carabali nodded vigorously. "Captain Desjani is right, sir. I'm sure of it. Look at the eyes of those Syndics, sir. They're on a suicide mission."

"I concur," Desjani stated. "We all agree those aren't merchant crews. They're combat troops, and they have only one weapon available to them on those ships."

Well, damn. Geary fought down an urge to curse loud and long. "Agreed. How can they overload their power cores while the Marines are watching?"

Desjani spoke again. "They'd have to have some sort of remote trigger rigged." Carabali nodded. "It could be anywhere and look like anything." Another nod.

"So should we take the crews down? Get them off the ships?"

Carabali shook her head this time. "If we start trying to herd them off the ships, they'll probably trigger the overloads right away. Your big ships might be safe enough, but we'd lose every Marine and all the boarding shuttles."

"What about killing them?" Desjani asked calmly.

Geary considered the question, and he considered what those Syndics were planning. "Yes. How good an option is that?"

Carabali grimaced. "Chancey, sir. We might be able to take them all down fast enough, but if they've got triggers tied to dead-man switches it'd just doom my Marines anyway."

"Dead-man switches? Couldn't we see—?"

Geary stopped speaking as Carabali shook her head again. "No, sir," the Marine stated. "The switches could be implanted and linked to their nervous systems or their hearts. If the Syndics died and their hearts or nervous systems shut down, it could well trigger the overloads."

"I see." *That's an advance over what was available in my time, though I wouldn't call it an improvement.*

Carabali's face brightened. "But there's another option. My Marines have a riot control load-out because we expected to be dealing with civilians."

"Meaning?" Geary pressed.

"Among other things, they have CRX gas dispensers. It's riot suppression gas, not riot dispersal, so it's odorless, colorless, and a tiny amount inhaled knocks someone out cold in a moment."

"You're suggesting we knock them out."

"Yes, sir. They'll be unconscious before they know we're acting."

"And you're certain this CRX won't cause some physical reaction that might trigger a dead-man switch?"

"Fairly certain. I can check with my medical personnel."

"Do so, please." Geary waited, trying not to let his impatience show, while the seconds crawled by until Carabali's image focused back on Geary.

"Medical staff says the CRX will be safe."

"*Will be* safe or *probably* will be safe?" Geary pressed.

Carabali grinned. "I asked them if they'd stake their lives on that assessment, and none of them hesitated."

"They're Marines," Desjani noted dryly.

"Not the medical staff," Carabali reminded her. "They're all seconded to the Marines from the fleet, so even though associating with the Marines so closely causes a bit of us to rub off on them, they're still not part of the same mind-set."

The brief exchange brought a grin to Geary's face. "Alright, then. We've established that the medical staff aren't quite as willing to die in the line of duty as the average Marine. So we can assume we can take down those alleged merchant sailors safely."

"That doesn't mean there still won't be a threat," Desjani interjected. "The ships could be rigged in a dozen ways to automatically overload their cores when they get near our big ships. A few smart proximity fuses hidden on the hulls would do the trick, and there's no way to guarantee we'd find them all in the time we've got." Desjani paused. "Merchant ships don't carry all the equipment that warships do, but they still have lots of different systems. There's no telling what else might've been rigged to set off the power cores."

Like maybe if we change the course or speed of those ships without some special input from the Syndic crew. I've got twenty flying bombs heading for the most vulnerable and valuable ships in this fleet. Geary thought about the situation. "Okay. Say we use the CRX. That'll leave us with twenty ships we can't let get close to our big units and twenty crews of unconscious Syndics." He knew Desjani was watching him, waiting for his decision and wondering how he'd square that decision with his expressed concern for prisoners. After all, he'd be justified in any action against people who planned a sneak suicide attack. *But that doesn't mean I have to do anything I don't want to. And what I do want to do is to make life difficult for the people who planned this, who sent those shock troops on a suicide mission while they're sitting safe and happy back near that inhabited world.* "How long do we have to work with?"

Carabali looked toward Desjani, who tapped rapidly on her controls. On Geary's display, large spheres appeared surrounding each Syndic merchant ship. "That's the estimated damage radius if one of those merchants blows its core. You can see the damage radius for each merchant bulged slightly to one side because of the movement vector of that ship. If our ships are farther away than that, their shields should be able to handle any debris that gets to them."

Geary judged the distances and the time left until the merchants got too close to the auxiliaries. The time remaining wasn't much, but hopefully it'd be enough. "Very well, Colonel. Here's what we'll do."

Twenty minutes later, Geary watched on the remote video feeds as the last of the unconscious Syndic crew members were dumped unceremoniously into the escape pods on their ships. Since none of them were strapped into the seats, they'd get banged up a bit when the pods blasted away. *But since they were planning on dying, I don't think they'll have any legitimate grounds to complain about bruises and broken bones.*

The pod hatches were left open as a precaution against a booby trap, and the Marines hastened back to their boarding shuttles, being met at the airlocks by the rest of the Marines in the boarding party who'd come from downloading instructions to the autopilots on the bridges of the merchant ships.

Geary let out a breath he hadn't known he was holding as the shuttles pulled away from the merchants. He

checked the time, willing the shuttles to move faster, wanting them as far as possible from the merchants and their
damage radii before the automated instructions that had
been sent to the Marines to download finally kicked in.

"Thirty seconds," Desjani advised unnecessarily.

Geary just nodded, his eyes flicking from the Marine
shuttles to the damage radii around the merchant ships to
the Alliance fleet auxiliaries that were drawing ever closer
to their rendezvous with the merchants.

"Mark."

Geary held his breath again, waiting to see if the instructions given the merchant ships' automated systems to
seal the escape pods would trigger the ships' destruction.
The Marine shuttles should be far enough away now to be
safe, if their estimates were right. *But "estimate" means it
can be wrong.*

"Pods should be launching," Desjani announced.

"There." Geary pointed at his display, where the *Dauntless*'s systems were tracking the escape pods that had shot
out from the merchants. They had another moment to wonder if launching the pods would cause the ships' power
cores to overload. But once again, the merchants continued
on, heading for the Alliance fleet in a steady way that was
almost unnerving. "Let's see what happens when we play
with the merchants' courses."

Moments later, the instructions the Marines had down-
loaded ordered the merchants' maneuvering systems to
start kicking them down and around. The big, slow merchant ships, heavily laden with the stores the Alliance fleet
had demanded, swung ponderously until their bows were
pointed down and away from the Alliance fleet. "One more
event left," Desjani noted.

The main drives on the Syndic ships lit off, pushing
against the mass and momentum of the merchant ships to
change their path through space. Geary tried to judge their
progress as the merchants continued getting closer to some
of the Alliance ships. "Should we maneuver *Titan* and *Jinn*
to make sure those things don't get too close?"

Desjani pursed her lips as she studied the relative movement of the vessels, then shook her head. "We should start seeing distances opening any minute now. Unless something causes those main drives to shut off, those merchants won't be a threat much longer."

The drives didn't shut off, continuing to push with all their capability against their ships. Slowly, the projected courses for the clumsy merchant ships began altering, the changes becoming clear as the actual courses diverged from the original paths, then changing faster as the big ships picked up speed in the new direction as fast as they were able.

"Where are they going?" Colonel Carabali's image asked.

Geary gave her a tight-lipped smile. "Home."

Carabali frowned.

"No, Colonel," Geary assured her, "we're giving the Syndics back their ships, but they won't appreciate the gesture. We had to do something with those twenty ships, and the people who launched the attack on us needed to get paid back. There are two military facilities orbiting the inhabited world. The orders we had your Marines download into the merchant maneuvering systems direct ten of those merchant ships to keep accelerating as fast as they're able, aimed directly at the point where one of those facilities will be when the merchants get there. The other ten are aimed at the other facility."

The Colonel's frown changed into an open smile. "Ten merchant ships packed full of cargo charging all-out at one target in a fixed orbit? The Syndics might have a little trouble stopping them all."

"They won't be able to stop them all, Colonel," Geary assured her. He gestured toward the images of the lumbering merchants. "Under normal conditions, the merchants would be too slow to worry about and easily destroyed on approach. But these ships won't be slowing down as they approach orbit. They'll keep speeding up as best they can until impact."

"And," Desjani added with her own smile, "any hits on the merchants will have a lot of mass to divert. If they manage to blow the merchants apart, they'll have to deal with all the cargo and wreckage still heading their way."

Geary smiled, too. "After all, we do need to conserve our supply of long-range weaponry. If in the process of breaking their word, the Syndics hand us something that will do the job of punishing them, they'll just have to live with the consequences." He glanced at the display. "We're just over thirty-two light-minutes from the inhabited world. It'll take a half hour for them to see that their suicide attack didn't come off as planned. Give them at least another ten minutes to track the merchants and figure out where they're headed. I'll wait a half hour to avoid tipping them off and then broadcast a message."

"Which will reach them in about an hour. That's far sooner than the merchant ships can reach their targets. They'll have time to evacuate their orbital facilities," Desjani sighed.

"Can't be helped," Geary noted with a shrug. "They'll have no trouble seeing the merchants coming long before they get there. Besides, any CEOs on those facilities would've gotten off first anyway. Not that I think they'll get off free. They'll have to explain to their superiors how they lost every Syndic space military asset in this system, and why they caused the destruction of the majority of the large merchant ships in the system as well, all without inflicting any losses on us or impeding our progress."

Carabali's smile grew grim. "Perhaps they'll be trading their boardrooms for labor camps."

"Maybe," Geary agreed. "And wouldn't that be a damn shame."

At the half-hour mark, Geary sat straight in his chair, making sure his uniform looked good, but not too good. He didn't want to look like one of the finely tailored bureaucrats who ran things in the Syndicate Worlds. "Begin transmission. People of Corvus Star System," he stated in his best command voice, pitched a little lower and louder than his usual speech, "this is Captain John Geary, commander of the Alliance fleet." He paused a moment, letting the fact of his identity sink in. He suspected that since the Alliance believed Black Jack Geary to be a savior, the Syndics would see him as a boogeyman or at least a threat with an air of the supernatural about him. It made him uncomfortable, but he wasn't about to discard something that could possibly help the fleet's chances of getting home.

"I wish to inform you of two things. The first is that the merchant ships we arranged to meet us here turned out to be booby-trapped. We negotiated with your leaders in good faith. They broke their word, and as a result those ships are forfeit. Even now, they are being returned with a vengeance to those who sent them. I want it clearly understood that even though we were betrayed by your leaders, we do not seek retribution against you."

"The other thing I must tell you is that the crews of the merchant ships were placed unharmed within the escape pods of the ships and ejected en route to your world. We did not sabotage or booby-trap those pods in any way. We did not turn them into weapons. They contain only your crew members."

"We could've killed the crews of those ships, who by planning a sneak attack while disguised as civilians placed themselves outside the protections granted by the laws of war. We could've retaliated against your world. This fleet had it within its power to wipe all traces of life from this system. We did not do any of those things. The Alliance fleet showed more concern for the lives of the citizens of Corvus System than did your own leaders. Remember that."

"To the honor of our ancestors," Geary recited, using the old formula even as he wondered if a phrase already old-fashioned in his day had become totally outdated by now. "This is Captain John Geary, commanding officer of the Alliance fleet. End transmission."

He relaxed, noticing as he did so that Captain Desjani had a small smile on her lips. "That should give the Syndics something to think about until the merchant ships start slamming into their targets. Especially the fact that you used the old, formal ending for your message."

"It isn't used anymore, then?"

"I've never seen it outside of historical documents." Desjani nodded, her smile not varying. "Yes. It's the sort of small touch that'll scare the hell out of the Syndics, because it'll make it clear that Black Jack Geary has returned."

Geary nodded as well, keeping his own thoughts to himself. *Yeah. Great. Knowing I'm probably something out of a nightmare to lots of people isn't something I ever wanted.*

But you use the weapons you've got.

SEVEN

ABOUT nine hours later, Geary made sure he was on *Dauntless*'s bridge to watch the Syndic merchant ships "come home."

"They blew a couple of them to star dust using some really big missiles," Desjani advised. "Too bad you missed it, but the recording of the events are in the tactical library if you want to catch a late showing."

"What kind of missile would do that kind of damage?" Geary wondered.

"My weapons techs say they must've been planetary bombardment weapons. No chance of hitting a warship, but the merchants were coming in on fixed courses and couldn't evade. Half the things still missed their targets, though."

Planetary bombardment weapons? Why would the Syndics have needed those in a backwater system like Corvus? They must've been based on one or both of those orbiting facilities since there's no big warships in the system, so the things were positioned here on purpose. Geary rubbed his chin as he pretended to study the positions of the fleet but actually tried to think through the puzzle. *The only thing the Syndics could've done with those weapons is employ them against one of the planets in this system. But why would . . . oh. Wake up, Geary. You know how the Syndic authorities maintain control. By any means necessary. I guess holding planetary bombardment munitions in orbit was just one more way of making sure the local population didn't get any ideas about not following orders.*

I never liked the Syndic leadership. I'm starting to really dislike them. He stared at the image of the inhabited world. It wasn't a perfect place for humans. *Not enough water, for one thing. Atmosphere's a little weak. But it's a good enough planet to sustain a decent population. I'm glad I didn't retaliate against those people. They've had enough to worry about from the threat posed by their own leaders.* "Any developments on the escape pods we launched from the merchant ships?"

"They're coming in behind the merchants now." Desjani looked as she'd tasted something foul. "The Syndic orbital defenses have taken out a few."

"Damn."

"It's a safe bet that they assumed we'd lied about not turning them into weapons somehow, and they'd rather kill some of their own than risk us tricking them. You know what they're like."

"Yes, I do." Geary shook his head. "But I had to try."

Desjani shrugged. "For what it's worth, the fact that the Syndic defenses have been forced to concentrate on the merchant ships means that it's reasonable to expect that maybe half the escape pods will reach the surface intact."

"Thanks. Once they get down, the Syndic population of that planet is going to find out we told the truth."

"I suppose that might make them feel bad about killing the Syndics in the other pods," Desjani stated doubtfully.

"I suppose it will." Geary hunched forward to study the images projected in front of his seat. "Not long until impact."

"No." Now Desjani sounded gleeful. "Orbital installations are always sitting ducks."

Despite his unhappiness at hearing the fate of some of the Syndic "merchant crews," Geary almost smiled himself at the truth in her statement. The military kept proving that objects in fixed orbits were not just sitting ducks but dead ducks when faced with mobile opponents, and the civil leaderships kept building orbital fortresses anyway. "They make the populations of the planets they're orbiting feel more secure. At least, that's what they told us the last time I was in Alliance space. I don't know if the rationale has changed since then."

"It hasn't. They still haven't learned. Maybe we should send them video of this," Desjani suggested with another grin.

Geary focused back on the visual display, where a highly magnified view of the area near the inhabited world was pocked with tags indicating the identities of various objects. Despite the best efforts of the Syndic defenders, several merchant ships were still rushing toward collisions with each of the military orbital installations. He'd worried a bit about hitting the planet by mistake, but the merchants had come up from the plane of the system to reach the Alliance fleet and had been sent back down. From that angle, the merchant ships were actually splitting to hit targets on either side of the planet. None were coming in at a high angle relative to the planet, so any that wandered into atmosphere ought to bounce off.

He glanced at the time and the distance, reminding himself that he was watching events that had played out about an hour and a half ago. The images seemed so immediate it was hard to recall that light from the events had been on its way out here for that long.

"Ten minutes to sighting of first impact," the weapons watch called out.

Small flashes of light were blinking into and out of existence near the bright dots that were all Geary could see of the merchant ships. He picked one orbital installation to focus on and increased the magnification of his view until the merchant nearest its target was visible as a ship rather than a point of light. A moment later, the ship started getting bigger, causing Geary to check his controls to make sure he wasn't still zooming in.

But he wasn't. "Lead merchant aiming for Syndic Orbital Installation Alpha has been destroyed," the weapons watch announced. The ship was getting bigger because its hull had been broken, and everything that had once made up the ship and its cargo was now spilling out into space, momentum still carrying the wreckage toward the target even though the engines had been silenced.

Something like hell-lances was being fired from the Syndic base, flaying the wreckage but unable to divert enough of it, and while the Syndic fire concentrated on the wreck of the lead merchant, the next in line, its engines still pushing it ever faster, came even with the debris of the first. Geary felt his jaws tighten as the Syndic close-in defenses shifted their fire to the still-intact merchant, though to what purpose he couldn't imagine. The installation was obviously doomed. He hoped the defenses were on automatic and no personnel had been left to die in a futile attempt to save the orbital facility.

Minutes later, the second merchant slammed into one side of the Syndic installation, shattering a large section into fragments of junk. The remains of the ship itself, also reduced to junk by the collision, bounced off and kept going.

On its heels, the huge cloud of wreckage from the former lead merchant started impacting. Geary stared, fascinated despite himself, as the Syndic orbital base staggered under repeated impacts, its whole structure warping and breaking as hundreds of tons of matériel rammed into it at very high speed. It looked oddly as if the Syndic base was dissolving under the impacts as the wave of debris tore it apart. The view shifted as the optics on the *Dauntless* followed the installation's movement. Under the force of the blows from the wreckage, the remains of the Syndic base were being shoved out of orbit, reeling farther and farther away from the planet it had both protected and menaced for who knew how long. The image became blurry as debris spread out from the impacts, hindering the Alliance fleet's view of the devastation.

Geary decreased the magnification so he could see a larger area, watching as the remaining merchant ships shot past where their target had been. As expected, the angle between the ships' courses and the planet meant none of the merchants plowed into the planet itself. One of the merchants hit the upper atmosphere of the planet at a high angle and glanced off, the friction and impact breaking its hull and spilling its cargo as the wreckage flew off into space. Three others drilled into the upper regions of the atmosphere at high speed, boring incandescent holes through the planet's sky as the ships' hulls vaporized into plasma, the slagged remnants of what had been a ship and cargo finally exiting back into space, still glowing brightly from radiated heat.

"That must've been quite a show from the planet's surface," Geary noted.

"Better show on the other side, Captain Geary," Desjani advised. "That side of the planet was in darkness. Do you want the replay?"

"Yeah." The details differed in that the first three surviving merchant ships all missed their target by varying distances, but the end result was the same, as by chance the fourth scored a direct hit, blasting a deep crater into the Syndic installation and surely destroying every piece of equipment on it by the force of its impact. This side only had two merchant ships enter and then exit atmosphere, but Geary had to concede that Desjani was right. Against the dark sky, the fiery trails of the dead ships stood out so bright that the optical systems on the *Dauntless* had to adjust sensitivity downward to keep the image from being whited out.

I wonder what the Syndic pursuit force thought of our little show? Geary checked their location. *They won't see it for another two hours. Then we won't see their reaction to it for at least another eight hours. Not that there's much they can do besides yell insults at us.*

"Why haven't we received another surrender demand?" Desjani wondered, just as if she'd been reading Geary's last thoughts. "There's been plenty of time for that Syndic force to get one to us."

"Good question. It wouldn't hurt them in any way to make another demand. Maybe they don't intend offering the opportunity to surrender anymore."

Desjani smiled crookedly. "With all due respect, sir, I don't think that the Syndics ever intended making a sincere offer to accept our surrender. Whatever terms they'd have offered, and whatever terms we'd have accepted, would've meant nothing."

"Based on what they did to Admiral Bloch and his companions in the Syndic home system, I'd have to agree with you."

"I was thinking as well of what just happened in this system."

"Another good example, Captain. You're quite right." Geary scratched behind one ear. "But if they never intended abiding by any terms of surrender, what would they have to lose by making offers or demands?"

He was answered this time by Co-President Rione. "They don't want to appear weak by making demands they can't enforce."

Geary looked back, seeing Rione seated in the observer's seat. "I'm sorry, Madam Co-President. I didn't know you'd come onto the bridge."

"I entered while the Syndic merchant ships were arriving at the inhabited planet, Captain Geary." Rione's face shadowed momentarily with some dark emotion. "I understand the agreement I negotiated was violated."

"You might say that," Desjani responded in a bland voice.

"But that's not your fault," Geary added, with a glance at Desjani.

"Nonetheless, I offer my apologies." Rione nodded her head toward the displays before Geary's and Desjani's seats. "As I said, the Syndicate Worlds commanders cannot continue demanding our surrender. It's a matter of politics and image. This fleet has escaped a trap at the Syndicate home system, and run through Corvus System without real hindrance. The appearance grows that the Syndicate commanders cannot bring us to heel. Under the circumstances, they must destroy us or force us to sue for surrender in order to reaffirm their strength."

Geary rubbed his lower face, contemplating Rione's words. "That sounds very plausible." He glanced at Desjani, who nodded back reluctantly. "There may be another reason, too. I'll bet you that right now the commander of that pursuit force knows there's a big reception party waiting for us at Yuon. He's figuring he'll come through to Yuon on our heels, while we're trying to fight our way through that ambush, and finish us. So he or she doesn't want to talk surrender when he or she sees themself as on the way to being the Hero of Yuon."

"That is certainly possible as well," Rione agreed.

He took another look at the display, pulling out the scale so that almost all of the Corvus Star System was visible on it, the Alliance fleet and the Syndic pursuit force both reduced to mere dots crawling across the great distances between jump exit and the new jump point. The Alliance force was most of the way through Corvus now, only a day away from being able to jump to hoped-for safety at Kaliban. *Which reminds me. There's some important unfinished business to attend to.* "I'll be in my stateroom."

Geary swept past Rione, who gave him a look that was just a shade shy of suspicion. Once safely alone, he began calling up the list of names Captain Duellos had forwarded to him, looking for a new commander for *Arrogant*. He'd vowed that Commander Vebos wouldn't be the captain of that ship when they left Corvus, and he meant to fulfill that vow.

With an entire fleet to draw from, there were plenty of

candidates. However, Duellos had taken the trouble to highlight certain names. Geary, checking the names against their service records and whatever brief memories (if any) he had of the individuals, realized those names belonged to officers who were good at their jobs but not among the worshippers of Black Jack Geary.

One caught his eye. Commander Hatherian, currently weapons officer on the *Orion*. One of Numos's officers, which would've made Hatherian automatically suspect in Geary's eyes. In Geary's experience, people like Numos tended to surround themselves with subordinates who were at least willing to pretend they thought their boss was the brightest star in the heavens. But Duellos thought Hatherian was worth considering. And Hatherian's last fitness report from Numos had been good but not glowing. Clearly, Hatherian wasn't Numos's favorite.

Hmmm. Hatherian's a commander. So is Vebos. I was wondering what to do with Vebos.

Geary crafted a pair of messages with great care, finally downloading them and then returning to the bridge where Rione still sat, her and Captain Desjani both apparently oblivious to the other's presence. "I'm sending orders to *Arrogant* and *Orion*," Geary informed Desjani.

"Yes, sir." Desjani obviously wondered why she needed to be told that, but she read the outgoing messages and then fought to keep her expression unremarkable. "Do you anticipate any trouble having these orders followed?"

"Not on *Orion*'s part." If he'd judged Numos right, the man thought himself an inspiring leader. Even if Captain Numos didn't think too highly of Commander Hatherian, Numos would likely assume that Hatherian would be more loyal to Numos than Geary. Having himself worked for people like Numos, Geary knew things often didn't work that way. Getting out from under such a commander was often a great relief, and little if any loyalty flowed from the past association.

Geary sat down, waiting.

Less than an hour later, a shuttle left *Orion*, heading for

Arrogant. Desjani ran some figures. "It'll take the shuttle about two hours to reach *Arrogant.*"

"I'll be back." Geary headed out, forcing himself back down to another mess area to pretend to eat another meal and pretend to be confident of their return to Alliance space. Then he vainly attempted to rest for a while before returning to the bridge.

"*Orion*'s shuttle is still a half hour out from *Arrogant.*"

"Thank you, Captain Desjani. Has *Arrogant* sent any messages to the shuttle?"

"No, sir. As far as we can tell, *Arrogant* hasn't acknowledged the shuttle at all."

Geary drummed his fingers on his chair arm, pondering what options he had if Vebos continued to act like an idiot. There were several, but he didn't want the situation to escalate any worse than it absolutely had to. Reaching a decision, he tapped in a communications address that was becoming all too familiar. "Colonel Carabali, I have a shuttle en route to *Arrogant* from *Orion.*"

"Yes, sir." Carabali eyed him, obviously curious as to why she should care.

"The shuttle carries Commander Hatherian to relieve Commander Vebos as commanding officer of *Arrogant.* Commander Vebos has orders to report to *Orion* as that ship's new weapons officer."

"Yes, sir."

"You're familiar with the fleet tradition of sideboys, Colonel Carabali?"

"Yes, sir."

"It occurs to me that it would be a nice gesture if your detachment of Marines onboard *Arrogant* were to give the departing commanding officer a ceremonial send off."

Carabali, who'd doubtless spent a career dealing with odd requests from superior officers, managed to keep from looking startled. "Sir?"

"Yes." Geary smiled in what he hoped was a benign manner. "Like sideboys. I think it would be a good thing if your Marines onboard *Arrogant* reported to Commander

Vebos and informed him that they were there to escort him
to the shuttle."

Colonel Carabali nodded slowly. "All of my Marines on
Arrogant? You want them to find Commander Vebos and
tell him they're . . . sort of an honor guard."

"Yes. Exactly. An honor guard. To escort him off the
ship."

"And if Commander Vebos declines to avail himself of
that honor? What should my Marines do then?"

"Should that happen," Geary stated, "have them maintain position around Command Vebos while they contact
you and you contact me. We'll decide on the proper way to
persuade Commander Vebos to accept the honor based on
the exact situation."

"Yes, sir. I will issue the necessary orders, sir. I assume
there's no chance of weapons-release authority being
given?"

Geary tried hard not to smile. Colonel Carabali hadn't
forgotten that it had been Vebos who had ordered the bombardment of her troops. "No weapons, Colonel. If we have
to, we'll frog-march him off the *Arrogant*. But I think even
Commander Vebos will realize his options are limited
when he's surrounded by Marines. Besides, he's going to
Orion."

Carabali's face lit with understanding. "I see. Yes. That
should help. I'll keep you informed, Captain Geary." Carabali saluted, and her image vanished.

Geary leaned back to see Desjani watching him and trying not to smile. "An honor guard?" she wondered.

"Yes," Geary replied with all the dignity he could
muster.

"Why to *Orion*, if I may ask?"

Geary looked around to make sure no one could hear
and lowered his voice. "It seemed one way to minimize the
number of places I need to keep my eye on. Besides, it
gives Numos the opportunity to work with Vebos. And
vice versa."

"I understand. They deserve each other. *Orion*'s shuttle

is on final approach. *Arrogant* still hasn't acknowledged it."

Arrogant, being smaller than *Orion*, didn't have a shuttle dock. Instead, the shuttle swung close to *Arrogant*'s main airlock, extended a mating tube and moored to the outside of *Arrogant*.

"According to our remote readings, *Arrogant*'s airlock hasn't opened yet."

Geary checked the time. "I haven't heard anything from Colonel Carabali. Let's give it a few minutes."

Five minutes later, Colonel Carabali called in, her expression carefully composed. "Commander Vebos and his honor guard are enroute to the airlock on *Arrogant*."

Geary nodded back solemnly. "Any problems?"

"Nothing that a dozen Marines in full dress uniform couldn't overawe. Though I must admit that the deciding factor was probably that *Arrogant*'s crew appeared unresponsive to Commander Vebos's orders regarding the matter."

"Naturally. They know Commander Hatherian has been appointed their new commanding officer. Commander Vebos no longer has command authority over them."

"Yes, sir," the Colonel agreed. "They don't appear to be in great distress over losing Commander Vebos."

"Somehow that doesn't come as a great shock to me, Colonel."

Geary glanced over at Desjani as she interjected. "*Arrogant*'s airlock has opened," Desjani reported. "Commander Hatherian is exiting. Commander Vebos is being marched— Excuse me, Commander Vebos is being escorted aboard the shuttle by his honor guard." Several moments passed. "The honor guard is leaving the shuttle. *Arrogant*'s airlock is closing."

Geary nodded to Carabali's image. "Thank you for the services of your Marines, Colonel."

Carabali saluted. "It was our pleasure, sir."

The shuttle detached from *Arrogant* and began making its way back to *Orion*. Geary felt a moment's pity for the crew of the shuttle, who were confined with a doubtlessly very unhappy Commander Vebos until they could off-load him. Then he pulled back the scale on his display, looking back to see the Syndic pursuers very slowly gaining on the Alliance fleet, and then ahead to where the jump point waited. *If only every thing I had to do could be as neatly and quickly done as removing Vebos from command.*

In seven more hours, the Alliance fleet would reach the jump point and bid farewell to Corvus. Assuming nothing went wrong before then. Assuming *Titan*'s propulsion systems didn't shift into full reverse and then fall off and spiral into a mini–black hole to be lost forever. Geary thought through that scenario twice, realized he'd not only thought of it but was actually taking it half-seriously, and realized just how tired he was. "I'm going to try to get some sleep."

He stood and headed off the bridge, slightly surprised to see Co-President Rione still in the observer's seat. She gave him an arch look as he passed. "An interesting show, Captain Geary."

"You mean the bit with Vebos?"

"Yes. I assume that was meant to encourage the others?"

He frowned, trying to remember where he'd heard the phrase. "Not exactly. Vebos demonstrated he isn't smart enough to be entrusted with command of a ship. That's not about me. It's about looking out for the crew of *Arrogant*, and looking out for anyone depending on *Arrogant* for anything."

Rione gave him back a look with just a trace of skepticism apparent. Geary flicked the briefest possible smile at her, then left the bridge.

He was back several hours later, having ensured the bridge would give him a wake-up call, when the Alliance fleet jumped out of the Corvus Star System, the Syndic pursuit force still far behind them.

• • •

HE'D been watching the strange lights in jump space for a while, slumped in a seat in his stateroom, knowing he had a couple of weeks ahead transiting jump space before he and the rest of the Alliance fleet would learn what, if anything, awaited them at Kaliban. *So much I need to do, and so little ability to do it in jump since I have only most rudimentary communications capability with the rest of the fleet until we return to normal space. I ought to just rest. Try to regain the strength I've never recovered since they woke me up from that survival pod.*

The fleet medics, *tsking* over Geary's physical state, had prescribed certain medications, exercise, and rest. Try to avoid stress, they'd advised. Geary had just stared at them, trying to figure out if they had any idea how ridiculous the prescription was in his case.

What made it all worse was the fact that he couldn't be sure how much weakness he could reveal to anyone else. Desjani worshipped the space he traversed, but Geary still didn't know how she'd take it if she truly came to be convinced that Geary wasn't a hero sent from the living stars. It'd be different if he had a long-term working relationship with Desjani or any other officer. But having almost literally fallen into the fleet from out of the past, he really knew none of them well.

Rione didn't worship Geary and would probably be unsurprised to hear Geary's worries. She might even have good advice, since so far Geary had been impressed by the quality of her thinking. But he still didn't know how much he could trust the Co-President of the Callas Republic. The last thing he needed was a politician knowing his secrets and capable of trading them to his enemies for whatever political advantage they might bring.

No one he could talk to, no one he could share the burden of command with.

No, that wasn't true. As a matter of fact, there was someone he was overdue for a conversation with. *Fine one I am to talk about honoring our ancestors when I haven't*

*even paid my formal respects to them since I was woken up
out of survival sleep.*

He called up directions to the right area of *Dauntless*,
certain that despite everything else that might've changed
there would still be the place he was looking for on the
ship. And there was. Checking the time to make sure the
area wouldn't be crowded at the moment, Geary pulled
himself out of the chair, straightened his uniform, took a
deep breath, then headed for the ancestral area.

Two decks down and near the *Dauntless*'s centerline,
the place Geary was heading for was located in one of the
most protected areas of the ship. Geary paused outside the
hatch leading into the ancestral area, grateful for the lack
of anyone else present to see him entering, then pushed
through, finding himself facing a comfortingly familiar series of small rooms. He picked an unoccupied one at random, closing the soundproofed door carefully, then taking
a seat on the traditional wooden bench facing the small
shelf on which a single candle rested. Picking up the
lighter on the shelf, he lit the candle, then sat watching it
silently for a while.

Finally, he sighed. "Honored ancestors. Sorry I've
taken so long," Geary apologized, speaking to the spirits
who'd supposedly been drawn by the candle's light and
warmth. "I should've rendered honors to my ancestors
some time ago, but as I'm sure you know, things have been
busy. And I've been dealing with many things I never expected to have to face. That's no excuse, but I hope you'll
accept my apologies."

He paused. "Maybe you've been wondering where I
was all this time. Maybe you knew. Maybe Michael Geary
has filled you in by now, if, as I fear, he died on his ship.
Let me tell you, he did you proud. Please tell him I wish
we'd had more time together.

"A lot of time has passed since I last spoke to you.
There've been a lot of changes. Most if not all of those
changes seem to have been for the worse. That's what I believe, anyway. I can't pretend I don't need all the guidance

and reassurance I can get these days. Whatever you can provide, I'll be grateful for. Thanks for whatever help you've provided in getting us this far."

Geary paused again, wondering not for the first time why speaking to his ancestors almost always brought comfort. He wouldn't have described himself as a deep believer of any kind, but nonetheless always felt that someone was listening at such times. And if a man couldn't trust his ancestors with confidences, who could he trust? "This is very difficult. I'm doing my best, but I'm not at all sure my best will be good enough. There's a lot of people depending on me. Some of them are going to die. I can't pretend that won't happen. Even if I somehow do absolutely everything just right, some ships are going to be lost before this fleet gets home. If I make mistakes—" He stopped, thinking of *Repulse*. "If I make more mistakes, a lot of these people could die.

"It's a long way back to Alliance space. I can't even be sure what we'll find if we get there. Hopefully I can tie up enough of the Syndicate Worlds fleet trying to catch us that they won't be able to exploit our defeat at the Syndicate home world. But we'll have no way of knowing whether the Syndics have gone after the Alliance using the advantage gained by their victory and by us being trapped out here, not until we get close enough to home to have a chance of getting fairly recent intelligence."

He paused again. "It's not that I'm worried about what'll happen to me. I feel like I should've died a century ago. But I can't give in to that feeling because I do care about what happens to the people who've placed so much trust in me. Please help me make the right decisions and do the right things, so I lose as few ships and sailors as possible. I swear I'll try my best to do right by you and by the living."

Geary sat for a while longer, watching the candle burn, then reached out, snuffed the flame, stood, and walked out of the room.

As he left the area, several sailors saw him. He nodded

in greeting while they watched him with awed expressions. *Hell, I ought to be one of the dead ancestors people are talking to, instead of walking these decks. They know that.*

But the sailors didn't act like they'd seen someone who didn't belong here. A couple of them saluted with the stiff awkwardness of someone who'd recently learned the gesture. Geary found himself smiling as he returned the salutes. Then he caught a flash of wariness in the eyes of two other sailors and his smile vanished. His own people shouldn't be afraid of him. "Is something wrong?"

The sailor he'd addressed went white. "N-no, sir."

Geary eyed the man for a moment. "Are you sure? You seem to have concerns. If you need to discuss them privately, I've got some time."

The sailor was still groping for a reply when his companion cleared her throat. "Sir, it's none of our business."

"Really?" Geary looked around, reading the disquiet in the others. "I'd like to know what's bothering you anyway."

The woman paled slightly as well, then spoke haltingly. "It's just, seeing you here. There'd been some talk."

"Talk?" Geary tried to keep from frowning. He didn't like making a public spectacle of his belief, but this seemed to be something beyond that. "About what?"

One of the sailors who'd saluted answered while he gave the worried ones an annoyed glance. "Sir, nobody'd seen you here since, uh, since we picked you up. And since we left the Syndic home system, well, sir, some people thought maybe what happened there had something to do with that."

Geary hoped he didn't look as annoyed as felt by the vagueness of the statement. "What in particular?" Then it struck him. "You mean *Repulse,* don't you?" The expressions on the sailors answered his question better than words could have. "You mean because my grandnephew probably died on *Repulse.*"

He looked down, momentarily not wishing to look at the others, and shook his head. "Did you think I was afraid to come here and deal with him? Deal with that?" Geary raised his head and once again read the answer in their expressions. "I don't know how much you all know, but Captain Michael J. Geary volunteered to keep *Repulse* back and hold off the Syndics. If he hadn't done that, I might've had to order it, because that would've been my responsibility, but I didn't order it. I didn't have to. He and his crew voluntarily sacrificed themselves for the rest of us."

Their faces told Geary they hadn't known that. *Great. They've been thinking that I'd ordered my grandnephew to his death. The hell of it is that I might've really had to do that.* "I have nothing to fear facing my ancestors. No more than anyone else, I guess. There's just been a lot going on. That's why I haven't been down here before."

"Of course, sir," one sailor replied quickly.

"You're not afraid of anything, are you, sir?" another asked in a rush.

One of my worshippers, Geary thought. *How do I answer that?* "Like anyone else, I'm worried about doing my best. It keeps me on my toes." He grinned to show it was meant to be a joke, and the sailors laughed on cue. Now all he had to do was get out of this conversation as quickly as possible without being too obvious about it. "I'm sorry to have kept you from your own observances."

The sailors offered a chorus of replies indicating the fault was theirs and then made way for Geary. He noted as he passed that the two worried sailors seemed much more comfortable around him now. To his own surprise, he realized he felt a little more comfortable around them. Perhaps, in his own way, he had been shying away from dealing with what had happened to *Repulse,* but by openly stating his feelings to others, he'd come to accept it somewhat.

He walked on toward his stateroom, feeling that the burdens on him were, for the moment, a bit lighter.

"CAPTAIN Geary, may I speak privately with you?"

Geary closed out the item he'd been working on, one of the simulations he wanted the fleet to use in practice for battle once it arrived at Kaliban. It was an older program, one whose ancestral forerunner he'd been familiar with a long time ago, but even this much newer version hadn't been updated for a while. He wanted the simulation parameters to match the state of this fleet and what he'd seen of Syndic capabilities nowadays. But there was still plenty of time to get that done before the fleet reached Kaliban, whereas Captain Desjani was doubtless stealing time from her duties as *Dauntless*'s commanding officer in order to talk to him now. "Of course."

Desjani paused as if ordering her thoughts. "I know this happened almost a week ago, but I was hoping you would tell me why you chose to send the crews of the Syndic merchant ships to safety. I understand your feelings regarding treatment of prisoners, but those individuals were not in uniform. They were in civilian garb. That made them saboteurs at best, and such people are not covered by the laws of war." She seemed done, but hastily added one more sentence. "I'm not questioning your decision, of course."

"Captain Desjani, I count on you to question me when you don't understand why I'm doing something. You may know something I need to know." Geary screwed his eyes shut for a moment and kneaded his forehead in an attempt to relieve the tension that had sprung up inside. "You're right, of course, that we weren't obligated to try to save the lives of those people. In fact, we could've executed the lot of them and not be held at fault." He grinned crookedly. "You didn't ask this directly, but I'll answer it anyway. I'm certain that your ancestors and mine wouldn't have looked askance at us if those Syndics had been dealt with in a much harsher and more permanent manner."

He could see the puzzlement in Desjani's eyes. "Then, why, sir? They were planning to kill many of our sailors, and destroy or disable some of our ships, in a sneak attack under the guise of civilians. Why show them mercy?"

"That's a valid question." Geary sighed and waved toward the starscape still displayed on one bulkhead. "I could say that sometimes it's good for the soul to show mercy when none is required or expected. I don't know about you, but sometimes I think my soul needs all the help it can get." Desjani looked momentarily startled, then smiled as if she'd decided Geary was joking. "But that's far from the only reason," Geary continued. "I had some very practical grounds for letting them go."

"Practical grounds?" Desjani looked from Geary to the starscape.

"Yeah." Geary hunched forward, pointing at the pictured stars. "What happened here is going to be heard about in every other Syndic system sooner or later. Oh, there'll be an official version in which the Alliance fleet was planning to crater the hell out of every population center in the Corvus System, only to be repulsed by the gallantry of the Syndic defenders. They'd put out that kind of nonsense regardless of what we did.

"However, even the Syndics can't stop unofficial news from making its way around. So what are Syndic populations in other systems going to hear through the grapevine? That we didn't try to bombard any cities. Of course, they might think that's because we didn't have time. But they'll also hear that we treated their people right when we made them prisoner. When we had the power to do anything we wanted to do, we respected the lives of every Syndic who came into our power."

Desjani let doubt show. "Surely the Syndics won't care. They'll probably see that as a sign of weakness."

"Will they?" Geary shrugged. "That's possible. It's possible that anything we did would've been seen as a sign of weakness. I remember being told that mistreating prisoners would be interpreted as a sign that we were too weak to stick to the rules, too frightened to risk any possible advantage."

"Really?" Desjani stared at him in open surprise.

"Yeah." Geary let his thoughts wander for a moment,

remembering a room and a lecture far distant in space and time. "That was what I was taught, that sticking to the rules would convey a sense of strength and confidence. I suppose that's arguable. But in practical terms right now, I believe that at a minimum, someone, somewhere, may treat Alliance prisoners better as a result of what we did. More directly important to us, someone we're fighting might not be as afraid of surrendering instead of fighting to the death. They're going to hear that we treated surrendered combatants right, that we avoided harming civilians, that we didn't cut a path of destruction through Corvus System, that even when sorely provoked, we only struck back directly at those who ordered a sneak attack on us. Somewhere along the line, someone who we need something from may remember that."

Desjani looked uncertain again. "I can see where that could possibly work to our advantage the next time we try to acquire supplies from a Syndic system we're passing through. But they're still Syndics, Captain Geary. They won't change their policies because we act differently."

"Won't they? I suppose their leaders might not. Between you and me, I detest the Syndic leaders I've encountered so far." Desjani grinned, doubtless reassured by Geary's statement. "But I'm sure there'll be no doubt in the minds of anyone who hears about this fleet, or sees this fleet, that we're not weak. They'll know we chose not to do certain acts that we could've done." Geary stared at the stars, feeling an edge of the coldness inside him again as he thought about the century of time and events that separated him from Desjani. "Ancestors help me, Tanya, the Syndic population is human, too. They've also got to be feeling the strain of this war. They've got to be sick to death of sending their sons and daughters and husbands and wives off to die in an apparently endless conflict." He looked directly at her. "Let's face it, we don't have much to lose by letting the average Syndic know we'll deal fairly with them."

"What about the fanatics who were willing to die? Surely they'll just make another such attempt."

"They might," Geary agreed. "But they went off antici- pating a glorious death. Instead, they came home uncon- scious, and their ships tore up their own bases. No glory there. What some of them got instead was death at the hands of their own side. Maybe all that'll make the next set of suicide volunteers a little less enthusiastic. When some- one's ready to die, killing them just furthers their own ob- jectives. Mind you, I'll grant their wish if it comes to that, but I'll do it on my terms. I don't want their deaths inspir- ing anyone."

Desjani smiled slowly. "You frustrated the Syndics' plan for a strike against the fleet, and frustrated the desire of some fanatics to die in the course of striking or trying to strike that blow. None of them got what they wanted."

"No." Geary looked at the stars again, wondering where among them the major elements of the Syndic fleet were currently located, and where those Syndic forces were cur- rently heading in their attempt to find and destroy the Al- liance fleet. "If they want to die at our hands so bad, they'll have to find another opportunity. And if it comes to that, we'll accommodate them. On our terms."

EIGHT

NOTHING.

They left jump space at full alert, ready for the worst, knowing they might find mines laid in their paths and a Syndic fleet right behind the mines. Knowing they might have to fight their way through that fleet if they wanted to survive another day. But only emptiness greeted the nervous searches of Alliance targeting systems.

The Kaliban Star System, as far as the best instruments available to the Alliance could tell, was totally lifeless. Nothing alive that could be seen, no spacecraft in motion, and not even the feeble warmth given off by a single piece of equipment even in standby mode could be detected. There had been people living here once, but now everything in Kaliban was cold, everything in Kaliban was silent.

"No mines, praise our ancestors," Captain Desjani exulted. "That means our arrival here was totally unexpected. You outguessed them, Captain Geary."

"I guess I did." *No sense in false modesty. We came here because I said so, and only because I said so.* "Kaliban's not much of a place now, is it?"

"It never was much of a place."

Five planets, two of them so small they barely qualified for the name. All hostile to human habitation because of temperatures either far too low or far too high, and atmospheres either nonexistent or toxic. Plus the usual assortment of rocks and ice balls, though even those didn't seem very numerous or noteworthy compared to other star systems. Nonetheless, people had built homes here. Kaliban didn't have anything special at all, except for the gravity well provided by its star that made jump points work. Geary could imagine the human history of Kaliban's system easily, because the same things had happened in so many other places.

Ships had been forced to come through Kaliban to get to other places before the hypernet. And because there'd been ships coming through, there'd been a shipyard or two or three built to handle emergencies and provide maintenance or supplies to the passing ships, as well as work on the ships that stayed in-system to transport workers and their families. The shipyards and the families had needed some services, so small towns had grown up in a few places. Buried under the soil of a hostile world or burrowed out of a large asteroid, they'd provided the things small towns had always provided. Some of the ships coming through would carry passengers or cargo bound for Kaliban. And of course there'd been mines to provide local raw materials instead of hauling mass from another star, and people to work in the mines, and a local government to keep things under control, and representatives of the central Syndic authority to keep the local government under control.

The rest Geary knew only from what he'd heard. The hypernet had come into existence and the ships didn't need to come through Kaliban, or the innumerable systems like it, anymore. The shipyards had closed as their lifeblood dwindled to a trickle, and without those jobs the small towns started dying. Once there'd been no particular reason to come to Kaliban except for the jump points. Now there wasn't any reason to stay at Kaliban. *How many years did the last holdouts hang on? Maybe not all that long. In a Syndic system, everyone would've been a company employee of some sort, and companies cut their losses long before most individual people are willing to give up. There's no one left now. All the installations we can see are cold. No energy usage, no environmental systems working. They shut down everything. I guess the last person who left Kaliban remembered to turn off the lights.*

Measured in the life span of a star, the human presence here had lasted the barest flicker of a moment. For some reason, seeing that and knowing it brought the sense of cold back to Geary.

Then he shook it off. Every sailor learned one thing quickly, and that one thing was that everything about space was inhuman. The sheer size of it, the emptiness of it, the death it carried everywhere except for those very, very small places amid the emptiness where humans could walk on a planet's surface with their faces bare to the wind and breathe the air. *It isn't good and it isn't bad,* the old saying went, *it just is.*

It's too big for us, and we're only here for the blink of eye as far as it's concerned, an old chief had told Geary when he was so young an officer it almost hurt to remember. *Someday, any day, it could take you, because even though it doesn't care about us, it'll kill us in an instant if it can. Then, if your prayers to the living stars are answered, you'll get to go live forever in their warmth and light. If not, you'd best make the best of the life you've got. Speaking of which, did I ever tell you about the time my old ship visited Virago? Now that was a party*

Geary became aware he was smiling, recalling that old chief and the often outrageous space stories he'd told. "Captain Desjani, I'm planning on putting the fleet in orbit around Kaliban. Please let me know if you have any recommendations regarding the exact orbit."

She gave him a mildly surprised look. "We're going to stay here?"

"Long enough to see what sort of equipment and materials the Syndics might've abandoned out here." He'd reviewed the status of the fleet's ships during the jump from Corvus and hadn't been happy to see how low some ships were getting on essentials. Nobody was close to critical yet, but then they were nowhere close to getting home, either. And there was something else he needed to do that required the ships to be in normal space. Something that had to be done before the fleet faced battle again.

Desjani nodded. "Good thing the food stockpiles at the Syndic base in Corvus were available. It seems unlikely we'll find much food here."

"I agree." Geary pondered his options, then ordered his ships to cut their speed to one hundredth of the speed of light and let the Alliance fleet drift slowly inward toward Kaliban. That would allow time to evaluate what the fleet's sensors were telling him about the shut-down Syndic facilities in the system. Time to learn what the Syndics might've left behind that his fleet could use. And time to talk to his ship commanders.

Captain Duellos called in. "I recommend posting some battle cruisers at the jump exit again to guard it."

Geary shook his head. "Not this time. I want the fleet together. We can't be positioned to exploit whatever the Syndics left in this system and also be positioned to support a force guarding the jump exit."

"Very well, Captain Geary."

Desjani gave Geary a hard-to-read look. "Duellos never liked Admiral Bloch, you know."

"I didn't know."

"He didn't think Bloch made wise decisions. It's interesting to see Duellos agreeing so readily to your decisions."

Geary smiled tightly. "I guess I haven't made too many mistakes yet."

Desjani grinned, then turned to study a message coming in on her display. "My operations officer recommends we take up position in the system at this orbital location."

Geary craned to look, seeing an area about two light-hours in-system from the jump exit. He compared the location to the orbits of the Syndic facilities that had already been spotted, then nodded. "Looks good for now. Let's head for there. Please let the other ships know the orbit we're planning to take up and that they should maintain formation on *Dauntless*."

"Yes, sir." Desjani started giving the necessary orders while Geary bent to his display, studying the data coming in.

He'd barely begun considering the reports being received on what could be learned about the Syndic facilities, and realizing he'd have to send scout teams down to find out enough about what was actually present at most of them, when he received a call from the commanding officer of *Titan*. *Great. Now what's wrong?*

But there wasn't any urgency or worry on the face of the officer calling Geary. *Titan*'s Captain seemed far too young for the job, but he acted and sounded confident enough. "Greetings, Captain Geary."

"Greetings. Is this about a problem with *Titan*?"

"No, sir. We're making more progress on the damage every day and have full propulsion capability back."

Geary actually smiled slightly at the news. "That's a relief. I have to admit that *Titan*'s been on my mind a lot."

Titan's Captain got the reference, making an exaggerated flinch. "We appreciate the efforts of our many escorts in keeping us safe. Well, relatively safe. We had considerable damage to deal with and appreciated not having to add to the list of things that needed fixed."

Geary grinned this time. The lack of opposition in the Kallban Star System had left him feeling in very good humor for once. "I can understand that. You've done a great job repairing your ship. What can I do for you now?"

"I'd like to offer a suggestion and a request." A small window popped up with a depiction of Kaliban's system. "We've been able to confirm that there were mining facilities here."

"Yeah. All shut down like everything else, of course."

"Yes, but assuming they're intact, I've got people who ought to be able to reactivate the automated mining equipment. From the looks of things, Kaliban's inhabitants never could've made a big dent in the supply of metals in the system, and we could really use those metals to fabricate new parts and weapons for the ships of this fleet."

Geary leaned back, considering the suggestion. "Can you refine whatever ore we get, or would we need to reactivate Syndic metal-handling facilities?"

Titan's Captain waved a dismissive hand. "Not a problem, sir. I'm certain of it. Some of the mines we've spotted are on asteroids. That means veins of pure metal. It won't need refining or purifying. We'd have to work it into alloys, but we can do that."

"How long? How long to reactivate the mines, get the metal out, and get it loaded on *Titan*? And I assume some of the other auxiliaries can use it, too?"

For the first time, *Titan*'s commanding officer hesitated. "If everything goes perfectly, I can have metals coming aboard in one week. And, yes, there are other ships in the auxiliary force that can use the metals as well. I know there's a risk involved in hanging around the system, but with that metal we could fabricate a lot of what we need to keep going."

Geary looked down, thinking. *If everything doesn't go perfectly, and it probably won't, then it'll be more than a week. Unfortunately, I have no real idea how long it'll take the Syndics to realize we went to Kaliban, and how long after that to get a significant combat force here. So it'll be a gamble. But I was planning to spend some time in this system anyway. And if I don't take this gamble, who knows when we'll have another opportunity to resupply the workshops on those auxiliaries?*

Speaking of the auxiliaries, who's in command of that division of ships? Who should've been the one calling me with this suggestion? Geary tapped some controls, feeling a surge of satisfaction when he managed to hit the right commands and the right data popped up in front of him. "One last question, I understand the commander of the auxiliaries division is Captain Gundel of the *Jinn*. Why isn't he making this proposal on behalf of all the ships that can benefit?"

Geary was certain he caught a very quick flash of guilt in the eyes of *Titan*'s Captain. "Captain Gundel is very busy, sir. There are many issues demanding his immediate attention."

"I see." *At least I think I do.* "Very well. Start preparations for putting this plan of yours into motion. Let me know before you launch any teams to physically check the mining facilities."

"Aye, aye, sir."

Geary spent a few moments staring at the space where the image had been while he thought about his options. Then he shrugged and called Captain Gundel directly. The watch on the bridge of the *Jinn* answered quickly, but there was a long delay before Gundel finally came on, looking cross. He'd plainly served in the fleet a long time, his uniform reflecting an odd mix of obsessiveness in the display of his many decorations and carelessness in the wearing. "Yes? What is it?"

Geary couldn't help noticing that despite Gundel's bellicose nature, none of Gundel's decorations were for heroism in combat. He kept his expression bland but raised one eyebrow. "Captain Gundel, this is Captain Geary, the fleet commander."

"I know that. What do you want?"

Give me much more talk like that, and I'll want you strung up by your heels. "I need a recommended course of action regarding reactivating the shut-down Syndic mining facilities in order to get raw materials for the auxiliaries."

Gundel's mouth worked irritably. "It'll need study. Say, one month. I may be able to complete a preliminary survey of those facilities and have a draft recommendation to you by then."

"I want it today, Captain Gundel."

"*Today?* Impossible."

Geary waited for a moment but Gundel obviously wasn't going to suggest any alternatives. "What are *Jinn*'s highest priority needs at this moment?"

Gundel blinked, apparently caught off guard by the question. "I can have that to you within a few days. Perhaps."

"You're commanding officer of *Jinn.* You should know that off the top of your head."

"I have many responsibilities! You and I obviously do not view the responsibilities of a division commander in the same light!"

You and I obviously don't view who's in command of this fleet in the same light. But Geary kept his face calm despite the heat rising inside him. "Thank you, Captain Gundel."

He broke the connection, knowing the abrupt ending would annoy Gundel no end, then spent some more time staring into space. If Gundel acted this way toward his superiors, it wasn't too hard to imagine how he treated subordinates. Which could be something you had to accept with a very competent officer, but not with someone who seemed lacking and refused to respond to clear direction. It seemed obvious that Gundel had to go, but relieving a senior officer like him would have to be done in a way that didn't give people like Captain Numos any excuses to foment more anger against Geary. Up and out would be the most diplomatic and direct way, but how to do that in a fleet that didn't have positions to promote the old fool into?

What would that old chief of mine have said? Besides "get drunk and see if it's better in the morning" that is. Wait. Regulations. He said you could always find something in regulations to justify what you wanted to do. That advice always worked for me before.

Geary called up the fleet regulations and started doing keyword searches, skimming the texts for whatever would serve his purpose. To his own surprise, the answer popped up fairly quickly. *But do I want to do that?* He turned to the personnel files, calling up data on the commanders of the other ships in the auxiliaries division. *Titan*'s commander was, as Geary had thought, pretty junior for such a position even given the relative youth of fleet officers nowadays. It helped explain his eagerness, and his rashness in going straight to Geary with his proposal on the Syndic mining facilities. On the other hand, Gundel was very senior to be commanding the smaller *Jinn*. *The difference between a competent, ambitious officer who's eager to get things done and one who just wants to hide in a comfortable burrow.*

But then there was Captain Tyrosian of the *Witch*. Experienced, but not exceptionally so. Highly rated as an engineer, good marks as an officer, senior enough to be qualified for higher command. She looked good on paper, for whatever that was worth.

Geary put in another call. Captain Tyrosian, on her bridge, was immediately available. She gave Geary a respectful look, though Geary thought he could see wariness in her eyes. "Yes, sir?"

Proper etiquette. That gives her points right off. "I'm just checking with auxiliaries commanders personally. How's *Witch* doing?"

"As our reports say, sir. We sustained little damage during the battle in the Syndic home system, so most of our work right now is aimed at rebuilding the fleet's supply of expendable weapons."

"How are you doing on supplies of raw materials?"

Captain Tyrosian didn't hesitate. "We need more."

"How long would it take you to give me a report on options for acquiring more?"

She eyed him with even more wariness. "Sir, I could produce that whenever you ask for it, but such a request should come through my division commander."

Very good, Captain Tyrosian. You know what's going on, you're willing to do what you're told, and you're will-

ing to remind me that I need to abide by the chain of command. "Thank you, Captain Tyrosian."

Geary checked the time. Give it a decent interval. Two hours.

He spent the interval working on his battle-training scenarios, as the fleet proceeded at a relaxed pace deeper into the Kaliban System, then Geary called *Jinn* once more. "Captain Gundel."

Gundel seemed even more irritable than he had before. "I have a lot of things I should be doing."

"Then you'll be happy to hear what I have to say, Captain Gundel. I've realized I need someone working on identifying the long-range needs of this fleet. Someone with the experience to put together everything that's needed into a comprehensive product, even if that takes a long time." Geary smiled at Gundel, who seemed to be trying to look approving of Geary's attitude in a patronizing sort of way. "But if that officer is constantly distracted by other responsibilities, they won't be able to focus on what needs to be done. Therefore, I'm appointing you to my staff, Captain Gundel, as chief engineering advisor." Geary smiled again.

Gundel seemed shocked now.

"Of course," Geary continued in a slightly apologetic voice, "you realize that fleet regulations prohibit having anyone in charge of a ship or higher level command being also assigned to a staff position. Too much distraction, too many conflicting responsibilities. A professional like you certainly understands. So in order for me to have the exclusive benefit of your advice, you'll have to relinquish command of *Jinn*. You'll need a good working office to produce your report for me, and I know a smaller ship like *Jinn* doesn't have much to spare, so you'll need to transfer to *Titan*. I'll make sure you get a good office on board her. And, also of course, since you'll not be in command of *Jinn* anymore, that'll make Captain Tyrosian of *Witch* the auxiliaries division commander."

Gundel simply stared back, speechless.

"No questions, then? Excellent. Since we're under time pressure here, please ensure you turn over command of *Jinn* to your executive officer prior to midnight. You'll transfer to *Titan* tomorrow."

At last, Gundel found his voice again. "You . . . you can't—"

"Yes, I can." Geary let his face grow stern and his voice get harsh. "My orders will be transmitted to *Titan*, *Jinn*, and *Witch* as soon as this conversation ends. I assume no officer of your experience would dream of balking at direct orders to proceed to a new assignment?" Geary paused, knowing his words would bring to Gundel's mind the example of Commander Vebos, former commander of the *Arrogant*. Then he held his peace a moment longer to let Gundel think through the advantages for an officer like Gundel of no longer holding command responsibility and being able to devote himself to an endless research project without any taint of having been relieved for cause. Geary could see Gundel's expression shift as the realization hit him that this was a great opportunity for an officer of his limited ambitions. "Will there be any problems?"

"No. Not at all." Geary watched as Gundel's eyes shifted again as he thought through the options once more, then as Gundel nodded to himself and regained his composure. "A wise use of personnel. I deeply regret leaving *Jinn*, it goes without saying."

"Of course."

"But my executive officer has been well trained by me. He should be able to benefit from having watched my period in command and make a capable commanding officer for *Jinn*."

"That's good to know."

"I believe Captain Tyrosian has also benefited from observing me as divisional commander."

"Then there should be no drawbacks," Geary stated, eager to end Gundel's apparently endless stream of self-aggrandizing statements.

"You realize of course that doing a proper job on the report you requested will be a lengthy process."

"You're to take however long it requires." *The longer the better, since that'll keep you out of mine and everyone else's hair.* "Thank you, Captain Gundel." Geary hastily broke the connection before Gundel could say anything else. *With any luck I'll never have to talk to him again. He can work on that report for however many years it takes until he retires and hands it to whatever poor sap has command of the fleet then.*

Geary transmitted the messages he'd prepared, then called *Witch* and *Titan* to personally inform their Captains of the new state of affairs. Captain Tyrosian seemed almost as stunned as Captain Gundel had been. But Tyrosian acknowledged the order to quickly produce a plan for possibly exploiting the Syndic mining facilities, and perked up as she realized she was now division commander and *Witch* was the new division flagship. Geary almost sighed with relief after he ended his conversation with Tyrosian, knowing he could work with her.

Titan's commanding officer, on the other hand, was clearly thrilled at the prospect of being out from under Gundel's thumb, but also just as clearly in dread of having his former divisional commander on his ship for an indefinite period. "He's no longer in your chain of command," Geary stated firmly. "Keep him supplied with all the research material he asks for and give him a nice place to work. You'll probably never see the man."

"Yes, sir. Thank you, sir."

"Thank me?" Geary prodded. "For what?"

The younger officer hesitated. "For not kicking me out the airlock for going over Captain Gundel's head to you, sir."

"If the Syndic mining facilities pan out, it'll be a very good thing for this fleet. You had good reason. But don't make a habit of it."

"I won't, sir."

A few hours later he remembered to call the new commanding officer of *Jinn*. Geary had deliberately moved Gundel to *Titan* to keep him from harassing his replacement in command. The former executive officer seemed competent enough. In fact, Geary was pretty certain he'd been the one actually running *Jinn* while Gundel pretended to be constantly busy. *Jinn*'s new captain managed to hide any happiness he felt at no longer being Gundel's subordinate, but then after working for Gundel, he probably had a lot of experience with hiding his feelings.

Geary glanced at the fleet's position within Kaliban. They'd been gliding slowly into the system for some hours. Even if the Syndic force pursuing them through Corvus had somehow made the decision to jump to Kaliban instead of Yuon, it'd still be quite a few hours from arriving in Kaliban. But the more Geary thought about it, the less he was worried about immediate pursuit. If the Syndics had developed even the slightest suspicion that the Alliance fleet would go to Kaliban, they would've managed to get something to Kaliban to at least detect the Alliance fleet's arrival there. The lack of even a scout ship capable of spotting the Alliance fleet and then fleeing to inform the Syndic command told Geary that the Syndics had thought themselves certain of Alliance intentions and put all of their effort into Yuon and Voss.

Unfortunately, reaching that conclusion meant he could no longer put off something that had needed doing since the fleet had arrived in the system, so Geary reluctantly sent orders to every ship for an immediate meeting with their commanding officers.

The conference room felt huge again, the table running off into the distance, with Geary wondering how long it would take his dislike of holding meetings here to mutate into hate. The virtual meeting process made it too easy to hold meetings, but Geary was slowly realizing it also made holding meetings too hard because it was so easy for everyone to attend and put their oar in if they desired. The software recognized anyone who wanted to speak, regardless of Geary's feelings on the matter, and he couldn't schedule meetings to deliberately make it difficult for his primary adversaries among the fleet captains to attend.

So here we all are again. One big happy family. Geary tried to avoid looking toward Captain Faresa, whom he was certain would be giving him one of her acidic looks. "I wanted to inform you all that my intentions are to remain in Kaliban for a while. We may be able to find useful matériel here, and there's little to no chance of rapid Syndic pursuit."

Captain Faresa interrupted, as Geary had expected her to. "If the Syndics show up here, will the Alliance fleet run away again?"

He gave Faresa a bland look, hoping it would discomfort her. "We didn't run away at Corvus. We declined battle."

"It's the same thing! And to a numerically inferior force!"

Geary tried to judge the attitudes around the table, studying the expressions of captain after captain and getting the feeling that entirely too many of them were betraying sympathy for Faresa's statements. The impression baffled him, but it seemed unmistakable. "If I may remind Captain Faresa, our sole purpose in Corvus was to transit the system in order to reach another jump point. I saw no reason to allow an inferior Syndic force to divert us from our intended plans."

"They believe we ran from them!"

Geary shook his head and smiled very briefly. "The Syndics believe a lot of ridiculous things." To his relief, the comment brought forth laughter from many of the captains. He'd thought over how to approach the issue of what had happened in Corvus if someone tried to make an issue of it, and dismissing the significance of the Syndic force had seemed to be the best angle.

Captain Faresa flushed, but before she could speak again, Captain Numos interceded. "The fact remains that the Syndics surely believe we were *scared* of fighting them."

Geary raised one eyebrow. "*I* wasn't scared of the Syndics." He let the statement hang a moment, while Numos glared daggers at him. "I don't believe in letting the enemy dictate our actions. If we'd turned to fight a battle simply because we were . . . concerned . . . about what the enemy would think, then we'd be letting them determine our course of action."

He pointed toward Faresa and Numos in turn. "I will remind you both that the Syndics knew we'd gone to Corvus. That was the only system we could reach from the jump point we'd used in the Syndic home system." He'd nearly used the word *escaped* but didn't want to feed the accusations that the fleet had run away from battles, even though it was one-hundred-percent true. "That force coming after us was surely only a first wave. There would've been more right behind them. What would we have done with our damaged ships when that second wave appeared? We had no safe harbor in a Syndic system. Any damaged ships would've been doomed along with their crews. How would that serve our cause? How would that serve the people we command? Would you fight a battle to the death of this fleet in an insignificant star system simply out of pride?"

Captain Faresa glared silently back at Geary, but Numos shook his head. "Pride is why this fleet fights. It holds us together. Without pride, we are nothing." His tone clearly conveyed that Geary should know this, and that Geary's ignorance of it was inexplicable.

Geary leaned toward the image of Numos, knowing his anger was showing. "This fleet fights for victory, not pride. It is held together by honor and courage, the belief in what we fight for and the belief in each other. *Pride* is nothing by itself. Nothing but a weapon in our enemy's hands, a weapon he will gladly use to help bring about our destruction."

Silence fell. Numos seemed to have a glint of satisfaction lurking in the back of his eyes, as if he thought he'd scored points against Geary. Geary calmed himself, know-

ing he couldn't afford to lose his temper. He looked along
the long, long lines of captains whose images appeared to
be seated at the table, trying to judge whether he'd harmed
his standing, and not knowing what else he could've said.
"If I may continue, the Syndics don't know we've come to
Kaliban. It'll be another few days before they even realize
we didn't go to Yuon. Only then will they start looking
elsewhere for us. We need to use that time to replenish
whatever stocks we can. Our auxiliaries," he nodded toward the place where Captain Tyrosian sat, "are going to
see what raw materials they can gather, while they also devote time to manufacturing more of the things this fleet
needs and getting it distributed to the ships that need it."

"Captain Tyrosian's in charge of the auxiliaries division? What happened to Captain Gundel?" an officer
asked. He was looking at Tyrosian with a puzzled, not hostile, expression.

"Captain Gundel has been assigned to assist me with a
long-range assessment of this fleet's needs," Geary answered. "He's transferring to *Titan*."

"I heard Gundel had been relieved of command," another officer challenged.

Word travels fast. That hasn't changed since my time.
Geary looked back toward Tyrosian. "Fleet regulations
prohibit having an officer serve as a ship's commanding
officer and in a staff assignment. Therefore, I was required
to give command of *Jinn* to Captain Gundel's executive
officer. Captain Gundel," Geary added, "agreed with all of
these changes."

Tyrosian, unused to being the center of attention at such
meetings, simply nodded.

"Will Captain Gundel say that if he's asked?" the officer continued.

"If you don't regard my own statements as sufficiently
reliable," Geary stated dryly, "feel free to contact Captain
Gundel. But I should advise you that he's likely to tell you
he's too busy to deal with many interruptions."

Smiles broke out around the table. As Geary had

guessed, many commanding officers had been forced to deal with Captain Gundel while he was in charge of the auxiliaries, and they all knew the point of Geary's half-disguised barb.

The challenger could see the smiles, too, and obviously realized he wouldn't have many allies in protesting against Gundel's transfer. "That's fine. I just wanted to be sure, that's all."

"Good." Geary looked slowly around the table. From the majority of the expressions, he'd maintained his hold on the fleet for now. *But too many seem to be sympathetic to what Numos was saying. Why? They're not stupid. But too many seem very unhappy that we didn't fight at Corvus, common sense and simple smarts be damned. All right. If they want to fight, they'll need to learn how.* "We're going to do something else while we're here."

Everyone watched him, some eagerly and some warily. "I've had the opportunity to watch the fleet in action." Now was the time for the most diplomatic language Geary could muster. He wished he'd been able to trust Rione enough on internal fleet politics to have her help him with the wording. "The courage of the personnel and the capabilities of the ships of this fleet are truly impressive. You have much to be proud of." He threw that last sentence in on the spur of the moment, trying to regain the high ground on that issue from Numos. "Our goal isn't just victory in battle. It's inflicting the heaviest possible losses on the enemy while suffering the fewest possible losses ourselves. There are things we can do to maximize our ability to win those kind of victories."

The wariness was still there on the faces of his ship commanders. Geary called up another display, showing battle formations he'd once practiced, learning how to coordinate groups of ships to bring them together at decisive points. He'd thought a long time about this, about how to tell them they didn't know how to fight a battle worth a damn. "Coordination, teamwork, and ship formations that allow us to take the best advantages of those qualities. It takes a lot of practice to carry these off right, but the pay-off will be that the Syndics won't be prepared to defend against them."

"We can put ships in those formations," someone objected, "but they're worse than useless without someone who can coordinate action across light-minutes in the face of an enemy who's acting and reacting. That's the problem. It always gets too difficult with the time-late information. We've got the basic concepts laid down in tactical guides, but nobody actually knows how to work those formations anymore."

Commander Cresida of the *Furious* spoke for the first time. "That's been true, but I believe we now have someone who does know how to do that. Someone who learned it a long time ago." She looked at Geary with a grim smile.

He could see the realization ripple around the virtual length of the table. Even Numos and Faresa seemed momentarily unable to come up with a rebuttal. *Time to seize the moment.* "We can do this. It'll take work. We're going to run simulations and exercises while we're in this system. Practice fleet engagements. Yes, there're some tricks I know that don't seem to have survived to this point in the war. I can show them to you, and then we can all surprise the Syndics."

Despite a scattering of skeptical expressions, most of the ship commanders seemed relieved and interested. "We'll go through formations, practice battles, maneuvering." At the mention of practice battles, even more of them perked up, as if Geary's interest in preparing for combat relieved them of some concerns. "I'll set up a schedule for those," continued Geary. "It'll be intense, because I don't know how long we'll have to practice. Any questions?"

"Where are we going from here?" Captain Tulev asked.

"That's still under consideration. As you know, we've got several options."

"Then you're not worried about having to leave Kaliban in a hurry?" Tulev gave Geary a look that clearly communicated that he knew the answer Geary was going to give.

Geary smiled slowly back, grateful for Tulev setting up an opportunity for a strong answer. "We'll leave Kaliban when we damn well feel like it, Captain."

A sort of cheer erupted around the table as most of the ship commanders expressed their approval of the sentiment. Geary kept his smile, even as he felt relief at apparently having succeeded in telling these men and women that they needed a lot of training without harming their pride in themselves and their abilities. "That's all. I'm working out the schedule for combat exercises and will transmit it to all ships when it's ready."

Captain Desjani stood, nodded to Geary, and walked quickly from the room, scanning her data pad for the latest actions required of the captain of the *Dauntless*. The images of the other ship commanders began vanishing rapidly as they raced off to let their own subordinates know the outcome of the meeting. Geary focused on one officer and held up a restraining hand. "Captain Duellos, a private word if you please."

Duellos nodded in assent, his image "walking" toward Geary while those of the other remaining commanding officers vanished like a rapidly bursting cluster of bubbles, and the apparent size of the compartment shrank back to its real proportions. "Yes, Captain Geary?"

Geary rubbed his neck, trying to decide how to ask his question. "I'd appreciate your assessment of something. During that meeting there was talk of pride and of us refusing to engage at Corvus. How do you feel about that?"

Duellos canted his head to regard Geary. "You particularly value my opinion? I cannot claim to be representative of the opinions of all of the other captains in the fleet."

"I know that. I'd like to know what you think, and what you think the others think."

"Very well." Duellos twisted up one corner of his mouth. "I understood what you said of pride. But you must understand that pride is one of the touchstones of this fleet."

"I never said they shouldn't be proud!" Geary threw his hands upward in annoyance.

This time both corners of Duellos's mouth twitched upward momentarily as if he were trying to find humor in the situation. "No. But the importance of pride cannot be discounted. There have been times, Captain Geary, when our pride was all that kept us going."

Geary shook his head, looking away. "I respect you far too much to think that empty pride is the only motivator you could call on. I think what you call pride is something much more than that. Belief in yourselves, perhaps, or perseverance in the face of adversity. Those are things to be proud of. That's not the same as being proud."

Duellos sighed. "I fear we've lost the ability to distinguish between those things. Lost it somewhere along the way from your time to now. War warps things, and human minds are far from the least of the things it twists."

"Then do you also think we should've engaged the Syndics in Corvus?"

"No. Absolutely not. That would've been foolish for the reasons you pointed out. But . . ." Duellos hesitated. "May I speak frankly?"

"Of course. I'm asking you this because I trust you to speak the truth to me."

Duellos made the very brief smile again. "I can't claim to always know what truth is. I can only tell you what I believe it to be. You must understand that while most of the commanding officers in the fleet believe deeply in Black Jack Geary, many wonder if you are still that man. Patience," he added as Geary made to speak. "I understand you never were that man. But they look for the qualities of Black Jack Geary in your actions."

Geary thought about that for a moment. "And if they don't see what they think of as Black Jack's qualities in me?"

"They will question your ability to continue in command of this fleet," Duellos stated flatly. "Since your assumption of command, there have been those who have spread rumors that you are a hollow man, damaged by the long period of survival sleep, an empty, wasted vestige of the great hero. If you come to be perceived to be lacking in the will to engage the enemy, it will give great strength to those rumors that your spirit has fled your body."

"Hell." Geary rubbed his face with both hands. As much as he hated being held up as a figure of legend, being labeled some sort of soulless zombie didn't strike him as any improvement. And such a label could critically damage his ability to command the fleet. "Is anybody contesting these rumors?"

"Of course, sir. But words from such as me mean nothing to those who doubt you. Those who can be swayed are looking to your actions."

Geary threw up his hands in exasperation again. "I can't fault that on principle, can I? I won't ask you who those rumor-mongers are because I'm sure you wouldn't tell me. Captain Duellos, I took this command to get the fleet home. If I can do that without fighting a big engagement, it'll mean I did that without losing any more ships."

Duellos eyed him for a long moment. "Captain Geary, getting the fleet home is hardly an end in itself. I won't pretend that it's not a matter of great importance, but the fleet exists to fight. The Syndics must be defeated if this war is to end. Any damage we can do to them on our way home will benefit the Alliance. And sooner or later, this fleet must engage the Syndics again."

Geary stood for a long moment, his head full of darkness, then nodded heavily. "I understand."

"It's not that we *want* to die far from home, you understand." Duellos actually mustered a wry smile this time.

"Actually, I do." Geary tapped his left chest, where few ribbons adorned his uniform in contrast to the row upon row of action awards that Duellos wore. The unmistakable pale blue of the Alliance Medal of Honor stood out among them, the award for his "last battle" that Geary didn't believe he'd earned but which regulations required him to wear. "You've all grown up with this. Fighting and dying is something you accept as a fact of life. My mind-set's still back a century ago, when peace was the norm and all-out war only a possibility. For me, combat was a theory game, where the referees would tote up points at the end to decide winners and losers, and then everybody would go have drinks together and lie about how brilliant their tactics had been. Now it's all real. Everything at Grendel happened so fast that I didn't have time to think about being in a war" He grimaced. "Your fleet is far larger than the fleet that existed in my time. I could, in one battle, lose more sailors than were in the entire fleet I knew. So I'm still adjusting to this, to being thrown into a very long-lived war."

A shadow fell across Duellos's expression. "I envy you, sir," he stated softly.

Geary nodded and gave Duellos a thin-lipped smile. "Yeah. I don't really have grounds to complain about that, do I? Thank you for your candor, Captain Duellos. I appreciate your frank insights."

Duellos made to step away in preparation for his image to vanish, then paused. "May I ask what you will do if a Syndic force appears in Kaliban?"

"Evaluate my options and choose the best one based on the exact circumstances."

"Of course. I am sure you will make a 'spirited' decision, sir." Duellos saluted, and his image disappeared.

Geary, alone again in a room where practically no one else had actually been present, spent a long time staring at the star display still floating above the conference table.

NINE

EVEN the Alliance engineering experts had to concede that the Syndic facilities in Kaliban had been efficiently moth-balled. Equipment had been powered down, power sup-plies disconnected or removed, everything else packed up or put away, the atmosphere inside the facilities rendered as dry as possible, then the atmosphere had been vented from the facilities before they were sealed again. Every-thing was in deep freeze, but also protected from the rav-ages of temperature variations, corrosive gases, and other threats.

Images from the facilities seemed at first glance to show darkened rooms that someone could've just left after a long day of work. It was only when Geary took note of the unnatural sharpness with which everything could be seen and the way in which light beams didn't diffuse as they would in atmosphere that he could tell from the im-ages alone that the facilities were airless.

"Look at that," Desjani commented. They were seated in the conference room, but this time the apparent size of the table stayed small. Instead, just off its end, a large window projected above the table displayed video from any of the scouts they cared to monitor as those scouts went through the Syndic facilities. The particular scout they were watching was going through what must have been the seat of Syndic political administration at Kaliban. Rows and rows of desks in identical cubicles, each left in identical shape, with every object on each desk positioned in the same spots in the same way. "They must've had people whose sole job was to inspect people's desks to make sure everything was left exactly right when they left."

"I've met people who'd enjoy doing that," Geary remarked.

"Me, too." Desjani suddenly grinned. "And here we come to the desks occupied by those who left last of all."

Geary couldn't help smiling, too. In the last row, several desks were in disarray, with long-ago dried-out drinking cups left standing amid scattered papers and documents, and some items that might have been leftover snack foods that had been desiccated and deep-frozen long ago. "It does look like the inspectors left before those desk jockeys did, doesn't it? Ah, this might be interesting." The Alliance scout was entering the main office. It still held an expensive-looking chair and a much more elaborate set of displays in addition to a workstation. "I wonder what that'd be like? Leaving a place forever. Some place you've worked at for who knows how long, and knowing odds were you'd never be able to come back. Knowing no one else would take your place because your place was gone."

"Sort of like being part of the decommissioning crew on a ship, I'd think," Desjani offered.

"Yeah. You ever done that?"

She hesitated for a moment. "We haven't had the luxury of retiring many ships while I've been in the fleet, sir."

Geary felt heat in his face and knew he was flushing, embarrassed at having asked such a boneheaded question. "Sorry. I should've known better than to ask that." When the fleet was building ships as fast as possible to replace losses, it was a safe bet no ships were being gently led out to pasture at the end of their optimum service lives.

But Desjani already seemed to have moved on. She nodded at the picture again. "You can see where personal items had been placed for a long time. Whoever occupied that office stayed there for many years."

Geary squinted, spotting the telltale darker squares and oblongs. "I guess so. I wonder where he or she went when they left Kaliban?"

"It hardly matters. Wherever it was, they went to help the Syndicate Worlds' war effort."

He didn't want to answer that for a moment, but he knew the truth of it, too. "Yeah. What's that?"

Desjani frowned, looking at the same object as Geary, a flat, white oblong resting on the surface of the desk. The scout they were monitoring walked carefully around the desk until he could focus on the object. "It's a note," he reported. "Faded but readable." He bent closer to read it. "Standard universal script. 'To Whom It May Concern. The left side . . . drawer . . . sticks. The . . . coffeemaker's . . . timer . . . does not work. There's . . . sweetener and coffee in the . . . right desk drawer . . . Take care of . . . everything.'" The Alliance scout straightened. "I can't read the signature."

Desjani's frown changed into a grin that slowly faded. "Captain Geary, for the first time I can remember, I actually wanted to have met a Syndic. Whoever wrote that note seems like someone I could like." She fell silent for a moment. "I've never thought of any Syndic as someone I could like."

Geary nodded at her words. "Someday, our ancestors willing, this war will end, and we'll get a chance to know the Syndics as people again. From what I know of this war, I don't imagine you've much interest in that, but it's necessary. We can't let hatred rule our relations with the Syndics forever."

She considered Geary's words before replying. "Or we'd be no better than they are. Just as you said about our treatment of prisoners."

"In a way, yeah." He tapped the communications tab to speak to the scout. "Can you tell yet how long ago they shut this place down?"

The scout pointed to the document. "The date on this uses the Syndic calendar. Just a moment, sir, while I run a conversion." After a moment, the scout spoke again. "Forty-two years ago, sir, if we assume this date is accurate. That coffee they left behind won't taste too fresh, I'm afraid, but it'll probably still be better than what they serve on our ships."

"You've got a point there. Thanks." Geary let go of the communications tab and looked over at Desjani. "Forty-two years ago. Whoever it was who wrote that note may well be dead by now."

"It's not as if there was a realistic chance of meeting the person," Desjani noted in a dismissive tone, her attitude now implying she wouldn't waste much time bemoaning the lost opportunity.

"Captain Geary?" Next to the scout's window, a smaller one appeared, with images of Colonel Carabali and a Marine Major standing in it. Both Marines, in full armor, appeared to be in a Syndic facility somewhere. Geary checked the system display next to the picture, zooming it in on the location of Carabali. They were somewhere in the same facility as the scout Geary had just spoken to. "There's something odd here."

Geary felt a sudden heavy sensation in his guts. "Dangerous?"

"No, sir. We don't think so. Just . . . odd." Carabali gestured to her companion. "This is Major Rosado, my best expert on Syndic computer systems." Rosado saluted smartly. "He tells me that not only have the data files for the Syndic systems been wiped clean and backup storage devices taken, but the operating systems have also been totally removed."

Geary thought about that. "That's odd?"

"Yes, sir," Major Rosado stated. "There's no sense in it. Why remove the operating systems? We've got copies of

Syndic code that've been acquired by various means, so we can get the stuff working again. And not having operating systems loaded and configured would make it that much harder to get things going for any Syndics who came back."

"The Syndics know we've got copies?"

"They know we've got copies of stuff a lot newer than what used to be on these antiques, sir."

Those "antiques" are likely younger than I am. "You can't think of any reason they would've wiped the operating systems?"

Major Rosado looked uncomfortable. "There's only one reason I could think of, sir."

"Which is?" Geary prodded.

"Sir," Rosado stated reluctantly, "they would've removed the operating systems if they were worried about someone besides us accessing these systems after they were abandoned. Someone they didn't think would have copies of their code."

"Someone besides us?" Geary looked from Desjani to Carabali. "Who?"

"A . . . a third party."

Desjani answered. "There isn't any third party. There's us and the planets allied with us, and there's the Syndics. There isn't anyone else."

"There's not *supposed* to be anyone else," Carabali corrected. "But it appears the Syndics were worried about someone. Someone who didn't have access to software that any human could be assumed to have."

"You're not suggesting intelligent nonhumans are you?" Desjani demanded. "We've never found any."

Carabali shrugged. "No. We haven't. But we don't know what's on the other side of Syndic space. They walled that off from us for so-called security reasons even before the war began."

Geary pivoted to study the star display. Stars like Kaliban were far from Alliance space, but measured from the outer edge of Syndic territory, they weren't all that far from the known limits of the Syndicate Worlds. "If this speculation was true, they'd have had to have known about these whatevers as of at least forty-two years ago when they shut down everything at Kaliban. Could they keep a secret like that for so long?"

The Marine commanding officer shrugged again. "It would depend on a lot of factors, sir. Neither I nor Major Rosado are saying such beings exist. We're pointing out that this is the only explanation we've been able to come up with for what the Syndics did when they left Kaliban."

"If there were such things out here," Desjani countered, "wouldn't we have run into them?"

"Maybe we will," Geary replied. "Are there any fleet procedures for dealing with nonhuman contact?"

Desjani looked baffled. "I don't know. There's never been any call for them, so I don't know of anyone who's looked into it. Maybe something exists, but it'd be really ancient, from before the war." Geary assumed he managed to conceal his reaction to that last statement since Desjani went on speaking, oblivious. "In any case, how could these nonhuman intelligences reach Kaliban if the Syndics didn't want them to? Kaliban isn't next door to the Syndic frontier."

Colonel Carabali looked apologetic but spoke again. "If there were nonhuman intelligences out here, they might have a different means of faster-than-light travel. Right now, humans have two such means. There could be other means, and one of those might make Kaliban accessible from the Syndic frontier. But I'm not saying that's the reason for the Syndics' actions. I'm not saying nonhuman intelligences exist or have been encountered by the Syndics. I'm just saying that's the only explanation we've been able to come up with that makes any sense at all for what the Syndics did here."

Geary nodded. "Understood, Colonel. I appreciate your sharing that idea, even though as you say there's no certainty at all to it. But you're telling me that we can get any of the Syndic systems running again despite what they did?"

Major Rosado smiled confidently. "Yes, sir. If you want it up, we can get it working."

"You're talking to the scout teams from the fleet auxiliaries?"

"Yes, sir. There's a team from *Jinn* with us here making an assessment on whether this site holds anything we can use."

"Good. Thanks for your information." The second window vanished, leaving only the scene from the Alliance scout as he painstakingly went over the office.

Desjani shook her head. "I never imagined I'd hear Marines worrying about two-headed aliens from the dark beyond."

Geary smiled but then sobered. "Yet they couldn't find any other reason for what the Syndics did. Can you think of a reason?"

"Perversity? Some stupid bureaucrat? People don't always do things for reasons that make any sense."

"True. Being in the fleet, we know all about that, right?"

Desjani grinned and nodded. "I really wouldn't waste time worrying about it, sir."

"No, I guess not, though frankly that's a lot of work to go to without any good reason." Geary checked the time. "We've got something else to worry about right now."

FOR at least the tenth time in the last half hour, Geary fought to suppress an angry comment. The ships that were supposed to have moved into a block-shaped formation to one side of the main body had gotten into some sort of dispute based on the seniority of ship commanders, so that instead of taking assigned stations, some ships were trying to wedge their way into locations where other ships were already in place. Geary counted to five slowly, then keyed his communications. "All units in formation bravo, be advised that everyone will get equal opportunity to engage the enemy. Proceed to your assigned stations."

He pondered taking something for the headache growing between his eyes while he watched the errant ships somewhat sheepishly alter their courses. Except for *Audacious*, which kept edging in toward *Resolution* in an apparent attempt to bull the other ship aside so that *Audacious* could lay claim to what looked like a leading position. "*Audacious*, did you copy my last?" He waited a minute to see if *Audacious* would respond, but the warship kept sidling in toward *Resolution*. *Fine. Let's see if a little humor will defuse this without my having to relieve another commanding officer.* "*Audacious*, be advised that if you are attempting to mate with *Resolution*, you might try buying her a few drinks first."

Off to one side, Geary heard Captain Desjani almost choke on her coffee. He heard no reply from *Audacious*, but the warship finally angled away and back toward its assigned station. A moment later, *Resolution* called in. "Alliance battle cruiser *Resolution* wishes to report that her virtue remains intact."

This time Desjani laughed, as did Geary. *Good. That's the sort of thing that indicates morale is okay. For the moment, at least.* He watched the other ships in formation bravo belatedly sliding into position, shaking his head. *Thank goodness I can do this by simulation. I wish I could do it for real, too, but I can't afford to burn the amount of fuel reserves that'd require.*

Geary waited until the laggard ships had reached their stations, then tapped his communications controls again. "All units, I'm going to put your simulated ship movements on automatic for a little while. I want to show you what happens when we employ these two formations in a coordinated fashion." He activated the sequence he'd programmed during the transit through jump space.

In the simulated version of the Kaliban System, a large Syndic force suddenly appeared near the Alliance formations. Geary let the simulation run, showing the two Alliance formations rotating to angles that maximized their firepower against opposite edges of the onrushing enemy.

He'd deliberately kept the scenario short, so twenty minutes later the remnants of the simulated Syndics were fleeing for their lives. Geary let another couple of minutes pass after the simulation paused, then spoke again. "There's a couple of points I want to make. First of all, you'll note that when the separate formations are properly employed, it maximizes our capability to employ the most ships and the most firepower against the enemy. You'll notice that every ship in formation bravo hit the enemy hard because of the way that formation swept across the enemy flank. Secondly, this scenario I just ran worked because every ship did what it was supposed to do."

He studied the vision of impossibly easy victory in the simulation. It'd been too painless, too uncomplicated, but he wanted the messages taught by it to be clear. "If we work as a disciplined fighting force, we can kick the Syndics so hard, they won't know what hit them. The simulations and formations we're going to practice over the next few weeks are going to get progressively more complex, but I wanted everyone to know the reason we're doing this. I promise you this fleet can beat any comparable force nine times out of ten if we have the same valor but apply it in a disciplined manner."

Desjani gave him a thumbs up from the other side of the simulation room. Geary nodded back at her, wishing that all of his ship captains had her unquestioning loyalty. "That's all. The next simulation will be run in two hours. I'll see you then." He stretched and stood up. "I think I can safely predict that within the next two days everyone will be sick to death of running these practice drills."

"Do you really think we can pull off that kind of maneuvering of independent formations in a time-late data situation involving an enemy who's reacting to our actions?" Desjani asked.

Geary nodded. "Yeah. So you spotted how the enemy force behaved in that simulation, huh?"

"Yes, sir. As much as I hate the Syndics, I don't think they're quite as stupid as that attacking force acted."

This time Geary grinned. "Maybe if we're lucky. But, no, I'm not planning on them actually acting that stupid. But, yes, I think I can call the orders. I learned the skill under some very good practitioners of the art." Then he remembered how long those men and women had been dead, and his smile faded.

By late the next day, Geary realized his prediction had been off by one day. Most of the ship commanders, burdened by their normal command responsibilities, had already gotten tired of simulating maneuvering and battles for a good portion of each day. It didn't help that Geary had set the simulations to get progressively more difficult. "Listen up," Geary admonished them after the last drill of the day. "We don't know how long we have before the Syndics show up here. We need to be ready. That means packing a lot of work into the shortest time possible. See you tomorrow."

He slumped back in his seat, feeling wearied from the constant effort involved in not only riding herd on all the ships under his command but also in massaging the egos of their commanders. "We have an update from *Witch*," Desjani advised. "The mining facility on Ishiki's Rock should be in working order tomorrow. They expect to be pulling out ore and sending it to the auxiliaries by late tomorrow afternoon."

"Great." Geary peered at the message. "Ishiki's Rock? Oh, that one. The asteroid mine. That isn't what the Syndics called it, is it?"

"No. There didn't seem any reason to go to the trouble of finding out what name the Syndics used. Ishiki is the senior enlisted who did the first reconnaissance and evaluation of the mining facility there."

"Then it's as good a name as any," Geary reflected. He called *Witch*. "Captain Tyrosian? If time permits, I'd like one of your machine shops to churn out a small plaque identifying the asteroid mining facility as Ishiki's Rock. We'll tack it up somewhere down there."

Tyrosian looked briefly startled, then smiled. "Chief Ishiki will surely appreciate that, sir. Do you want any ceremony when we put the plaque up?"

"If you want to improvise something, feel free. Everybody in this fleet is working their butts off, and we can use an excuse for a little fun."

"Yes, sir. There's some good metal in that rock. How long will we have to exploit it?"

Geary thought about the question. "That's still undetermined at this time. Assume you have to work fast, but if possible, I want to top off the bunkers in the auxiliaries with raw materials before we leave."

Tyrosian raised her eyebrows. "That's a lot of raw material, Captain Geary. At the rate we can mine and transport it here, it'd take weeks."

"I can't promise weeks, but we'll take every day we can."

"I feel obligated to remind you as well that all the extra mass will adversely affect the maneuvering capabilities of my ships. *Titan*, in particular, since she's the largest. But *Witch, Jinn,* and *Goblin* will all get a lot more sluggish as well."

Geary felt an increasingly familiar pain behind his eyes. "How bad will *Titan*'s ability to accelerate be if her raw material bunkers are topped off?"

Tyrosian looked to one side, apparently working some controls. "Here's *Titan*'s performance at full load, Captain Geary."

Geary exhaled as he read the data Captain Tyrosian displayed. "She'll be a real flying pig, won't she?"

"We usually use the term *flying elephant.* A flying pig would probably be much more maneuverable than *Titan* with a full load."

"Thanks. I appreciate the heads-up."

Tyrosian looked questioning. "Do you still want *Titan*'s bunkers topped off, sir?"

Geary rubbed the place between his eyes to try to push back the throbbing there. "Yes. If we can't manufacture what we need for the long haul, it won't matter how fast we can move for the short haul. If I have to choose, I want to be prepared for the long run."

"Yes, sir. You need it, we build it."

The old motto of the fleet engineers, unchanged since Geary's time, brought a smile to his face. "Thank you, Captain Tyrosian. I know I can always count on you and your ships." The statement made Tyrosian smile as well.

Geary made his way back to his stateroom, cheered by his dealings with Captain Tyrosian but still looking forward to relaxing and pretending to be away from the demands of being in charge of the fleet. But he found someone waiting outside of the hatch leading to his stateroom. "Madam Co-President." Geary hoped his weariness and lack of desire for conversation didn't come through too clearly. "To what do I owe the honor of your presence?"

She inclined her head to acknowledge the greeting, then gestured toward the hatch. "I wish to speak to you privately, Captain Geary."

"I don't want to seem unwelcoming, but is there another time we can do that? I've been pretty heavily occupied lately."

"So I've noticed." Rione gave him an arch look. "You've been so heavily occupied, that I've been frustrated in my other attempts to meet with you. I would very much like to speak with you now."

Geary managed not to sigh too heavily. "Okay. Please come in." He let her enter first, then waved her to one seat while he unceremoniously flopped into another.

That earned him another look from Rione. "You don't seem to be the iron-willed hero of legend today, Captain Geary."

"The iron-willed hero of legend is damned tired today, ma'am. What can I do for you?"

Rione seemed a little surprised by Geary's directness,

but she finally sat down in the offered seat. "My question is a simple one. What are you planning, Captain Geary?"

Geary shrugged. "As I've stated every time I've been asked that question, I'm planning on getting this fleet home."

"Then why are we lingering at Kaliban?"

The woman does have a gift for asking awkward questions. Geary considered her for a moment before answering. "We need some time. We're not sitting idle. As I'm sure you're aware, we're getting raw materials to the ships that can use them, *Titan* and her sisters are churning out new fuel cells as well as replacements for the equipment we've had damaged or destroyed and the weapons we've expended, we're getting some major external repairs done to some of our ships that couldn't be accomplished in jump space, we're scavenging through the abandoned installations here for anything we can use, and most important of all, we're training."

"Training." Rione's eyes narrowed. "For what?"

"As I'm also sure you're aware, Madam Co-President, we're training for combat. The next time we face a large Syndic force, I want this fleet to operate like a military organization instead of an untrained mob of well-intentioned but overaggressive warriors." Damn. He had to be careful not to be too blunt with Rione. It wouldn't do to have a phrase like that repeated too widely.

"Captain Geary, I told you when first we met that this fleet is brittle. You agreed with me. How can you now speak of facing a large enemy force?" Rione's voice had gotten flatter and harder as she spoke.

Geary, wishing he could strengthen shields around himself against the force of Rione's words, simply nodded. "I agreed with you then. But brittle metal can be reforged, Madam Co-President. It can be made strong again."

"To *what* purpose?"

Okay. She doesn't trust me at all when it comes to things like this, I guess. Fine. Trust me or not, all she'll get from me is the truth. "To get home. I mean that. Look." Geary reached forward far enough to push in a command he'd learned by heart, then waved at the display of stars that appeared over the table between them. "We're a long way from home by system jumps. I can keep trying to outguess the Syndics and try to plan far enough ahead to keep them from trapping us, but I can't count on them never second-guessing me, never getting lucky. That means I can't count on never running into some Syndic force that could hurt us badly. What's going to happen then? If this fleet is still the force I led out of the Syndic home system, it'll run the risk of being broken and destroyed. But, Madam Co-President, if I can teach these sailors to fight smart as well as brave, then we'll be able to fight our way through that Syndic force."

She watched him for a long time without speaking, her thoughts impossible for Geary to read. Finally, she spoke in a slightly less harsh voice. "You believe you can do this?"

"I hope I can." Geary hunched forward, trying to project his feelings. "These are good sailors. Good officers. Good captains. For the most part, good captains. I'm sure you know there are some exceptions, but there always have been and always will be. All they need is someone they believe in, who they'll listen to, to show them how to win."

"Because they trust you."

"Yes, dammit! What the hell's the matter with that? I've yet to take one single action to betray that trust, and I never will."

"Is that an oath, Captain Geary?" Rione's voice had become very soft but also very clear. "Do you swear that on the honor of your ancestors?"

Geary wondered if Rione knew about his occasional visits to the ancestral spaces, and guessed she'd probably picked up as much information about them as anyone could. "Of course I do."

"And the Alliance itself? The elected leadership of the peoples of the Alliance?"

Geary stared at her. "What about them?"

Rione glared back, exasperation showing in an uncharacteristic display of emotion. "If I only knew whether you were truly naïve or simply playacting! Captain Geary, you are a figure of legend. What sort of power do you think you will be able to wield if you return to the Alliance with this fleet at your back? Black Jack Geary, the paragon of Alliance officers, the hero of the past, the man every Alliance youth is taught to revere, back from the dead with a mighty fleet he has literally saved from total loss! A fleet you say will be trained to be far better than other Alliance forces. What will become of the Alliance then, Captain Geary? You will hold the Alliance within the palm of your hand, to dispose of as you wish. You know this is true! What will you do?"

"I . . ." Geary looked away, discomforted by her words and the intensity of the feelings behind them. "I'll . . . I don't know. I hadn't really thought that far . . . but, no. No! I don't want that kind of power. I don't want to tell the elected leaders of the Alliance what to do. I want . . ." To get home? Home, for him, was dead and gone. What would be left for him when this mission was done? What life could he hope for? "I want . . ."

"What, Captain Geary? What do you want, more than anything?"

Geary, worn out mentally and physically by the exertions of the last few days, felt a wave of cold washing over him. "More than once, Madam Co-President, I have wanted more than anything to have died on my ship a century ago." He regretted the words as soon as he'd spoken them, words and thoughts he hadn't revealed to anyone else, but which had broken through internal barriers weakened by tiredness and stress.

Rione seemed taken aback for a moment. She watched him silently for a while, then nodded. "Could you walk away from it, Captain Geary? If we get home, can you walk away from the power to decide the fate of the Alliance?"

He took a long, deep breath. "In all honesty, I think I have that power already. If I can get this fleet back, with the device you know is on *Dauntless,* the Alliance has a real good chance of forcing the Syndics to negotiate in earnest to end this war. But if I don't, if we're lost out here, the Syndics will have a very large military advantage, and I can't imagine they won't press that advantage for all it's worth. So, one way or the other, what I manage to do is going to determine a lot about what happens to the Alliance." Geary looked straight into Rione's eyes. "I swear I'd walk away from it this instant if I could. But I can't. You know that, don't you? There's no one else here who has a chance of getting this fleet home. I've tried to tell myself I'm not indispensable, that there are other officers here who could get this fleet back. But I know it's not true."

Rione's eyes and expression were unyielding. "Democracies and republics cannot live with indispensable men or women, Captain Geary."

"It's only until I get this fleet back! Once we get back to the Alliance, Madam Co-President, I fully intend turning over command to the first admiral I meet and then finding a nice quiet planet to hide on for the rest of my life." Geary stood up and paced despite his weariness. "That's all anyone can ask of me. That's all the honor of my ancestors can possibly demand. I'll resign this command and my commission and go to . . . to . . ."

"Where, Captain Geary?" Rione sounded weary now, too, though Geary couldn't imagine why. "What planet do you think would grant you refuge against the ancient glory of Black Jack Geary and the modern adulation for the man who saved the Alliance fleet and perhaps the Alliance itself?"

"I . . ." Geary cast about for a name, knowing his own home world would never be such a refuge, knowing it might well have changed beyond recognition in a century's time and actually fearing to see the sort of monuments to Black Jack Geary that surely existed there, and settled on the one planet he'd heard the most of in the last several weeks. "Kosatka."

"Kosatka?" This time Rione laughed, though with more disbelief than humor. "I told you before, Captain Geary. Your fate does not lie on Kosatka. Kosatka is a good world, but it is not a mighty world. Kosatka could not hold you now."

"I'm not—"

"No one planet could hold you now, regardless of where you believe your duty must take you." Rione stood as well, her eyes still fixed on Geary. "But if it proves necessary to hold you, if someone must act to contain your power, then I will do my best."

He stared back at her, not believing what he'd heard. "Are you threatening me?"

"No. I'm merely informing you that should you attempt to reach out and take what could be yours, I will be there to stay your hand." She turned to go, then faced him again. "And lest you doubt, Captain Geary, I am not indispensable. Even if I am lost, there will be others."

"I haven't done anything."

"There you are surely wrong. Don't mistake me. I'm not prejudging you, and what you have done are arguably things that needed to be done to save this fleet. If you hold to your vow to reject the power that will be yours, you'll have no truer ally than me. But you must not pretend there will be no temptation, Captain Geary. You must not pretend that there won't be those urging you to take certain actions allegedly for the sake of the Alliance, actions that may then appear justifiable to you but that will destroy everything you claim to honor."

He glared at her. "I'm not the kind of person who'd do that sort of thing."

"Is Black Jack Geary that kind of person?"

"What?" He shook his head several times as if to clear it, puzzled that she'd actually posed the question. "I have no idea. I don't know who that imaginary hero is. I don't know what he's like. All I know is he's not me."

Rione shook her own head, but slowly in clear negation of Geary's last statement. "I regret to say that you are wrong. No matter who you think you are, you must realize that, in every way that matters in this universe, you *are* Black Jack Geary."

"Then perhaps you'd care to explain to me why I have to work so hard to keep most of these commanding officers happy if they believe in Black Jack Geary so damn much!"

Rione's mouth twisted. "You said it yourself. They believe in Black Jack Geary, Captain. In their minds, that person must be exceptional in every way. If they come to believe that you are not Black Jack Geary as they imagine that person must be, they would no longer believe in you."

"So you're saying I'm damned if I do and damned if I don't? That in order to save this fleet, I have to be exceptional in every way? I have to effectively become the person they think Black Jack Geary is or this fleet will be lost? But just how am I supposed to be exceptional in every way?"

"I'm afraid I cannot help you there, Captain Geary." Rione inclined her head again, then departed.

Geary watched her leave, then collapsed again onto the nearest seat, two thoughts warring in his mind. *What if she's right? And what the hell did I ever do to deserve this?*

"ALL units in formation sigma roll port twenty degrees at time three four." Geary waited, then buried his head in his hands as half of the ships rolled in place while the other half moved as if the entire formation were pivoting twenty degrees to port. *Listen to the message! Please listen to the message! It's not like you don't have time to think about it before the execution time!*

Outwardly, Geary spoke as calmly as he could. "All units, take care to execute the order as given." He checked the time, rubbed his eyes, then broadcast again. "All units. That's enough for today. Thanks for all your hard work." *I just hope they're learning something. Not just about keep-*

ing formation, either. If they're paying attention to how I'm calling the maneuvers to account for time-late data, they should be picking up some of that as well.

Captain Desjani looked tired, too, but smiled encouragingly. "I've never seen our units actually maneuver like this under battle conditions."

"You still haven't," Geary noted, trying not to sound as sour as he felt. "It's all simulated and not under the stress of actual combat."

"I still think we've seen a lot of improvement."

Geary thought for a moment, then nodded. "Yes. You're right. We have. Given the amount of time we've been working on this, everyone has progressed quite quickly." He checked the final disposition of the ships on the simulator, now frozen in place. "There's been a lot of progress for just less than two weeks of running drills. But then there's a lot of good ship handlers in this fleet." He nodded again, this time toward Desjani. "Present company included."

"Thank you, sir." Desjani looked both pleased and embarrassed by the praise.

"I mean it. You can really handle this ship. You can train some people in ship handling for a star's lifespan, and they'll still jerk a ship around like it was a sack of lead. But you've got skill. You feel the ship and work with her motion." Geary levered himself out of his seat. "I'm going to take a break before I review the next simulation scenario. How about you?"

Desjani shook her head. "There're some things I need to take care of as commanding officer of *Dauntless*. No rest for the wicked, as they say."

"I don't know about wicked, Tanya, but I do know ship captains never get much rest. Thanks for all the help you've given me lately."

"It's my pleasure, sir." She sketched an informal salute and left.

Geary sat back down, fought a brief internal battle between a desire for downtime and the need to catch up on his own responsibilities, then called up the latest fleet status reports. There were three former Syndic asteroid mines being worked now, and a gratifying amount of pure metal had been transferred to the auxiliaries, which had kept their own workshops going to provide the fleet with desperately needed spares and replacements for expendable weapons. In addition, some food stocks had been found, still preserved by the cold in the abandoned towns where they'd been left, doubtless because shipping the food out had made no economic sense when the Syndics had left Kaliban. *I have a feeling we're all going to get very tired of Syndic food before we get home. Especially since they undoubtedly ate the stuff that tasted best first and left the stuff no one wanted.* A notation on one report advised that scouts had located a storehouse of electronic components that had yielded some useful matériel that could be reworked to meet some Alliance requirements. All in all, the fleet had spent its time in Kaliban well.

An internal communication circuit chimed urgently. "Captain Geary, this is Captain Desjani."

"Roger. What's up?"

"They're here."

Geary headed for *Dauntless*'s bridge as fast as he could get there. It was somewhat irrational to rush since the nearest jump exit was two light-hours away, but he still felt the need.

He was still taking his seat when Desjani started briefing him. "Initial sightings indicate the Syndic force is comparable to the one that followed us through Corvus."

Geary nodded, not commenting on the fact that he'd noticed every Alliance sailor on the *Dauntless* had stopped talking about the Syndic force "chasing" the Alliance fleet through Corvus. Now they always said the Syndics had simply followed. Within another few weeks, the Alliance sailors would probably be saying the Alliance fleet had somehow been chasing the Syndic force out of Corvus. As long as it salved their pride, Geary wouldn't correct anyone. "It could actually be the same force. If it is them, they've gotten to Kaliban the hard way around, and they're likely to be a little perturbed with us."

Desjani grinned. "Per your instructions, we've already ordered all shuttles and personnel back to their ships."

"Good. Have they initiated destructive shutdowns of all the equipment we reactivated?"

"Yes, sir." Desjani's approval of the scorched-earth tactic was clear. "That equipment won't be working for anyone again."

"That's the idea." It was a pity in a way, but he couldn't leave industrial assets behind for the Syndics to possibly use again for their own purposes. Geary studied the situation for a long moment. "Coming out of that exit, they must've come from Saxon or Pullien, and they could've reached either of those stars from Yuon, right?"

Desjani checked her display. "Pullien would take an extra jump, but yes. Either way, they've come in using the jump exit closest to us."

Just as I could've predicted from my experience with the perversity of the universe. The Syndics came out of the closest jump exit to the Alliance fleet, only two light-hours away. We just saw them, which meant the Syndics actually arrived at Kaliban two hours ago. The Alliance ships hadn't been able to see the suddenly arriving Syndic ships until light made its journey, but the Syndics would've instantly been able to see the Alliance fleet and its position as of two hours before. *The amount of blue shift on the light from the Syndic ships indicates they were doing point-one light coming out of jump. If they've maintained that speed, that'd put them point two light-hours closer to us by the time we saw them first arrive. It still means they're eighteen hours away from reaching us at that speed, though.*

There's no doubt we could accelerate away and avoid action on our way out of the system. It'd be easy.

And it'd give a lot of strength to those rumors that I'm not fit to command this fleet. I've spent the last couple of weeks trying to decide what to do when the Syndics ar-

rived. I couldn't really make up my mind until I saw how big the Syndic force turned out to be. Now I know. It's significantly smaller than us, but still powerful. It could do a lot of damage.

Geary glanced over at Captain Desjani, seeing how her muscles were tensed in anticipation of combat even though it was at least several hours away even if Geary accelerated the Alliance fleet to meet the Syndics. He knew she and most of his other ship captains would be disappointed to leave Kaliban without engaging the Syndics. More than disappointed. He took another look at the latest estimate of the enemy force's size. *I'm not sure the fleet's ready to take on a force like that. We outnumber them by quite a bit, but if we screw things up anything like the engagements at Corvus, we could take terrible losses. Can I trust my ships to keep formation and follow orders?*

I know what prudence dictates, but these people I'm commanding need to believe I'm the one who can lead them to victory. How long will they follow me if they think I'm afraid of combat? Should I give in to that concern despite my doubts? Or are my doubts greater than they really should be? Am I afraid to risk these ships because of the mistakes they might make, or because of the mistakes I might make?

Run or fight. Which would be right? Which would be best?

Ancestors, send me a sign.

"Captain Desjani," the *Dauntless*'s communications watch called out. "*Witch* reports there's a dead bird on Ishiki's Rock."

Geary took a moment to process the modern slang through his brain. "Bird" was what the sailors called shuttles, and "dead" meant . . . "There's a shuttle that can't rise?"

"Yes, sir. On Ishiki's Rock. One of the big cargo haulers."

"Tell them to abandon the cargo. Just get the personnel out."

"They tried, sir. It's not a mass issue. Propulsion and control systems went dark when they tried to lift. They're troubleshooting now."

"How many of our people are on Ishiki's Rock?"

"Thirty-one, sir, counting the shuttle crew."

Geary looked at Desjani. "You know these shuttles better than I do. What're the odds they'll get it fixed soon?"

She shook her head. "I wouldn't place bets on it," Desjani advised. "Two major systems dead means multiple junction failures." She gestured toward the engineering watch-stander. "Your assessment, please?"

The watch-stander grimaced. "That bird won't be going anywhere until a full maintenance unit can get a look at it. Exact time to get it flying again will depend on how many subsystems did a meltdown, but I'd assume four hours minimum once the maintenance team gets there, assuming they've got all the parts they'll need."

"I had a feeling it'd be that bad." Geary looked back at the display, running through possible options in his head. Ishiki's Rock was thirty light-minutes closer to the Syndics than the Alliance fleet's main body. *Titan* had finished topping off its raw materials storage a day and a half ago and moved back with the fleet, but *Witch* was still out there near Ishiki's Rock.

Five hours transit time at .1 light, and while *Witch* massed less than *Titan*, it had less propulsion capability so it couldn't accelerate much better than *Titan*. He could order *Witch* to send another shuttle out to pick up the people on Ishiki's Rock and abandon the dead bird in place. Or he could send in a maintenance team to fix the bird. *Witch* was close enough to Ishiki's Rock that they could probably revive the dead bird and still get it back to *Witch* in time for the fleet to take off ahead of the Syndics. Though that could well be a close thing. The safest thing to do would be to abandon the bird.

And wouldn't that look bad in the eyes of people who already didn't like to see the Alliance fleet "running away" from Syndics.

But staying long enough to try to salvage or fix the bird could run a real risk of having Syndic HuKs catching up with *Witch* if anything went wrong. He could bring up some ships to defend *Witch*, but how many would he need? If the Syndics were pushing their propulsion to maximum, they could shave significant time off their transit by accelerating half the way to *Witch* and then decelerating back to .1 light in time to engage her.

And what would happen to anyone left on Ishiki's Rock if the Syndics came charging in faster than anticipated? The closer the Syndics got, the less time Geary would have to react.

Thirty-one people. One cargo shuttle. I can get the people out. No problem. Unless something else messes up. Which it could, and then we could face trouble. And if I try to save face by saving the shuttle, too, I'll be risking more people. If we have to pull out fast . . .

Pull out fast, Geary? Try running away. Because no matter what label you put on it, that's what it means. You know it, and so will everyone else. And you don't really like it any more than they do.

The fleet's trusted me to lead them this far. I have to trust them. I have to trust them to win if I can lead them competently.

And I can't lead them unless they continue to believe in me.

And they won't continue to believe in me unless I show them they can win by listening to me.

And I can't win unless I take risks.

Captain Desjani was looking at him, having surely reached the same conclusions he had about the options available and wondering how Geary would handle it.

Geary took a deep breath, then activated the fleet command communications circuit. "Alliance fleet, this is Captain Geary. All units, assume Combat Formation Alpha. I say again, assume Combat Formation Alpha. Execute order immediately upon receipt. Take stations relative to fleet flagship *Dauntless*, formation axis aligned to *Daunt-*

less's long axis. All ships prepare for action. Estimated time to battle is"—he did a quick estimate of how quickly the two forces would come together if the Alliance fleet headed directly for an intercept—"eight hours." He glanced over at Desjani. "Captain Desjani, please have your communications watch inform the personnel on Ishiki's Rock that the fleet is coming to get them. Then please bring *Dauntless* around so her bows point toward an intercept with the projected course of the Syndic formation entering the system."

"Aye, aye, sir!" Desjani looked exultant, and so did everyone else Geary could see on the bridge.

"Captain Geary!" He hadn't seen that Co-President Rione had also arrived on the bridge. Now he turned to look as she spoke, her face appalled. "Are you intending to fight a full-scale battle for control of this system?"

"Yes. That's exactly what I'm planning. I have thirty-one personnel and a fleet cargo shuttle marooned on one of the asteroids in the system."

"And with the Syndic ships well over half a day away, you believe a full-scale battle is your only option?"

Geary gave her a brief, humorless smile. "I believe it's the best option for a variety of reasons."

"You can't risk the loss of hundreds or thousands of sailors and who knows how many ships for thirty-one people who could be easily rescued and a cargo shuttle that could be easily abandoned on that asteroid!"

"None of the available options are foolproof, Madam Co-President. We don't know what the Syndics are doing this very minute. Even a simple rescue, if delayed by other unforeseen events, could place *Witch* or some other ship in peril. Yes, I'm risking the entire fleet to cover those personnel and that shuttle and the ships working to take them off that asteroid. It's a matter of responsibility and keeping faith. The Alliance fleet does not leave anyone behind."

Sudden cheers startled Geary and Rione. Looking around, he saw *Dauntless*'s bridge team holding fists upward as they roared approval.

He turned toward Captain Desjani, catching her just as she finished muttering something into her communications system. "Pardon me, Captain Geary. I was just transmitting the record of your statement to the fleet." Even after spending almost a couple of months with her, Geary was still shocked to see the admiration shining in her eyes.

But he knew she'd done something right. As much as he hated to admit it, those words he'd blurted out would steel the fleet through this battle. And no doubt be added to the inspirational sayings of Black Jack Geary. Which, he prayed to every ancestor he had, he'd never have to actually hear repeated by anyone else.

Rione looked like she was praying, too, though Geary suspected they were prayers for what she thought of as sanity to prevail. "Captain Geary, what can I say to convince you that this fleet's survival is the most important factor to consider?"

"Madam Co-President, I understand your concerns. I must ask you to trust my judgment that this fleet's survival will depend ultimately on many factors."

"Captain." Rione stepped close and spoke very quietly. "You know how critical it is for *Dauntless* to return safely to Alliance space. The item it carries is of incalculable value."

"I haven't forgotten that," Geary replied in an equally quiet tone.

"Have you forgotten that I have it in my power to pull from your command the ship contingents from the Callas Republic and the Rift Federation?"

"No. I'd strongly urge you not to do that." Geary tried to look like he imagined someone should look when they knew the risks but could still be confident. "I'd wanted more training time, but the fleet can handle this well. There are good reasons for why I'm doing this. I'd like to have your ships participate."

"And if I refuse to allow that?"

Geary exhaled heavily. "There'd be nothing I could do about it. You know that."

She eyed him for a long moment while Geary ached to get back to the developing battle, but he knew he had to resolve this situation first. "Very well, Captain Geary. Your actions thus far have earned you the benefit of the doubt from me. You have your battle and you have the ships of the Callas Republic and the Rift Federation. May the living stars grant that neither of us regrets our decision."

"Thank you." Geary took another deep breath and turned back to his display. It would be several hours before the fleets clashed, but he'd already set events in motion that would make that battle inevitable. He needed to use the intervening time to maximize his chances of winning. And planning for what to do if disaster struck and he had to pull another desperate retreat out of his hat.

TEN

DECIDING to fight started the adrenaline flowing, though combat was still several hours away even if both sides rushed toward each other at maximum acceleration. Geary ached to immediately order the fleet out of the generic Alpha formation into the actual battle formation he planned on using, but he knew that would be a mistake. His old commanders had drilled that into him. *The three things you need to worry about the most during the hours leading up to an engagement are acting too early, acting too early, and acting too early.*

And here was Desjani wanting to do just that. "Will we be fighting in this formation?" she asked dubiously.

"No." Geary caught the look of frustration that flashed across her face and relented. "We won't move into the battle formation until shortly before contact. I want to leave just enough time, with a small margin of error, for our ships to reach their new stations and then be able to accelerate to battle speed."

"Why not do it now? You've told me you're concerned about the fleet's ability to maneuver properly in an actual combat situation. Why wait until we're almost in contact with the enemy?"

He'd asked the same question a long time ago. "Because we don't want to give the enemy hours of leisure time to study our formation and figure out our plan of engagement."

"But we could be in one usable formation and then shift to another, couldn't we? Then we'd be ready even if the ships didn't get into the new formation in time. We could shift a lot and keep the enemy guessing as to our intentions."

Geary laughed softly, drawing a puzzled look from Desjani. "I'm sorry, but I'm just remembering wanting to do the same thing. It took me a while to learn the flaw in that approach." He waved at the display, where the symbols representing the Alliance and Syndic forces were slowly converging across the huge distances between them. "We decide to fight and then usually have quite a while to prepare. There's a tremendous temptation during that time to keep messing with things. Keep changing formations, keep making minor adjustments, keep altering plans. And if you do that, you end up wearing out your crews and drawing down your fuel reserves before you even get into contact with the enemy. It's far better to discipline yourself to wait, to give your ships a chance to rest a bit before battle."

"I see." Desjani shifted in her seat. "Yes, I do understand. I want to do something *now,* but it'd be premature. That's how we've fought, you know. Immediately assume battle formation, almost always something simple, and then charge straight at the enemy."

"I figured that." He looked again at the display, where the Syndic force seemed to be following that kind of approach. *Two opposing forces just hurling themselves straight at their opponents and beating the hell out of each other. Brute force against brute force. No wonder these people value pride and courage so much. In that kind of battle, the side that keeps fighting the hardest and longest is likely to win. But at a terrible price in casualties and ship losses.*

Geary checked the time, then called the fleet again. "All units. Updated estimated remaining time to contact with enemy force is seven hours. Recommend all ships rest their crews for the next few hours." He grinned at Desjani. "Did you ever get held at maximum alert for half a day?"

She looked away. "That's actually been common. To ensure everyone was fully ready."

"You're joking." The look on Desjani's face told him she wasn't. "That wears everybody out before the battle's even joined. There are situations where you don't have any choice, but with something like this, where we know the enemy can't engage us for close to seven hours, it makes sense for everybody to get what rest they can." Geary made a show of standing up. "I'm going to take a walk," he announced to the entire bridge, "and get something to eat." Aware of all their eyes upon him, Geary sauntered off of the bridge, wondering how well he'd be able to fake an interest in food. He'd have to pretend to be resting for at least the next couple of hours, too, though he knew the chances of actually getting any sleep were nonexistent. "Please keep me informed of any changes in the Syndic force's formation or movement, Captain Desjani."

"Of course, sir." Desjani hesitated, but as Geary was leaving the bridge he heard her standing down a good part of *Dauntless*'s crew so they could get some food as well.

After spending hours wandering through *Dauntless* to visit compartments and talk to the sailors in them, after pretending to eat in three different meal areas, and after periodically checking with the bridge to make sure there weren't any new developments, Geary finally gave in and returned to the bridge. Desjani was still in her seat, having apparently not left the bridge the entire time.

Desjani gave him a sheepish look. "Force of habit."

"You're a ship's captain, Tanya. I know that means you have to be here even when you shouldn't have to be here." Geary sat down, then forced himself to lean back and study the display again. The two opposing fleets had gotten much closer, but were still hours from contact. The Syndic formation remained unchanged. "We're going to fight in Fox Five," he advised her.

"Fox Five?" Desjani grinned in anticipation. "I can't wait to see this fleet carry that off."

Me, too. I hope they can *carry it off.* He ran calculations, using the latest estimates of the velocity at which the Syndics were traveling and the point at which the two formations would come together if nothing changed between now and then. *Two more hours. Too long. I can't order the fleet into Fox Five yet.* Dreading the thought of spending the next hour staring at the display, Geary called up the simulation program and began running it using his fleet and the actual Syndic force. *This should keep me busy, and maybe I'll spot something I need to know.*

It still seemed to take forever for the next hour to crawl by. "Okay, Tanya. Let's get ready to kick some Syndic butt." She bared her teeth in an eager smile as Geary called the fleet. "All units, this is Captain Geary on the *Dauntless*. Execute Formation Fox Five at time four zero. I say again, execute Formation Fox Five at time four zero. *Dauntless* remains the formation guide."

Fox Five was an old formation, though as far as Geary could tell it hadn't been used for a long time. It seemed perfectly suited to what the Syndics were doing and to what he wanted to do in the upcoming engagement, and it was one of the formations he'd included in the simulations, so his ship commanders weren't totally unfamiliar with it.

"Fox Five?" a voice queried. Co-President Rione, on the other hand, wasn't at all familiar with it. "What does that involve?"

Geary turned to smile at her, unaware until now that she'd come onto the bridge sometime in the last hour. "It's a way of arranging my forces. A fairly complex way compared to the manner in which battles have been fought recently, but it should be very effective."

"How so?"

"I have superior numbers," Geary assured Rione. "The trick is getting those superior numbers to hit the enemy together so his defenses are overwhelmed."

She looked skeptical. "If I understand what I'm seeing on the displays, your ships are heading off in different directions."

"That's the idea. Too many ships in one formation means you can't employ them all together. An enemy force engaged on one side of the formation can't be engaged by ships on the other side of the formation."

Rione shook her head. "I see you breaking your force into pieces. How does this help them work together?"

"I'm afraid you'll have to watch it in practice." Geary felt too nervous and excited to want to try to further explain fleet tactics to a civilian. He'd practiced moving fleets around, he'd trained at it under some captains and admirals who awed him with their skill, and he'd done a lot of simulating such maneuvers in the last couple of weeks. But this was the first time he'd be doing it in earnest, the first time large numbers of ships would actually be moving and engaging the enemy on his orders, the first time his decisions would decide the fates of many ships and perhaps the entire fleet.

He concentrated on the display to calm himself. As the ships moved in response to his order, the main body of the fleet was splitting into three sections. The section centered on *Dauntless* was significantly larger than the other two, a flattened oval facing the oncoming Syndic force. Moving to a position a million kilometers, or a bit over thirty light-seconds, above and forward of *Dauntless* were ships that were gradually forming a flat circle containing the second section of the main body, while another flat circle consisting of the rest of the main body was forming up thirty light-seconds below and forward. Together, the three formations resembled a huge nutcracker awaiting the Syndics, with the base centered in *Dauntless* and the two jaws positioned above and below the course the Syndics were taking.

Off to either side, also thirty light-seconds away, two smaller discs aligned at right angles to the main body were rapidly coming into existence as lighter units, mainly light cruisers and destroyers, with a leavening of heavy cruisers, raced into position to form the cheeks of the nutcracker.

Moving back, behind the lines of combatants, were the auxiliaries and the warships designated as their escorts.

And all six pieces of the Alliance fleet were moving at a still-deliberate pace of .03 light speed, following the course and speed set by *Dauntless*, having abandoned the orbit around Kaliban that they'd occupied for the last two weeks and headed through space toward an intercept with the Syndic force.

Geary gave a quiet sigh of relief as he saw the ships responding to orders. No one seemed to be pushing into an unassigned station, no one was charging off to be first to engage the Syndic force. Geary grimaced as he reviewed the formations, though. There was another command he had to send, to confirm the command arrangements for the coming battle, and he'd had to make a decision in that respect that he feared he'd regret. "All units, this is Captain Geary on the *Dauntless*, confirming the command structure for the upcoming engagement. In addition to exercising overall command of the fleet, I will exercise direct command of the main body."

He looked at the display as he continued speaking, focusing on the powerful formation forward and above the main body. "Formation Fox Five One will be commanded by Captain Duellos on the *Courageous*." His gaze shifted, looking at the lower jaw of the fleet. "Formation Fox Five Two will be commanded by Captain Numos on the *Orion*."

Desjani gave Geary a sympathetic look. "Captain Numos is a senior captain."

"Yeah. I didn't have any choice but to give him command of that formation." *No choice since I had no grounds for dishonoring him by bypassing him for that responsibility. But if he screws this up, I'll have those grounds and damn the consequences.*

Geary activated his communications again. "Formation Fox Five Three is under the command of Commander Cresida on the *Furious*. Formation Fox Five Four is under the command of Commander Landis on the *Valiant*." That took care of the light forces in the cheeks of the formation. "Captain Tulev in *Leviathan* is in command of Formation Fox Five Five." The auxiliaries had needed someone in command of their escorts that Geary could count on, and he felt sure Tulev was that man. A dashing commander, even one as reliable as Duellos, might be tempted at some point to leave the auxiliaries unguarded in order to hurl the escorts into the battle. Tulev, steady and calm, should stick with the lightly armed auxiliaries to the death.

Geary took another satisfied look at the display, pleased to see the disparate elements of the fleet going exactly where they all should go. Then he noticed some concern on the face of Captain Desjani. "What's the matter?" Geary asked quietly. She hesitated. "I need to know your thinking, Captain Desjani. Candid and direct."

"Very well, sir." Desjani spoke half-apologetically. "I know we've done simulations using this formation, but I'm still concerned about the distances between our forces. We seem to be spread out far enough to invite defeat in detail."

He nodded. "That's a legitimate concern. Dividing the fleet and remaining passive would allow the enemy to hit each piece in turn and have local superiority when they did so. If we didn't move, that'd be exactly what would happen. But we're not going to be sitting still waiting for the Syndics to hit us. Or rather," Geary corrected, "the other formations won't be sitting still. The main body is going to offer itself as a target for the Syndic assault."

Oddly enough, the assurance that her ship would be charging straight into contact with the enemy clearly reassured Desjani. "*Dauntless* is to hold this course until contact?"

"Right." Geary smiled again. "We're going to adjust the course as necessary if the Syndics don't head right for us, and we'll modify our speed at the right points. But when the Syndics get to us they're going to have a lot of other things to worry about, too. Trust me."

She smiled back. "We do, Captain Geary."

For some reason, having that said almost rattled Geary again. The trust some of these people had in him was so absolute, it was unnerving. But he focused back on the maneuvers of his ships, seeing the individual discs forming up nicely. On a whim, he pivoted the display in front of him so he could look sideways down the ranks of ships in the main body oval centered on *Dauntless*. Normally such a formation would have destroyers to the lead, cruisers behind, then the grim, steady mass of battleships and battle cruisers. But since Geary had sent the lighter units off to the other pieces of the Fox Five formation, the main body consisted of just the heavy hitters, battleships and battle cruisers arrayed in an open formation with interlocking fields of fire in front and to the sides. *Have the Syndics seen what I'm doing yet? Do they understand?*

He checked the Syndic formation. Still about six light-minutes away, the time-late images showed the Syndic force hadn't altered formation in response to the movements of the Alliance fleet. The Syndic ships were spread into the flat bar that thinned and extended forward toward the edges. In some ways, it resembled a hammerhead bearing down on the Alliance fleet. Geary recognized the general concept behind it. Simple, and effective against an enemy who didn't take the right countermeasures, the hammer would concentrate the attacking force's assault against a relatively small but critical area, allowing close-ranked successive waves of warships to sweep through the center of the defending force and batter it repeatedly with no chance for the defenders to recover between waves. Very simple, indeed. The Syndic commander wouldn't have to give any maneuvering orders to his or her fleet until it had swept completely through the Alliance forces, and then they could simply turn the entire formation to come back and repeat the battering if needed. Or release the formation into individual ships with orders to independently run down and overwhelm the scattered survivors of the first attack.

Unfortunately for you guys, I have no intention of letting you get in that kind of blow.

Geary waited until his ships had all reached their assigned stations. "All units assume full combat readiness. At time zero seven, all units accelerate to point zero five light speed and proceed along formation axis defined by *Dauntless*." Two minutes later, the entire Alliance fleet accelerated in unison, pushing its speed upward. "Damn, that looks nice."

"It does." Desjani grinned as Geary showed his surprise. "Didn't you realize you'd said that out loud?"

"No." But he smiled again as he watched the display, showing the vast formation of the Alliance fleet rushing onward in perfect unison, while the Syndic force continued to charge straight toward the center of the main body, and thereby straight into the jaws of the nutcracker. *It never hurts to have an arrogant or foolish opponent, does it?*

And now the really hard part had come, making sure he ordered the next maneuvers at the right times and in the right ways. Geary watched the data and the displays as the two opponents hurtled toward each other, trying to let his training and instincts feel the right moments to call the next orders. The images of the closest Syndic warships were still five minutes old by the time the Alliance saw them. Five minutes wasn't a huge amount of time, especially given the momentum of those massive warships, but it was enough time for the Syndics to make some last-minute moves to mess up Geary's carefully coordinated attack. Especially if he moved his formations just a little too early and gave the Syndics the warning they needed.

Minutes passed. At one point, he thought Desjani might've asked him something, but he stayed focused on the feel of the fleets rushing together, and she didn't speak again.

A few more minutes. Just a few more.

Geary's hand reached out and touched the communications control, his eyes never leaving the display. "Formation Fox Five One. At time four five accelerate to point one light speed and alter course down six zero degrees. Align your formation axis perpendicular to the Syndic formation. Adjust course as necessary to enter the top of the Syndic formation about one-third of the way behind its leading edge."

He paused, wanting to get the timing right. "Formation Fox Five Two. At time four five point five accelerate to point one light speed and alter course up five zero degrees. Align your formation axis perpendicular to the Syndic formation. Adjust course as necessary to enter the bottom of the Syndic formation about two thirds of the way behind its leading edge."

Forty seconds later came Captain Duellos's cheerful acknowledgment of the orders to Formation Fox Five One. One minute after that, Captain Numos in command of Formation Fox Five Two acknowledged his orders with no apparent emotion.

Geary waited, trying to keep his mind in that place where it could operate with all the distances and time delays in play. "Formations Fox Five Three and Fox Five Four. At time five zero accelerate to point one light speed and alter course to intercept the leading edges of the Syndic formation on your sides. Align formations to maintain right angles to the Syndic formation."

As the other formations began accelerating toward the enemy, he could almost physically feel the ships of the main body straining to leap forward at maximum acceleration and join in the attack. "Main body, hold your formation. Reverse headings and prepare to execute braking maneuver."

He might've caught a glimpse out of the corner of his eye of the shock on Desjani's face or just imagined it. He waited as the Alliance ships swung one hundred and eighty degrees so that their sterns faced the enemy. *Come on, come on,* he urged the big warships. *Get your butts around.*

Good. "Main body, brake velocity down to point two light, then reverse headings and prepare to engage." Again he had the sense that the main body's ships were straining at the leash. "All ships hold formation. You'll have the entire Syndic attack coming through you in a few minutes and all the combat your hearts can handle."

Dauntless shuddered as her engines thrust against her motion, slowing her, then she swung up and around another time to face the enemy head-on once again.

By this time, momentum had heavily committed the Syndics to their attack, but they could still react in minor ways if they figured out what Geary was doing. But because of the time-lag in being able to see the movements of the Alliance ships, it would take them a few minutes to spot that the jaws above and below their course had started closing. Minutes later, they'd see the cheeks of the nut-cracker closing in from the sides. Even then, they might think they could engage the main body of the Alliance fleet before the jaws could bite down on them, but Geary's braking maneuver had just altered the time to contact enough that the jaws would actually hit minutes before the van of the Syndic force hit the Alliance main body.

They can try veering up or down to engage one of the jaws separately, but if they do that, I should be able to get the main body on them anyway, and the light units will still be able to hit their flanks. They're not going to get out of this without getting hurt.

"Blue shift on the Syndic ships," the tactical watch reported.

"They're speeding up?" Desjani wondered.

"Trying to counteract the effect of our braking maneuver and come to contact quicker. Maybe they think they'll be able to blow right through the main body here and out of the trap," Geary noted. "I don't think they'll make it. Duellos and Numos shouldn't have any trouble compensating for the Syndics' acceleration by increasing the angle of their intercept."

"We'll have a harder time dealing with them at those speeds, though."

"Not really. We know where they're going. They're the one's who'll have a harder time, because they'll have more trouble seeing us through the distortion."

As the last minutes to contact scrolled down, Geary had to imagine events in his mind's eye, because time lag meant he wasn't really seeing it as it happened. *Dauntless*'s sensors and Geary's eyes told him that the two jaws of the nutcracker were still closing to contact, when at that moment the upper disc of Alliance ships was already cutting down through the Syndic hammer at a high angle even as the second disc should be cutting upward farther back. While the Alliance ships shot through the Syndic formation along its shortest axis, each Alliance ship was in contact with the enemy for only a few minutes, able to flay any ships within range and then racing onward before its own defenses were too heavily stressed. But while the Alliance ships were continuing outward, allowing time for their shields to recover, the Syndic ships were getting hit again and again by new Alliance warships as the narrow disc of the Alliance formation swept through the Syndic formation.

But he couldn't get lost in that vision. "All units in main body open fire as enemy ships enter your weapon engagement envelopes. Ensure first volley is grapeshot, followed by specters."

He feared for a long minute that he'd cut the timing too fine, left the final open-fire command too late, in his desire to make sure a concentrated barrage hit the Syndic formation that had just been savaged by two Alliance buzz saws. Then he heard *Dauntless*'s weapons officer reporting that the projected paths of Syndic ships were entering the engagement envelopes of the flagship's weapons, and moments later reporting that *Dauntless*'s weapons systems were firing. Even given the time lag needed for his command to reach every ship in the main body, they should all have opened fire at the optimum time.

Space between the Syndic force and the Alliance main body was suddenly populated by rapid bursts of light as a missile volley fired by the Syndics against the main body ran into and was wiped out by the wave of Alliance grapeshot. Moments later, space in front of the *Dauntless* lit up in a broad area as the charging Syndic warships ran head-on into the barrage of grapeshot, the ball bearings flashing into gas as collisions with Syndic shields converted their kinetic energy to heat and light. It looked for all the world like someone had painted a sweep of space with light.

The huge flare was still fading when brighter and bigger lights started flaring like flashbulbs. Geary kept his expression dispassionate, knowing he was looking at the deaths of Syndic minor combatants whose shields had been overwhelmed, leaving the ships exposed to more grapeshot slamming them at high relative speeds.

Right behind the grapeshot came the wave of specters, hammering weakened shields and in many cases breaking through to hit the Syndic ships.

Within moments, the van of the Syndic force had been wiped out.

Geary swallowed, trying not to think of how many lives had just been ended in those flashes of light. He glanced over at Desjani, who was studying the display intently, her hands clenching and unclenching.

Holding their courses, though momentum left them little choice, follow-on waves of Syndic ships battered their way through the wreckage of the ships that had once made up their van. Instead of hitting an already softened-up Alliance main body with fresh attackers, the follow-on Syndics had themselves been hit by the two Alliance buzz saws even before they'd been further depleted by encountering the debris field. On the Alliance side, Geary's ships were still almost untouched, their shields still at maximum.

Then the Syndic charge came within range of the hell-lances of the Alliance fleet, and space was filled with blazing shafts of energy converging toward the paths the

Syndic ships were taking. Almost immediately thereafter, Geary saw null-fields being hurled out to also meet the on-rushing Syndics.

He could never be sure how much he'd actually seen and how much he'd imagined in snapshot fashion as the two fleets swept through each other at a combined speed of well over .1 light, the moments of actual closest approach flashing by too fast for humans to register. But by that time, the damage had been done.

As the Alliance ships absorbed a heavy barrage against their bow shields, the outgunned Syndics had already run into the much heavier fire of Geary's ships. Previously weakened and without time to rebuild, Syndic shields failed or let through damaging shots. Null-fields carved sudden gaps in ships while hell-lances flayed the oncoming Syndic warships.

Dauntless's instruments, detecting and calculating damage at superhuman speed, told her crew that most of the Syndic ships racing past Geary had taken damage. Many appeared to be little more than wrecks, still carried along with their living comrades by the force of momentum. As the Alliance main body swept through the space once occupied by the Syndic force, Geary realized many of the impacts registering on Alliance shields were actually pieces of shattered Syndic warships.

Forcing himself to ignore the human cost of what had just happened, Geary scanned his display for summaries of the estimated damage to the Syndic force even as he gave new orders. "Main body, reverse course at time one five, turning up through zero nine zero." That would bring the ships of his main body bending their courses upward in unison, up and over until they were going back in the other direction, chasing after the Syndic force that had passed through them, but slightly above them because of the turning radius required at the speeds they were traveling. They'd also be upside down relative to their former positions, of course, but in space that didn't matter in the slightest.

It was tempting, very tempting, to break the formation and let the fastest ships charge ahead, but until he knew the Syndic force had been broken, he couldn't take that risk. He also had to make sure the rest of his fleet was still acting in coordination. And despite the damage already done to the Syndics, the enemy force was still heading toward the auxiliaries formation. "Formation Fox Five Five. Take evasive course minimum down angle two zero at time one . . . seven." That would bring the auxiliaries toward the formation led by Captain Duellos, which had altered course after diving through the Syndic formation and was now swinging back up toward the bottom and rear of the Syndics. "Formation Fox Five One, close on Formation Fox Five Five and lend support."

Geary turned his attention to the smaller discs of cruisers and destroyers that had made up the cheeks of the nutcracker. As the Syndics had charged forward, the Alliance light units had sliced off the escort units making up the edges of the Syndic formation. "Formations Fox Five Three and Fox Five Four. Maneuver independently and close on the enemy. Ensure any stragglers or detached units are destroyed. Do not, repeat do not, break formation until given orders to do so."

Geary took a deep breath, glaring at the depiction of the formation commanded by Captain Numos. After carrying out Geary's orders, Fox Five Two should've been well above the path taken by the Syndics. Instead, it had leveled out early and was now proceeding along the same path the Syndic ships had taken, though far behind them and still a few light-seconds from even Geary's main body formation. Apparently, Numos had tried to pivot his formation even as it crossed through the Syndics, bleeding off much of its speed to achieve a tight turn, and as a result had failed to make as heavy a strike against the enemy as he should have. *He fell outside engagement range while trying to single-handedly run up the enemy's formation from the rear. Idiot.* "Formation Fox Five Two, continue pursuit and close with the enemy formation as soon as possible."

*That fool's handling of his formation kept a good chunk of
my heavies out of contact during the first encounter and
robbed me of some of my numerical advantage. He'll never
command another formation under me unless the living
stars themselves order me to let it happen.*

*Now, are the Syndics going to continue charging at the
auxiliaries before turning, or are they going to run for
open space to buy time to recover from their pass through
us?*

Over the next few minutes, Geary could only watch as
time-late images confirmed that the auxiliaries had altered
course as commanded, their path curving downward toward Captain Duellos's oncoming warships. Captain
Tulev's escorts for the auxiliaries had formed a slightly
concave disc, his entire formation of warships pivoting
slowly to keep its central focus on the badly hurt Syndic
force. The two smaller Alliance formations were far behind but coming around, edge-on toward the Syndics.
Geary's own main body was still swinging through its
course reversal.

The Syndics, as far as he could tell, had continued heading for the auxiliaries even though the Syndic formation
was increasingly ragged, as wrecked and heavily damaged
ships wavered off their courses even though their momentum had kept them with the rest of the formation. Judging
from the damage assessments still coming in and the
raggedness of the Syndic formation, they'd lost a lot of
ships. *But they're still sticking to their plan, apparently.
Rigid thinking. What would they have been planning on
doing after making a firing run through the auxiliaries?*

*Course reversal and come back through us en masse.
They'd turn about . . . there.*

*And they still have to do that if they're going to get out
of here. There are no jump points anywhere near their current course. Their only near-term chance to escape us is if
they can blow through us again going back toward the
jump point they used to enter the system.*

The main body finished its course reversal, steadying

on a vector leading back toward the Syndics, though of course the main body was still going far slower than the Syndic force. *But now that we're through the turn, I can crank up the engines on this force and go get those bastards.* "Main body, accelerate to point one light at time three zero." He turned to Desjani. "Captain, please adjust *Dauntless*'s course to keep this formation headed for an intercept with the projected path of the Syndic force."

Desjani seemed dazed, but nodded. "We'll never catch them at point one light."

"Assume they'll turn here," Geary advised, pointing out his earlier conclusion. "They'll come back toward us."

Her face lit up with bloodlust at the implications. "Yes! And that'll be the last maneuver any of them will ever manage."

Geary looked away, then activated his command circuit again. "All units remain in formation," he ordered again, haunted by the images of the chaos when his fleet fell apart at Corvus. "Formation Fox Five Five, increase down angle by two zero at time three eight." That should force the Syndics to bend their own course enough to help Geary's formations reach them in a coordinated assault. "Formation Fox Five One, alter course one zero down at time three eight. Adjust formation axis four zero degrees to starboard at time three eight. Maintain velocity of point one light." That should bring Duellos's formation edge on against the Syndics if they kept heading for the auxiliaries. "Formation Fox Five Three, alter course one zero to port and two zero down at time four zero and increase velocity to point one light. Formation Fox Five Four, alter course one five to port and one zero down at time four zero and hold present velocity." Which should bring the two lighter formations in from where they were sweeping up crippled Syndic strays, so they could rake across the flanks of the remnants of the Syndic formation, and where they could do the most damage to any Syndic ships having trouble staying in formation.

He couldn't help glaring at Numos's formation, even

though he'd realized he could use its position to his advantage. "Formation Fox Five Two, adjust course starboard three zero, down zero point five and increase velocity to point one light at time four zero. Roll formation axis six zero to port." If the Syndics tried to run for some of the other jump points on the other side of the system they'd have to veer off toward the inner system of Kaliban. The odds of them making that long a run were slim anyway, but now if they tried that, Numos's ships should be able to intercept their track and rake them as they ran.

If they didn't try to run, Geary's other formations would hit them in quick succession.

He sat back, breathing heavily as if he'd just physically exerted himself, knowing he'd have to just watch for a while and see what happened. It would be perhaps a half hour before the formations swept into contact again.

"Captain Geary?" Geary looked back to see Co-President Rione still on the bridge, apparently calm, but her eyes very alert. "Do you have one moment?"

"Yes, ma'am." Geary flashed a tense smile. "It'll be at least a few minutes until I can tell if everyone's following orders and if the Syndics are doing anything unexpected. It's a very old military dilemma. Hurry up and wait."

"Could you explain something for me, then?" She gestured around vaguely. "You gave orders in terms of 'up' and 'down,' 'port' and 'starboard,' yet the ships of your fleet are in a wide range of aspects. You are upside down relative to the ships in Captain Tulev's force, for example. How do they know which way you mean?"

Desjani, unseen by Rione, rolled her eyes at the Co-President's ignorance, but Geary just pointed at the display. "It's a standard convention, Madam Co-President, one every sailor learns by heart. It had to be established to provide a common frame of reference in an unbounded three-dimensional environment." He sketched the shape of Kaliban's system. "Every star system has a plane in which its planets or other objects orbit. One side of that plane is labeled 'up,' and the other side 'down.' So up and down within the system doesn't change regardless of how your ship is oriented. By the same token, the direction toward the star is 'starboard' while the direction away from the star is 'port.'" Geary shrugged. "I've been told that early on they tried to use 'starward' instead of 'starboard,' but the older expression stuck."

"I see. You take your orientation from the outside, not from yourself or from the aspect of the ship."

"It's the only way it could work. Otherwise, no two ships could be counted on to figure out what the other one meant by directions."

"What if you meet outside a star system? Where there is no such reference?"

Desjani looked startled. Geary also felt a shock of surprise at the question. But, then, how could Rione know better? "It doesn't happen. How could two ships meet up in interstellar space? Why would they be there, too far from the nearest star to use it for reference? Why would two ships, or fleets, fight where there was no reason to fight? Nothing to defend, nothing to attack, no jump points or hypernet gates. The weaker side could just run away indefinitely."

Rione stared back, her own surprise visible. "You always *choose* to fight?"

"You saw what happened at Corvus. We just kept going, and the Syndics couldn't catch us before we left. Space, even within star systems, is too big, and ships are still far too slow relative to that, for combat to be forced if one side refuses to engage and can't be blocked from running. If we'd wanted to defend a planet in Corvus or deny use of its jump points, we'd have had to stay and fight, but that wasn't the case."

Rione's stare shifted to the display. "As you chose to fight here."

"That's right. If we'd run instead, the Syndics wouldn't have caught us." *And it increasingly looks like I made the right decision to fight. Don't get too cocky, Geary. It's not over yet. But we've done a tremendous amount of damage to them.* He checked the information on his display. "They're still headed for our auxiliaries."

"You don't seem worried."

"No. If they'd immediately scattered and run after their pass through us, some of them might've gotten away. But now they've given me time to bring my ships back at them." He didn't add something that he knew to be true. The fate of the Syndic force had been sealed. All of those Syndic ships would be destroyed in the near future.

Desjani pointed at her display, emphasizing something to Geary. Geary's orders to formation Fox Five Five had forced the Syndic formation to alter course to keep closing on the auxiliaries and their escorts. As it did so, the Syndic wrecks and ships that were too heavily damaged to maneuver kept going along the old course, gradually separating from their less-damaged comrades. The Syndic formation had begun to look as if it were melting, the increasingly disordered hulls of the wrecks and badly damaged ships spreading onward and outward while the remaining warships headed down, still in their rectangular block, which had lost a third of its length when the Syndic van was annihilated, and contained large ragged gaps where lost ships had once been.

He became aware Rione was watching, too, as the two groups of Syndic ships separated, the still-functioning warships continuing on their doomed charge while the wrecks diverged from their original course. "I've seen detailed reports of space battles, Captain Geary. Why haven't I seen one like this?"

"It's not over yet, Madam Co-President."

"I'm aware of that. But this formation you used, the way you ordered your ships to move and fight. I haven't seen that. Why?"

This time Desjani smiled at Geary, and he knew she'd declare him to be the greatest fleet commander of all time unless he answered the question himself. "Fox Five, and formations like it, haven't been used for a long time. It took me a while to figure out why. It's because it requires a special kind of training and experience with judging exactly when to transmit orders to forces deployed across light-minutes of space, when to have those orders take effect, how to compensate for the small, but real, relativistic distortions that can creep into coordinated time lines, how to estimate what the enemy must be doing based on time-late visual images that vary depending on which part of the enemy formation you're looking at." He remembered a show he'd once attended. "Think of it as a ballet in four dimensions, with the different parts staggered through different layers of time delays in seeing and communicating with them."

Rione didn't bother trying to hide her reaction. "Very impressive. How did you learn this skill?"

Geary exhaled slowly before answering. "I learned how to do it from old hands, officers who'd trained at it for decades."

It took her a moment to connect the dots. "All of whom are dead now."

"Yes." He gave her a flat look. "Everyone those officers trained died in battle. The officers that group had started to train also died."

"I see. Like a trade secret in the world of peace. If those who know it die before passing on their skills, the chain of expert knowledge and experience is broken. The craft is lost and must be reinvented if it is to be seen again."

Geary simply nodded in reply this time. For decades there'd been no one left who knew the tricks and the methods. So the fleet had been forced to fall back on simple formations using simple tactics. *Until I came back, like some ancient general who remembers ways of fighting that the barbarians forgot long ago.*

There was nothing to do for a few minutes but watch the Alliance formations converge on the Syndics, with occasional glances at the fleet status information to see how much damage his ships had taken, as well as the latest estimates of Syndic damage and losses. So far, the two sides of the ledger were grossly unbalanced in the Alliance's favor.

"Captain Geary, this is Captain Numos. I demand that the ships under my command be allowed to engage the enemy!"

Desjani managed to convert a laugh into a cough, then carefully avoided betraying any other emotion.

Geary grabbed for his communications controls, then stopped himself and took a few moments to think before he reached again, then spoke with a bland tone. "Captain Numos, your formation is playing an important role in this battle by blocking any Syndic retreat. Since your formation, along with Fox Five One initiated contact with the enemy in this battle, I fail to understand your implication that your ships have not engaged the enemy."

There was a pause before the reply came, Numos's voice this time cold instead of heated. "You have deliberately placed the ships under my command in positions where they had the least chance to engage the enemy."

"No, Captain Numos." Geary realized with some surprise that his voice had remained level and calm. "I ordered your formation into an attack that would've resulted in substantial engagements for all of the ships in that formation. Unfortunately, my orders were not followed, with the result that the formation you command found itself out of position and out of the action. If you wish to complain about your current position relative to the battle, Captain Numos, I suggest you direct your complaints to the officer in command of Formation Fox Five Two. I believe you will find him on *Orion*." He cut the link to Numos, not wanting further distraction.

Captain Desjani made a small pointing gesture, her expression still controlled. "I believe that conversation was somehow accidentally carried out on a fleetwide communications circuit instead of a private command circuit. How unfortunate."

Geary glanced down to check, then shook his head. "Numos actually called me on a fleetwide circuit? Did he think I'd just let him claim his honor had been besmirched and not point out that he's the one responsible for where Fox Five Two is right now?"

"Yes, sir, I believe he did think that."

"Well, damn." Desjani gave Geary a surprised look. "I know Numos deserved to get chewed out, Tanya, but I was always taught to chew out in private and praise in public."

"I see." But Desjani shook her head. "Normally, I'd agree, but in this case, the charges would've otherwise been whispered in quarters where you'd have been unaware of them even as they served to undermine your authority. It's best that Numos's charges were rebutted so clearly and so publicly."

"You may be right," Geary conceded. "But I'm still not happy it happened that way."

Another message arrived on the heels of his words, but this time the tone was professional. "Captain Geary, this is Captain Tulev on *Leviathan*. The Syndic force is continuing down a course to intercept the auxiliary ships I am charged with protecting. I believe I can best keep the Syndics from closing within weapons range by pushing my heaviest units out five light-seconds from the auxiliaries. Request permission to do so."

Interesting idea. Geary checked the display, imagining how the situation would change if he granted Tulev permission for the maneuver. *He'll still be close enough to the auxiliaries, but in a position to engage the Syndics before the enemy can get within range of the auxiliaries. But why is this necessary? Fox Five Five should've been able to keep the range open longer than this.*

Titan. I should've guessed. All that mass she took on has reduced her performance as much as taking out half her propulsion systems would've done. Not that Witch *and the others are dancing around like space fairies, either.* "Captain Tulev, permission granted to extend your escort range to five light-seconds from the auxiliaries. Captain Duellos, be advised that Formation Fox Five Five's escorts will be closing on the enemy to engage them at a distance of five light-seconds from the main body of Fox Five Five. Request you adjust your intercept of the Syndic formation accordingly."

Duellos's reply, sounding very cheerful indeed now, came over a half minute later. "We are adjusting course and will coordinate our next strike with Captain Tulev, sir."

With *Leviathan* a good light-minute away, Tulev's reply took a little while longer. "Thank you, sir."

It took another few minutes before Geary could see Tulev's ships arcing up toward the Syndics, as well as Duellos's formation altering their course and accelerating a little more so that both Alliance forces would be in position to engage the enemy at about the same time.

Geary shook his head, imagining himself on the bridge of the Syndic flagship and trying to think through options, none of which were particularly good at this point. With Tulev's escorts heading to intercept the Syndics from in front and below, while Duellos's formation swung ever closer from behind and below, the Syndics faced two options. They could continue their original plan and get caught by both Alliance forces hitting them almost simultaneously from two different angles, or they could turn away from the Alliance auxiliaries and try to make it back to the jump point from which they'd entered Kaliban. "What would you be thinking if you were them?" Geary asked Desjani.

She considered the question for a moment. "Their objective is clear enough."

"They won't reach the auxiliaries. We've got too much heading to intercept them."

Desjani shrugged. "If their orders are to get to the auxiliaries, they'll do it or die trying."

Senseless. Totally senseless. But I don't see any sign the Syndics are having second thoughts. Perhaps I can add a little pressure and see if that'll change their minds. "Formation Fox Five Three, adjust course and speed as needed to strike the upper edge of the Syndic formation. All units in Formation Fox Five Four, break formation and head for the cluster of Syndic wrecks. I want you to ensure they're all really dead."

It took time for the formations to converge, but he finally saw the images of Tulev's escorts engaging the Syndics which had occurred less than a minute before. Using the same tactics as Geary had employed with the main body, Tulev's heavies had fired grapeshot, then followed up with a barrage of specters. The Syndics were still reeling from the impact of those volleys when Captain Duellos's formation sailed past, angling upward to slide through the rear of the Syndic formation and pound the ships there. Taken together, Tulev's and Duellos's formations outgunned the surviving Syndics almost two to one without even taking into account the damage to many of the Syndic ships.

As Tulev's escorts slid by beneath the Syndics and Duellos's warships rolled up through the enemy formation, the lighter Alliance ships in Formation Fox Five Three glided in from above. Against fresh heavy combatants, the Alliance destroyers and cruisers would've been outmatched, but by this point the Syndic force had been hurt so badly that it could offer little effective defense. The remnants of the Syndic destroyers and cruisers tried to block Fox Five Three's firing run but were quickly overwhelmed, their shields swamped and their hulls broken.

As the third Alliance formation in quick succession engaged the Syndics, the enemy formation suddenly fell apart. Geary saw the surviving Syndic warships scattering, most of them turning frantically back toward the Alliance main body that blocked their way to the jump point and safety. Hardly daring to believe the enemy force had been so decisively broken, Geary evaluated the way the Syndic ships were dispersing. Trying to catch them all using big formations would be difficult at best and very likely impossible. "All units, this is Captain Geary. Break formation. General pursuit. I say again, general pursuit. Make sure we get all of them."

There were triumphant cheers on the bridge of *Daunt-*

less, but Geary barely registered them as he watched his fleet on the display. Even though he'd known how badly those ships wanted to be cut loose, he was still surprised to see just how rapidly his neat formations dissolved, as the individual ships sped away to engage targets of opportunity.

Dauntless surged forward herself under Desjani's orders. Geary leaned over to see which target had been highlighted by the battle cruiser's combat system. A Syndic D-Class battle cruiser, looping upward in an attempt to pass over the main body. *Why isn't he going faster? According to what I've read, a D-Class should be able to do a lot better than that.* Geary highlighted the target on his own display, getting the estimated damage readout. *Ah. He's been hit hard. Looks like he's lost a lot of propulsion capability.*

Zooming in the view of the Syndic battle cruiser from *Dauntless*'s optical sensors, Geary could see the damage that had blasted holes in the enemy ship. At one time, the enemy ship had been a good-looking ship, displaying clean lines and smooth menace, but now its hull was torn and bent. *A D-Class versus* Dauntless *would be a roughly even match, except that Syndic warship has already been beat to hell.*

Then he thought of something else, pulling back the range scale on his display again and checking the movement vectors of nearby Alliance ships. As far as he could tell without asking, the battleship *Vanguard* and the battle cruiser *Fearless* were both also aiming for the same Syndic warship. Geary called up remote data from the other ships, confirming that they were also targeting the D-Class battle cruiser and getting their estimated times to intercept as well. "They're going to get to it first," he remarked out loud.

Captain Desjani nodded, her frustration clear. "I can't beat them to it without accelerating to the point that my aim will be lousy. I'd rather get in the third blow than risk missing the bastard completely."

Geary looked back as his display, where the curving lines through space that marked the projected paths of both Alliance and Syndic warships formed an oddly beautiful pattern against the backdrop of the stars. At this scale, he could easily see how the paths of multiple Alliance ships were converging on the courses of every individual Syndic ship. *This isn't a battle any more. The surviving Syndics are so badly outnumbered and already so damaged that this is just a massacre.*

I know we have to destroy the Syndic fighting forces to survive, but why can't the Syndics have the brains to surrender when the situation is obviously hopeless?

On the other hand, the Alliance fleet's situation seemed hopeless back in the Syndic home system and surrender was a lousy option then.

The irony finally hit him that this one-sided slaughter was what would've happened to the Alliance fleet in the Syndic home system if it had fallen apart and tried to run as individual ships.

Vanguard reached the D-Class battle cruiser first, pounding it with a barrage of hell-lances and then sweeping onward with its sights set on another target. *Fearless* came in next, from a different angle, its shots hitting the Syndic battle cruiser in the stern. Secondary explosions ripped pieces off of the Syndic warship's stern as it began rolling erratically through space, apparently no longer under control.

"Our turn," Desjani breathed. "Combat systems watch, is there anything left on that hulk that still needs killing?"

Dauntless swept down on the crippled Syndic battle cruiser, which was tumbling through space while escape pods burst from it in irregular volleys. "Captain," the combat systems watch reported, "we're picking up powered systems still active amidships."

"He's not dead yet, then," Desjani observed with a grim smile. "Hell-lances target midships section of the battle cruiser. Fire when the target enters range."

The great tumbling shape of the battle cruiser made for

a difficult target, but *Dauntless*'s hell-lances flashed out
and punched into the Syndic ship's hull as *Dauntless* rock-
eted past, nearly every shot slamming into the midships
area of the battle cruiser.

"No systems activity registering now," the watch reported as the wreck of the battle cruiser receded behind
them, still fitfully spitting out occasional escape pods.

"He's not worth another pass," Desjani decided. "Shifting target to heavy cruiser bearing zero two zero degrees
relative, three one degrees up, range point three light-
seconds." *Dauntless* swung in response to her maneuvering systems, arcing up and slightly to the side in a smooth
curve. The Syndic cruiser, which also displayed the marks
of damage already inflicted earlier in the battle, tried
rolling and diving away, but was too close and didn't have
enough of a relative speed advantage. Desjani adjusted
Dauntless's course and slashed over the fleeing heavy
cruiser at close range. *Dauntless*'s shields easily absorbed
the ragged series of shots fired by the damaged cruiser,
while the Alliance ship sent a heavy series of barrages at
the Syndic ship that first collapsed the cruiser's remaining
shields, then ripped into the ship.

"Damage assessment," Desjani rapped out as *Dauntless*
and the cruiser rushed away from each other on diverging
courses.

"Heavy damage to Syndic cruiser," the watch hastily reported. "Confirmed hits on all areas of the hull. Ma'am, we
just spotted escape pods leaving the cruiser."

"Do we have a confirmed kill on that cruiser?" Desjani
demanded.

The watch hesitated, pouring over the information
being collected by *Dauntless*'s sensors. "Heavy damage,
and the cruiser no longer appears to be under control, but I
cannot confirm a kill."

Desjani frowned in thought. "It could be a ruse." She
scanned the area. "And there're no other Syndic ships
nearby that aren't being brought to battle or haven't been

taken out already. Let's bring *Dauntless* back around for another pass at the cruiser."

Dauntless began laboriously curving around for another run on the Syndic ship, using her propulsion systems to brake and allow for a tighter, though still gigantic, turn. The turn had barely begun, when an Alliance destroyer flashed past the Syndic cruiser and slapped it with several more hits. Then, two-thirds of the way through *Dauntless*'s turn, the watch called out again. "More escape pods leaving that cruiser. Lots of them."

Geary gave a lopsided smile to Desjani. "I guess they figured out you were coming back."

"As if we'd let them get away in any case," Desjani replied before issuing another order to her crew. "Continue firing-run maneuver but hold further fire until I give orders to shoot." Geary and Desjani watched the target intently as *Dauntless* swung farther back, now closing on the battered heavy cruiser again, but almost .2 light-seconds away after the wide turn her velocity had required. "Two more escape pods, I see," Desjani commented. Moments later, light flared as the cruiser's power core overloaded. "That might've been an accident, but if they'd intended on hurting us with that, they did it way too soon."

"Hard to tell," Geary replied. "Maybe they were just scuttling the ship to keep it out of our hands."

Desjani snorted. "An abandoned heavy cruiser isn't going to have anything on it that we're interested in. They'd have destroyed anything of intelligence value. All we'd do with it is set the power core to overload so the Syndics couldn't use it again. They just saved us the trouble." She glared at her display in frustration. "There're no more targets near us."

Geary checked his own display again. The number of Syndic ships still active had dwindled rapidly, with the destruction of more being registered by *Dauntless*'s sensors even as Geary watched. A few Syndics were still trying to flee, but Alliance pursuers were closing in on them from multiple angles. The remaining Syndic ships would be wiped out in short order.

It's over. He stared at the cloud of debris that was all that remained of the heavy cruiser that *Dauntless* had last targeted. *I don't want to know how many human beings died over the course of the last few hours. The great majority who died were our enemies who were trying to kill us, and the ugly truth is that's all that matters right now.*

ELEVEN

THE star that humans had named Kaliban had acquired a great many more objects in orbit. Most of those objects were small, the shattered debris that was all that was left after Syndic warships had either blown themselves apart or Alliance boarding parties had done the same thing to prevent the ships from being salvaged and reused by the enemy. Also among the remnants of battle were a swarm of Syndic escape pods scattered through a wide area of space, carrying the survivors who'd managed to leave their ships before the end. Small, unarmed, and with just enough range to reach safety within the Kaliban System, the pods were no threat to the victorious Alliance fleet.

"Those crews could fight again. They *will* fight again," Desjani argued. "I'm not saying we should have target practice on the escape pods, but rounding them up and taking the crews prisoner would be a good idea."

Geary let her see he was considering the idea before he shook his head. "Where would we put them? They'd fill every brig on every ship and have large numbers left over. And we'd have to feed them."

Desjani grimaced but nodded. "Security and logistics. Those two things keep getting in the way of a lot of good ideas."

"You got that right." Geary grinned. "Though I've seen plenty of plans that didn't take reality into account, and that didn't seem to bother the people who created the plans."

"Of course not. Why spoil a great plan by letting reality intrude?" Desjani smiled as well. "This is a wonderful victory, Captain Geary."

"Thank you. There's some unfinished business, though. How can we find out which one of those pods contains whoever's the senior surviving Syndic officer?"

It took a little while, bouncing messages around various escape pods until the one containing the Syndic commander was located and a communications link established. As fate would have it, the overall commander had survived the battle, though Geary wondered whether that officer would be grateful for the fact for very long.

The Syndic CEO's carefully tailored uniform had suffered the indignities of several rips and burns. His face, as pale as if he were in shock, had the stunned look of someone who hadn't been able to absorb what had happened. Geary didn't recognize the CEO, but the CEO stared at Geary with eyes filled with disbelieving recognition. "It's true," the Syndic commander whispered.

"What's true?" Geary asked, knowing the answer already.

Instead of giving that answer, the Syndic CEO appeared to try to steel himself. "My force will not s-surrender," he stuttered.

Geary couldn't help raising both eyebrows in a surprised expression. "That's not really an option anymore. There's nothing to surrender. Your force has ceased to exist. All of your ships have been destroyed."

"We can s-still fight."

"Hand to hand, you mean? But, you see, *we're* not interested in fighting *you* any longer," Geary explained.

"Your former command no longer possesses any military capability, and to be perfectly frank, we have no interest in taking on responsibility for a large number of prisoners." The CEO somehow paled a little more, but he stayed silent. "There are two things I need to tell you. The first is that I still have some personnel on an asteroid in this system. I'm sending you the orbital data for the asteroid I'm speaking of. If you still have any doubts as to which asteroid it is, make sure you contact us. Try to ensure none of the escape pods from your fleet land there. I'll be taking off my personnel and have no wish to confront refugees from your fleet, as that could inadvertently lead to further bloodshed."

The Syndic CEO nodded, still silent.

"The other thing is that we surveyed all of the abandoned Syndicate Worlds facilities within the Kaliban Star System, and I want you to know that the former towns at these locations I'm now sending you remain in good condition. Your people will have no trouble restarting life support. I regret to state we drew down the supplies of foodstuffs that had been left behind when the towns were abandoned, but enough should remain for your personnel until other Syndicate Worlds units arrive in the system to discover the fate of your command. In order to ensure word of your presence here is known, I assure you that when next we contact any Syndicate Worlds planets or other representatives, we will also inform them that you are awaiting rescue."

Another nod. The Syndic CEO seemed increasingly confused, as if waiting for the other shoe to drop.

"I regret that my fleet cannot linger much longer in this system," Geary continued, "and that therefore offering medical care to your injured is out of the question. But the mothballed medical facilities we examined in this system, while limited and outdated, all appear fully functional and still contain an adequate supply of expendable materials."

The CEO finally found his voice again. "Why are you telling me all this?"

"I am fulfilling my obligations under the rules of war," Geary stated in a slow, firm voice, "as well as the obligations incurred by my personal honor and the honor of my ancestors. Now, one last thing." Geary leaned forward. "Once you are back in communication with your superiors, please inform them that any other Syndicate Worlds force that attempts to engage this fleet will suffer the same fate as yours."

The CEO just stared back for a long moment. "Who are you?" he finally asked in a voice so dry it was almost unintelligible.

"You know who I am. I saw you recognize me."

"You're— He's dead!"

"No. *I'm* not." Geary jabbed a finger at the CEO's image. "My name is John Geary. I used to be known as Black Jack Geary a long time ago. I'm in command of this fleet now, and I'm taking it home. Anyone who wishes to try to stop this fleet will have to deal with me."

Geary could see several of the Syndic personnel within the CEO's escape pod make sudden gestures over their chests. It took a moment, then he realized they were making ancient warding signs against forces of darkness. *Believe that if you want, as long as it makes you afraid to mess with this fleet again.*

But it ought to bother me more to see it. Is what Co-President Rione said true? Am I starting to like being regarded as something more than human?

After a victory like this, am I going to start believing it myself? He nodded to the Syndic CEO. "No offense, but hopefully we won't meet again until this war is ended." Then he broke the connection and stared at the space where the CEO's image had been.

Maybe a little reality check will keep me grounded. Geary worked the controls on his display until he got a readout of the losses the Alliance fleet had suffered. He gazed at the report, then punched his controls again. "Are loss reports still coming in?"

Captain Desjani looked surprised at the question. "Loss

reports are updated continuously based on ship status feeds."

"This can't be right."

She called up the same data. "I don't see any indications the data stream has been compromised. Communications watch, double-check the ship status feeds to ensure we're getting everything."

"Yes, ma'am." A minute later, the watch gave his report. "No problems with the ship status feeds, Captain. All feeds confirmed active, except for those feeds lost due to loss of the ship."

Desjani gave Geary a long look. "It was an amazingly one-sided battle," she noted. "I find the results hard to believe myself, but that is an accurate tally of our losses and damage throughout the fleet."

"Thank the living stars." Geary ran his eyes over the list again, the gratifyingly short list, of ship losses suffered by the Alliance fleet. "That's the way it's supposed to work. In theory. By taking full advantage of our superior numbers, exploiting the weaknesses of the enemy formation, and concentrating fire at the decisive point, we overwhelmed the Syndic ships and prevented them from doing the same to us. It didn't hurt that the Syndic commander fought stupidly."

"I believe he assumed we'd fight the same way we have in the past." Desjani noted, shaking her head in apparent disbelief. "I never would've believed the difference it made."

"If courage alone decided battles, the course of human history would've been a lot different." Geary forced himself to read the list of lost ships slowly. *One-sided it may have been, but even a one-sided victory costs the winner.* "Damn." Geary just looked at the warship name at the top of the list, feeling a numbness inside. *The* Arrogant. *Lost with all hands. Commander Hatherian. I'm sorry.*

"Sir?" Captain Desjani looked over. "Oh. *Arrogant.* Power core overload."

Geary couldn't look at her. "Do we have any idea what happened?"

"It's in the summary file, sir. See? During the first pass-through of the Syndic formation by Fox Five Two, *Arrogant* was near several lighter units that came under sustained fire from a number of heavy Syndic warships. *Arrogant* moved to cover them and took the fire herself." She nodded, her expression sober. "Commander Hatherian proved himself to be a good commanding officer."

"Yes." Geary didn't trust himself to say anything else, knowing that if he hadn't transferred Hatherian to *Arrogant*, then that officer would have been on *Orion* and still alive. But then if he hadn't given command of Fox Five Two to Captain Numos, and if Numos hadn't squandered his maneuvering advantage and allowed some of his ships to be caught under concentrated enemy fire, then *Arrogant* wouldn't have had to sacrifice herself to protect those ships. *That's also my fault. I decided to let Numos take that command even though I didn't trust him with it.* "We also lost some light units. *Dagger, Swift, Venom.* And another heavy cruiser. *Invidious.*"

"Yes, that's too bad. We need every escort we have. But we did recover some of their crews."

Geary just stared at her, trying to understand how a fleet officer, how a citizen of the Alliance, could so calmly deal with the losses of ships and their crews. Desjani seemed partly somber over the losses yet also partly jubilant at the same time. *Have my people really become so barbaric that it doesn't matter to them when ships and crews die?*

Then Desjani indicated the list of losses, and her face went sad in a way that relieved Geary. "No victory comes without a price, not even one of yours, sir. None of those we lost today need fear facing their ancestors, though." She shook her head, her gaze distant. "After the battle at Easir, we didn't know what to think. We'd kept possession of the system, but the cost was so high. Every single battle cruiser in the system and half of our battleships lost, the light escorts decimated. We'd traded losses almost ship for ship with the Syndics, but had we truly done honor to our ancestors by losing so many? You never really know in a case like that." Desjani paused again. "I was a junior lieutenant, then. I made lieutenant commander the next day. They needed a lot more officers."

Oh, damn. I didn't understand at all. Geary nodded without speaking, trying to mask his embarrassment and shame at thinking Desjani and the others didn't care about losses. *They care. But they're used to it. They've seen so many die, so many times. It's a fact of life, so they don't let it overwhelm them.*

He wondered how many ships and how many sailors had died at Easir. He wondered if he'd ever have the guts to look up the history of the battle to find out. *You knew this, Geary. You knew they'd taken horrible losses, year in and year out. But you didn't really feel it. Didn't understand how it must feel to them. They're used to it, as used to seeing their friends and comrades die as anyone can ever be. I'm not used to it. War, this war, is still new to me even though it's a century old.* He felt the cold inside again, thinking about his crew members who had died long ago in that battle at Grendel. And then, for the first time, he wondered if Desjani ever felt the cold when she remembered dead comrades.

He reached out and clasped Desjani's shoulder, drawing a look of surprise from her. "They all did honor, Tanya. To themselves, to their ancestors, to those of us who've survived to win this battle. Thank you."

She looked puzzled, now. "For what, sir?"

"For honoring their memory by your own efforts. For continuing the task they died for."

Desjani looked away and shook her head. "I'm not unique, Captain Geary."

"I know." He let his hand drop. "But I'm honored to know you and every other sailor in this fleet."

He looked down at the list again, going past the ships destroyed and on to the long tally of damage suffered by other ships. That was a much longer list, but none of the ships on it had been badly hurt. Still, men and women had died on ships when compartments were breached by enemy fire. He became aware that Desjani was watching him intently. "What is it?"

"I don't know if you understand what's happened here, Captain Geary. I told you about Easir. Those who were still alive after that battle count themselves as survivors. There's no pride in it, and as I said no glory. But you've done something at Kaliban." She indicated the list of dead. "Their descendents will be very proud their ancestors died here, just as everyone in this fleet will carry the pride in having been here for the rest of their lives."

But Geary shook his head. "It wasn't a closely matched battle. We outnumbered the Syndics by a good margin from the start. Even if you don't factor in the lousy tactics of the Syndic commander, it wasn't that great a victory." He didn't go on to add that he suspected some people might not be all that impressed by it.

GEARY paused a moment, looking down, closing his eyes and breathing slowly and deeply to relax himself. *I am really getting to hate these fleet conferences.* He raised his head again and looked around the table.

Most of the officers present seemed to at least out-wardly share Desjani's elation at the recent victory. The glaring exception was a block of ship commanders seated on either side of Captain Numos and Captain Faresa, who were stone-faced at best and actively glowering at worst. Geary looked from one of them to the next, reading their ship's names, and realizing all had been assigned to Formation Fox Five Two during the battle. Some of the officers met his gaze when he looked at them, but most managed to avoid his eyes.

Geary leaned back, taking a moment to sweep his gaze across the rest of the officers "seated" at the table, and Captain Desjani, the only other person physically present in the room. "We'll be leaving the Kaliban System soon.

Our work here is done, and we've given the Syndics a bloody nose. I want to personally congratulate every ship in the fleet for the parts they played in winning the recent battle." The words were met by a lot of smiles and an increase in the antipathy from Numos's group. "My intent is to leave Kaliban tomorrow. We'll head for the jump point that provides access to a system named Sutrah. Sutrah probably hasn't been abandoned, as there's a good habitable world there, but its unlikely to have much in the way of defenses."

Numos finally spoke, his voice icy. "Why are we not going to Cadez?"

Geary gave Numos a long look. "Because Cadez is too obvious an objective. It's on a straight line back to Alliance territory, and it's on the Syndic hypernet."

Faresa spoke this time, her tone as acidic as usual. "We can access the Syndic hypernet from there and get home very quickly. Why don't you want to do that?"

Geary felt heat building in his head. "I want to get home as quickly as any of you."

"Do you?" Faresa challenged.

"Yes. I'll remind you, Captain, that any Syndic system on the hypernet can be very easily and quickly reinforced by the Syndics. If I were the Syndic commander and I knew we were at Kaliban, I would have very substantial forces sent to Cadez in order to guard against our arrival there and to prevent our use of the hypernet gate at Cadez."

Commander Cresida spoke with exaggerated casualness. "Since the Syndics have a gate at Cadez, they don't need the jump points, do they? They could mine the hell out of the jump exits."

Captain Tulev nodded. "True."

Numos made a dismissive gesture. "I for one am not afraid to confront a *strong* Syndic force." The words and tone clearly implied that the recent victory at Kaliban didn't count for much since the Syndic force had been badly outnumbered.

Captain Duellos, looking off into the distance, spoke

blandly. "Yet you didn't do a very impressive job of confronting the Syndic force in the recent battle."

Numos's face reddened with anger. Captain Faresa answered, though. "It's not the fault of Captain Numos that the ships under his command were deliberately mispositioned so as to deny them a proper role in the battle."

Tulev shook his head. "The fleet commander gave proper orders to all formations. I could hear them as well as you."

"You were far away from my formation, and far away from the Syndics as well at the time!" Numos snapped.

It was Tulev's turn to flush. "The ships under my command engaged more enemy units than yours did!"

Geary spoke loudly enough to cut across the argument. "Ladies and gentlemen, we're not here to question anyone's courage."

Numos focused on Geary again, acting as if he'd not heard Geary's admonition. "Had I been given proper opportunity to engage the enemy, I would've left no grounds for anyone to imply I lacked courage!"

"Your orders, if properly followed, would've given you ample opportunity," Geary replied, trying to keep his temper in check.

"You were many light-seconds from the scene of my engagement, yet you insisted on maintaining absolute control of my ships' movements."

"I had no trouble doing that with every other formation engaged in the battle, Captain Numos. They followed the orders they were given."

Numos leaned forward, his voice rising. "Are you saying that the duty of the Captain of a ship of the Alliance fleet is to do nothing except follow orders exactly? That we have no discretion to employ our ships as our many years of combat experience dictates?"

Geary barely refrained from snarling back at Numos, taking a long moment to calm himself before he spoke. "You are well aware that your instructions for this battle included the authority to alter movements as necessary if you believed the tactical situation so required. You had that discretion, Captain Numos. Don't attempt to blame me or anyone else for the results of your own actions."

Numos stared back at Geary, his face hard. "Are you accusing me of incompetence? Are you trying to imply that I bear the responsibility for the losses we suffered? Are you—"

"Captain Numos," Geary ground out, not aware of how his voice sounded until he saw the reactions of others, "the responsibility for all losses in this battle lie with me. I was in command, and I do not shirk from accepting the responsibilities that come with that!" Numos made to speak again, but Geary cut him off. "As for you, sir, you are perilously close to being relieved of your command and all authority if you continue to behave in an insubordinate and unprofessional manner. Do I make myself clear?"

Numos's jaw worked, but he stayed silent. On one side of him, Captain Faresa was giving Geary a look so fierce that it seemed capable of driving a hole through heavy armor.

Geary looked around the table again. He expected those gathered around Numos would still side with him, but he was surprised to note that many other officers seemed discomforted by Geary's threat. Then he saw in their faces, in the way they carried themselves, something else, something that shocked him. *They're not entirely happy with the victory, are they? They're not happy that we won by fighting in a different way. They wanted to win, but not at the cost of changing the way they're used to fighting, with all its emphasis on individual courage and freewheeling combat. Now they don't want me cracking down on one of their own and insisting he act with more discipline.*

There were exceptions, like Captain Desjani, who still glowed with unalloyed pride at the victory they'd won. It finally hit Geary that the worshippers of Black Jack Geary fell into two camps. The smaller camp, officers like Desjani, were willing to do whatever Geary said because they believed he could do no wrong. The larger camp, though, wanted Geary to lead them to victory without changing anything. They just wanted a legendary hero to lead them in the same glorious charges against the enemy that they'd always employed. And they were having a lot of trouble with the fact that their hero was demanding they fight a type of battle where individual ships truly worked as parts of a greater whole.

They want a hero who'll reaffirm everything they've done before and somehow make it work better. But now they're realizing I'm not that kind of hero.

The silence stretched, and Geary finally became aware that everyone was still waiting for him to speak again. "I want everyone to know that I've never seen a more courageous group of officers. All of you are individually brave and aggressive." *To a fault. Being too willing to die is as bad as being too afraid of dying. How do I convince them of that?* "I hope the recent battle has demonstrated how using good tactics—" *No. Damn. They'll think I'm saying they've been using bad tactics. Which they have been, but I don't want to say it.* ". . . effective tactics can enable us to inflict far more serious losses than we receive. We're a fleet. A combat organization. That gives us immense strength if we use it. I never want any of my captains to feel they can only follow orders exactly. Initiative is very important. Reacting to changing circumstances is very important. Commander Hatherian, may his ancestors honor him, did exactly what I think he should've done when he brought *Arrogant* out of her assigned station in order to protect other ships in peril."

He couldn't tell how they were reacting to his words. He was starting to wonder if he'd ever be able to really understand these Alliance sailors, whose thoughts and habits differed from his own by a century's worth of time and all the changes that had wrought.

"We will go to Sutrah. We'll evaluate conditions there and whatever we can learn about Syndic movements in deciding on our next objective." There were some nods of agreement, but everyone stayed silent. "That's all. Congratulations again on how well you all fought yesterday."

Geary sat this time, watching the images vanish rapidly. Captain Desjani, seeming slightly puzzled by Geary's depressed attitude, bade him farewell and hurried off to deal with ship's business. He became aware that one officer's image remained in the room once everyone else had disappeared. "Captain Duellos."

Duellos nodded in response to Geary's acknowledgement of his continued presence. "You've figured it out, haven't you?"

"I think so. Pardon me for being blunt, but how can they be so damned stupid?"

Duellos sighed and shook his head. "Habit. Tradition. I told you before how important pride is to this fleet. Pride and honor, the last things you can hold on to when everything else is failing. Well, they're proud of how they've fought."

Geary also shook his head. "Couldn't they see there's a better way to fight?"

"Ah, that will take time, if enough time is granted to us." Duellos quirked a small smile as Geary stared at him. "I decided after we arrived in the Syndic home system and were badly hurt that we'd probably never see home again. So, I've accepted we may not make it."

"We'll make it."

"I dare not believe that completely, but if we should make Alliance space once more, I'll buy you every drink you can handle." Duellos looked tired. "You must realize the officers you command are not used to firm hands. It's fortunate you're not a strict disciplinarian. I've read of such. A commander like that would've already lost command of the fleet. These officers truly need to be led, but they will not accept the whip."

"I'm not a whip-employing kind of officer, but I need to show them the old ways work," Geary stated.

"Yes. But it'll take time, as I said. Time to forget one set of habits and acquire a new set. Time to gather victories that reinforce the new habits." Duellos stood, preparing to leave. "Do not despair, I beg you. We all need you, even those who don't think they need you. Perhaps I should say, especially those who don't think they need you."

Geary gave Duellos a tight-lipped smile. "I can't afford to give up."

"No. You can't." Duellos saluted, then his image vanished.

Geary pushed himself up from his seat, glaring at the now empty compartment. *I need to hold fewer meetings. No. As much as I hate them, I have to keep holding meetings. It's my only chance to see all of these officers, even though I'm not liking what I'm seeing.*

He walked back to his stateroom, so lost in thought that he was surprised to find himself at the hatch. Rubbing his eyes, he considered a med-patch but decided against it. The meds were guaranteed not to cause physical addiction, but the last thing he needed was psychological addiction to the temporary comfort they brought.

This day's already gone to hell, so I might as well catch up on paperwork. Geary called up his message queue and cycled through incoming material as fast as possible, until he came to one that made him pause. *"Intelligence exploitation report regarding Syndicate Worlds facilities in the Kaliban System." I didn't think the Syndics had left anything worth exploiting.*

He began reading, then started skimming as it became apparent the Syndics had indeed left little of interest behind, and what there was of interest was decades old and therefore of doubtful use.

Wait a minute. Geary stopped scrolling and paged back to find whatever had caught his attention. *There it is. The security vault at the headquarters facility had been breached at some point long after the departure of the Syndicate Worlds authorities. This assessment was reached after examining damage done to the vault by its physical breaching via the use of power tools. Analysis of the stress fracturing of the metal cut through indicates it was at am-*

bient environmental temperature when the power tools were employed, which could only have been the case after the facility had been mothballed and abandoned for some time. As far as could be determined, the vault was empty when sealed, so the reasons for the breach are undetermined. Since attempted intelligence collection by Alliance assets could not account for the damage, it was most likely caused by criminal elements, though their reasons for trying to access a security vault in an abandoned facility cannot be understood. It is also impossible to know why those breaching the vault made use of drill bits whose diameters match none of those used within the Syndicate Worlds or the Alliance. We can only assume the nonstandard drill bits were employed to prevent their source from being identified."

Geary read through that section of the report several times, trying to figure out what bothered him. The fact that the security vault had been breached long before the Alliance fleet had arrived at Kaliban made no sense at all, of course. Someone must've believed something valuable would be in there, but the Syndics were fanatical about following standard procedure, and surely anyone associated with the Syndics would know that standard procedure presumably included removing everything from the security vault before the star system was abandoned.

The speculation about using nonstandard drill bits to avoid being traced. That was it. The conclusion stood logic on its head. It'd be far easier to trace nonstandard drill bits than it would standard bits, since uncounted millions of such standard bits existed in both the Syndicate Worlds and the Alliance.

But that left the question begging. Why go to the immense trouble of using nonstandard drill bits?

Unless those were the only drill bits you had. Because you didn't belong to the Syndicate Worlds or any worlds known to the Alliance.

That's quite a leap, Geary. You wouldn't have even thought of that if the Marines hadn't raised the possibility that the Syndics were worried about some nonhuman intelligences. But even the Marines didn't want to stand by that conclusion. They just felt they had to bring it up. Wiped operating systems and nonstandard drill bits aren't exactly strong proof that there's alien intelligences wandering around Syndic space.

But I have to wonder. This report about the nonstandard drill bits made them fit a predictable scenario even though it didn't really make sense. How many other small things like that have been filed away and forgotten because someone came up with an alternate explanation? An explanation that didn't involve making an assertion, that alien intelligences might be involved, which would've gotten people laughed at? I've gone through the classified files on Dauntless *and found nothing about evidence of nonhuman intelligences. But even in my time the overriding assumption was that we were alone out here, and facts tend to be bent until they corroborate overriding assumptions.*

The chime on his hatch announced the presence of a visitor. He didn't really feel like talking to anyone, but couldn't justify turning away what might be important business. "Come in."

Victoria Rione entered, her face composed, as usual giving no clue to her inner thoughts. "Captain Geary, may we speak?"

He stood up, suddenly uncomfortably aware of how rumpled his uniform was. "Sure. I hope it's nothing too serious." *Like accusing me of being a dictator in training again.* "Is there something I can ask you first?"

"Certainly."

He waved her to a seat, then took his own again. "Madam Co President, I assume you'd be willing to share any classified information with me if I asked."

She gave him a questioning look. "You have access to every classified piece of information on this ship, Captain Geary."

Geary lowered his head so she couldn't see his grimace. "There may be things too sensitive to be in the databases of even a fleet flagship. Information kept within governing channels."

Rione shook her head slowly. "I don't know which information you might be referring to."

"Is there anything known to the Alliance, that you are aware of, regarding any nonhuman intelligences?"

Her head froze in midshake. "Why are you asking this?"

"Because something at Kaliban led some of my officers to speculate about it."

"I'd like to hear what it was. In response to your question, I'm not aware of anything like that. I've certainly never seen anything along those lines." She looked upward as if expecting to see signs of an alien intelligence somehow visible there. "Encountering a nonhuman intelligence would be a very significant event in human history. They might be able to tell us a great deal. Perhaps help explain things we don't understand. Maybe even explain things about ourselves we don't understand." She gave a brief, humorless laugh. "Such as why we've spent a hundred standard years fighting a war. Or even why it started in the first place."

Geary had been about to say more, but he stopped at her last words. "We never learned why the Syndics launched their first attacks?"

Rione gave him a speculative look. "No. Not the timing, anyway. As I think you can confirm, the first attacks were a total surprise because there'd been no indications that tensions had risen to such a level."

He brooded on her statement, remembering so clearly the shock he'd felt at Grendel when it became clear that a Syndic attack was underway. *Total surprise, just as she said.* "I'd assumed the reasons had become clear by now."

"No. Our best assessments provide complex answers, Captain Geary. There's no clarity. There appear to have been many factors."

"'Appear to have been.'" He chewed his lower lip for a moment. "Then we still don't know exactly why they did it? Why they attacked when they did? Why they attacked at all?"

"No," Rione repeated. "Not for certain. Their Executive Council doesn't share its deliberations with anyone. The answer is surely buried in the secret records of the Syndicate Worlds' leadership."

Geary nodded at her words, but his mind had generated a question he couldn't ignore. "Then we don't know of any . . . external factors that might've influenced the Syndics' actions?"

She spread her hands in a gesture of incomprehension. "I don't know what you could be speaking of. External factors?" Her eyes widened. "You're not talking about nonhuman intelligences, are you? Is that why you asked about them? You're not suggesting they were somehow involved or caused the war, are you?"

"No. No, of course not." *I'm a long way from wanting to openly suggest such a thing. But I'm wondering. If the Syndics did encounter nonhuman intelligences, how long ago was it? More than forty-two years ago, certainly, if what the Syndics did when they shut down Kaliban means what it might mean.*

Did the Syndics encounter alien intelligences? When did they find them? What happened?

Did it have anything to do with the start of this war? Could it perhaps explain why the Syndics attacked, and why this war has continued even though victory seems impossible for either side? But how could it have had anything to do with either of those things?

Outwardly, Geary smiled politely. "Thank you, Madam Co-President. Now, what did you need from me?"

Rione seemed a bit surprised that Geary had changed the subject, but she went along without protest. "I feel I should tell you what the commanders of my ships have told me. Those loyal to Captain Numos are attempting to spread a tale around the fleet that you deliberately kept him and the ships in his formation out of the battle so you could claim all the glory."

Geary found himself laughing for a moment. "Unfortunately, I already know that. I'm sure your ship commanders will soon provide you with the ugly details of my latest conference."

"Then you've already confronted the issue?"

"Confronted it? Yes." Geary let his feelings show. "Dealt with it? That's another thing. There are some larger issues involved."

"You mean the discontent over your changes to the Alliance fleet's manner of fighting?"

Geary just stared at her for a long moment. "Just how many spies do you have inside my fleet, Madam Co-President?"

She actually managed to look slightly shocked at the question. "Why would I have spies in a friendly fleet, Captain Geary?"

"I can think of a lot of reasons," he suggested, "many involving keeping track of what the fleet commander is up to. I'm beginning to think you didn't entirely trust Admiral Bloch, either."

Rione made a noncommittal expression. "Admiral Bloch was an ambitious man."

"And I already know what you think of ambitious men."

"I feel the same way about ambitious women, Captain Geary. Are you proud of your victory here at Kaliban?"

He started to simply say yes, surprised by sudden question, but then paused as other thoughts overtook him. "In some ways," he finally admitted. "It was my first fleet action. I think I called the maneuvers pretty well. I did a decent job of predicting the enemy's moves. But it wasn't perfect." He paused again. "I wish I could've done the same without losing a single ship or sailor. But I'm proud of this fleet. They fought well."

"Indeed. The results of the battle were gratifying."

"Is that how you feel now, Madam Co-President? Do you have no regrets about letting me retain control of the ships from your republic and the Rift Federation?"

She shook her head. "No. As long as we're being candid . . . and we are being candid, aren't we, Captain Geary? . . . I should tell you something you may learn regardless. My ship commanders are impressed with our victory in the battle, though a majority of them share with many Alliance officers unease regarding the way it was fought. They had a greater skepticism of this Black Jack Geary person than sailors of the Alliance did, of course, since to them you were a foreign hero. Now," she blew out a long breath, "they are more inclined to believe there is some truth behind the myth."

"Ancestors help me." Geary let his feelings show, trusting Rione now to that extent. "There's no truth behind that myth, as you well know."

She clenched her teeth so tightly her jaw muscles stood out. "On the contrary, and as I have told you, Captain Geary. You are that figure of myth."

"You *know* that's not true!"

"I *know* you saved this fleet in the Syndic home system, I know you have brought it this far and won an overwhelming victory, and I *know* no ordinary man could've done that!" Rione was glaring at him as if daring Geary to deny her statement.

Instead of responding with anger, Geary found himself laughing in self-mockery. "My dear Madam Co-President, I'd never have made it this far if a lot of people hadn't thought I was the living stars' gift to the Alliance fleet. But you know as well as I, there are plenty of people with growing doubts as to the truth of that."

Rione smiled back, though her voice had more sarcasm than humor to it. "I have a feeling you'll find a way to cope, Captain Geary."

He returned the sarcasm full force, bowing slightly toward her. "Thank you for your confidence in me."

She stood up, walking away a few steps before turning to look at him again. "I notice you said 'confidence' and not 'trust.'"

He shrugged. "Same thing."

"No, it's not. I'll share one more confidence with you, Captain Geary. I'm not superhuman. I very much want to believe in you, to believe you *are* the hope we all need, a gift from our ancestors. But I don't dare do so."

Geary's smile vanished, and he looked down at the deck for a moment. "That makes two of us who don't dare believe that. If I do, I'll be more dangerous to this fleet than the enemy."

"Agreed. You make it hard to doubt you." She smiled again, and this time it seemed genuine. "You have won your victory at Kaliban. What are you going to do now, Captain Geary?"

Geary walked over to stare at the starscape. For the first time in a long time, he searched through it until he recognized some of the stars in Alliance space. So far to go yet. His grandnephew Michael Geary, who'd died on his ship *Repulse* in the Syndic home system, would never see Alliance space again. Nor would the crew of the *Arrogant*. But there were a lot of ships' crews left who were still counting on him, believing Black Jack could get them back to their homes, and a grandniece back in Alliance space who could tell him about the family he'd lost to time. "What am I going to do? As I'm sure you've already heard, I'm going to take this fleet to Sutrah. Eventually, I'm going to take this fleet home, no matter who or what stands in the way."